SCHILD'S LADDER

■

Other Books by Greg Egan

SCHILD'S LADDER

∎

Greg Egan

An Imprint of HarperCollins*Publishers*

A hardcover edition of this book was published in 2002 by Eos, an imprint of HarperCollins Publishers.

HarperCollins books may be purchased for educational, business, or sales promotional use. For information please write: Special Markets Department, HarperCollins Publishers Inc., 10 East 53rd Street, New York, NY 10022.

First paperback edition published 2004.

The Library of Congress has cataloged the hardcover edition as follows:

Egan, Greg, 1961–
   Schild's ladder / by Greg Egan.
      p. cm.
   ISBN 0-06-105093-8 (hardcover)
   I. Title.
   PR9619.3.E35 S35 2002
   823'.914—dc21   2001055583

ISBN 0-06-107344-X (pbk.)

04 05 06 07 08 ❖/RRD 10 9 8 7 6 5 4 3 2 1

Thanks to John Baez, Jennifer Brehl, Caroline Oakley, Anthony Cheetham, John Douglas, Simon Spanton, Oisín Murphy-Lawless, Devi Pillai, Peter Robinson, Russell Galen, Carol Jackson, Emma Bailey, Diana Mackay, Philip Patterson, Christodoulos Litharis, Nicola Fantini, Giancarlo Carlotti, Albert Solé, Petr Kotrle, Makoto Yamagishi, Florin Pîtea, and Mihai-Dan Pavelescu.

SCHILD'S LADDER

■

Part One

Chapter 1

In the beginning was a graph, more like diamond than graphite. Every node in this graph was tetravalent: connected by four edges to four other nodes. By a count of edges, the shortest path from any node back to itself was a loop six edges long. Every node belonged to twenty-four such loops, as well as forty-eight loops eight edges long, and four hundred and eighty that were ten edges long. The edges had no length or shape, the nodes no position; the graph consisted only of the fact that some nodes were connected to others. This pattern of connections, repeated endlessly, was all there was.

In the beginning? Waking more fully, Cass corrected herself: that was the version she remembered from childhood, but these days she preferred to be more cautious. The Sarumpaet rules let you trace the history of the universe back to the vicinity of the Diamond Graph, and everything you could ask for in a Big Bang was there: low entropy, particle creation, rapidly expanding space.

Whether it made sense to follow these signposts all the way back, though, was another question.

Cass let the graph's honeycomb pattern linger in the darkness of her skull. Having relinquished her child's-eye view of the world, she was unable to decide which epoch of her life she actually inhabited. It was one of the minor perils of longevity: waking could be like to trying to find your way home on a street with ten thousand houses, all of which had once been your own. That the clues on the other side of her eyelids might be more enlightening was beside the point; she had to follow the internal logic of her memories back into the present before she could jolt herself awake.

The Sarumpaet rules assigned a quantum amplitude to the possibility of any one graph being followed by another. Among other things, the rules predicted that if a graph contained a loop consisting of three trivalent nodes alternating with three pentavalent ones, its most likely successors would share the same pattern, but it would be shifted to an adjoining set of nodes. A loop like this was known as a photon. The rules predicted that the photon would move. (Which way? All directions were equally likely. To aim the photon took more work, superimposing a swarm of different versions that would interfere and cancel each other out when they traveled in all but one favored direction.)

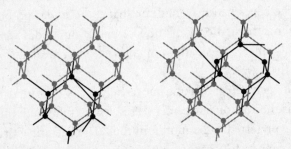

Other patterns could propagate in a similar fashion, and their symmetries and interactions matched up perfectly with the known fundamental particles. Every graph was still just a graph, a collection of nodes and their mutual connections, but the flaws in the diamond took on a life of their own.

The current state of the universe was a long way from the Diamond Graph. Even a patch of near-vacuum in the middle of interstellar space owed its near-Euclidean geometry to the fact that it was an elaborate superposition of a multitude of graphs, each one riddled with virtual particles. And while an ideal vacuum, in all its complexity, was a known quantity, most real space departed from that ideal in an uncontrollable manner: shot through with cosmic radiation, molecular contaminants, neutrinos, and the endless faint ripple of gravitational waves.

So Cass had traveled to Mimosa Station, half a light-year from the blue subgiant for which it was named, three hundred and seventy light-years from Earth. Here, Rainzi and his colleagues had built a shield against the noise.

Cass opened her eyes. Lifting her head to peer through a portal, still strapped to the bed at the waist, she could just make out the Quietener: a blue glint reflecting off the hull a million kilometers away. Mimosa Station had so little room to spare that she'd had to settle for a body two millimeters high, which rendered her vision less acute than usual. The combination of weightlessness, vacuum, and insectile dimensions did make her feel pleasantly robust, though: her mass had shrunk a thousand times more than the cross sections of her muscles and tendons, so the pressures and strains involved in any collision were feather-light. Even if she charged straight into a ceramic wall, it felt like being stopped by a barricade of petals.

It was a pity the same magical resilience couldn't apply to her encounters with less tangible obstacles. She'd left Earth with no guarantee that the Mimosans would see any merit in her proposal, but it was only in the last few days that she'd begun to face up to the possibility of a bruising rejection. She could have presented her entire case from home, stoically accepting a seven-hundred-and-forty-year delay between each stage of the argument. Or she could have sent a Surrogate, well briefed but nonsentient, to plead on her behalf. But she'd succumbed to a mixture of impatience and a sense of proprietorship, and transmitted herself blind.

Now the verdict was less than two hours away.

She unstrapped herself and drifted away from the bed. She didn't need to wash, or purge herself of wastes. From the moment she'd arrived, as a stream of ultraviolet pulses with a header requesting embodiment on almost any terms, the Mimosans had been polite and accommodating; Cass had been careful not to abuse their hospitality by pleading for frivolous luxuries. A self-contained body and a safe place to sleep were the only things she really needed in order to feel like herself. Being hermetically sealed against the vacuum and feeding on nothing but light took some getting used to, but so did the customs and climate of any unfamiliar region back on Earth. Demanding the right to eat and excrete, here, would have been as crass as insisting on slavish re-creations of her favorite childhood meals, while a guest at some terrestrial facility.

A circular tunnel, slightly wider than her height, connected her spartan quarters to a chamber where she could interact with the software she'd brought from Earth, and through it the Mimosans themselves. She bounced down the borehole, slapping the wall with her hands and feet, bumping her head and elbows deliberately.

As she entered the chamber, she seemed to emerge from the mouth of a burrow to float above a lush, wide meadow beneath a cloud-dappled sky. The illusion was purely audiovisual—the sounds encoded in radio waves—but with no weight to hold her against the ceramic hidden beneath the meadow, the force of detail was eerily compelling. It only took a few blades of grass and some chirping insects to make her half-believe that she could smell the late-summer air.

Would it really have been an act of self-betrayal, if this landscape had stretched all the way inside her—right down to the sensations of inhabiting her old, two-meter body, gorging on a breakfast of fruit and oats after swimming across Chalmers Lake? If she could drift in and out of this soothing work of art without losing her grip on reality, why couldn't she take the process a few steps further?

She pushed the argument aside, though she was glad that it never stopped nagging at her. When the means existed to transform yourself, instantly and effortlessly, into anything at all, the only way to maintain an identity was to draw your own boundaries. But once you lost the urge to keep on asking whether or not you'd drawn them in the right place, you might as well have been born *Homo sapiens*, with no real choices at all.

A short distance from the burrow stood a marble statue of Rainzi, arms folded, smiling slightly. Cass gestured at the messenger and it came to life, the white stone taking on the hue and texture of skin. Rainzi himself was several generations removed from anyone who'd bothered to simulate a living dermis, let alone possess one, but Cass was not equipped to make sense of the Mimosans' own communications protocols, so she'd chosen to have everything translated into the visual dialect used back on Earth.

"We'll give you our decision at nine o'clock, as promised," the messenger assured her. "But we hope you won't mind if we precede this with a final review session. Some of us feel that there are matters that have yet to be entirely resolved. We'll begin at half past seven." The messenger bowed, then froze again, expecting no reply.

Cass tried not to read too much into the sudden change of plan. It was unnerving to discover that her hosts still hadn't been able to reach a verdict, but at least they weren't going to keep her waiting any longer than she'd expected. The fact that she'd already briefed them in detail on every aspect of the experiment that had crossed her mind during three decades of preparation, and they now hoped to hear something new and decisive from her in twenty minutes' time, was no reason to panic. Whatever loose ends they'd found in her analysis, they were giving her the chance to put things right.

Her confidence was shaken, though, and she couldn't stop thinking about the prospect of failure. After a month here, she still wasn't lonely, or homesick; that was the price she'd pay upon returning. Even at the leisurely pace of the embodied, seven hundred and forty years cut a deep rift. It would be millennia before the changes that her friends on Earth had lived through together would cease to set her apart from them. Millennia, if ever.

She still believed that she could come to terms with that loss, so long as she had something to weigh against it. Being a singleton meant accepting that every decision had its cost, but once you understood that this state of affairs was a hard-won prize, not a plight to rail against, it gave some dignity to all but the most foolish choices.

If the Mimosans turned her down, though? Maybe there was something daring and romantic in the mere act of traveling hundreds of light-years, inhabiting the body of a vacuum-dwelling insect, and alienating herself from the world where she belonged, all in the hope of seeing her ideas tested as rapidly as possible. But for how long would she be able to take comfort from the sheer audacity of what she'd done, once that hope had come to nothing?

She curled into a ball and tried to weep. She could not shed tears, and the sobs rebounding against her membrane-sealed mouth were like the drone of a mosquito. But the shuddering as she worked her vestigial lungs still provided some sense of release. She had not entirely erased the map of her Earthly body from her mind; too much of the way she experienced emotions was bound up in its specific form. So everything she'd amputated lingered as a kind of phantom—nowhere near as convincing as a true simulation, but still compelling enough to make a difference.

When she was spent, Cass stretched out her limbs and drifted over the meadow like a dandelion seed, as calm and lucid as she'd been at any time since her arrival.

She knew what she knew about Quantum Graph Theory, backward. Whatever insights she was capable of extracting from that body of knowledge, she'd extracted long ago. But if the Mimosans had found a question she couldn't answer, a doubt she couldn't assuage, that in itself would be a chance to learn something more.

Even if they sent her home with nothing else, she would not be leaving empty-handed.

It was Livia who asked the first question, and it was far simpler than anything Cass had anticipated.

"Do you believe that the Sarumpaet rules are correct?"

Cass hesitated longer than she needed to, a calculated attempt to imbue her response with appropriate gravity.

"I'm not certain that they are, but the likelihood seems overwhelming to me."

"Your experiment would test them more rigorously than anything that's been tried before," Livia observed.

Cass nodded. "I do see that as a benefit, but only a minor one. I don't believe that merely testing the rules one more time would justify the experiment. I'm more interested in what the rules imply, given that they're almost certainly correct."

Where was this heading? She glanced around at the others, seated in a ring in the meadow: Yann, Bakim, Darsono, Ilene, Zulkifli, and Rainzi. Her Mediator had chosen appearances for all of them, since they offered none themselves, but at least their facial expressions and body language were modulated by their own intentional signals. By choice, they all looked politely interested, but were giving nothing away.

"You have a lot of confidence in QGT?" Clearly, Livia did realize just how strange her questions sounded; her tone was that of someone begging to be indulged until her purpose became apparent.

Cass said, "Yes, I do. It's simple, it's elegant, and it's consistent with all observations to date." That handful of words sounded glib, but other people had quantified all of these criteria long ago. QGT as a description of the dynamics of the universe with the minimum possible algorithmic complexity. QGT as a topological redescription of some basic results in category theory—a mathematical setting in which the Sarumpaet rules appeared as natural and inevitable as the rules of arithmetic. QGT as the most probable underlying system of physical laws, given any substantial database of experimental results that spanned both nuclear physics and cosmology.

Darsono leaned toward her and interjected, "But why, in your heart"—he thumped his chest with an imaginary fist—"are you convinced that it's true?" Cass smiled. That was not a gesture in the staid vocabulary her Mediator used by default; Darsono must have requested it explicitly.

"In part, it's the history," she admitted, relaxing slightly. "The lineage of the ideas. If some alien civilization had handed us Quantum Graph Theory on a stone tablet—out of the blue, in the eighteenth or nineteenth century—I might not feel the same way about it. But *general relativity* and *quantum mechanics* were among the most beautiful things the ancients created, and they're still the best practical approximations we have for most of the universe. QGT is their union. If general relativity is so close to the truth that only the tiniest fragment can be missing, and quantum mechanics is the same . . . how much freedom can there be to encompass all of the successes of both, and still be wrong?"

Kusnanto Sarumpaet had lived on Earth at the turn of the third millennium, when a group of physicists and mathematicians scattered across the planet—now known universally as the Sultans of Spin—had produced the first viable offspring of general relativity and quantum mechanics. To merge the two descriptions of nature, you needed to replace the precise, unequivocal geometry of classical space-time with a quantum state that assigned amplitudes to a whole range of possible geometries. One way to do this was to imagine carrying a particle such as an electron around a loop, and computing the amplitude for its direction of spin being the same at the end of the journey as when it first set out. In flat space, the spins would always agree, but in curved space the result would depend on the detailed geometry of the region through which the particle had traveled. Generalizing this idea, crisscrossing space with a whole network of paths taken by particles of various spins, and comparing them all at the junctions where they met, led to the notion of a *spin network*. Like the harmonics of a wave, these networks comprised a set of building blocks from which all quantum states of geometry could be constructed.

Sarumpaet's quantum graphs were the children of spin networks, moving one step further away from general relativity by taking their own parents' best qualities at face value. They abandoned the idea of any preexisting space in which the network could be embedded, and defined everything—space, time, geometry, and matter—entirely on their own terms. Particles were loops of altered valence woven into the graph. The area of any surface was due to the number of edges of the graph that pierced it, the volume of any region to the number of nodes it contained. And every measure of time, from planetary orbits to the vibrations of nuclei, could ultimately be rephrased as a count of the changes between the graphs describing space at two different moments.

Sarumpaet had struggled for decades to breathe life into this vision, by finding the correct laws that governed the probability of any one graph evolving into another. In the end, he'd been blessed by a lack of choices; there had only been one set of rules that could make everything work. The two grandparents of his theory, imperfect as they were, could not be very far wrong: both had yielded predictions in their respective domains that had been verified to hair's-breadth accuracy. Doing justice to both had left no room for errors.

Livia said, "Conceptually, that argument is very appealing. But there could still be deviations from the rules—far too small to have been detected so far—that would change the outcome of your experiment completely."

"So it's a sensitive test," Cass agreed. "But that's not why I've proposed it." They were talking in circles. "If the rules hold, the graph I've designed should be stable for almost six-trillionths of a second. That's long enough to give us a wealth of observations of a space-time utterly different from our own. If it doesn't last that long, I'll be disappointed. I'm not doing this in the hope of proving Sarumpaet wrong!"

Cass turned to Darsono, seeking some hint that he might share her exasperation, but before she could gauge his mood, Livia spoke again.

"What if it lasts much longer?"

Finally, Cass understood. "This is about *safety*? I've addressed the potential risks, very thoroughly—"

"On the basis that the Sarumpaet rules are correct."

"Yes. What other basis should I have used?" *Phoenician astrology? Californian lithomancy?* Cass resisted the urge to lapse into sarcasm; there was too much at stake. "I've admitted that there's no certainty that the rules hold in every last untested circumstance. But I have nothing better to put in their place."

"Nor do I," Livia said gently. "My point is, we mustn't overinterpret the success of the Sarumpaet rules. General relativity and quantum field theory confessed from the start that they were just approximations: pushed to extremes, they both yielded obvious nonsense. But the fact that QGT doesn't—the fact that there is no fundamental reason why it can't be universally applicable—is no guarantee that it really does stretch that far."

Cass gritted her teeth. "I concede that. But where does it leave us? Refusing to perform any experiment that hasn't been tried before?"

Rainzi said, "Of course not. Livia is proposing a staged approach. Before attempting to construct your graph, we'd move toward it in a series of experiments, gradually bridging the gap."

Cass fell silent. Compared to outright rejection this was a trivial obstacle, but it still stung: she'd worked for thirty years to refine her own proposal, and she resented the implication that she'd been reckless.

"How many stages?"

"Fifteen," Livia replied. She swept a hand through the vacuum in front of her, and a sequence of target graphs appeared. Cass studied them, taking her time.

They'd been well chosen. At first one by one, then in pairs, then triples, the features that conspired to render her own target stable were introduced. If there *was* some undiscovered flaw in the rules that would make the final graph dangerous, there could be no more systematic way to detect it in advance.

"It's your choice," Rainzi said. "We'll vote on whichever proposal you endorse."

Cass met his eyes. The openness of his face was an act of puppetry, but that didn't mean he was insincere. This wasn't a threat, an attempt to bully her into agreeing. It was a mark of respect that they were letting her decide, letting her weigh up her own costs, her own fears, before they voted.

She said, "Fifteen experiments. How long would that take?"

Ilene answered, "Perhaps three years. Perhaps five." Conditions varied, and the Quietener wasn't perfect. Planning an experiment in QGT was like waiting for a stretch of ocean to grow sufficiently calm that a few flimsy barriers could block the waves and keep out the wildlife long enough to let you test some subtle principle of fluid dynamics. There was no equivalent of a laboratory water tank; space-time was all ocean, indivisible.

In terms of separation from her friends, five years was nothing compared to the centuries she'd already lost. Still, Cass found the prospect daunting. It must have shown on her face, because Bakim responded, "You could always return to Earth immediately, and wait for the results there." Some of the Mimosans had trouble understanding why anyone who found life in the station arduous would feel obliged to be here in person at all.

Darsono, empathetic as ever, added quickly, "Or we could give you new quarters. There's a suitable cavity on the other side of the station, almost twice as large; it's just a matter of rerouting some cables."

Cass laughed. "Thank you." Maybe they could build her a new body, too, four whole millimeters long. Or she could abandon her scruples, melt into software, and wallow in whatever luxuries she desired. That was the hazard she'd face every day, here: not just the risk that she'd give in to temptation, but the risk that all the principles she'd chosen to define herself would come to seem like nothing but masochistic nonsense.

She lowered her gaze toward the illusory meadow, laser-painted on her retinas like everything around her, but her mind's eye conjured up another image just as strongly from within: the Diamond Graph, as she saw it in her dreams. She could never reach it, never touch it, but she could learn to see it from a new direction, understand it in a new way. She'd come here in the hope of being changed, by that knowledge if by nothing else. To flee back to Earth out of fear that she might test her own boundaries more rigorously here, in a mere five years of consciousness, than if she'd spent the same three-quarters of a millennium at home, would be the greatest act of cowardice in her life.

"I'll accept the staged experiments," she declared. "I endorse Livia's proposal."

Rainzi said, "All in favor?"

There was silence. Cass could hear crickets chirping. *No one? Not Livia herself? Not even Darsono?*

She looked up.

All seven Mimosans had raised their hands.

Chapter 2

Riding her ion scooter the million kilometers to the Quietener, Cass found herself reveling in the view for the first time in years. The scooter was doing one-and-a-quarter gees, but the couch pressed against her back so gently that she might have been floating. Floating in dark water, beneath an alien sky. Even at half a light-year, Mimosa punched a dazzling violet hole in the blackness, a pinprick ten times as bright as a full moon. Away from its glare, the stars were far too plentiful to suggest constellations; any stick-figure object that she began to sketch between them was soon undermined by an equally compelling alternative, then a third, then a fourth—like a superposition of graphs, each with a different choice of edges between the same nodes. When she'd first arrived, she'd homed in on her own star, watching with a mixture of fear and exaltation as it hovered at the edge of visibility to her thousandth-scale eyes. Now, she'd forgotten all the cues she'd need to find it, and she felt no urge to ask her navigation software to remind her. The sun was no beacon of reassurance, and she'd be seeing it close-up again soon enough.

Each time one of Livia's staged targets had been achieved, Cass had dispatched a small army of digital couriers to pass on the news to seven generations of her ancestors and descendants, as well as all her friends in Chalmers. She'd received dozens of messengers herself, mostly from Lisa and Tomek, full of inconsequential gossip, but very welcome. It must have grown strange for her friends as the years had passed, and they no longer knew whether or not there was any point continuing to shout into the void. If she had traveled embodied, as a handful of ancients still did, she could have caught up with centuries of mail on the return voyage. Reduced to a timeless signal *en route*, though, she'd have no choice but to step unprepared into the future. Her homecoming was going to be the hardest thing she'd ever faced, but she was almost certain now that her time here would prove to have been worth it.

Half an hour before arrival, Cass rolled onto her stomach and poked her head over the edge of the couch. Her engine's exhaust was a barely perceptible flicker, fainter than a methanol flame by daylight, but she knew that if she reached down and placed her hand in the stream of plasma, she'd rapidly lose any delusion that her Mimosan body was indestructible.

She watched the Quietener growing beneath her, the silvery sphere glinting Mimosa-blue. Surrounding it was a swarm of smaller, twinned spheres, unevenly colored and far less lustrous. Tethers, invisibly slender, allowed the twins to orbit each other, while ion jets balanced the slight tug of the Quietener's gravity, keeping each pair's center of mass fixed against the stars.

The Quietener made it possible to perform experiments that could never be carried out elsewhere. The right distribution of matter and energy could curve space-time in any manner that Einstein's equations allowed, but creating a chosen state of quantum geometry was a very different proposition. Rather than simply bending space-time in bulk, like a slab of metal in a foundry, it had to be controlled with the same kind of precision as the particles in a two-slit interference experiment. But the "particles" of geometry were twenty-five orders of magnitude smaller than atoms, and they could never be vaporized, ionized, or otherwise coaxed apart to be handled one by one. So the same degree of delicacy had to be achieved with the equivalent of a ten-tonne lump of iron.

Refining the starting material helped, and the Quietener did its best to screen out every form of impurity. Ordinary matter and magnetic fields absorbed or deflected charged particles, while a shell of exotic nuclei, trapped by gamma-ray lasers in states from which they could not decay without absorbing neutrinos, mopped up a greater fraction of the billions wandering by than would have been stopped by a galaxy's-worth of lead.

Gravitational waves passed through anything, so the only antidote was a second train of waves, tailored to cancel out the first. There was nothing to be done about sporadic cataclysms—supernovae, or black holes gorging on star clusters in the centers of distant galaxies—but the most persistent gravitational waves, coming from local binary stars, were cyclic, predictable, and faint. So the Quietener was ringed with countersources, their orbits timed to stretch space at the center of the device when the bodies they mimicked squeezed it, and vice versa.

As Cass passed within a few kilometers of one of the countersources, she could see the aggregate rocky surface that betrayed its origins in Mimosa's rubble of asteroids. Every scrap of material here had been dragged out of that system's gravity well over a period of almost a thousand years, a process initiated by a package of micron-sized spores sent from Viro, the nearest inhabited world, at ninety percent of lightspeed. The Mimosans themselves had come from all over, traveling here just as Cass had once the station was assembled.

The scooter's smooth deceleration brought her to a halt beside a docking bay, and she was weightless again. Whenever she was close enough to either the station or the Quietener to judge her velocity, it seemed to be little more than that of a train, giving the impression that in the five-hour journey she might have traveled the width of a continent on Earth. Not to the moon and back, and more.

One wall of the bay had handholds. As Cass pulled herself along, Rainzi appeared beside her. The Mimosans had dusted projectors and cameras all over the walls of the places she visited in the Quietener, rendering guest and host mutually visible.

"This is it!" Rainzi said cheerfully. "Barring untimely super-novae, we'll finally get to see your graph complete." The software portrayed him with a jet pack, to rationalize his ability to follow her uneven progress up the wall without touching anything.

Cass replied stoically, "I'll believe it when it happens." In fact, from the moment Ilene had scheduled the run, twelve hours be-fore, Cass had felt insanely confident that no more hurdles re-mained. Eight of the fourteen previous targets had been achieved at the first attempt, making the prospect of one more tantalizingly plausible. But she was reluctant to admit to taking anything for granted, and if something did go wrong it would be easier to swal-low her disappointment if she'd been pretending from the start that her expectations had always been suitably modest.

Rainzi didn't argue, but he ignored her feigned pessimism. He said, "I have a proposition for you. A new experience you might like to try, to celebrate the occasion. I suspect it will be against all your high-minded principles, but I honestly believe you'd enjoy it. Will you hear me out?"

He wore a look of such deadpan innocence that Cass felt sure he knew exactly how this sounded in translation. If that *was* his meaning, the idea wasn't entirely absurd, or unwelcome. She'd grown fond of Rainzi, and if he'd never been quite as solicitous or as eager to understand her as Darsono, the truth was, that made him more intriguing. If they could find enough common ground to become lovers, it might be a fitting way to bid Mimosa farewell:

sweeping away the mutually distorted views they had of each other. To remain loyal to the ideals of embodiment, here, she'd been forced to adopt a kind of asceticism, but that was definitely not a quality to which she'd ever aspired, let alone one for which she hoped to be remembered.

She said, "I'm listening."

"For special events like this, we sometimes go nuclear. So I thought I'd ask whether you'd like to join us."

Cass froze, and stared at him. "Nuclear? *How?* Has someone solved all the problems?" Femtomachines built from exotic nuclei had been employed as special-purpose computers ever since the basic design had been developed, six thousand years before. For sheer speed, they left every other substrate in the dust. But as far as Cass knew, no one could make a femtomachine stable for more than a few picoseconds; they could perform a great many calculations in that time, but then they blew themselves apart and left you hunting through the debris for the answer. Gamma-ray spectroscopy could only extract a few hundred kilobytes, which was orders of magnitude too small even for a differential memory—a compressed description of experience that could be absorbed by a frozen reference copy of the person who'd actually lived through it. Cass might have missed the news of a breakthrough while she'd been on her way here from Earth, but if word had reached Mimosa Station at all she should have heard by now.

"Nothing's changed in the technology," Rainzi said. "We do it freestyle. One-way."

Freestyle meant implementing your mind on a substrate that underwent quantum divergence. *One-way* meant none of the end products of any version of the computation could be retrieved, and transferred back into your usual hardware. Rainzi was asking her to clone herself into a nuclear abacus-cum-time-bomb that would generate a multitude of different versions of her, while holding out no prospect of even one survivor.

Cass said haltingly, "No, I'm sorry. I can't join you." So much for feeling smugly unshockable for daring to contemplate cross-modal sex. She joked, "I draw the line at any implementation where I experience detectable weight changes every time I learn something." Femtomachines shuffled binding energies equivalent to a significant portion of their own mass; it would be like gaining or losing half a kilogram several times a second, from the sheer gravity of your thoughts.

Rainzi smiled. "I thought you'd say no. But it would have been discourteous not to ask."

"Thank you. I appreciate that."

"But you'd see it as a kind of death?"

Cass scowled. "I'm embodied, not deranged! If a copy of my mind experiences a few minutes' consciousness, then is lost, that's not the death of anyone. It's just amnesia."

Rainzi looked puzzled. "Then I don't understand. I know you prefer embodiment, for the sake of having honest perceptions of your surroundings, but we're not talking about immersing you in some comforting simulation of being back on Earth. Your experiment should last almost six picoseconds. Running on a strong-force substrate, you'd have a chance to watch the data coming in, in real time. Of course, you'll receive a useful subset of the same information eventually, but it won't be as detailed, or as immediate. *It won't be as real.*"

He smiled provocatively. "Suppose the ghost of Sarumpaet came to you in your sleep, and said: 'I'll grant you a dream in which you witness the decay of the Diamond Graph. You'll travel back in time, shrink to the Planck scale, and see everything with your own eyes, exactly as it happened. The only catch is, you won't remember anything when you wake.' You say you don't believe that the dreamer would be dying. *So wouldn't you still want the dream?*"

Cass let go of one handhold and swiveled away from the wall.

There wasn't much point objecting that he was offering her a view billions of times coarser than that, of a much less significant event. It wasn't a ringside seat at the birth of the universe, but it was still the closest she could hope to get to an event for which she'd already sacrificed seven hundred and forty-five years of her life.

She said, "It's not the fact that I wouldn't remember the experience. If you've lived through something, you've lived through it. What worries me is all the other things I'd have to live through. All the other people I'd have to become."

Cass dated the advent of civilization to the invention of the quantum singleton processor. The Qusp. She accepted the fact that she couldn't entirely avoid splitting into multiple versions; interacting with any ordinary object around her gave rise to an entangled system—Cass plus cloud, Cass plus flower—and she could never hope to prevent the parts that lay outside her from entering superpositions of different classical outcomes, generating versions of her who witnessed different external events.

Unlike her hapless ancestors, though, she did not contribute to the process herself. While the Qusp inside her skull performed its computations, it was isolated from the wider world—a condition lasting just microseconds at a time, but rigidly enforced for the duration—only breaking quarantine when its state vector described *one outcome, with certainty*. With each operating cycle, the Qusp rotated a vector describing a single alternative into another with the same property, and though the path between the two necessarily included superpositions of many alternatives, only the final, definite state determined her actions.

Being a singleton meant that her decisions counted. She was not forced to give birth to a multitude of selves, each responding in a different way, every time she found her conscience or her judgment balanced on a knife edge. She was not at all what *Homo sapiens* had actually been, but she was close to what they'd believed themselves to be, for most of their history: a creature of choice, capable of doing *one thing and not another.*

Rainzi didn't pursue the argument; he followed her in silence as she clambered into the display chamber. This was a small cavity in the Quietener's outer structure, not much larger than her room at the station, equipped with a single chair. There was no question of Cass being allowed any closer to the action; even the processor on which the Mimosans were running, scrupulously designed to spill as little noise into the environment as possible, was banished to the rim of the Quietener. Lacking the same antinoise features herself, she had to agree to be snap-frozen to a few Kelvin, three minutes before each run. Apart from being immobilized, this had no unpleasant side effects, but it served as an uncomfortable reminder of the fact that the closed-cycle "breathing" of her Mimosan body was pure placebo. Still, she'd been willing to put up with it twenty times so far, merely for the sake of sparing herself the three-second time lag for data to make its way back to the station.

As she took her place in the cryogenic chair, the other Mimosans began to appear around her. Teasing her, congratulating her on her stamina. Livia joked, "We should have had a wager as to whether or not the incremental targets would turn out to be a waste of time. You could have relieved me of all my worldly goods by now." Livia's sole material possession was a replica of an ancient bronze coin, carved from leftover asteroid metal.

Cass shook her head. "What would I have put up? My left arm?" They'd been right to do things Livia's way, and Cass had long ago ceased resenting it. Not only was it safer, it was better science, testing each novel structure one by one.

It turned out that Livia was alluding to a real wager: Bakim admitted that he'd made a bet with Darsono that Cass would not remain at Mimosa to the end. But he was unable to explain the stakes to her; her Mediator couldn't find a suitable analogy, and nothing she suggested herself was even close. No precious object or information would change hands, nor was there any token act of servitude or humiliation in store for the loser. Cass was amused by the bet itself, but it bothered her that she could only grasp half of what was going on. When her friends asked her about the Mimosans, would all her stories end with apologies for her own incomprehension? She might as well have visited one of the great cities back on Earth and spent her time living in a storm-water drain, having shouted conversations through a narrow grill with the people at street level, full of misunderstandings about objects and events she couldn't even glimpse.

Rainzi had clearly been delegated to put the Nuclear Question to her, because no one else broached the subject. Cass found it slightly galling that they wouldn't even suffer a moment's embarrassment when they took up their superior vantage point. They wouldn't depart, they wouldn't abandon her; they'd simply clone their minds into the nuclear substrate. With no expectation of recovering the clones, the originals would have no reason to pause, even for a picosecond, while their faster versions ran.

The target graph appeared on the wall in front of her. The four distinctive node patterns they'd tried in every other combination were all present now. Just as virtual particles stabilized the ordinary vacuum—creating a state of matter and geometry whose most likely successor was itself—Cass's four patterns steered the novo-vacuum closer to the possibility of persistence. The balance was only approximate: according to the Sarumpaet rules, even an infinite network built from this motif would decay into ordinary vacuum in a matter of seconds. At the Planck scale, that was no small achievement; a tightrope walker who managed to circumnavigate the Earth a few billion times before toppling to the ground might be described as having similarly imperfect balance. In reality, any fragment of novo-vacuum they managed to create would be surrounded from the start by its older, vastly more stable relative, and would face the inevitable about a trillion times faster.

Ilene reeled off a list of measurements from the instrument probes that were monitoring their environment, out to a radius of more than a light-hour. There was nothing on its way that could wreck the experiment—or at least, nothing traveling slower than ninety-five percent of lightspeed. Zulkifli followed with a status report from the machinery deep inside the Quietener. Systems that had been preparing themselves for the last twelve hours were now minutes away from readiness.

The single graph on the wall was just a useful shorthand for the state they were hoping to create; the novo-vacuum itself was the sum of equal parts of forty-eight variations of the target graph, all generated by simple symmetry transformations of the original. All the individual variations favored one direction over another, but the sum combined every possible bias, canceling them all out and giving rise to a perfectly isotropic state. Since none of the graphs could be found in nature, this elegant description was useless as a recipe, but it wasn't hard to show that the same state vector could also be described by a different sum: forty-eight regions of ordinary vacuum, each slightly curved, oriented in forty-eight different directions.

Inside the Quietener, an asteroid's-mass worth of helium had been cooled into a Bose–Einstein condensate, and manipulated into a state where it was equally likely to be found in any of forty-eight different places. These alternative locations were distributed across the surface of a sphere six kilometers wide. Ordinary matter—or any kind of matter interacting with the outside world—would have behaved as if each distinct position had already become the sole reality; if a swarm of dust particles wandering by had made themselves part of the system, or if the helium's behavior *en masse* had merely hinted at the detailed motion of its own atoms, then that behavior could only have told half the story—the classical half—and all the quantum subtleties would have been lost in the fine print. But the condensate was isolated as scrupulously as any cycling Qusp, and it had been cooled to the point where the states of all its individual atoms were dictated completely by its macroscopic properties. With no hidden complications, inside or out, the result was a quantum-mechanical system the size of a mountain.

The geometry of the vacuum in the Quietener inherited the helium's multiplicity: its state vector was a sum of the vectors for forty-eight different gravitational fields. Once the condensate's components had all been nudged into place, the quantum geometry at the center of the sphere would be equivalent to the novo-vacuum, and a new kind of space-time would blossom into existence.

That was the idealized version: a predictable event in a known location. In reality, the outcome remained hostage to countless imperfections and potential intrusions. If the experimenters were lucky, sometime over a period measured in minutes, somewhere over a region measured in meters, a few thousand cubic Planck lengths of novo-vacuum would be created, and survive for an unprecedented six-trillionths of a second.

Yann turned to Cass. "Are you ready to freeze?" The first time he'd asked her this, she'd been almost as nervous as the moment before she'd been transmitted from Earth, but the question had rapidly become a formality. *Of course she was ready. That was how things were done.* Just a few minutes of numb immobility, watching the data appear on the screen in front of her, and the odds were good that it would be the last time. A five-hour trip back to the station, a day or two of analysis, a brief celebration, and she would depart. Her Earth body, frozen more deeply than this one had ever been, was waiting for her. She'd step across the light-years in a subjective instant, a new set of memories to sweep away the icy cobwebs of her old self.

She said, "No. I'm not ready."

Yann looked alarmed, but only for a moment. Cass suspected that he'd just conferred privately with someone better able to guess what she had in mind. Though the Mimosans didn't think any more rapidly than she did—running on Qusps themselves, they faced the same computing bottlenecks—they could communicate with each other about five times faster than her own form of speech allowed. That only annoyed her when they used it to talk about her behind her back.

She added dryly, "Tell Rainzi I've changed my mind."

Yann smiled, clearly delighted, and then his icon was instantly replaced by Rainzi's. Fair enough: with the countdown proceeding, the Mimosans had better things to do than fake inertia for its own sake.

Rainzi's response was more cautious than Yann's. "Are you certain you want to do this? After everything you told me?"

"I'm the quintessential singleton," Cass replied. "I weigh up all my choices very carefully."

There was no time to spell out in glacial words everything she was feeling, everything that had swayed her. Part of it was the same sense of ownership that had brought her all this distance in the first place: justifiably or not, she didn't want the Mimosans to have a better view than she did of the thing they were about to create together. There was the same longing for immediacy, too: she would never see, or touch, any graph as it really was, but to remain locked in a body that could only perceive a fraction of the data, milliseconds after the fact, would leave her feeling almost as detached from the event, now, as if she'd stayed on Earth, waiting for the centuries-old news of an experiment conducted light-years away. Every viewpoint was a compromise, but she had to be as close as she could get.

Beyond the experiment itself, though, it was clear to her now that she couldn't leave Mimosa without doing at least one thing that went against the grain. After five years of monastic restraint, five years of denying herself the dishonest comforts of virtual reality, she was sick of placing that principle above everything else. Beyond the fact that *this* disembodiment would be entirely in the service of honesty, she needed, very badly, to drag herself out of the absolutist rut she'd been digging from the moment she'd arrived. If she'd compromised a little from the start, maybe she wouldn't have felt the same sense of desperation. But it was too late now for half-measures. If she returned to Earth *unchanged*, it wouldn't be a triumph of integrity. It would be a kind of death. She'd implode into something as hermetic and immutable as a black hole.

All this, weighed against the thing she hated most: lack of control. Every choice she made rendered meaningless. *What choices, though?* Her clones would run for a few subjective minutes, most of them in rapt attention as the data poured in. What was the worst that one of these transient selves might do? Utter a few unkind words to Livia or Darsono? Disclose some small guilty secret from her past to people who either wouldn't understand, wouldn't care, or at the very least, wouldn't have the chance to reproach her for long? She wasn't opening up the gates to the old human nightmare: endless varieties of suffering, endless varieties of stupidity, endless varieties of banality. She would diffuse a very small distance into the space of possibilities, and whatever unhappiness she might experience, whatever misdemeanors she might commit, would be erased beyond recovery.

Rainzi looked skeptical, and she couldn't blame him. But there was no time left for him to play devil's advocate, to test her resolve. Cass stood her ground, silently, and after a moment he nodded assent.

She felt a stream of low-level requests for data, and she willed her Mediator to respond. She'd been through the same process before her transmission from Earth: sending the preliminaries first, things that needed to be known about the structure of her mind before it could be implemented in a new environment.

Rainzi said, "Take my hand. We'll step through together." He placed his ghost-fingers over hers, and asked her for everything.

Cass examined his face. It was pure chance that her Mediator had given him an appearance that inspired trust in her, but the faces of the embodied were no better guides to character, whether they'd been sculpted by genes or by their wearer's wishes. If Rainzi's eyes still seemed kind to her, after five years, wasn't that because he'd shown her genuine kindness? This was not the time for paranoid delusions about the unknowable mind behind the mask.

She said, "Are you ever afraid of this, yourself?"

"A little," he admitted.

"What frightens you the most? What is it that you think might happen?"

He shook his head. "There's no terrible fate that I fear is lying in store for me. But however many times I do this, I come no closer to knowing what it's actually like. Don't you think there's something frightening about that?"

She smiled. "Absolutely." They weren't so different that she'd be insane to follow him, the way it would be insane to follow an armored robot into a volcano. This would not be strange or painful beyond her power to bear. If she truly wanted it, she had nothing to fear.

Cass opened the floodgates.

Rainzi's hand passed through her own, intangible as ever. Cass shuddered. *She was who she always was*, and the part of her who valued that above all else could not disguise its relief.

"Don't worry," he assured her, "you won't be hanging around waiting. And you won't be disappointed. The femtomachine will only start up on a definite signal from the Quietener; if there's nothing, it won't ever be run."

Cass protested, "Aren't you telling the wrong person?" He might have mentioned this before she'd been split.

Rainzi shrugged. "To the clone, it will be self-evident. If it gets the chance to think anything at all."

If the vacuum at the heart of the Quietener changed, her other self would wake, watch the whole event unfold in slow motion, bifurcate a million times, then vanish, before Cass had even noticed the good news. Neither the price nor the payoff were part of her own future, now.

Yet they would all be one person: awake, asleep. The dream she would not remember would be her own.

Here and now, though?

She would have to make do with whatever glimpses she could steal.

She turned to Yann. "Freeze me. One last time."

Chapter 3

Cass looked around the simulated chamber. The display on the wall was densely inscribed with new data, but nothing else appeared to have changed. The Mimosans were the usual icons drawn by her Mediator; she still had no hope of perceiving them as they perceived themselves. The structures in her mind where sensory data was represented hadn't changed; they simply weren't coupled to genuine sense organs anymore. It was only the touch of Rainzi's nonexistent skin against her own—a translation interacting with a simulation—that proved she'd stepped from her world into his.

Or rather, they'd both stepped together into a new world, from which neither of them could hope to emerge.

Cass felt no anxiety, just a bittersweet sense of everything her newfound freedom did and didn't mean. If she'd abandoned embodiment a year or two earlier, she might have had some prospect of going further: finding a path of gradual change that led to new abilities, such as the power to interpret the Mimosans' language firsthand. As it was, she didn't even have time for the smallest act of self-indulgence: a simulated swim, a solid meal, a glass of cool water. After five years, all the pleasures she'd been pining for had become attainable at the very moment when they would be nothing but unwelcome distractions.

She slipped her hand free of Rainzi's and turned to examine the display. A faint spray of particles was radiating out from the center of the Quietener, the sign of an unstable boundary between old vacuum and new.

The data had only been coming in for a few hundredths of a picosecond, so the statistics were still ambiguous. As she watched, rows of figures were updated, the sprinkling of points on half a dozen charts grew denser, curves shifted slightly. Cass knew where every number and every curve was heading; it was like watching the face of a long-awaited friend materialize out of the darkness, having pictured the reunion a thousand times. And if the face might yet turn out to be a stranger's, that had nothing to do with the way she felt. There was pleasure enough in anticipation; she didn't need to conjure up traces of doubt just to savor the added suspense.

"What we're doing isn't all that unusual," Darsono mused. "I think everyone lives in at least two time scales: one of them fast and immediate, and too detailed to retain in anything but outline; the other slow enough to be absorbed completely. We think our memory has no gaps, we think we carry our entire past inside us, because we're accustomed to looking back and seeing only sketches and highlights. But we all experience more than we remember."

"That's not true of everyone," Bakim countered. "There are people who record every thought they have."

"Yes, but unless every part of that record has the potential to be triggered automatically by subsequent thoughts and perceptions—which no one ever allows, because the barrage of associations would drive them mad—it's not true memory. It's just a list of all the things they've forgotten."

Bakim chortled. " 'True memory'? And I suppose if I perceive something with so much spatial resolution that I can't give immediate, conscious attention to every last detail simultaneously, it's not a 'true' perception—it's just a cruel taunt to drive home all the things I've failed to perceive?"

Cass smiled, but stayed out of the argument. *With certainty?* Probably not. But it was pointless dwelling on every potential branching; if and when she experienced something unpleasant, firsthand, or did something foolish herself, she could regret it. Anything else was both futile and a kind of masochistic double-counting. (And she would not start wondering if *that* resolution was universal—a constant across histories, an act of inevitable good sense—or just the luck of one branch.)

Livia said, "I don't understand what's happening with the energy spectrum." In the feigned weightlessness of the chamber, she appeared upside down, her face at the upper edge of Cass's vision. "Does that make sense to anyone?"

Cass examined the histogram showing the number of particles that had been detected in different energy ranges; it did not appear to be converging on the theoretically predicted curve. She'd noticed this earlier, but she'd assumed it was just an artifact of the small sample they'd collected. The histogram's rim was quite smooth, though, and its overall shape wasn't fluctuating much, so its failure to match the curve really didn't look like an accident of noise. Worse, all the high-powered statistics beneath the chart suggested that there was now enough data to give a reliable picture of the underlying spectrum.

"Could we have miscalculated the border geometry?" Rainzi wondered. The particles they were seeing reflected the way the novo-vacuum was collapsing. Cass had first modeled the process back on Earth, and her calculations had shown that, although the border's initial shape would be a product of both pure chance and some uncontrollable details of conditions in the Quietener, as it collapsed it would rapidly become spherical, all quirks and wrinkles smoothed out.

At least, that was true if some plausible assumptions held. She said, "If the converted region had a sufficiently pathological shape to start with, it might have retained that as it shrank. But I don't know what could have caused that in the first place."

"Some minor contaminant that wasn't quite enough to wreck coherence?" Ilene suggested.

Cass made a noncommittal sound. It would be nice to have a view from several different angles, allowing them to pick up any asymmetry in the radiation. But they'd been woken by the arrival of data from the cluster of detectors closest to the femtomachine; information from the second-closest would take almost another microsecond to reach the same spot, by which time they'd be long gone. Her old embodied self would get to see the big picture, albeit more coarsely grained. Her own task—her own entire *raison d'être*—was to make what sense she could of the clues at hand.

The energy spectrum wasn't jagged and complicated, or even particularly broad. It didn't look *wrong enough* to be the product of a sausage- or pancake- or doughnut-shaped region of novo-vacuum, let alone some more exotic structure with a convoluted fractal border. The peak had about the same width, and the same kind of smooth symmetry as the predicted curve; it was merely displaced upward along the energy scale, and the shoulders on either side were reversed. It wasn't literally a mirror image of the expected result, but Cass felt sure it was the product of some fairly simple transformation. If you changed a single plus sign to a minus, somewhere deep in the underlying equations, *this* would be the outcome.

Zulkifli was one step ahead of her. "If you modify the operator that acts on the border, swapping the roles of the inside and outside of the region, you get a perfect match."

Cass experienced a shiver of fear, all the more disturbing for evoking the phantom viscera of her Earth body. *If Zulkifli's claim was true, then the region was expanding, not collapsing.*

She said, "Are you sure that works?"

Zulkifli made his private calculations visible, and superimposed the results on the histogram. His curve ran straight through the tops of all the bars. He'd found the plus sign that had turned into a minus. Except—

"That can't be right," she declared. The simple role reversal he'd suggested was elegant, but nonsensical: it was like claiming that they were seeing the light from a fire in which ashes were burning into wood. Conservation of energy was a subtle concept, even in classical general relativity, but in QGT it came down to the fact that the flat vacuum state remained completely unchanged from moment to moment. An awful lot of physics flowed from that simple requirement, and though it was remote from everyday notions of work, heat, and energy, a billion commonplace events that Cass had witnessed throughout her life would have been impossible, if the truth were so different that Zulkifli's border operator was the right choice.

There was silence. No one could contradict her, nor could they deny that Zulkifli's curve matched the data.

Then Livia spoke. "The Sarumpaet rules make our own vacuum perfectly stable; that's the touchstone Sarumpaet used from the start. But the novo-vacuum is *not* decaying in the way those rules predict. So what's the simplest way to reconcile the contradictions?" She paused for a moment, then offered her own solution. "Suppose *both* kinds of vacuum are perfectly stable, on their own. If there's a wider law that makes that true—with the Sarumpaet rules as a special case—we would never have stumbled on it in the staged experiments, because we never had the full set of virtual particles that constituted a viable alternative vacuum."

Yann grinned appreciatively. "All states with the potential to be a vacuum must be treated equally? However exotic we might think they are, they're all eternal? Very democratic! But wouldn't that imply a stalemate? Wouldn't that freeze the novo-vacuum, leaving the border fixed?"

Ilene said, "No. The dynamics needn't be that evenhanded. One side could still convert the other at a boundary. The one with the fewest species of particles, I expect."

By any count, the novo-vacuum was the more streamlined of the two. Cass was more angry than afraid, though. Talk of a runaway vacuum conversion was intolerable; they'd spent five years ruling that out, validating the Sarumpaet rules for every related graph. They could not have been more cautious.

Rainzi said calmly, "Suppose the novo-vacuum is growing. What happens when it encounters some contamination? It's a coherent state that could only be created in perfect isolation, in the middle of the purest vacuum in the universe. It's fragility incarnate. Once it hits a few stray neutrinos and decoheres, it will be forty-eight flavors of ordinary vacuum—all of them in separate histories, all of them harmless."

Livia glanced warily at Cass. It was as if she wanted Cass to be the bearer of bad news for a change, rather than always hearing it from her.

Cass obliged her. "I wish you were right, Rainzi, but that argument's biased. It's just as correct to say that our own vacuum is a superposition of different curved versions of the novo-vacuum. If there really is a new dynamic law at work here, and if it preserves the novo-vacuum precisely, then according to *that* law, it's *our* vacuum that's the delicate quantum object waiting to decohere."

Rainzi pondered this. "You're right," he conceded. "Though even that doesn't tell us much about the border. Neither of the specialized laws that apply on either side can hold there. We'll only understand the fate of the border if we can understand the general law."

Cass laughed bitterly. "What difference does it make, what *we* understand? We won't be able to tell anyone! We won't be able to warn them!" The border wasn't traveling at lightspeed—or they wouldn't have been woken at all before it swept over the femtomachine—but it was unlikely to be spreading so slowly that their originals would see it coming, let alone have a chance to evacuate. In any case, what she and her fellow clones knew was worthless; they had no way to share their knowledge with the outside world. The femtomachine was designed to do no more than compute its inhabitants, for their own benefit. All it would leave behind was debris. Even if they could encode a message in the decay products, no one would be looking for it.

A lifetime's worth of defensive slogans about the perils of VR started clamoring in her head. She wanted to scrape this whole illusion off her face, like a poisonous, blinding cobweb; she wanted to see and touch reality again. *To have real skin, to breathe real air, would change everything.* If she could only see the world through her own eyes, and react with the instincts of her own body, she knew she could flee from any danger.

It was so perverse it was almost funny. She was perceiving the danger a billion times more clearly than she could ever have hoped to if she'd been embodied. She had all her reflexes at her disposal, and all her powers of reasoning, operating a billion times faster than usual.

It was just a shame that all of these advantages counted for nothing.

Zulkifli said, "The brightness is increasing."

Cass examined the evidence as dispassionately as she could. A slow, steady rise in the rate of particle production was apparent now, clearly distinguishable from the background fluctuations that had initially masked it. That could only mean that the border was growing. Short of some freakishly benign explanation for this—a fractal crinkling that allowed the border to increase in area while the volume of novo-vacuum itself was shrinking—this left little room for doubt about which vacuum was being whittled away to produce the particles they were seeing. The thing she had always thought of as an elegant piece of whimsy—as charming and impractical as a mythical beast that might be bioengineered into existence, and kept alive briefly if it was pampered and protected, but which could never have lasted five minutes outside its glass cage—was now visibly devouring its ancient, wild cousin. She had summoned up, not a lone, defenseless exile from a world that could never have been, but the world itself—and it was proving to be every bit as autonomous and viable as her own.

Rainzi addressed her, gently but directly. "If the station is destroyed, we all have recent backups *en route* to Viro. What about you?"

She said, "I have my memories back on Earth. But nothing since I arrived here." The five years she'd spent among the Mimosans would be lost. *It had still happened. She had still lived through it all. It would be amnesia, not death.* But if that argument had been enough to let her step willingly into the *cul-de-sac* she inhabited now, she wasn't sure she could push it far enough to reconcile herself to the greater loss. She had finally become someone new, at the station—someone different enough from her old self to be here now, beside the Mimosans. But the Cass who had steeled herself to leave the solar system for the very first time would wake from her frozen sleep unchanged, to learn that the emboldened traveler she'd hoped to become was dead.

"I don't know how to help you make peace with that," Rainzi said. "But I can only think of one way to make my own peace with the people we've endangered." Mimosa was remote from the rest of civilization, but the process they'd begun would not burn itself out, would not fade or weaken with distance. With vacuum as its fuel, the wildfire would spread inexorably: to Viro, to Maeder, to a thousand other worlds. To Earth.

Cass asked numbly, "How?"

"If we can see a way to stop this," Rainzi replied, "then it doesn't matter that we can't enact it ourselves, or even get the word out to anyone else. We can still take comfort in uncovering the right strategy. I know we have certain advantages—in the time resolution with which we're seeing the data, and in being the only witnesses to this early stage—but on balance, I think the combined population of the rest of the galaxy constitutes more than an even match. If we can find a solution, someone out there will find it, too."

Cass looked around at the others. She felt lost, rootless. Not guilty, yet. Not monstrous. The Mimosans would all wake on Viro, missing a few hours' memories but otherwise unscathed, and though she'd robbed them of their home, they'd understood the risks as well as she did when they'd chosen to conduct the experiment. But if the loss of the Quietener and the station was something she could come to terms with, it was still surreal to extrapolate from her own few picoseconds of helplessness to the exile of whole civilizations. She had to face the truth, but she was far from certain that the right way to do that was to hunt for a solution that would at best be a plausible daydream.

Darsono caught her eye. "I agree with Rainzi," he said solemnly. "We have to do this. We have to find the cure."

"Livia?"

"Absolutely." Livia smiled. "Actually, I'm far more ambitious than Rainzi. I'm not willing to concede yet that we can't stop this ourselves."

Zulkifli said dryly, "I doubt that. But I want to know if my family will be safe."

Ilene nodded. "It's not much, but it's better than giving up. I'm not bailing out just to spare myself the sense of being powerless—not while data's pouring in, and we can still look for an answer."

"The danger doesn't seem real to me," Yann admitted. "Viro is seventeen light-years away, and we can't be sure that this thing won't snuff itself out before it even grazes the shell of the Quietener. But I would like to know the general law that replaces the Sarumpaet rules. It's been twenty thousand years! It's about time we had some new physics."

Cass turned to Bakim.

He shrugged. "What else are we going to do? Play charades?"

Cass was outnumbered, and she wanted to be swayed. She ached to get her hands on even the smallest piece of evidence that the disaster could be contained, and if they failed, it would still be the least morbid way to go out: struggling to the end to find a genuine cause for optimism.

But they were fooling themselves. In the few subjective minutes left to them, what hope did they have of achieving that?

She said simply, "We'll never make it. We'll test one hunch against the data, find it's wrong, and that will be it."

Rainzi smiled as if she'd said something comically naive. Before he spoke, Cass recalled what it was she had forgotten.

What it was she had become.

He said, "That's how it will seem for most of us. But that shouldn't be disheartening. Because every time we fail, we'll know that another version of ourselves will have tested another idea. There will always be a chance that one of them was right."

Part Two

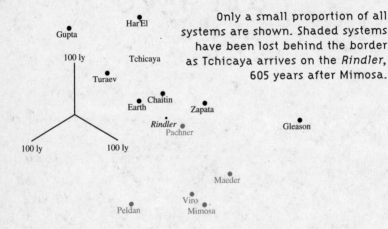

Inhabited Space

Only a small proportion of all systems are shown. Shaded systems have been lost behind the border as Tchicaya arrives on the *Rindler*, 605 years after Mimosa.

Gupta

Har'El

100 ly

Tchicaya

Turaev

Chaitin

Earth

Zapata

Rindler

Pachner

Gleason

100 ly

100 ly

Maeder

Viro

Peldan

Mimosa

Chapter 4

By choice, Tchicaya's mind started running long before his new body was fully customized. As his vision came into focus, he turned his gaze from the softly lit lid of the crib to the waxen, pudgy template that he now inhabited. Waves of organizers swarmed up and down his limbs and torso like mobile bruises beneath the translucent skin, killing off unwanted cells and cannibalizing them, stimulating others to migrate or divide. The process wasn't painful—at worst it tickled, and it was even sporadically sexy—but Tchicaya felt an odd compulsion to start pummeling the things with his fists, and he had no doubt that squashing them flat would be enormously satisfying. The urge was probably an innate response to Earthly parasites, a misplaced instinct that his ancestors hadn't got around to editing out. Or perhaps they'd retained it deliberately, in the hope that it might yet turn out to be useful elsewhere.

As he raised his head to get a better view, he caught sight of an undigested stretch of calf, still bearing traces of the last inhabitant's body hair and musculature. "Urrggh." The noise sounded alien, and left a knot in his throat. The crib said, "Please don't try to talk yet." The organizers swept over the offending remnant and dissolved it.

Morphogenesis from scratch, from a single cell, couldn't be achieved in less than three months. This borrowed body wouldn't even have the DNA he'd been born with, but it had been designed to be easy to regress and sculpt into a fair approximation of any-one who'd remained reasonably close to their human ancestors, and the process could be completed in about three hours. When traveling this way, Tchicaya usually elected to become conscious only for the final fitting: the tweaking of his mental body maps to accommodate all the minor differences that were too much of a nuisance to eliminate physically. But he'd decided that for once he'd wake early, and experience as much as he could.

He watched his arms and fingers lengthen slightly, the flesh growing too far in places, then dying back. Organizers flowed into his mouth, re-forming his gums, nudging his teeth into new loca-tions, thickening his tongue, then sloughing off whole layers of excess tissue. He tried not to gag.

"Dith ith horrible," he complained.

"Just imagine what it would be like if your brain was flesh, too," the crib responded. "All those neural pathways being grown and hacked away—like a topiary full of tableaux from someone else's life being shaped into a portrait of your own past. You'd be having nightmares, hallucinations, flashbacks from the last user's memories."

The crib wasn't sentient, but pondering its reply made a useful distraction from the squirming sensation Tchicaya was beginning to feel in his gut. It was a much more productive rejoinder than: "You're the idiot who asked to be awake for this, so why don't you shut up and make the best of it?"

When his tongue felt serviceably de-slimed, he said, "Some people think the same kind of thing happens digitally. Every time you reconfigure a Qusp to run someone new, the mere act of loading the program generates experiences, long before you for-mally start it running."

"Oh, I'm sure it does," the crib conceded cheerfully. "But the nature of the process guarantees that you never remember any of it."

When Tchicaya was able to stand, the crib opened its lid and had him pace the recovery room. He stretched his arms, swiveled his head, bent and arched his spine, while the crib advised his Qusp on the changes it would have to make in order to bring his expectations for kinesthetic feedback and response times into line with reality. In a week or two he would have accommodated to the differences anyway, but the sooner they were dealt with, the sooner he'd lose the distracting sense that his own flesh was like poorly fitted clothing.

The clothes that were waiting for him had already been informed of his measurements, and the styles, colors, and textures he preferred. They'd come up with a design in magenta and yellow that looked sunny without being garish, and he felt no need to ask for changes, or to view a range of alternatives.

As he dressed, Tchicaya examined himself in the wall mirror. From the whorl of dark bristles on his scalp to the glistening scar running down his right leg, every visible feature had been reproduced faithfully from a micrometer-level description of his body on the day he'd left his home world. For all he could tell, this might as well have been the original. The internal sense of familiarity was convincing, too; he'd lost the slight tension in his shoulder muscles that had been building up over the last few weeks before his departure, but having just rid himself of all the far more uncomfortable kinks he'd acquired in the crib, that was hardly surprising. And if this scar was not the scar from his childhood, not the same collagen laid down by the healing skin in his twelve-year-old body, nor would it have been the same in his adult body by now, if he'd never left home. All an organism could do from day to day was shore itself up in some rough semblance of its previous condition. The same was true, from moment to moment, for the state of the whole universe. By one means or another, everyone was an imperfect imitation of whatever they'd been the day before.

Still, it was only when you traveled that you needed to dispose of your own past, or leave behind an ever-growing residue. Tchicaya told the crib, "Recycle number ten." He'd forgotten exactly where the tenth-last body he'd inhabited was stored, but when his authorization reached it, the memories sitting passively in its Qusp would be erased, and its flesh would be recycled into the same kind of waxen template as the one he'd just claimed as his own.

The crib said, "There is no number ten, by my count. Do you want to recycle number nine?"

Tchicaya opened his mouth to protest, then realized that he'd spoken out of habit. When he'd left Pachner, thirty years before—a few subjective hours ago—he'd known full well that his body trail would be growing shorter by one while he was still in transit, and he wouldn't have to lift a finger or say a word to make it happen.

He said, "Keep number nine."

As he stepped out of the recovery room, Tchicaya was grateful for his freshly retuned sense of balance. The deck beneath his feet was opaque, but it sat inside a transparent bubble a hundred meters wide, swinging for the sake of gravity at the end of a kilometer-long tether. To his left, the ship's spin was clearly visible against the backdrop of stars, all the more so because the axis of rotation coincided with the direction of travel. The stars turning slowly in the smallest circles were tinted icy blue, while away from the artificial celestial pole they took on more normal hues, ultimately reddening slightly. The right half of the sky was starless, filled instead with a uniform glow that was untouched by the Doppler shift, and so featureless that there was nothing to be seen moving within it: not one speck of greater or lesser brightness rising over the deck in time with the stars.

From the surface of Pachner, the border of the Mimosa vacuum had appeared very different, a shimmering sphere of light blazing a fierce steely blue at the center, but cooled toward the edges by its own varied Doppler shift. The graded color had made it look distinctly rounded and three-dimensional, and the fact that you could apparently see it curving away from you had added to an already deceptive impression of distance. Because it was expanding at half the speed of light, the amount of sky the border blotted out was not a reliable measure of its proximity. Looking away from its nearest point meant looking back to a time when it had been considerably smaller, and starlight that had grazed the sphere centuries before—skirting the danger, and appearing to delineate it—actually told you nothing about its present size. When Tchicaya had left, Pachner had been little more than two years away from being engulfed, but the border had barely changed its appearance in the decade he'd spent there, and it would still have occupied a mere one hundred and twenty degrees of the view at the instant the planet was swallowed.

Tchicaya had been on Pachner to talk to people on the verge of making their escape. He'd had to flee long before the hard cases, who'd boasted that they'd be leaving with just seconds to spare, but as far as he knew he'd been the only evacuee who was planning to end up closer to the border than when he left. Doomed planets were useless as observation posts; no sooner did the object of interest come near than you had to retreat from it at the speed of light. The *Rindler* was constantly retreating, but no faster than was absolutely necessary. Matching velocities with the border transformed its appearance; from the observation deck, the celestial image that had become an emblem of danger for ten thousand civilizations was nowhere to be seen. The border finally looked like the thing it was: a vast, structureless, immaterial wall between two incomparably different worlds.

"Tchicaya!"

He looked around. There were a dozen people nearby, but they were all intent on the view. Then he spotted a lanky figure approaching, an arm stretched up in greeting. Tchicaya didn't recognize the face, but his Mediator picked up a familiar signature.

"Yann?" Tchicaya had known for centuries that Yann was also weaving his way toward the *Rindler*, but the last place he'd expected to run into him was the observation deck. In all the time they'd been in contact, exchanging messengers across decades and light-years, Yann had been strictly acorporeal.

The half-stranger stood before him. "How are you?"

Tchicaya smiled. "I'm fine. You seem to have put on weight."

Yann shrugged apologetically. "Conforming to local fashions. I still think it's an absurdity: boosting millions of tonnes of furniture into a trajectory like this, when a few hundred kilograms of instrumentation and Qusps could have achieved as much. But given that they've gone ahead and done it anyway, and given that most of the people here are wearing flesh, I have to take account of that. I need to be in the thick of things, or there's no point being here at all."

"That makes sense," Tchicaya conceded. He hated the idea of anyone being forced out of their preferred mode, but the political realities were undeniable.

If the optimists were right, and the border's current velocity was the highest it would ever be, the simplest way to avoid the threat would be to flee from it. If your whole world already consisted of compact, robust hardware that was designed to function in interstellar space, the prospect of engineering in the necessary shielding against relativistic collisions with gas and dust, accelerating to a suitable velocity—half c plus a chosen safety margin—then simply coasting away from the danger, was not unthinkable at all. A dozen acorporeal communities, and countless scattered individuals, had already done that.

For people accustomed to dwelling on a planetary surface, though, the notion of entering a permanent state of flight was more likely to be horrifying. So far, the Mimosan vacuum had swallowed more than two thousand inhabited systems, and while most of the planet-hopping refugees were willing to transmit themselves at lightspeed from point to point, in less than two millennia all the old, established colony worlds that had taken them in would themselves be gone. In principle, the process could be prolonged indefinitely: new, habitable planets could be prepared in advance by high-velocity spore packages, with people following close behind. Each temporary home would last a little longer than the one before, as the border was outpaced. People might even grow accustomed to the fact that every world they set foot upon would be obliterated, not in billions of years, but in a few thousand. It would take six times as long as recorded history before the entire Milky Way was lost, and by then, the gulf between neighboring galaxies might seem less daunting.

Even assuming a watertight proof, though, that the border would not speed up without warning and turn that whole scenario into a rosy-hued fantasy, exile was not a fate to be accepted lightly. If it was physically possible to turn back the novovacuum—to seed its destruction, the way the Mimosans had seeded its creation—Tchicaya's fellow embodied had by far the greatest stake in making that happen. It was not going to be easy to persuade them that they shouldn't try.

Yann said, "You've just come from Pachner?"

Tchicaya nodded. He was pleased to have met up with Yann, but he was having trouble maintaining eye contact; the spinning sky kept drawing his gaze. "When did you get here?" He'd lost track of Yann's recent movements; communication between interstellar travelers had always been difficult, with line-of-sight time lags and transit insentience, but having to route signals around a constantly growing obstacle had added a further level of delays and fragmentation.

"Almost nine years ago."

"Ha! And there I was thinking you were the one out of your element."

Yann took a moment to interpret this. "You've never been in space before?"

"No."

"Not even planetary orbit?" He sounded incredulous.

Tchicaya was annoyed; it was a bit rich for a former acorporeal to put such stock in where he had or hadn't been, in the flesh. "Why would I have been in space? Vacuum never used to be much of an attraction."

Yann smiled. "Do you want to take the grand tour, while I fill you in?"

"Definitely." Everything Tchicaya had heard about the state of play on the *Rindler* was out of date—though not by the full sixty years that his thirty-year journey would normally have implied. He did a quick calculation before confirming the result with the ship: fifty-two years had elapsed here, since the last bulletin that he'd received on Pachner had been sent.

Stairs led down from the observation deck to a walkway. The ship was made up of sixteen separate modules arranged in a ring; the tethers joining them to the hub were not traversable, but there were umbilicals linking adjacent modules. Once they'd left the shelter of the deck behind, Tchicaya could see the engines sitting at the hub as dark outlines clustered at the zenith. They were unlikely to be used again for some time; if the border suddenly accelerated, it would probably move too fast for the *Rindler* to escape, and everyone onboard would evacuate the way they'd arrived: as data. Even if the ship was destroyed without warning, though, most people would only lose a few hours' memories.

Tchicaya had instructed his Qusp to transmit daily backups, and no doubt Yann was doing something similar, having escaped from the Mimosan vacuum once already that way.

The view from the narrow walkway was disorienting; without an expanse of deck imposing a visual horizon, the rim of the border became the most compelling cue. Tchicaya began to feel as if he was walking inside a huge horizontal centrifuge, hovering an indeterminate distance above an ocean shrouded in white fog. Any attempt to replace this mildly strange hypothesis with the idea that he was actually keeping pace with a shock wave six hundred light-years wide did nothing to improve his steadiness.

"The factions have names now," Yann began.

Tchicaya groaned. "That's a bad sign. There's nothing worse than a label, to cement people's loyalties."

"And nothing worse than loyalties cementing while we're still in the minority. We're Yielders, they're Preservationists."

" 'Yielders'? Whose idea was that?"

"I don't know. These things just seem to crystallize out of the vacuum."

"With a little seeding from the spin doctors. I suppose it's a step up from being Suicidal Deviants, or Defeatist Traitors."

"Oh, those terms are still widely used, informally."

Without warning, Tchicaya's legs buckled. He knelt on the walkway and closed his eyes. He said, "It's all right. Just give me a second."

Yann suggested mildly, "If the view's that unsettling, why not paste something over it?"

Tchicaya scowled. His vestibular system wanted him to curl up on the ground, block out all the contradictory visual signals, and wait for normality to be restored. He spread his arms slightly, reassuring himself that he was prepared to take action to recover his balance at short notice. Then he opened his eyes and rose to his feet. He took a few deep breaths, then started walking again.

"Both stances remain purely theoretical," Yann continued. "The Preservationists are no more prepared to erase the Mimosan vacuum than we are to adapt to it. But the team working on the Planck worms has just attracted a fresh batch of recruits, and they're running experiments all the time. If it ever does come down to a technological race, it's sure to be a close one."

Tchicaya contemplated this prospect glumly. "Whoever first gains the power to impose their own view decides the issue? Isn't that the definition of barbarism?" They'd reached the stairs that led up to the deck of the next module. He gripped the rails and ascended shakily, relieved to be surrounded by the clutter of ordinary objects.

They emerged at the edge of a garden, engineered in a style Tchicaya hadn't seen before. Stems coiled in elaborate helices, sprouting leaves tiled with hexagonal structures that glinted like compound eyes. According to the ship, the plants had been designed to thrive in the constant borderlight, though it was hard to see how that could have required some of their more exotic features. Still, the embellishments did not seem overdone here. Pure-bred roses or orchids would have been cloyingly nostalgic in the middle of interstellar space.

There were more people in the garden than on the observation deck. When strangers caught his eye, Tchicaya smiled and offered whatever gestures his Mediator deemed appropriate to greet them in passing, but he wasn't ready for formal introductions, sorting everyone into opposing camps.

"Isn't there a level where both sides can still cooperate?" he asked. "If we can't agree on the theory that's going to underpin whatever action finally gets taken, we might as well all give up and join the wagon train to Andromeda."

Yann was apologetic. "Of course. Don't let my moaning give you too bleak a picture. We haven't reached the point of hostility for its own sake; we still pool resources for the basic science. It's only the goal-directed experiments that make things a little frosty. When Tarek started scribing graphs at the border that he believed stood a good chance of being viable proto-worms, we cut him out of all the theoretical discussion groups and data sharing agreements—though none of us thought he was in any danger of succeeding. Since then, he's backed off slightly, and agreed to limit himself to graphs that can test his hunches without running amok if they happen to confirm them."

Tchicaya began to protest, but Yann cut him off. "Yes, I know that's a treaty full of holes: it wouldn't take much disingenuousness to pretend that success was just a terrible mistake. But who am I to lecture anyone about the results they should or shouldn't have expected?"

Tchicaya muttered, "Everyone's wise about the accident, after the fact." He'd met people who'd claimed they'd happily obliterate every extant version of Cass and her accomplices, though that was the rare, extremist view. More commonly, it was conceded that the Mimosans had been cautious, and could not be judged by the magnitude of the force they'd unleashed. Few people could honestly claim that in the Mimosans' place, they would have treated the Sarumpaet rules—inviolate for twenty thousand years—as being subject to serious doubt, let alone erasure.

The last Tchicaya had heard, seventeen people out of the billions of evacuees had chosen to stand their ground and die. He knew that these suicides weighed on Yann's conscience—as did the distress of all those who'd been driven from their homes—but that didn't dictate his attitude to the phenomenon. It might have been tactful to withdraw from the debate entirely, as the other seven had, but Tchicaya understood his refusal to do so. The fate of the vacuum had to be argued on its merits, not treated as a surrogate through which its creators could be condemned or absolved, and Yann intended the fact that he'd dared to take sides to highlight that distinction.

"So there's been no theoretical progress while I was in transit?" A definitive breakthrough would have been the first thing Yann mentioned, but there might still have been promising developments.

Yann shrugged. "Three steps left, four steps down. We scribe these elaborate probe graphs and drop them through the border, then hope that whatever we can see of their decay will tell us something useful. Even when we make an inspired choice of probe and get a clean set of data, as evidence for competing models it's all hideously indirect."

In the immediate aftermath of the accident, it had been easy to devise candidates for meta-rules that stabilized both the old and new vacuum in bulk. In those days, the theorists' biggest problem had been an excess of possibilities. The borderlight's spectrum had helped narrow the choices somewhat, and even the single, fortunate fact that the border was traveling slower than light had ultimately been shown to rule out a class of theories in which the accident had merely changed some particle masses and triggered a boring old Higgs field collapse. In that case, the Mimosan vacuum would have been nothing but a lower-energy version of the ordinary vacuum, and coming to terms with its physics would have been as simple as altering a few numbers in the old equations. A careful analysis, though, had eventually confirmed most people's instinctive hunch: any single kind of vacuum—even one that was undergoing such a collapse—had to appear exactly the same to anyone who was coasting through it, an ancient principle known as Lorentz invariance, dating back to the abolition of the aether. The only velocity at which a change could spread while satisfying that criterion was lightspeed.

Since the *Rindler* had provided a stable platform from which to probe the border experimentally—while vividly driving home the point that it was *not* Lorentz-invariant—the embarrassment of riches had proved illusory. Once it had become possible to put the new theories to the test, the only ones that hadn't been falsified were those that remained too ill-defined to offer clear predictions. That provisional vagueness wasn't necessarily a flaw, though; it could easily be the case that the correct grand generalization of the Sarumpaet rules simply *couldn't* be pinned down from one example of a stable vacuum and a murky glimpse of another, and it was better to be forced to confront that fact than to be lulled for a second time into a false sense of security.

Yann said thoughtfully, "I suppose we could always stop messing about trying to peek behind the border, and just resurrect the Quietener." He punched his hands together enthusiastically. "A few well-planned experiments in the old style might cut straight to the heart of things."

"Oh, that's a great idea. We could do it right here." A second seeding of the novo-vacuum, from a starting point that was already moving rapidly in the same direction as everyone who was fleeing the first, would be twice as difficult to escape. Yann's sardonic suggestion was sobering, though, since it was far from being the only way in which the disaster might be magnified. However careful they were, whatever their motives, there was always the chance of simply making things worse.

"We're dropping the next probe in about twelve hours' time," Yann said. "If you're interested, I could probably swing it."

"Swing what?"

"Bringing you along."

Tchicaya's throat tightened. "You mean, you go down there? In person?"

"Absolutely."

"*Why?*"

Yann laughed. "Don't ask me! You're the one with the flesh fetish; I thought you'd understand. That's how they do things here. I just play along."

Tchicaya looked past him, into the opaque pearly light, more featureless than any darkness he'd ever encountered. The eyes relished darkness, conjuring up hints of what it might contain, but the borderlight flooded his vision with incontrovertible blankness.

And he believed he could live in that light? He believed the embodied should end their flight, end their resistance, and march straight into that blinding whiteness?

The borderlight was a surface phenomenon, a distractingly perfect veil. Whatever lay behind it could easily be as richly structured and complex as the universe he knew.

He said, "Let me sleep on it."

Half the *Rindler*'s sixteen modules were devoted to accommodation. The ship informed Tchicaya of the cabin he'd been allocated, but he declined detailed directions, since Yann seemed eager to continue as his guide.

"I'll show you where I am, myself, first," Yann offered. "It's on the way, and you're always welcome to drop by." The accommodation modules were all split into multiple levels; away from the edges, where you could still glimpse the sky, it was like being in a high-rise building. When they left the stairwell, Yann paced briskly down a corridor, and pointed out the room.

Tchicaya's heart sank. The cabin was divided into two banks of narrow slots, each about a meter wide and half as high. A number of the slots contained inert figures. Rows of handholds between the pigeonholes were apparently intended to assist the occupants in gaining access. Yann followed his gaze and said, "It's not that hard, once you're used to it." He demonstrated, clambering up and sliding into his coffin-sized bunk, the fifth in a stack of eight.

Tchicaya said forlornly, "My embodiment request had the standard clause: if there was no room for me here at full size, the ship was meant to bounce me to the nearest alternative destination. Maybe I'm going to have to start spelling out the meaning of some of those terms." In four millennia of traveling between planetary surfaces, he'd encountered a wide range of living conditions deemed acceptable by the local people, whether through custom or necessity. On rare occasions, he'd even been provided with deliberately inhospitable accommodation. He'd never seen people squeezed together as tightly as this.

"Mmm." Yann's response was noncommittal, as if in retrospect he wasn't surprised by the complaint, but it honestly hadn't occurred to him that a newcomer would see the *Rindler* as cramped. He deftly reversed his insertion maneuver and joined Tchicaya on the deck.

"I'd suggest they ease things by scrapping the garden," Tchicaya mused, "but given how little difference that would make, they probably should keep it, for sanity's sake."

Yann squeezed past him, back into the corridor. Tchicaya trudged after him dejectedly. He'd felt no sense of panic upon waking in the confinement of the crib, but he hadn't realized he'd soon be moving into something smaller.

He crossed the final walkway with his eyes locked straight ahead, still faltering every ten or fifteen meters when the false horizon became impossible to ignore. He was angry that he was letting these petty tribulations weigh on him. He was lucky: he was used to travel, he was used to change, and he should have been inured to this kind of minor disappointment. Most of the evacuees on the verge of leaving Pachner had lived there all their lives, and change of the kind they were about to confront was something metaphysically foreign to them. Never mind what lay behind the borderlight; those people knew the shape of every rock within a thousand-kilometer radius of their homes, and even if they ended up on a world miraculously similar by any planetologist's standards, they'd still feel alienated and dispossessed.

As they climbed the stairs, Tchicaya joked, "Let's head back to the garden. I can sleep in the bushes." His shoulders were already aching at the thought of having to lie so still. He could modify himself to lose his usual urge to turn over repeatedly as he slept, but the prospect of needing to do that only made him feel claustrophobic in a deeper sense. You could whittle away a hundred little things like that, and not miss any of them individually, but then you woke one day to find that half your memories no longer rang true, every minor joy and hardship drained of its flavor and significance.

"D37, wasn't it?" Yann asked cheerfully. "That's left here, then fourth door on the right." He stopped and let Tchicaya walk past him. "I'll talk to you again soon about the probe drop, but I'm sure the others won't object."

"Yeah. Thanks." Tchicaya raised a hand in farewell.

The doors he passed were all closed, but the fourth recognized him and opened to his presence.

In front of him stood a desk, two chairs, and a set of shelves. He stepped into the room, and saw one, quite spacious, bed. Behind a partition, there was a shower, toilet and basin.

He sprinted after Yann, who started fleeing halfheartedly, then gave up and doubled over with laughter.

"Bastard!" Tchicaya caught up with him, and thumped him on the arm, hard enough to elicit a satisfying yelp.

"Show some cultural sensitivity!" Yann pleaded. "Pain isn't part of my traditional gestalt." Which made it unlikely that he'd actually felt any; even among the embodied, it was a shade conservative to let anything short of structural damage register as genuine discomfort.

"Nor is space, apparently."

Yann shook his head, and tried to appear earnest. "On the contrary. I've always had a sophisticated self-and-environment map; us ex-acorporeals just aren't hung up about its correlations with the physical world. Whatever it looks like to you, what we experience in that crowded cabin is ten orders of magnitude beyond any luxury you've ever known." He said this without a trace of gloating or pomposity. It wasn't hyperbole, or wishful thinking; it was simply true.

"You know I almost turned around and left the ship?"

Yann snickered, completely unconvinced.

Tchicaya was at a loss for any suitable parting threat, so he just raised his arms in resignation and walked back to his cabin.

Sweeping his gaze around the modest few square meters made him beam like an idiot. It was one-thousandth the size of the house he'd lived in on Pachner, but it was everything he needed.

"Bastard." He lay down on the bed and thought about revenge.

Chapter 5

The shuttle separated from the *Rindler,* sending Tchicaya's stomach into free fall. He watched the docking module retreat, knowing full well that he'd been flung off at a tangent, backward, but so viscerally convinced that he'd fallen straight down that the sight of the module—continuing along its arc of rotation, yet dropping from the zenith in front of him rather than disappearing behind his head—scrambled his sense of balance and direction completely. At first he felt as if he was tumbling backward, which would at least have explained what he was seeing, but when his inner ears failed to confirm the motion, the illusion vanished—only to return a moment later, to take him through the same cycle again. The lurching fits and starts that followed might have made him less queasy if they'd actually been happening; it was the inability to make sense of his perceptions that was disturbing, far more than any direct, physical effect of the lack of gravity.

He began to get his bearings once the whole ship was visible, edge-on. A minute later it had shrunk to a sparse necklace of glass beads, and the newly fixed stars finally crystallized in his mind as cues worth taking seriously. The infinite plane of whiteness on his right might have been a moonlit desert seen through half-closed eyes. He'd once flown a glider high over sand dunes at night, on Peldan, nearly free-falling at times in the thin air. There'd been no moonlight, of course, but the stars had been almost as bright as these.

Yann, sitting beside him, caught his eye. "You okay?"

Tchicaya nodded. "In the scapes you grew up in," he asked, "was there a vertical?"

"In what sense?"

"I know you said once that you didn't feel gravity . . . but was everything laid out and connected like it is on land? Or was it all isotropically three-dimensional—like a zero-gee space habitat, where everything can connect in any direction?"

Yann replied affably, "My earliest memories are of CP^4— that's a Kähler manifold that looks locally like a vector space with four complex dimensions, though the global topology's quite different. But I didn't really grow up there; I was moved around a lot when I was young, to keep my perceptions flexible. I only used to spend time in anything remotely like this"—he motioned at the surrounding, more-or-less-Euclidean space— "for certain special kinds of physics problems. And even most Newtonian mechanics is easier to grasp in a symplectic mani- fold; having a separate, visible coordinate for the position and momentum of every degree of freedom makes things much clearer than when you cram everything together in a single, three-dimensional space."

So much for being a seasoned traveler. Tchicaya didn't envy Yann's upbringing, but it probably rendered the world behind the border less exotic to him than the notion of a jungle had been to Tchicaya as a child. It shook his confidence to be reminded that there were measures by which his millennia of experience had been laughably narrow.

He couldn't have it both ways, though: he couldn't claim that the embodied needed the shock and the strangeness of this burgeoning universe, and then wish it could be no more daunting to confront than one more mundane planetary surface.

Kadir turned around and interjected testily, "I can analyze the flows in a symplectic manifold perfectly well without pretending to inhabit it. That's what mathematics is for. Imagining that you need to float through every last abstract space that shows up in a physics problem is just being literal-minded."

Yann smiled, unoffended. "I'm not going to argue with you. I haven't come here to proselytize for acorporeality."

Zyfete, seated in front of Tchicaya, muttered, "Why bother, if you can render embodiment just as barren?"

Tchicaya bit his tongue. He'd been forewarned about the level of acrimony, and at some point everyone on the *Rindler* was going to have to wade waist-deep through their opponents' venom on their way to a resolution, but spur-of-the-moment bickering in a confined space wasn't his idea of productive disharmony.

The shuttle's drive kicked in, delivering a mild push that Tchicaya succeeded in interpreting as a precipitous dive, rather than a complete inversion of land and sky. He scanned the eye-watering whiteness, hunting for their destination, but the glare was impenetrable. It seemed miraculous to be skimming kilometers above an object that dominated the sky for hundreds of light-years—without being burnt to a cinder, as he would have been this close to the surface of a star—but it was sheer size that made the border visible from afar. Each square kilometer didn't have to blaze fiercely for the total luminosity to outshine any supernova. Without the usual Doppler shift to boost the light's power, a pinhole view looking straight at the border would actually have been dimmer, here, by a factor of three, than the equivalent view from any planet he'd visited. What dazzled was the fact that it filled his vision, leaving room for nothing else. On Pachner, for much of the year the border had been partly hidden by daylight, but even when it reached its furthest angle from the sun there'd always been a narrow strip of washed-out darkness left over somewhere on the horizon, with a few pallid stars on which to rest your eyes.

As the drive reversed, he finally spotted the silhouette of the Scribe. He made a mask against the surrounding glare with his hands, and managed to discern some structure. At the top of the machine was a sphere, rainbow iridescent in the light that grazed it. He knew it was embossed with a fine pattern of microjets, trillions of tiny devices capable of firing as few as one or two atoms in any direction. While the *Rindler* could keep pace with the border well enough simply by cruising, the Scribe's stylus hovered so close that collisions with interstellar gas, and even the pressure of the borderlight itself, would have ruined the alignment if left uncompensated. Presumably, the visitors' own influence would be well within the machine's defensive capacities, but to Tchicaya it was both marvelous and comical that their presence could be accommodated—like a calligrapher inscribing *Gravitation* on the head of a pin, while four fat infants clambered onto the artisan's shoulders and proceeded to wrestle.

As the shuttle drew nearer, the Scribe's modest size became apparent; it was smaller than one of the *Rindler*'s modules, forty or fifty meters across, with the sphere of microjets held out on a boom above a flat deck. The shuttle's drive made one last perceptible correction before a series of maneuvers too gentle to feel brought them into contact with the deck.

Kadir unstrapped himself, and approached the hatch in the floor of the shuttle. Tchicaya followed him.

"You keep an atmosphere in there?"

Kadir nodded. "People come and go, it's easiest just to maintain the pressure."

Tchicaya frowned. "I'm never going to get to use this, am I?" He pinched the back of his hand to tug on the near-invisible membrane that he'd sprayed all over his skin; he'd been told it would let his body survive for up to a week in vacuum, and since it took three months to grow a new one, that had seemed like a precaution worth taking. The one thing the suit lacked was reaction mass. If he found himself drifting toward the border, the best thing to do would be to broadcast a final backup and resign himself to an interesting local death.

Kadir said, "I'll see if I can arrange an opportunity on the way back." The remark was delivered without obvious malice, but it was still hard to know how to take it. Since Tchicaya had allowed Yann to introduce him to the two Preservationists as a fellow partisan, the tension he'd felt had ebbed and flowed, and he was never sure when to expect a bit of good-natured teasing, and when to brace himself for a genuinely chilly rebuff as an enemy of the cause.

Zyfete and Yann joined them as the hatch irised open, revealing a softly lit tunnel lined with handholds. Tchicaya hung back until last, not wanting to block anyone's progress if he froze. The others all went feetfirst, as if they were descending a ladder, but he felt more secure crawling along the tunnel, imagining himself more or less horizontal. He recalled a playground back on Turaev, a maze of interconnected pipes. When Zyfete glanced up at him and scowled, he poked his tongue out at her and recited a few lines of childish rhyme. In spite of herself, she smiled.

The Scribe's control room was octagonal, with eight slanted windows facing down toward the border. Judging the distance by eye was difficult, with no texture to the light to set the scale, but Tchicaya guessed he was now floating just five or six meters from the novo-vacuum. He suddenly noticed the beating of his heart, though the rhythm didn't feel abnormal; it was a shift in his attention, rather than a rush of adrenaline. He wasn't afraid, but he was acutely aware of his body: the softness and fragility of it, compared to most other things in the world. It was the way he felt when he found himself stranded in the middle of a harsh landscape, insufficiently prepared for its rigors, but not so threatened that he'd simply write off his current incarnation as unsalvageable. It would take a cosmic disaster even larger than Mimosa to rob him of more than a few minutes' memories, but while he inhabited a body he identified with it wholly. He was in a place where a mishap could shred him into something smaller than atoms, and under the circumstances he was more than happy to let instincts predicated on absolute life and death come to the fore and do their best to protect him.

A bank of displays in the center of the room surrounded an octagonal dome, the housing for the stylus. Tchicaya watched as Kadir and Zyfete issued a long series of spoken commands. The lack of automation was almost ritualistic; he glanced inquiringly at Yann, who whispered, "It's a kind of transparency. There are more sophisticated ways we could monitor each other, but having observers from both sides at every experiment, and controlling everything with words, keeps the proceedings out in the open on one level—while we check the equipment and audit the software with a thousand different kinds of high-powered tools, offstage."

"That's so much like Earth-era diplomacy it's depressing."

Yann smiled. "I knew your arcane knowledge would come in handy here."

Tchicaya snorted. "Don't look at me to spout Machiavelli. If you want that shit, go and dig up an ancient."

"Oh, I'm expecting anachronauts to arrive at the *Rindler* any day now—preceded by a few megatonnes of fusion by-products—and announce that they've come to save the universe."

"Any day, or any millennium." It was an eerie prospect to contemplate. Scattered remnants of pre-Qusp civilization, twenty thousand or so years old, still chugged between the stars in spluttering contraptions, spewing spent fuel and taking thousands of years for every journey. Tchicaya had never met any of the ancients himself, but his father had encountered one group, which had visited Turaev long before he was born. None had traveled more than eighty light-years from Earth, so as yet they hadn't been endangered by the novo-vacuum, but unless the Preservationists triumphed, within decades the anachronauts would face a decision between adopting some of the hated new technologies and annihilation.

Kadir shot them a disapproving look, as if their chattering meant they weren't taking their monitoring role seriously. Tchicaya had full-sensory recall, regardless of conscious attention, and Yann would undoubtedly boast something even fancier, but he disciplined himself and fell silent.

Zyfete was describing a sequence of particles to be emitted by the stylus. The disaster at Mimosa had provided at least one compensatory boon: experiments in quantum gravity had become far easier to perform. The border was only a few Planck lengths deep, providing experimenters with a tool compared to which an atomic blade would look wider than a planetary system. While the highest-energy particles the Scribe could create were laughably blunt instruments, the border itself could be made to carve them into shrapnel vastly more effective than each innocuous whole. When the stylus fired a coherent beam of mesons at the border, the razor wire of disrupted graphs sliced fragments of their own surreal dimensions from the knot of virtual quarks and gluons making up each meson, and it was possible to exploit coherence effects to make some of these fragments act in unison to modify the border itself. Natural sources of noise had no prospect of accidentally triggering the same effect, so the kind of exorbitant shielding the Quietener had used was no longer required.

Kadir turned to look at them inquiringly. Yann nodded approval. "That's all as we agreed. Go ahead."

Zyfete addressed the Scribe. "Execute that."

With no perceptible delay, the Scribe began to answer with the results. Tchicaya's skin tingled; he'd had no time to remind himself between risk and reprieve, but they'd just tickled a tiger that might have responded by raking the four of them into geometric quanta, swallowing the *Rindler* a fraction of a millisecond later, and redoubling its efforts to devour all their distant backups and more prudent friends.

Kadir started cursing, his Mediator politely tagging the words with a cue that would shut off translation for anyone inclined to be offended. Zyfete watched him, anguished but silent.

When the tirade stopped, Tchicaya asked cautiously, "Not what you were hoping for, but did it tell you anything?"

Kadir kicked the stylus housing, the recoil driving him back to hit the window behind him with a thud. Tchicaya couldn't help wincing; however robust the participants in these collisions, precision machinery, living flesh, and windows facing interstellar vacuum all seemed to merit gentler treatment.

Zyfete said, "This sequence was meant to confirm a previous experiment, but it didn't yield the same results as the last time we ran it. Our model can't explain the discrepancy, either as a statistical variation, or any predictable change in the novo-vacuum."

Kadir turned and blurted out, "Either you genocidal traitors have corrupted this machine, or—"

Yann pleaded, "Or *what*? Give us the more likely alternative!"

Kadir hesitated, then smiled grimly. "I think I'll keep that hypothesis to myself."

Tchicaya was dismayed, though he was prepared to put the outburst down to frustration, rather than genuine contempt. Both sides were equally helpless. If this went on, no one was going to get their own way, and no one was going to forge a compromise. The novo-vacuum would simply roll on over them.

Halfway back to the *Rindler*, Kadir apologized. Tchicaya didn't doubt his sincerity, though the words were more formal than friendly. Yann tried to joke with him, making light of the incident, but Kadir withdrew from the conversation.

When they reached the dock and disembarked, the group broke apart. Yann wanted to observe some tests on a new spectrometer package that were being conducted in a workshop higher up in the same module, but Tchicaya didn't feel like tagging along, so he headed back toward his cabin.

He hadn't expected to witness a breakthrough on the trip, let alone gain some kind of dramatic insight himself from mere proximity to the border; he might as well have hoped to learn the secrets of the ordinary vacuum by gazing into thin air. Nevertheless, he felt a pang of disappointment. Before he'd arrived, there'd been an undeniable thrill to the notion of cruising just beyond reach of the fatal shock wave, and then compounding the audacity by turning around and studying it. Dissecting the danger, laying it bare. It was like a legend his mother had told him: in the Age of Barbarism, when humans had rained bombs on each other from the sky, people called Sappers had dived from airplanes to fall beside them and defuse them in midair, embracing the devices like lovers as they reached into their mechanical hearts and seduced them into betraying their malign creators. But if aerodynamics rendered this romantic fable unlikely, at least no one had expected the Sappers to teach themselves nuclear physics from scratch as they fell, then reach inside each atom of fissile material and pluck out the destabilizing protons one by one.

Zyfete caught up with Tchicaya on the stairs leading down to the walkway. She said, "Kadir's home is this far away from the border." She held up her hand, thumb and forefinger almost touching. "Nine thousand years of history. In less than a year, it will be gone."

"I'm sorry." Tchicaya knew better than to respond with platitudes about history living on in memory. He said, "Do you think I want to see Zapata destroyed?" She didn't need to name the planet; everyone knew the awful schedule by heart. "If we can halt the border without wiping out the entire novo-vacuum, I'll back that. I'll fight for that as hard as anyone."

Zyfete's eyes flashed angrily. "How very evenhanded of you! You'd let us keep our homes, so long as there was no danger of you losing your precious new toy!"

"It's not a toy to me," Tchicaya protested. "Was Zapata a 'toy' nine thousand years ago, when it lay on the frontier?"

"*That* frontier spread out from Earth, and it was made up of willing settlers. It didn't incinerate anyone who dared to stay put." She scowled. "What do you think you're going to find in there? Some great shining light of transcendence?"

"Hardly." *Transcendence* was a content-free word left over from religion, but in some moribund planetary cultures it had come to refer to a mythical process of mental restructuring that would result in vastly greater intelligence and a boundless cornucopia of hazy superpowers—if only the details could be perfected, preferably by someone else. It was probably an appealing notion if you were so lazy that you'd never actually learned anything about the universe you inhabited, and couldn't quite conceive of putting in the effort to do so: this magical cargo of transmogrification was sure to come along eventually, and render the need superfluous.

Tchicaya said, "I already possess general intelligence, thanks. I don't need anything more." It was a rigorous result in information theory that once you could learn in a sufficiently flexible manner— something humanity had achieved in the Bronze Age—the only limits you faced were speed and storage; any other structural changes were just a matter of style. "All I want to do is explore this thing properly, instead of taking it for granted that it has to be obliterated for our convenience."

"*Convenience?*" Zyfete's face contorted with outrage. "You arrogant piece of shit!"

Tchicaya said wearily, "If you want to save people's homes, you have greater obstacles than me to overcome. Go and comfort your friend, or go and work on your model. I'm not going to trade insults with you."

"Don't you think it's insult enough that you come here and announce your intention to interfere, if we ever look like we might be on the verge of succeeding?"

He shook his head. "The *Rindler* was built by a coalition with no agenda beyond studying the novo-vacuum. The individual members all had their personal goals, but this was meant to be a platform for neutral observation, not a launching pad for any kind of intervention."

They'd reached the walkway. Tchicaya kept his eyes cast down, though he knew it made him look ashamed.

Zyfete said, "The bodiless I can understand: what lies outside their Qusps is irrelevant to them, so long as they can keep the same algorithms ticking over. But you've felt the wind. You've smelled the soil. You know exactly what we have to lose. How can you despise everything that gave birth to you?"

Tchicaya turned to face her, angered by her bullying but determined to remain civil. He said, "I don't despise anything, and as I've said, if it's possible, I'll fight to preserve all the same things as you. But if all we're going to do with our precious embodiment is cling to a few warm, familiar places for the next ten billion years, we might as well lock ourselves into perfect scapes of those planets and throw away the key to the outside world."

Zyfete replied coldly, "If you think a marriage has grown too stale and cozy, I suppose you'd step in and stave one partner's head in?"

Tchicaya stopped walking and held up his hands. "You've made yourself very clear. Will you leave me in peace now?"

Zyfete faced him in silence, as if she'd run out of venom and would have been happy to depart at precisely this moment, if only he hadn't asked her. After a delay long enough to preclude the misconception that she might be doing his bidding, she turned around and strode back along the walkway. Tchicaya stood and watched her, surprised at how shaken he was. He'd never concealed his views from the people he'd lived among—apart from keeping his mouth politely shut in the presence of anyone in genuine distress—and over the decades he'd had to develop a thick hide. But the closer he'd come to the source of the upheaval, the harder he had found it to believe that he was witnessing an unmitigated tragedy, like the floods and famines of old. On Pachner, where the sorrow and the turmoil had been at their most intense, he'd also felt most vindicated. Because beneath all the grief and fear, the undercurrent of excitement had been undeniable.

If Zyfete's attack had stung him, though, it was mostly through the things she hadn't said. Just being here meant that she had already left her own home behind, already tasted that amalgam of liberation and loss. Like Tchicaya, she had paid once, and no one was going to tell her that the price had not been high enough.

Tchicaya took a shower to wash off his vacuum suit, then lay on his bed, listening to music, brooding. He didn't want to spend every waking moment on the *Rindler* questioning his position, but nor did he wish to grow impervious to doubt. He didn't want to lose sight of the possibility that he had chosen the wrong side.

If the Preservationists did achieve their goal, the possibilities offered by the novo-vacuum need not be lost forever. Whatever was learned in the process of destroying it might open up the prospect of re-creating it, in a safer, more controlled fashion. In a few tens of millennia, there could be a whole new universe on their doorstep again, but this time it would pose no threat to anyone. No one would be forced from their homes. No one would be made to choose between exile and adaptation.

And in a few tens of millennia, how much tighter would the

deadening spiral of familiarity have wound itself? If the nine-thousand-year history of Zapata was too precious to lose, after ninety thousand years every tradition, every grain of sand on every inhabited planet, would be positively sanctified.

Still, those who believed they were being smothered could always flee, as he'd fled Turaev. Those who were happy sleepwalking into eternity could stay. He had no right to force this cusp on anyone.

He didn't have the right, but he didn't have the power either, nor did he aspire to it. He was only here to state an unpopular case, and see if anyone could be swayed. If he believed that the novo-vacuum offered the greatest wealth of opportunities the species had faced since leaving Earth, what else would it be but cowardice and dishonesty if he failed to argue against its destruction?

The cabin was beginning to feel less spacious by the minute. He left it and made his way around the ship, heading for the garden. He still felt jittery on the walkways, but his confidence was slowly improving.

The garden was almost deserted. He found a bench that faced away from the border, offering a view he could take in without vertigo. The reel of the blue polar stars was slow enough to be soothing, and with the foliage to break up their perfect arcs the whole sight seemed less mechanical.

The Doppler shift was a novelty to him, but the motion of the stars was familiar. The night sky on Turaev had looked just like this, during a mild Slowdown. The only thing missing was the sun, rising and setting with each turn.

He'd stood by the crib that would prepare his body for storage, and his mind for transmission. It had asked him to state his wishes on the eventual recycling of this, his birth flesh. His father had pleaded gently, "We could still wait for you. For a thousand years, if that's what you need. Say the word, and it will happen. You don't have to lose anything."

Someone passing glanced his way, curious at the sight of an unfamiliar passenger. Their Mediators interacted, and the stranger requested an introduction. Tchicaya hadn't asked not to be interrupted, and he allowed the exchange of information to proceed. Protocols were established, translators verified, mutually acceptable behavior delineated. There were no local customs to defer to, here, so their Mediators virtually flipped a coin to decide the manner in which they should greet each other.

"I don't believe we've met. My name's Sophus."

Tchicaya stood and gave his own name, and they touched each other lightly on the left shoulder. "I've only been here a day," he explained. "It's my first time off-planet; I'm still adjusting."

"Do you mind if I join you? I'm waiting for someone, and this is the nicest spot to do it."

"You'd be welcome."

They sat on the bench. Tchicaya asked, "Who are you waiting for?"

"Someone who'll usurp your present role as most junior arrival. In fact, technically, I suppose she's already done that, but she's not yet in a state to show herself and claim the position."

Tchicaya smiled at the memory of his own appearance in the crib. "Two arrivals in as many days?" That wouldn't have been so strange if someone had been following him from Pachner, but he hadn't come across anyone there who'd shared his travel plans. "They'll be running out of bodies if this keeps up. We'll have to squeeze the ex-acorporeals right into the ship's processors."

Sophus frowned, mock-reprovingly. "Hey, no discrimination, please! It's up to them to volunteer, not us to suggest it."

"The way they offered to share those cabins, to make room for new arrivals?"

Sophus nodded, apparently amused by the gesture. Tchicaya felt a twinge of unease, unsure whether he had just endeared himself to Sophus with some remarks that had been taken as evidence of bigotry, or whether he was just being hypersensitive. He wondered how long it would take Sophus to quiz him about his allegiance; either the answer had spread through the grapevine already, or Sophus was polite enough to make small talk for a while, and see if he could extract the information indirectly.

"Actually, we'll start some new bodies growing soon," Sophus explained. "We were expecting a rush about now—give or take a decade. People will want to be here, it's what the models predicted."

Tchicaya was puzzled. "What, because of Zapata?"

Sophus shook his head. "It's far too late to save Zapata. Maybe not literally, but most people are realistic enough not to think that they can turn back the tide at the very last moment. Look a bit further down the track. A century, a century and a half."

"Ah." In the right company, Tchicaya might have made a joke of the prospect Sophus was raising, but it wasn't the kind of casual blasphemy he'd try out on a stranger. And the truth was, he did feel genuine sorrow, in some ways deeper than his feelings about Turaev's eventual demise. Like the uprooting of some much-loved, long-sedentary ancestor through whom a scattered family remained in touch, the exodus of Earth's people, and the destruction of its soil, would scar the hearts of even the most cosmopolitan travelers.

"There's still talk of moving it," Sophus said casually. "Pushing a white dwarf into the solar system, to carry it away. Sirius B is the obvious candidate." Tchicaya blinked at him, incredulous. "It wouldn't be impossible," Sophus insisted. "When you dump matter on a white dwarf, it undergoes tidal compression heating. If you do it in the right way, a significant amount squirts off in jets. If you arrange for asymmetric jets, and if you have enough mass to play with, you can achieve a modest net acceleration. Then you get the Earth into orbit around the star; the acceleration displaces the orbit, but it can still be bound."

"But to get Sirius B up to *half the speed of light*—"

Sophus raised a hand. "I know, I know! You'd have to gather so much reaction mass, and move all of it so swiftly into place, the damage would rival Mimosa. To wreak that kind of havoc just to put the whole ball of rock into exile as an unbroken whole would be like saving New York from the floods by blasting it all the way to Io. The only sane response is to work on designing an effective sandbag, while being prepared to give up gracefully and watch the place sink if that proves to be impossible."

"Yeah." If Tchicaya remembered the story correctly, though, while New York hadn't quite ended up on Io, *gracefully watching the place sink* would be putting things charitably. Hadn't some famous statue ended up in Paris, and various bridges and buildings gone to scattered theme parks?

Sophus attended briefly to an internal perception. "My colleague is on the brink of emerging. Would you like to meet her?"

"I'd be delighted." They rose together and headed for the stairs. On the walkway, Tchicaya forced himself to keep pace with Sophus, as if no one would make allowances for his lack of experience now that he'd ceased to be literally the rawest recruit.

"Where's she come from?"

"You mean, directly?"

"Yeah. I was on Pachner, and no one else there was talking about traveling to the *Rindler*. Maybe I just didn't bump into her—"

Sophus shook his head. "She's been in transit almost a century, standard time."

That was a long journey. Though it cost you more lost years in total to travel by an indirect route, breaking up the trip with as many stops as possible eased the sense of alienation. Whatever faction she supported, she had to be serious about the cause.

Tchicaya pictured a map of the region. "She's come from Chaitin?"

"Right."

"But she wasn't born there?"

"No. You know, you'll be able to ask her for her life's history directly, in a couple of minutes."

"Sorry." Maybe it was absurd to be so curious about the newcomer when he still knew next to nothing about the *Rindler*'s other passengers, but Yann's gloomy summary, and his own limited experience, had already made him long for someone who'd shake up the *status quo*.

As they crossed the observation deck, the door to the recovery room opened. Tchicaya smiled in recognition at the newcomer's posture: loose-limbed and confident after the kinesthetic retuning, seizing up for a moment at the sight of the border.

Then he recognized something more, and his own body turned to stone again.

He didn't need to check her signature; she hadn't changed her appearance since their paths had last crossed. In fact, she hadn't changed in four thousand years, since the day they'd first parted.

Tchicaya broke into a run, blind to everything around him, calling out her name.

"Mariama!"

She turned at the sound. He could see that she was shocked, and then uncertain how to respond. He halted, not wanting to embarrass her. It had been twelve hundred years since they'd set eyes on each other, and he had no idea what she'd make of his presence.

Mariama held out her hands, and he ran forward to grip them in his own. They whirled around, laughing, surefooted on the polished floor, leaning back into their own centrifugal force, moving ever faster, until Tchicaya's arms ached and his wrists burned and his vision blurred. But he would not be the one to stop moving, and he would not be the one to let go.

Chapter 6

Something unseen stung Tchicaya's hand, a vibration like a tuning fork held against the bone. He turned and stared at the empty space beside him, and a dark blur shivered into solidity.

"Quickly! Give your Exoself this code."

No sooner had the data passed between their Mediators than Tchicaya wished he'd rejected it. He felt as if he'd been tricked into catching something incriminatory thrown his way, the reflex action triggered by the object in flight turning out to have been the wrong response entirely.

"I can't!"

Mariama said, "No one will ever know. They're like statues. You'll be invisible."

Tchicaya's heart pounded. He glanced at the door, and caught himself straining his ears for footsteps, though he knew there'd be nothing to hear. Could she have really walked through the house undetected, marching right past his parents in that scandalous state?

"Our Exoselves scan for danger," he protested. "If anything happens at ordinary speed—"

"Did your Exoself detect me?"

"I don't know. It might have."

"Did it signal you? Did it bring you out of Slowdown?"

"No." He wasn't an adult, though. Who knew how differently theirs were programmed?

"We'll stay clear of them," Mariama explained. "I'm not doing this to pick their pockets. If we're not a threat to anyone, we won't trigger any alarms."

Tchicaya stared at her, torn. He had never feared his parents, but he basked in their approval. It only took the faintest shadow of disappointment on his father's face to make him ache with unhappiness. His parents were good people; valuing their high opinion was not just childish narcissism. If he did well in their eyes, he would be respected by everyone. Mariama was only Mariama: a law unto herself.

She inclined her head. "Please, Tchicaya. It's fun doing this, but I'm lonely without you."

"How long have you been out of Slowdown?"

Mariama averted her eyes. "A week."

That hurt. How lonely could she be, if it had taken her a week to miss him?

She put a hand over her mouth and mumbled, "Or two."

Tchicaya reached out to grab her arm, and she danced back and vanished from sight. He froze for a second, then rushed for the door, and stood with his back pressed against it.

He searched the room with his eyes, knowing that it was pointless looking for her if she did not want to be seen. Shadows slid across the walls and floor with hypnotic regularity. Lighting panels in the ceiling came on at night, and softened the changes at dusk and dawn, but even when he looked away from the window the diurnal cycle was obvious, everywhere.

Another week had passed, while he stood there. She could not still be in the room with him; even if she was able to go that long without food and water, she would have gone mad from boredom.

She reappeared in front of him like a trembling reflection in a pan of water, jolted into turbulence but quickly stilled.

"How did you get in?" he demanded.

She pointed a thumb at the window. "The same way I left."

"You're wearing my clothes!"

Mariama grinned. "They fit me nicely. And I'm teaching them lots of new tricks." She ran a hand down one sleeve and erased the old pattern, supplanting it with golden starbursts on black.

Tchicaya knew she was goading him, hoping to prod him into giving chase. She'd handed him the key; he didn't need anything more in order to pursue her. If he gave in and joined her now, at least he'd be spared an elaborate game of hide-and-seek.

He said, "Two weeks." That sounded more than generous, and the risk of his parents noticing his absence would be microscopic.

"We'll see."

Tchicaya shook his head. "I want you to agree to it. Two weeks, then we both come back."

Mariama chewed her lower lip. "I'm not going to make a promise I might not be able to keep." Then she read his face, and relented slightly. "All right! *Barring exceptional circumstances*, we'll come back in two weeks."

Tchicaya hesitated, but he knew that this was the closest thing to a guarantee he could hope to extract from her.

She held out a hand to him, smiling slightly. Then she silently mouthed the word *Now*.

Their Mediators were smart enough to synchronize the process without needing to be told. Tchicaya sent the code to his Exoself, and the two of them dropped out of Slowdown together. Switching the metabolic modes of cells throughout his body, and reconfiguring all the higher-level systems responsible for maintaining posture, breathing, circulation, and digestion took nearly fifteen minutes. The time passed imperceptibly, though, since his Qusp only resumed its normal rate once his body had completed the shift.

The light in his room had frozen into a late-winter's afternoon. He could hear a breeze moving through the trees beside the house, a different sound entirely to the throb of barometric pressure changes to which he'd grown accustomed. They were only six civil days into the Slowdown, but the new rhythms had seeped into his mind more rapidly than they'd had any right to, as if abetted by some process that his Exoself had neglected to retard.

Mariama tugged on his hand, pulling him toward the door. "Come on!" Her expression made a joke of it, but she couldn't disguise the note of genuine impatience. They were like lightning now, their least purposeful meanderings a dazzling feat in everyone else's eyes, but that still wasn't fast enough.

"Not that way." He gestured at the window.

Mariama said accusingly, "You're afraid to walk past them."

"Of course." Tchicaya gazed back at her calmly. It was perfectly reasonable not to want to be discovered, and however skillful she was at manipulating him, he wasn't going to be made ashamed of every last instinct of his own. "It's safer to use the window. So we'll use the window."

Mariama managed to look both amused and martyred, but she didn't argue. Tchicaya climbed out, then she followed him, carefully pulling the hinged pane closed behind her. He was puzzled for a moment; no one was going to notice an open window in the short time they'd be gone. But in two weeks, the night frosts would have left an indelible mark on some of his more fragile possessions.

As they crossed the garden, he said, "Don't you go home to sleep?"

"No. I've set up camp in the power station. All my food's there." She turned to face him, and Tchicaya was sure she was on the verge of demanding that he go back to the house to pilfer some supplies of his own, but then she said, "You can share it. I've got plenty."

The bright afternoon was eerily quiet, though Tchicaya doubted that he would have been unsettled if he'd heard no other voices for a minute, or an hour, on an ordinary day. As they stepped onto the road, he spotted two other pedestrians in the distance. During Slowdown, his Exoself had not only reprogrammed his own gait, it had tweaked his expectations of other people's appearance: moving with both feet constantly on the ground, positioning the arms to maximize stability, had looked as normal as it had felt. With his old notions of bodily dynamics restored, the pedestrians appeared, not merely frozen, but cowed and timid, as if they expected an earthquake at any moment.

He looked back at his house, quickly lowering his eyes from the windows to inspect the garden. Wind and rain could shift soil and pebbles into unwanted places on a time scale of decades, but the plants were engineered to herd those unruly elements; he'd watched the process with his own eyes. Out in the fields, the crops would be tending themselves, collectively arranging whatever changes they needed in irrigation and drainage, glorying in the strange seasons of unharvested bounty.

Tchicaya said, "How did you find the code?" It was the first Slowdown for both of them; she couldn't have stored it on a previous occasion.

Mariama replied casually, "It's not a big secret. It's not buried deep, or encrypted. Don't you ever examine your Exoself? Take apart the software?"

Tchicaya shrugged. He'd never even dream of tinkering with things on that level: his Exoself, his Mediator. Next thing you were probing the workings of your own Qusp, dissecting your own mind. He said, "I only take things apart if I can survive not putting them back together."

"I'm not stupid. I make backups."

They'd reached the park. Four giant hexapods huddled motionless in a corner. The decorative robots consisted of nothing but six coiled legs, arranged as three pairs that met at right angles in the center. If they'd been endowed with even the mildest form of sentience, they would have gone insane from the lack of stimulation, but they were little more than pattern-recognizers on springs.

Mariama ran up to them and clapped her hands. The nearest one stirred sluggishly, shifting its center of mass and wobbling on the tripod of the three legs currently touching the ground. She started dancing back and forth, encouraging it, and it began to tumble for her.

Tchicaya watched, laughing, biting back an admonition: *someone would notice that they'd moved, and know that the Slowdown had been violated*. He doubted that the hexapods had memories, but there was machinery everywhere, monitoring the streets, guarding the town against unlikely dangers. The fact that they hadn't woken anyone didn't prove that they wouldn't be found out in the end.

Mariama weaved between the robots. "Aren't you going to help me?"

"Help you do what?" She'd managed to get all four of them moving simultaneously, without his aid. Tchicaya hadn't played with them since he was an infant, but he'd never been able to hold the attention of more than one at a time.

"Make them collide."

"They won't do that."

"I want to get their legs tangled together. I don't think they understand that that can happen."

"You're a real sadist," he protested. "Why do you want to confuse them?"

Mariama rolled her eyes. "It can't hurt them. Nothing can."

"It's not them I'm worried about. It's the fact that you enjoy it."

She kept her eyes on him without breaking step. "It's just an experiment. It's not malicious. Why do you always have to be such a prig?"

Tchicaya felt a surge of anger, but he fought it down and replied pleasantly, "All right, I'll help you. Tell me what to do." He caught the flicker of disappointment in her eyes before she smiled and started issuing detailed instructions.

The hexapods were primitive, but their self-and-environment model was more reliable than Mariama had imagined. After fifteen minutes trying to trick them into tying their legs into knots, she finally gave up. Tchicaya collapsed on the grass, breathless, and she joined him.

He stared up into the sky. It had grown pale already, almost colorless. It had been summer when the Slowdown began; he'd forgotten how short the winter days were.

Mariama said, "Has anyone you know even *heard* of Erdal?"

"No."

She snorted, her expectations confirmed. "He probably lives on the other side of the planet."

"So? Do you want half the planet to go into Slowdown, and the other half not?" Everyone on Turaev was connected somehow. While Erdal traveled, the whole world would wait for him, together. It was either that, or they broke into a thousand shards.

Mariama turned to face him. "You know why they do it, don't you?"

It was a rhetorical question. People always had an ulterior motive, and Tchicaya had always been taken in by their explanations. He squirmed like an eager child and asked with mock excitement, "No, tell me!"

Mariama shot him a poisonous look, but refused to be sidetracked. "*Guilt.* Cosmic apron strings. Do you think poor Erdal would dare not come home, with nine million people holding their breath for him?"

Tchicaya knew better than to dispute this claim directly; instead, he countered, "What's so bad about Slowdown? It doesn't hurt anyone."

Mariama was venomous. "While every other civilized planet is flowering into something new, we do nothing and go nowhere, ten thousand times more ponderously than before."

"Lots of other planets do Slowdown."

"Not *civilized* ones."

Tchicaya fell silent. A faint star had appeared directly above him, even before the sun had fully set.

He said, "So you'll leave one day? For good?" The question produced an odd, tight sensation in his windpipe. He'd never lost synch with anyone; he couldn't imagine that kind of unbridgeable separation.

"No."

He turned to her, surprised. She said, "I plan to whip the whole planet into life, instead. Anything less would just be selfish, wouldn't it?"

The machinery inside the power station was robust and intelligent enough to defend itself, and to safeguard any visitors, without the need for high fences or locked doors. Tchicaya remembered the place as being noisier the last time he'd explored it, but Slowdown had reduced the flow of waste from the town to an inaudible trickle. Energy was extracted from the waste by an enzyme-driven electrochemical process that he was yet to study in detail; fortunately, some of the energy ended up as heat, and even the diminished output was enough to make the building habitable at night. Mariama had made a nest of blankets right up against the coolant pipes that led to the radiator fins on the roof.

Tchicaya sniffed the air cautiously, but there was no trace of the usual offensive odor, maybe because there was not only less sewage passing through, but the undiminished runoff from the fields was diluting it. There was a strange, boiled-vegetable smell to the place, but it was nothing he couldn't tolerate.

Mariama had stockpiled cans of food, self-heating rations of the kind people took into the untouched, frozen lands to the south. It must have taken her a while to build up the collection without attracting suspicion. She handed him a can, and he pressed the tab to start it heating.

"How long were you planning this?" he asked.

"A bit more than a year."

"That's before I even knew Erdal would be traveling."

"Me too. I just wanted to be prepared, whenever it happened."

Tchicaya was impressed, and a little daunted. It was one thing to watch the sun and the stars racing around the sky, and think: *what if I could be as fast as them?* Plotting to break out of Slow-down before she'd even experienced it required an entirely different line of thought.

"What were you doing? Before you came to my house?"

She shrugged. "Just exploring. Messing about. Being careful not to wake the drones."

Tchicaya felt his face harden at this contemptuous phrase, but then he wondered how much allowance to make for the fact that she was always striving to provoke him. The calculations became so difficult at times, it drove him mad. He wanted the two of them to be straightforward with each other, but he doubted that would ever be her style. And he didn't want her to be different, he didn't want her to change.

He opened the can and hunched over his meal, unsure what his face was betraying.

After they'd eaten, they switched off the lamp and lay beneath the blankets, huddled together. Tchicaya was self-conscious at first, as if the contented glow he felt at the warmth of her body against his was at risk of turning into something more complicated, but he knew that it was still physically impossible for anything sexual to happen between them. The prospect of that guarantee eventually failing disturbed him, but it couldn't vanish overnight.

Mariama said, "Two weeks isn't long enough. You need to walk out of your room a centimeter taller: just enough to make your parents feel something is wrong, without being able to put their finger on it."

"Go to sleep."

"Or learn something you didn't know. Amaze them with your erudition."

"Now you're just mocking me." Tchicaya kissed the back of her head. He immediately wished he hadn't done it, and he waited, tensed, for some kind of rebuke. Or worse, some attempt to move further along a path on which he'd never meant to set foot.

But Mariama lay motionless in the darkness, and after a while he began to wonder if she'd even noticed. Her hair was thick at the back, and his lips had barely brushed a few loose strands.

In Tchicaya's view, the town's effective desertion didn't render it more interesting, and the freedom to wander the streets and fields at any hour was less appealing now, in winter, than in the ordinary summers when it was barely curtailed by parental authority anyway. Tchicaya thought of suggesting that they drop back into Slowdown and reemerge when the weather was warmer, but he was afraid of compromising their original deal. If he didn't stick to the letter of it, he could forget about holding Mariama to her word.

Mariama wanted to catch a train to Hardy, further if possible, preferably circumnavigating the entire continent. In one weird concession to practicality, the trains moved at their ordinary speed, whisking commuters to their destinations in an eye blink.

Understandably, though, departures were rare, and on examining the schedules it turned out that they could not have traveled anywhere and back in less than ten years.

Tchicaya did his best to keep Mariama distracted, terrified that she might harbor a yearning for sabotage that went beyond playground equipment. She'd know it was futile to hope to succeed in damaging any of the town's infrastructure, but he could picture her delight at sirens wailing and people shuddering into motion around her. This image might have been unfair, but there was no point asking her for assurances; at best, that would only offend her, and at worst it might tempt her to act out his fears. So he tried to go along with any suggestions she made that weren't completely outlandish, but only after putting up enough resistance to keep her from becoming too bored, or too suspicious of his compliance.

On their tenth night out of Slowdown, Tchicaya was woken by lukewarm fluid dripping onto his face. He opened his eyes in the pitch blackness, and rashly poked his tongue out to sample the fluid. It was water, but it had a complicated, slightly metallic taint. He pictured a crack in the ceiling, the heat from the radiator fins above them on the roof melting the surrounding frost.

He slid out from the blankets without waking Mariama, and groped for the lamp. When he held it up, a faint liquid sheen was visible snaking down one thick coolant pipe, collecting in drops at a right-angled bend above the cushion where his head had lain.

Mariama stirred, then shielded her eyes. "What is it?"

"Just some water from the roof. We might have to shift." He moved the lamp about, hunting for leaks along the other pipes. Then something different caught his eye, a flash of iridescent colors at the very top of the pipe that had proved to be the original culprit. "Is that oil?" Why would there be oil leaking from the roof? As far as Tchicaya knew, the plant's few moving parts were all inside the building, and they'd all be molecularly smooth if they made physical contact with each other at all. Maybe flakes of ice could catch the light like that. But what could make them thin and flat enough?

There was sure to be a simple answer, but the puzzle gnawed at him. It was cold, and part of him wanted nothing more than to curl up beneath the blankets again—but what was the point of achieving a state in which no one could tell him to stop worrying and leave it till morning, if he didn't take advantage of his freedom to act on his curiosity immediately?

He said, "I'm going up on the roof."

Mariama blinked at him in the lamplight, apparently at a loss for words.

Tchicaya put on his shoes and walked outside, taking the lamp with him.

He circled the building twice, before settling on a sturdy-looking drainpipe. The lamp was attached to a chain; he hung it around his neck, like a pendant worn backward, and gripped the drainpipe between his forearms and knees. There were no handholds, and the frosted surface was slippery. The first time he found himself sliding back down, he panicked and almost let go, but the friction from the polymer surface was never enough to really hurt him. After ending up back on the ground twice, he found that if he tightened his grip the instant he began to slip, he could bring himself to a halt in a fraction of a second, and retain most of his hard-won altitude.

He reached the roof with his limbs numb and his chest soaked in icy perspiration. He crouched on the sloped tiles, flapping his arms vigorously to try to restore the circulation, until he realized that this was driving him slowly backward toward the seven-meter drop behind him. If he did real damage to his birth flesh, there'd be no prospect of concealing it from his parents. And to take on a new body at the age of twelve would make him a laughingstock for centuries.

He rose up on his haunches and waddled across the roof, as wary of gravity now as if he'd been back in Slowdown. He had no idea whether he was heading in the right direction; the dark shapes looming ahead of him might have been anything. He stopped to work the lamp around from his back to a more useful position, and noticed a long gash along the inside of his right leg, wet with blood. Something had cut him as he'd slipped along the drainpipe, but the wound wasn't painful, so it couldn't be too deep.

Up close, the radiator fins were massive, each as wide as his outstretched arms. He ambled around the structure, shining the lamp into the angled gaps between the fins, hunting for the source of the leak.

Mariama called out to him, "What have you found?" She was outside, on the ground somewhere.

"Nothing, yet."

"Do you want me to come up?"

"Suit yourself." He felt a twinge of guilt at the way that would sound, but it was hardly an expression of lofty disdain by the standards she'd set. This was the first thing he'd done since he'd joined her that wasn't part of some complicated strategy to please her, or confound her. He had to be indifferent to her, just this once, or he'd go mad.

When the lamplight finally returned the rainbow sheen he'd glimpsed from inside the building, it was unmistakable. An irregular, glistening patch of some filmy substance covered half the fin. Tchicaya approached, and touched it with a fingertip. The substance was slightly sticky, and the film clung to his finger for a fraction of a millimeter as he pulled away. When it parted from his skin he could feel it snap back elastically, rather than tearing like something viscous and treacly. He held his finger up for inspection; the skin was unstained, and when he rubbed it against his thumb there was no moisture or slickness at all. This wasn't any kind of oil he'd seen before, and it definitely wasn't ice.

He held the lamp closer to the surface, hunting for some sign of a damaged coolant channel. This had to be the residue left behind by a leak, though why the coolant would contain some sticky impurity was beyond him. Antifreeze? He was shivering with cold, but he was in a stubborn frame of mind.

A small hole appeared in the film at the center of the circle of lamplight, and grew before his eyes. He held the lamp as still as he could; once the boundary of the film had retreated into the penumbra cast by the lamp's housing, the hole stopped growing.

Tchicaya moved the lamp to another spot. The same thing happened: the lamplight seemed to melt the film away. But the beam carried no heat whatsoever. Was it driving some kind of photochemical reaction?

He turned back to the original rent in the film. It had shrunk to half the size it had grown to when he moved the lamp away. He made a hole in the film in a third location, then took the lamp back to inspect the second hole. It was closing up, too.

Tchicaya stepped out from the gap between the fins and sat huddled on the roof tiles, his teeth chattering. Maybe the light broke up whatever molecules the film was made from, while the chemical process that had formed it in the first place rebuilt it when he took the light away. Some mixtures of simple chemicals could behave in a complicated fashion. He had no right to start summoning up phrases from his biology lessons, like *negative phototropism.*

His arms were shaking. Mariama had been silent since their last exchange; she had probably gone back to bed.

He rose to his feet, and scrupulously searched the other parts of the radiator, but it was only one side of one fin that bore any visible trace of the film.

He took a knife from his pocket, opened it, and scraped it over the film. The surface appeared unchanged, but when he lifted the knife there was a waxy residue visible along the edge of the blade.

He walked around the structure, counting the fins as he went, orienting himself with the stars. He closed his eyes and pictured the arc the sun would make as it crossed the sky; it was an easier task now than it would have been before he'd sat for a year in the front room of his house and watched the ribbon of fire shift with the seasons. He stepped between two of the fins and dislodged whatever had adhered to the knife onto the clean surface of the radiator.

He looked up at the sky again. A million stars, a million dead worlds. Only four planets had ever held anything different. His hunch was sure to be disproved, but the prospect only made him smile. There were some things so large and outlandish that you could only wish for them with your tongue in your cheek, and to be disappointed when they failed to appear would be like throwing a tantrum and cursing the world because the sun failed to rise at your beck and call.

He made his way to the edge of the roof, his breath frosting in front of him.

As he was climbing down the drainpipe, his leg began to throb. His body had managed to close the wound, and now it was warning him not to break the temporary seal of collagen it had woven across the gap in his skin. As he adjusted his legs to shift the pressure away from the cut, Tchicaya made a decision: he wanted to remember this night, he wanted it to leave a mark. He instructed his Exoself never to permit the cells of his skin to grow back in their normal pattern across the wound. For the first time, he would let the world scar him.

"Why do we need to borrow your parents' ladder?"

Tchicaya waved Mariama back from the toolshed. "I'm hoping it won't trigger any alarms. If I tried to borrow someone else's, that might look like I was stealing." He didn't want her taking part in the act, though. That the house had permitted her to enter un-invited, and even borrow his clothes without his permission, proved that it was prepared to show some tolerance toward his friends. His parents had never been obsessed with safeguarding their possessions, so it was not surprising that they hadn't pro-grammed any paranoid, hair-trigger responses. He didn't want to push his luck, though.

When he emerged from the shed, Mariama said, "Yes, but what do we need it *for*? What's so interesting, up on the roof?"

Tchicaya swung the ladder toward her, making her jump back. "Probably nothing." He had planned to show her the film on the coolant pipes inside the building when she woke that morning, but by daylight the sight had been so drab and uninspiring that he'd changed his mind; she'd probably looked herself, and seen nothing but a mild discoloration. She'd laugh at his naiveté when he finally described his experiment, but he didn't care. "We'll find out tonight."

Mariama was puzzled. "What's to stop me going up there be-fore nightfall?"

Tchicaya tightened his grip on the ladder, but even if he could keep it from her, she wouldn't need it.

He said, "Nothing. I'm asking you to wait, that's all."

This answer seemed to please her. She smiled back at him sun-nily.

"Then I'll wait."

The ladder couldn't stretch to the full height of the roof, and Tchicaya had to argue with it before it would extend itself at all.

"It's not safe," the ladder wailed.

"I've already been up there once, without any help from you," he protested. He showed it his new pink scar. "I'll climb up the drainpipe again if I have to. You can either make this as safe as possible, or you can stay on the ground and be completely use-less."

The ladder gave in. Tchicaya gripped the bottom end firmly while a wave of deformation swept along the length of the device. As the side rails stretched, material was redistributed into new rungs. In its final shape, paper-thin, the ladder was still a meter too short to touch the edge of the roof, but it would bring it within reach.

Mariama said, "After you."

Tchicaya had planned to follow her up, so he'd have a chance to catch her if she slipped, but he'd been assuming that she'd demand to go first anyway, so he had no argument prepared. He mounted the ladder and began to ascend. He didn't need to look down to know when she'd joined him; he could feel the structure vibrating with a second load.

If she did fall and injure herself, she could retreat at will into the painless world of her Qusp. An accident would mean discovery and shame, but no great suffering. Yet Tchicaya's hands shook at the thought of it, and he could not imagine feeling differently. The structure of his mind had been passed down with only a few small modifications from the original human form, shaped by evolution in the Age of Death, leaving him with the choice between embracing its impulses in all their absurdity—like ancient figures of speech whose literal meaning bore no resemblance to anything people still did—or struggling to invent a whole new vocabulary to replace them. If you cared about someone, what could replace the sick feeling of the misery you'd feel if they came to harm? The bodiless, he knew, had found their own, varied answers, but the idea that he might one day do the same made him giddy.

He peered down.

Mariama said, "What?"

"Nothing."

The long climb was far easier than it had been the night before, but Tchicaya found the act of reaching back to grab hold of the gutter a lot more disconcerting while perched on the top rung of the ladder than when he'd gripped the drainpipe firmly with his legs. He hoisted himself up and clambered onto the roof, then moved away from the edge quickly so he wouldn't be in Mariama's way. Seconds later, she was beside him.

"We should have used ropes, and grappling hooks," she said. "Like they do on mountains."

"I never thought of that," Tchicaya admitted.

"I was joking."

"It might have been fun, though." It might have been safer.

"Are you going to let me in on the big secret now?"

Tchicaya feigned indifference. "I did warn you: there's probably nothing to see." He aimed the lamp's beam across the roof, but deliberately kept it low. "This way."

They crossed the tiles together in silence. When they reached the radiator, Tchicaya showed her the patch of iridescent film he'd discovered the night before.

Mariama examined it. Tchicaya had half-expected her to identify the substance immediately, puncturing his fantasy with a far simpler explanation, but she was as baffled as he was. When he showed her how the film responded to the lamplight, she said, "Is that why you thought there'd be nothing here? You expected the sunlight to destroy it?"

"No. This surface ought to be in the shade all day."

"It would still get some light from the sky, though."

"That's true," he conceded. "But if it was there last night, it either had to be able to survive that much indirect sunlight, or it had to have formed after sunset, at least once. So why wouldn't it be here again?"

Mariama nodded patiently. "All right. So what were you warning me not to expect?"

Tchicaya's throat tightened. "I scraped some off, and put it on another fin. One that should have been about equally shaded. To see if it would . . ." He couldn't say the word.

"To see if it would grow?"

He nodded stupidly.

Mariama whooped with delight. "Where!" She clutched at the lamp, but when he held on to it she didn't fight him for it. Instead, she took hold of his arm and said, "Will you show me? Please?"

They stumbled around the radiator, helping each other stay balanced. Tchicaya told himself he didn't care what they found; when there turned out to be nothing, they could laugh at his grandiose delusions together.

"This is the one." He aimed the lamp into the wedge-shaped space between the fins, but he couldn't hold it still. "Do you see anything?"

Mariama put an arm around him, steadying his whole body to steady the lamp.

There was a patch of the film in front of them, an oval about the size of his hand, at exactly the height where he would have scraped the knife clean.

Mariama took the lamp, and knelt to inspect the patch more closely. It began to shrink immediately; she pulled the light away. "This wasn't here last night?"

"No."

"So it must be a new . . ." She struggled for the right word. "Colony? Do you think that's what it is?"

"I don't know."

She turned to him. "But it is alive? It has to be!"

Tchicaya was silent for a moment. He'd thought the result would settle the issue, but now he was having second thoughts. The evidence was still too flimsy to support the extraordinary conclusion. "There are chemicals that do some strange things," he said. "I'm not sure what this proves."

Mariama rose to her feet. "We have to wake someone, and show them. Right now."

Tchicaya was horrified. "But then they'll know what we did. They'll know we broke Slowdown."

"No one will care. Don't you know how rare this is?"

He nodded. "But you promised me—"

Mariama laughed. "We're not going to be in trouble! This is a thousand times more important!"

Apart from Earth itself, native life had only been found on three worlds. Simple and microbial, but in each case unique. Every biosystem used different chemistry, different methods of gathering energy, different structural units, different ways of storing and transmitting information. On the crassest, most pragmatic level, this knowledge might be of little value: technology had long ago surpassed nature's ability to do all of these things efficiently. But each rare glimpse at a separate accident of biogenesis cast light on the nature and prospects of life. The roof of this building would become the most talked-about location for a hundred light-years.

Tchicaya said, "What if it's something we brought ourselves? That wouldn't be much of a discovery."

"Such as what? Nothing we brought can mutate freely: every cell in every crop, every cell in our bodies, has fifty different suicide enzymes that kill off the lineage at the first genetic error. This could no more be *ours* than if they found some strange machine out in the ice that nobody owned up to making."

Tchicaya was growing tired of trying to keep his balance on the sloping roof; he sat down, his back slumped against the fin. It was lukewarm, body temperature. Once Slowdown ended, it would be hotter than the boiling point of water. *So which extreme did the native life favor?* Had it grown here before the Slowdown, and then managed to cling on in the relative cool? Or had it blown out of the icy wastes and only colonized the radiator once the Slowdown had rendered this tiny niche benign?

Mariama sat beside him. "We'll have to leave," she said.

"Can't that wait until morning?"

"I don't mean us, now. We'll have to leave Turaev. *They'll evacuate the planet.* We'll all have to go somewhere else." She smiled, and added with a kind of mock jealousy, "I always wanted to be the one to shake this place out of its stupor. But it looks as if you've beaten me to it."

Tchicaya sat motionless, scowling slightly. The words refused to sink in. He knew that she was right: it was a universal principle, accepted by every space-faring culture. In each of the other three cases, the planet in question had been strictly quarantined and left to its own fate. Only one of those worlds had been settled, though. Native life was supposed to have been ruled out, long before the colonists' first spores were launched. However microscopic, and however sparsely distributed, it should have left some detectable chemical signature in the atmosphere.

Tears stung his eyes. In his euphoria, he'd never thought beyond the unlikely confirmation that his own world, his own town, held the fourth known example of extraterrestrial life. He could have lived down the shame of this childish escapade, half-excused by that serendipitous discovery. But he'd been more than disobedient, more than disrespectful of the customs that bound the people of Turaev together. He'd destroyed their whole world.

He didn't want to weep in front of Mariama, so he stammered out an incoherent stream of words instead. Everything he'd planned, everything he'd pictured for the future, had just turned to ashes. He might have traveled one day, like Erdal, but he would never have left his friends and family behind, never lost synch. Fifty-nine generations had made this planet their home; he could never belong anywhere else. Now it would all be torn away from him. And nine million people would suffer the same fate.

When he stopped to catch his breath, Mariama said soothingly, "Everything here can be moved! Every building, every field.

You could wake up on New Turaev, a thousand light-years away, and if you didn't check the stars you'd never know."

Tchicaya replied fiercely, "You know it will never happen like that! Five minutes ago, you were crowing about it!" He wiped his eyes, struggling not to turn his anger against her. He'd always understood what she wanted; he had no right to blame her for that. But any reassurance she offered him was hollow.

Mariama fell silent. Tchicaya buried his head in his hands. There was no escape for him: only adults had the right to shut down their Qusp, to choose extinction. If he threw himself from the roof and broke his spine, if he doused himself in oil and set himself alight, it would only make him more contemptible.

Mariama put an arm around his shoulders. "On how many worlds," she said, "do you think they've found life?"

"You know the answer. Three, since Earth."

"I don't know that. There might have been ten. There might have been hundreds."

Tchicaya's skin crawled. He looked up and searched her eyes in the starlight, wondering if she was testing him. What she was proposing now was infinitely worse than anything they'd done so far.

She said, "If you believe it will hurt so many people, so badly, then I'll listen to you." Tears were trickling down his cheeks again; she wiped them away with the back of her hand. "I'll trust you."

Tchicaya looked away. She had the power to incinerate everything around her, the power to break through every stifling absurdity she'd railed against from the day they'd met. When they'd spoken of the future, it was all she had ever talked about: finding a way to force the world to change. Now she could gut the planet with its own stupid rules, and nothing would ever be the same.

Unless he asked her to stay her hand.

* * *

Tchicaya slept through the end of Erdal's Slowdown, and woke from deep dreams, refreshed but disoriented. He lay in bed, listening to the wind, thinking over what had happened in the last two hundred and seventy-two years.

Erdal had traveled to Gupta, a hundred and thirty-six light-years away, and stayed for ten days. When he rose from the crib, back in his birth flesh, he would find that ten days had passed on Turaev, too. He would be the one bearing news, eagerly describing his travels to his family and friends. He would not be a stranger to them, greeted with an incomprehensible litany of change.

The whole planet had waited for him. What else should they have done? Turaev's sun would burn for four billion years. How much greed and impatience would it take to begrudge the wait, to cast someone aside for the sake of a few centuries?

Tchicaya felt more pride than guilt. Despite his lapse, his heart was still in the right place, and he had resolved never to be so weak again.

As he was dressing, his gaze ran over the scar on his leg. His was sure that his parents had noticed it, but neither of them had asked him to explain its meaning. It was his right to decide who to tell, and when.

Above the scar, between his legs, the skin was newly red and swollen. Tchicaya sat on the edge of his bed and probed the swelling gingerly. Touching it was like tickling himself; it made him smile faintly, but there was no disguising the fact that he'd much rather be tickled by someone else.

He finished dressing, moving about the room slowly. He hadn't thought it would happen so soon. Some people were fourteen, fifteen, sixteen. He was tall, but he wasn't strong for his age. He was nothing like his mother or father yet. He wasn't ready. It was some kind of sickness, some kind of mistake.

He sat down on the bed again, trying not to panic. Nothing

was irreversible yet. Whatever his body was constructing might take another year to be completed; the first time always took longer. And he could still change his mind, change his feelings. Everything was voluntary, his father had explained. Unless you loved someone deeply, and unless they felt the same way toward you, neither of you could grow what you both needed to make love together.

Tchicaya exposed the raw skin again, and stared down glumly at the formless nub. Every couple grew something different, just as every couple would have a different child. The molecules that had already passed between them in the air would determine the pair of shapes that formed. The two of them would be bound together then, literally remade for each other, even the chemical signals that gave them pleasure fitting together in a complementary pattern as unique as their interlocking flesh.

Tchicaya whispered, "I don't love you. You're nothing to me. I don't love you." He would picture her face and recite the words every day, once when he rose and once before he slept. If he was strong enough, stubborn enough, his body would have to listen.

Chapter 7

Sophus was far too tactful to ask Tchicaya how he and Mariama knew each other; it must have been obvious that the answer was long, complicated, and largely none of his business. Tchicaya volunteered the bare minimum that the situation seemed to require. "We grew up together, in the same town on Turaev," he explained. "It's been a while since we last ran into each other."

When Mariama asked to hear what was happening on the *Rindler*, Tchicaya deferred to Sophus, who took up the task of outlining some seventeen decades' worth of advances and disappointments. Tchicaya listened politely, hoping Mariama was taking in more than he was. His thoughts were still so scattered by the shock of her arrival that he gave up trying to pay attention; he could replay the whole conversation later.

As Sophus talked, the three of them strolled around the ship. Mariama was unfazed by the view from the walkways; she might not have been this close to the border before, but apparently she'd become accustomed to space. Then again, it would not have surprised him if she had decided to choose equanimity in the new environment by fiat, even if this was her first time off-planet.

When Tchicaya tuned in to the discussion again, Mariama was

saying, "So there's no prospect of using universality-class arguments to design a generally effective Planck worm, before we pin down the detailed physics?"

Sophus said, "Tarek has looked into that, and even tried some experiments, but I believe it's a dead end. For a start, we still don't know what the bulk symmetries of this system are. I've more or less given up talking about 'the novo-vacuum'; it's too misleading. What vacuum? We don't know that there's a state that lies in the null space of all annihilation operators for the Mimosan seed particles. And if there is such a state, we don't know that it will obey anything remotely analogous to Lorentz invariance. Whatever's behind the border might not even possess any kind of time-translation symmetry."

"You're joking!"

"No. In fact, it's looking more likely every day." Sophus glanced at Tchicaya meaningfully, as if he was waiting for the Preservationists' laudable openness to be acknowledged.

Tchicaya said, "That's right. I watched one experiment myself, just a few hours ago." Mariama smiled at him, envious at this slight head start.

He smiled back at her, hoping his face wasn't betraying his confusion. At the instant he'd seen her standing on the observation deck, he hadn't consciously assumed anything about the faction she'd be joining; such ephemeral concerns had been swept from his thoughts entirely. Now that she'd casually revealed in passing that she'd come here to support the side that he would have sworn she'd be committed to opposing, the one part of his mind that resonated with this fact was the oldest, crudest model he had of her: someone whose only role in life was to confound and unsettle him. The original Mariama, who he had imagined would go to any lengths, not so much to spite him as to prove that he had no hope of pinning her down.

Tchicaya dragged his thoughts back to Sophus's comments.

Kadir and Zyfete had been nowhere near as explicit, but then they'd not been in the friendliest of moods. Kadir's despair made more sense now, though; it went beyond his growing fears for his home world, and one more ordinarily frustrating encounter with the border.

Time-translation symmetry was the key to all their hopes of predicting how the novo-vacuum would behave. In ordinary physics, if two people performed the same experiment, one starting work at midnight while the other began at noon, their separate versions could be compared, very easily: you merely added or subtracted half a day, and all their data could be superimposed. That sounded too obvious to be worth stating, but the fact that it was possible, and the fact that any laws of physics had to be compatible with this process of sliding the two sequences of events together, was a powerful constraint on the forms such laws could take.

Everything that happened in the universe was unique, on some level. If that were not true, there'd be no such thing as memory, or history; there'd be no meaningful chronology at all. At the same time, it was always possible to unpick some features of an event from the complicated tapestry of its context, and demand that this tiny patch of reality look the same as countless others, once you knew how to orient them all for the purpose of comparison. Taking a step north on Turaev on your eighteenth birthday could never be the same as taking a step west on Pachner four thousand years later, but in analyzing these two admittedly singular activities, you could safely abstract the relevant joints and muscles from the surrounding thicket of biographical and planetological detail, and declare that the applicable laws of mechanics were precisely the same in both cases.

It had been obvious since the accident that whatever the Mimosans had created in the Quietener did not possess the same symmetries as ordinary space-time, which allowed the unique location, time, orientation, and velocity of any physical system to be stripped away, revealing its essential nature. Still less had anyone expected the Mimosan vacuum to obey the "internal" symmetries that rendered an electron's phase or a quark's color as arbitrary as the choice of a planet's prime meridian.

But everyone studying the novo-vacuum had been relying on the assumption that these familiar regularities had merely been replaced by more exotic ones. Mathematicians had long had a catalog of possibilities on offer that dwarfed those realized in nature: more or fewer dimensions, different invariant geometric structures, novel Lie groups for the transformations between particles. All of these things would be strange to encounter, but ultimately tractable. And at the very least, it had been taken for granted that there was some prospect of using the results of sufficiently simple experiments to deduce what would happen when those experiments were repeated. Once you lost *that*, prediction in the conventional sense became impossible. You might as well try to guess who you'd meet in a crowded theater on Quine by consulting the guest list for an opening night of Aeschylus.

Tchicaya said, "If you're right, we're wasting our time here."

Sophus laughed. "I wish all Yielders were so easily discouraged."

Tchicaya caught the change in Mariama's demeanor as he was finally labeled for her. She did not appear surprised, or cooler toward him, but a look of resignation crossed her face, as if she was letting other possibilities slip away.

He replied, "I didn't say I believed you. Now I know you're just spreading misinformation."

Sophus said, "The data's all public; you should judge for yourself. But I'm giving a presentation later today that might interest you."

"On why we should all give up and go home? Yielders first, of course."

"No. On why we shouldn't, even if I'm right."

Tchicaya was intrigued. "Dishing out despair with one hand, taking it away with the other. You're never going to drive us away like that."

"I'm really not interested in driving anyone away," Sophus protested. "The more people there are working on this, the sooner we'll understand it. I'm happy to share my ideas with everyone— and if some Yielder beats me to the punch line because of it, and fails to show reciprocal generosity, what have I lost?"

"You're not afraid we'll get through the border first? And shore up what you hope to annihilate?"

Sophus smiled amiably. "There might come a point when that's a real threat. If I'm ever convinced that we've reached it, I suppose I might change my strategy. For now, though, it's like a game of Quantum Pass-the-Parcel: all the players work simultaneously to tear off the wrapping, and all the players share the benefits. Why convert to the classical version? This is faster, and much more enjoyable."

Tchicaya let the argument rest. It would have been impolite to state the obvious: when Sophus finally decided that sharing his insights had become too risky, it would not be to his advantage to announce the fact. At that point, the most logical strategy would be to continue displaying the same generosity as he'd shown in the past, but to replace the genuine, hard-won conjectures he'd revealed to his opponents in the past with equally well-crafted red herrings.

When they reached Mariama's cabin, Sophus left them. Tchicaya hung back in the corridor, unsure whether she wanted him to stay or go.

She said, "Would you come in, if you're coming in?"

He sat cross-legged on the bed while she moved around the

cabin. She'd included some physical ornaments in her transmission—a handful of carved rocks and blown-glass objects that the *Rindler*'s reception unit had obligingly re-created for her from spare materials—and now she couldn't decide where to put them.

"I traveled light, myself," Tchicaya said teasingly. "It didn't seem fair to ask them to cannibalize the ship to provide me with knickknacks."

Mariama narrowed her eyes. "Aren't you the puritan? Not to the point of amnesia, I hope."

He laughed. "Not these days." In the past, he'd left some rarely used memories behind in the Qusps of his body trail. With full-sensory recall, the amount of data mounted up rapidly, and there'd come a point when knowing precisely what it had been like to shake water out of his ears in a river on Gupta or roll over and fart while camping in a desert on Peldan didn't really strike him as a crucial part of his identity.

Yet he'd gathered up all the trivia again, before any of the Qusps were erased. And now that there was nowhere he could store his memories in the expectation that they'd remain secure—even if he archived them with a fleeing acorporeal community, their safety would come at the price of accessibility—they all seemed worth dragging around with him indefinitely.

Mariama finally settled on the shelf by the bed as the place for an elaborately braided variant of Klein's bottle. "Holding on to your memories is one thing," she said. "It doesn't stop you going over the horizon."

Tchicaya snorted. "Over the horizon? I'm four thousand and nine years old! Take out Slowdowns and travel insentience, and I've barely experienced half of that." Information theory put bounds on the kind of correlations anyone could sustain between their mental states at different times; the details depended on the structure of your mind, the nature of its hardware, and, ultimately, on the recently rather plasticized laws of physics. If there were unavoidable limits, though, they were eons away. "I think I can still lay claim to doing a far better job of resembling myself—at any prior age—than a randomly chosen stranger."

Mariama folded her arms, smiling slightly. "In the strict sense, obviously. But don't you think people can cross another kind of horizon? The strict definition counts everything: every aspect of temperament, every minor taste, every trivial opinion. There are so many markers, it's no wonder it takes an eternity for all of them to drift far enough to change someone beyond recognition. But they're not the things that define us. They're not the things that would make our younger selves accept us as their rightful successors, or recoil in horror."

Tchicaya gave her a warning look that he hoped would steer her away from the subject. With a stranger, he might have asked his Mediator to handle the subtext, but he didn't believe either of them had changed so much that they couldn't read each other's faces.

He said, "Any more children?"

She nodded. "One. Emine. She's six hundred and twelve."

Tchicaya smiled. "That's very restrained. I've had six."

"Six! Are any of them with you here?"

"No." He took a moment to realize why she was asking; he'd always sworn that he'd never leave a child before a century had passed. "They're all on Gleason; large families are common there. The youngest is four hundred and ninety."

"No travelers among them?"

"No. What about Emine?"

Mariama nodded happily. "She was born on Har'El. She left with me. We traveled together for a while."

"Where is she now?"

"I'm not certain." She admitted this without a trace of reticence, but Tchicaya still thought there was a hint of sadness in her voice.

He said, "One thing about being planet-bound is, once you've committed to the place, that's it. Even if you wander off to the other side of the world, everyone else who's chosen to stay is just a few hours away."

"But two travelers? What does that guarantee?" Mariama shrugged. "Chance meetings, every few hundred years. Or more often, if you make the effort. I don't feel like I've lost Emine."

"Of course not. Nor the others. What's to stop you visiting the ones who've stayed put?"

She shook her head. "You know the answer to that. You're like a cross between a fairy-tale character and some kind of . . . rare climatic disaster."

"Oh, come on! It's not that bad." Tchicaya knew there was a grain of truth in what she said, but it seemed perverse to complain about it. When he was made to feel welcome, it was as a visitor, a temporary novelty. When your child had lived with three or four generations of their own descendants, for centuries, you were not a missing piece of the puzzle. But he never expected to *slot in*, anywhere. Once he'd told the crib on Turaev that his birth flesh could be recycled, he'd given up the notion that somewhere there'd always be a room waiting for him.

He said, "So what about Emine's other parent?"

Mariama smiled. "What about your partner back on Gleason? The one you raised six children with."

"I asked first."

"What is there to say? She stayed on Har'El. Not even Emine could drag her away." Mariama lowered her eyes and traced a fingertip over the edges of one of the abstract carvings.

Tchicaya said, "If you could drag everyone with you, what would be the point of leaving? There were cultures back on Earth that traveled across continents, whole extended families together—and they were usually more conservative than the ones that stayed put, or the ones that spawned diasporas."

Mariama scowled. "If two travelers happened to have a child, would that constitute a tribe?"

"No. But traveling is not about a change of scenery. It's about breaking connections." Tchicaya felt a sudden sense of *déjà vu*, then realized that he was quoting her own words back at her. He'd got into the habit long ago of using them on other people. "I'm not saying that there'd be anything wrong if six whole generations uprooted themselves together, if that's not a contradiction in terms. But they wouldn't stay together for long—or at least, they wouldn't without imposing rules on themselves a thousand times more restrictive than any they'd needed when they were planet-bound."

Mariama said irritably, "You're such a fucking ideologue some-times! And before you call me a hypocrite: it's always the converts who are the worst."

"Yeah? That's not such a convenient axiom for you, if you re-member that it cuts both ways." Tchicaya raised his hands in apol-ogy; he wasn't really angry or offended yet, but he could see where they were heading. "Just . . . forget I said that. Can we change the subject? Please?"

"You can tell me what happened on Gleason."

Tchicaya thought for a while before replying. "Her name was Lesya. I was there for a hundred and sixty years. We were in love, all that time. We were like bedrock to each other. I was as happy as I've ever been." He spread his arms. "That's it. That's what hap-pened on Gleason."

Mariama eyed him skeptically. "Nothing soured?"

"No."

"And you don't wish you were still there?"

"No."

"Then you weren't in love. You might have been happy, but you weren't in love."

Tchicaya shook his head, amused. "Now who's the ideologue?"

"You just woke up one morning and decided to leave? And there was no pain, and no rancor?"

"No, *we* woke up one morning, and we both knew I'd be gone within a year. Just because she wasn't a traveler doesn't mean it was all down to me. What do you think? I lied to her at the start?" He was becoming so animated he was messing up the bed; he stroked the sheet, and it tightened. "You know how I think she'll feel, if the border reaches Gleason?"

Mariama resisted answering, knowing that she was being set up. After several seconds, she succumbed anyway.

"Terrified?"

"No. I think she'll be grateful." Tchicaya smiled at Mariama's expression of disgust. It was strange, but she'd probably given him more confidence in his stance, now that she'd turned out to be his opponent, than if they'd been allies willing to reassure each other endlessly.

He continued. "You don't take a traveler for a partner if you hope that the world will always stay the same. You do it because you can't quite break away, yourself, but you can't live without the promise of change hanging over you every day.

"That's what the border means, for a lot of people. The promise of change they'd never be able to make any other way."

Sophus's presentation took place in a theater that the ship had improvised in the middle of one of the accommodation modules, folding up all the cabins that happened to be unoccupied to create a single large space. When Mariama realized that this included her own, she was not pleased.

"I have glass in there!" She pointed across the theater. "Right where that person's sitting."

"It'll be protected," Tchicaya reassured her, as if he were a veteran of the concertina effect. "Anyway, what's there to lose? If anything's broken, it can be reconstructed."

"They've never been *broken*," she complained.

Tchicaya said, "I hate to be the one to point this out, but—" He held up his thumb and forefinger and adjusted the spacing to atomic size.

Mariama glared at him until he dropped his hand. "It's not the same thing. But I wouldn't expect you to understand."

Tchicaya winced. "So now I'm an all-round philistine?"

Mariama's face softened. She reached over and ran a hand affectionately across his stubbled scalp. "No. Your failings are much more specific than that."

Tchicaya spotted Yann coming through the entrance with a small group of people. He raised a hand and tentatively beckoned to him. Yann responded by bringing the whole group along to sit beside them.

Rasmah, Hayashi, Birago, and Suljan had been involved in designing the new spectrometer. Catching the tail end of the conversation they'd been having made it clear that all but Birago were Yielders; the other three were joking about his plans to sneak in a filter to conceal the telltale signature of Planck worms devouring the scenery. Birago seemed to be taking their teasing with equanimity, though it struck Tchicaya that he had the quietness of someone outnumbered, who had decided that there was no point in speaking his mind.

Perhaps Mariama felt outnumbered, too, but she appeared genuinely amiable toward the Yielders as introductions were made; she was certainly more than diplomatically polite. Tchicaya had been wondering whether their friendship had caused her to conceal the full measure of her distaste for his position, but whatever effort she was making for his benefit, she was nowhere near the point that Kadir and Zyfete had reached.

Yann said, "The new spectrometer looks good. We'll be able to resolve a whole new band of gamma rays, and with twice the precision of the old machine."

Tchicaya nodded, unsure how much difference that would make. "Do you know what this is all about?" He gestured at the podium that was now growing before their eyes. His Mediator had explained that the timing was meant to encourage people to stop talking among themselves—like a change of lighting, or the raising of curtains—but apparently this was an aspect of the *Rindler*'s local culture that had been documented without ever being practiced.

"Not really," Yann admitted. "There's usually something on the grapevine about these talks, weeks in advance, but this one has come out of the blue. Sophus is always interesting, though. I'm sure he'll be worth listening to."

"He said something to me earlier about time asymmetry."

"What, time-reversal asymmetry? He's talking about an arrow of time in the novo-vacuum?"

"No, time-translation asymmetry."

Yann's eyes widened. " 'Interesting' might have been an understatement."

Sophus appeared and made his way to the podium, but then he stood to one side. People were still entering the theater, and it looked as if they'd keep on streaming in until it was completely full.

Mariama surveyed the latecomers irritably. "Why can't they watch this in their heads?"

"It's a flesh thing," Yann confided. "I don't understand it either."

Tchicaya glanced up. People were sitting in chairs suspended from the ceiling, accessed via corridors through higher levels that would otherwise have come to a sudden end. The ship had made use of every square meter of available surface, even though there was no prospect of cramming every last passenger in. Rasmah caught Tchicaya's eye and joked, "I always wanted to be at a performance where people were hanging from the rafters."

Sophus cleared his throat, and the audience fell silent almost immediately. Tchicaya was impressed; even if he'd known everyone on the ship personally, he would probably have asked his Mediator to plead on his behalf for their attention.

Sophus began. "We've been scribing probes and gathering data now for more than two hundred and fifty years, trying to understand what's going on behind that wall." He motioned with a raised fist, as if pounding against the border. "The results are there for everyone to see. Theories come and go, and all we have gained is the ability to rule out ninety-nine percent of new models without performing a single new experiment, because we already have enough data to kill off most of our ideas at birth.

"To some people, it's beginning to look hopeless. How can the laws we've failed to understand be so difficult to grasp? It only took three and a half centuries to get from Newton to Sarumpaet. What's wrong with us? We have the mathematical tools to model systems far more arcane than anything nature has ever actually thrown at us, before. The acorporeals grew bored with physics ten thousand years ago; expecting them to live with such meager intellectual stimulation was like asking an adult to spend eternity playing with a child's numbered blocks. But even their boundlessly flexible minds can't make sense of the new toy they've come here to admire."

Tchicaya glanced at Yann, who whispered plaintively, "Maybe I should be grateful whenever it slips someone's mind that acorporeals were running the Quietener."

"The Sarumpaet rules survived *twenty thousand years of scrutiny!*" Sophus marveled. "How flawed, how misguided, could they possibly be? So we began with the sensible, conservative approach: we'd find a new set of rules that extended the old ones, very slightly. The smallest change we could possibly make, the tiniest correction, or expansion, that would encompass all their past successes—but also explain what happened at Mimosa.

"Fine. That's a simple enough piece of mathematics; people solved the equations within days of hearing the news. Then we built the *Rindler* . . . and that minimal extension didn't quite fit what we found. So we tweaked the rules a little more. And a little more.

"In essence—and I know this is unfair to some of you, but I'm going to say it anyway—most of what's been done here has consisted of repeating that process, over and over, for a quarter of a millennium. We've raised ever more elaborate theoretical towers on the same foundations, and most of them have been toppled by the very first prediction they made."

Sophus paused, frowning slightly. He looked almost apologetic, as if he'd been surprised by the tone of his own rhetoric. When he'd spoken to Tchicaya earlier, he'd appeared casually optimistic, but now his frustration was showing through. That sentiment was understandable, but it risked undermining the reception of whatever he said next: to claim any kind of fundamental new insight now would sound like arrogance, after so many people before him had struggled and failed. Still, if he honestly believed that they'd all been misguided, and that progress would come not from standing on their shoulders but from digging in the opposite direction entirely, there was a limit to how graciously that opinion could be expressed.

He collected himself and continued, loosening his posture, visibly striving to make light of his subject, however many worlds, and egos, were at stake.

"Sarumpaet was right about everything that happened before Mimosa. We have to hold on to that fact! And in one sense, *we* were right, to aim to tamper with his work as little as possible. But what we shouldn't have done was paint ourselves into a corner where we just kept building ever more baroque and elaborate 're-finements' of the original rules.

"What do the Sarumpaet rules really *say*?" Sophus looked around the theater, as if expecting volunteers, but he'd caught everyone off-balance, and there were no takers. "We can write them half a dozen ways, and they're all equally elegant and compelling. A combinatorial recipe for transition amplitudes between quantum graphs. A Hamiltonian we exponentiate to compute the way a state vector evolves with time. There's a Lagrangian formulation, a category-theoretic formulation, a qubit-processing formulation, and probably a hundred more versions cherished by various en-thusiasts, who'll never forgive me for leaving out their favorite one.

"But what do they all say, in the end? They say that *our vacuum is stable*. And why do they say that? Because Sarumpaet required them to do so! If they'd implied anything else, he would have con-sidered them to be a failure. The stability of the vacuum is not a prediction that emerges from some deep principle that had to be satisfied, regardless; it was the number one design criterion for the whole theory. Sarumpaet certainly found some simple and beautiful axioms that met his goal, but mathematics is full of equally beautiful axioms that don't get to govern everything that happens in the universe."

Sophus halted again, arms folded, head inclined. To Tchicaya he seemed to be pleading for forbearance; what he'd just stated was so obvious and uncontroversial that half the audience had probably found it baffling, if not downright offensive, that he'd wasted their time spelling it out for the thousandth time.

"Our vacuum is stable: that was the hook on which Sarumpaet hung everything. So why did he have such unprecedented success, despite basing his entire theory on something we now know to be false?"

Sophus let the question hang in the air for a moment, then changed tack completely.

"I wonder how many of you have heard of 'superselection rules'? I only learned the phrase myself a month ago, while doing some historical research. They're an arcane notion from the dawn of quantum mechanics, and they only persisted in the vocabulary for the first couple of centuries, before people finally got things straightened out.

"Everyone knows that it's an axiom of quantum mechanics that you can form superpositions of any two state vectors: if V and W are possible physical states, then so is aV + bW, for any complex numbers a and b whose squared magnitudes sum to one. If that's true, though, then why do we never see a quantum state with a fifty-percent probability of being negatively charged, and a fifty-percent probability of being positively charged? Conservation of charge is not the issue. Long after people could routinely prepare photons that were equally likely to be on opposite sides of a continent, why couldn't they manage to prepare a system that was equally likely to be an electron here and a positron here"— Sophus held up his left hand, then his right—"or *vice versa?*

"For a hundred years or so, most people would have answered that question by saying: 'Oh, there's a superselection rule for charge! You can *usually* combine state vectors . . . but not if they come from different superselection sectors of the Hilbert space!' Apparently there were these strange ghettos that had been cordoned off from each other, and whose inhabitants were not allowed to mix. Cordoned off *how?* There was no mechanism, no system; it was just an inexplicable fact dressed up in some fancy terminology. But people went ahead and developed methods for doing quantum mechanics with these arbitrary borders thrown in, and the lines on the map became something to be memorized without too much scrutiny. If some innocent novice asked a jaded elder student, 'Why can't you have a superposition of different charges?' the reply would be, 'Because there's a superselection rule forbidding it, you idiot!' "

Sophus lowered his gaze slightly before adding acerbically, "We're far more sophisticated now, of course. No one would tolerate mystification like that—and besides, every child knows the real reason. An electron and a positron in the same position would be correlated with vastly different states for the surrounding electric field, and unless you could track all the details of *that field* and incorporate them into your observations, you'd have no hope of recognizing the state as a superposition. Instead, the two different charge states would decohere, and you'd be split into two versions, one believing that you'd detected an electron, the other that you'd detected a positron. So although there *are no* superselection rules, the world still looks so much like the way it would look if there were that all the mathematics that revolved around the term lives on, in various guises."

Tchicaya sensed a sudden change in the atmosphere around him. When he'd glanced at people before, most had seemed puzzled that they were being offered such mundane observations. Tolerant, and prepared to go on listening for a while, thanks to Sophus's reputation, but clearly not expecting much from yet another tortured reexamination of their field's basic assumptions. Now there was a shifting of bodies, a creaking of seats, as people felt compelled to transform their postures of indifference or mild disappointment into something altogether more vigilant.

As this mood swept the room, Tchicaya felt gooseflesh rise along his spine. He couldn't claim to have anticipated the words he heard next, but they thoroughly merited his body's reaction.

"I believe there are no Sarumpaet rules," Sophus proclaimed. "Not the originals, and not some grander, more perfect version that will explain what happened at Mimosa. But the world still looks so much like the way it would look if there were that we couldn't help but think such rules existed."

In the silence that followed, Tchicaya turned to Mariama, wondering if she'd picked up more from Sophus's earlier remarks than he had, but she appeared to be equally stunned. Tchicaya was beaming with delight at the audacity of Sophus's claim. Mariama looked dismayed, almost fearful.

Sophus continued. "How can the Sarumpaet rules seem to be true, when they're false? How can our vacuum seem to be stable, when it isn't? I believe that the right way to answer these questions is virtually identical to the resolution of another paradox, one that was dealt with almost twenty thousand years ago. How can the universe appear to obey classical mechanics, when it really obeys quantum mechanics?

"What creates the illusion of classical mechanics is our inability to keep track of every aspect of a quantum system. If we can't observe the whole system—if it's too large and complex in itself, or if it's coupled to its surroundings, making *them* part of the system—we lose the information that distinguishes a genuine superposition, where alternatives coexist and interact, from a classical mixture of mutually exclusive possibilities.

"I believe the same effect is responsible for the Sarumpaet rules. How can that be? The Sarumpaet rules are quantum rules. They apply to systems that have *not* been rendered classical by decoherence. How can interaction with the environment explain anything *wholly quantum-mechanical*?"

Sophus smiled wearily. "It's been staring us in the face for twenty thousand years. An electron—a charged particle, which transforms the ordinary vacuum around it into an entirely different state—still obeys quantum mechanics in all of its *other* degrees of freedom. Its position is quantum-mechanical, its charge is classical. Even when we do our best to isolate an electron from its surroundings, we actually fail miserably at half of the task, while succeeding at the other half. So decoherence hides superpositions of different charge states from us, but *not* different position states. Our failure looks classical, our success is quantum-mechanical.

"We thought the Sarumpaet rules were pure quantum mechanics: the final story, the lowest level, the rules that held for a system in perfect isolation. Of course, we accepted the fact that, *in practice*, we could never isolate anything from its surroundings completely, but that wasn't the point. The universe itself, the total system, was assumed to be obeying the Sarumpaet rules—because whenever we did our best to examine any small part of it, separated out as scrupulously as possible, those were the laws that held.

"That was the wrong conclusion to reach. The electron shows how quantum and classical properties can coexist. The fact that you can demonstrate *some* quantum behavior in a system doesn't mean you've uncovered all that there is to be found.

"I believe that the Sarumpaet rules are *classical rules*. Part of the total state vector of any system obeys them, but not the whole. The part that does follow the Sarumpaet rules interacts with the environment one way: transforming its surroundings into what we think of as our own vacuum. But there are other parts that interact differently, creating other states. Because we can't begin to track what's really happening to the environment on the Planck scale, what we see is a single, certain, classical outcome: the Sarumpaet rules hold absolutely true, and our vacuum is absolutely stable."

A member of the audience stood, and Sophus acknowledged the request. "Tarek?"

"You're claiming that the vacuum has been stabilized by something like the quantum Zeno effect?"

Tchicaya craned his neck to observe the questioner more closely. Tarek was the Preservationist who'd been trying to scribe Planck worms to devour the novo-vacuum, without waiting to discover what it was, or what it might contain. There was nothing fanatical about his demeanor, though; he merely radiated an impatience that everyone in the audience shared.

"It's similar to that," Sophus agreed. "The quantum Zeno effect stabilizes systems through constant measurement. I believe that part of the total graph in which everything's embedded 'measures' the part we see as the vacuum, which also determines the dynamic laws that govern matter moving through that vacuum. It's like the vapor in a cloud chamber, condensing in droplets around the path of a subatomic particle. The particle only appears to follow a definite trajectory because each path is correlated with a particular pattern of droplets—and the droplets have too many hidden degrees of freedom to exhibit quantum effects themselves. But we know there are branches where the particle follows different paths, surrounded by different trails of droplets."

Tarek frowned. "So why can't we discover the path, the rules, that are holding sway behind the border?"

Sophus said, "Because what lies behind the border is *not* another vacuum, another set of rules. It has no classical properties like that to discover. It's not that it couldn't be divided up—formally, mathematically—into a sum of components, each obeying a different analog of the Sarumpaet rules. But we're not correlated with any particular component, the way we are with our own vacuum, so we can't expect to uncover any particular set of rules."

Tchicaya was exhilarated. It was too soon to take Sophus's idea seriously, but there was something deeply appealing in the simplicity of the notion. Behind the border was a superposition of *every possible dynamic law*.

Tarek said, "We can't measure those properties? Make them definite, if only for different branches of ourselves? When we interact with the novo-vacuum—or whatever you now wish to call it—shouldn't we end up as a superposition of observers who each find definite laws?"

Sophus shook his head firmly. "Not by dropping a few Planck-scale probe graphs into a system six hundred light-years wide. If there *were* preexisting laws behind the border, we might hope to discover them that way, but that's not what we're dealing with. On our side of the border, there's a tight correlation stretching across all of space-time: the dynamics being followed at different times and places has become a tangle of mutual interdependence. What lies behind the border isn't correlated from place to place, or from moment to moment. What we're sampling with our probe graphs might as well be random noise at every level."

Rasmah stood, just ahead of a dozen other people. The others resumed their seats, and Tarek begrudgingly followed.

She said, "This is wonderful speculation, Sophus, but how do you plan to test it? Do you have any solid predictions?"

Sophus gestured at the space behind him, and a set of graphs appeared.

"As you see, I can match the borderlight spectrum. That's not claiming much. I can match the half-c velocity of the border, which is slightly harder. And I can match the pooled results of all the experiments performed here so far: namely, their complete failure to identify anything resembling a dynamic law.

"So much for retrodiction. I'm making the following prediction: when we repeat the old experiments, re-scribe the old probe graphs, and monitor the results with your new spectrometer . . . we'll find exactly the same thing, all over again. No patterns will emerge, no symmetries, no invariants, no laws.

"We've already discovered that there's nothing to be discovered. All I can predict is that however hard we look, that absence will be confirmed."

Chapter 8

Yann rolled off the bed and landed on the floor, laughing.

Tchicaya peered over the edge. "Are you all right?"

Yann nodded, covering his mouth with a hand but unable to silence himself.

Tchicaya didn't know whether to be annoyed or concerned. Acorporeals taking on bodies often mapped them in unusual ways. Perhaps laughter was Yann's only available response to some terrible psychic affront that Tchicaya had unwittingly inflicted.

"You're sure I haven't hurt you?"

Yann shook his head, still laughing helplessly.

Tchicaya sat on the edge of the bed, struggling to regain his own sense of humor. "This is not a reaction I'm accustomed to. Rejection and hilarity are perfectly acceptable responses, but they're supposed to occur much earlier in proceedings."

Yann managed to regain some composure. "I'm sorry. I didn't mean to offend you."

"I take it you're not interested in finishing what you started?"

"Umm." Yann grimaced. "I could try, if it's important to you. But I think it would be very difficult to take seriously."

Tchicaya planted a foot on his chest. "Next time you want an authentic embodied experience . . . just simulate it." He still felt a pang of lust at the touch of skin on skin, but it was fading into a kind of exasperated affection.

He crouched down and kissed Yann on the mouth, meaning it as a gesture of finality. Yann smiled, puzzled. "That was nice."

"Forget it." Tchicaya stood and started dressing.

Yann lay on the floor, watching him. "I think I'm getting all the signals you talked about," he mused. "But they're so crude, even now. And before, it was just a single message, repeating itself endlessly: 'Be happy, be happy, be happy!' Do you think there's something wrong with this body?"

"I doubt it." Tchicaya sat cross-legged on the floor beside him. "You expected more?"

"I was already happy, so it was a bit redundant."

"How happy?"

"As happy as it's possible to be, for no particular reason."

"I have no idea how to interpret that. What gets to count as a particular reason?"

Yann shrugged. "Something more than being told by my body: 'Be happy.' Be happy . . . why?"

"Because you're with someone you like. And you're making them happy, too."

"Yes, but only if they accept the same reasoning. That's circular."

Tchicaya groaned. "Now you're being disingenuous. It's a tradition, passed down from reproductive biology. Every tradition's arbitrary. That doesn't mean it's empty."

"I know. But I still expected something more subtle."

"That takes time."

"What, hours?"

"Centuries."

Yann narrowed his eyes with suspicion.

Tchicaya laughed, but made a face protesting his honesty. "On

Turaev, it takes six months of attraction before anything's physically possible." Like most generic bodies, the *Rindler*'s were promiscuous: any two of them could develop compatible sexual organs, more or less at will. You could wire in your own chosen restraints while you inhabited them, but since leaving home, Tchicaya had never felt the need to delegate the task. "The waiting was nice, in its own way," he admitted. "You might think it was risking an awful anticlimax, but I think the buildup improved the sex itself almost as much as it raised expectations. Acting on the spur of the moment is more likely to be disappointing."

Yann protested, "I've been contemplating this for almost six months."

"Since I arrived? I'm flattered. But then, who else would you dare to ask?"

Yann smiled abashedly. "How could I not be curious? It's what flesh is famous for. However undeservedly." He watched Tchicaya carefully, serious for a moment. "Have I hurt you?"

Tchicaya shook his head. "That usually takes longer, too." He hesitated. "So what do acorporeals do, instead? When I was a child, I used to imagine that you'd all have simulated bodies. Sex would be just like embodied sex, but there'd be lots of colored lights, and cosmic bliss."

Yann guffawed. "Maybe twenty thousand years ago there were people that vacuous, but they must have all decayed into thermal noise before I was born." He added hastily, "I'm not saying you're wrong to continue the tradition. You've mapped some stable mammalian neurobiology, and it's not too pathological in its original form. I suppose it still serves some useful social functions, as well as being a mild existential placebo. But when you have a malleable mental structure, intensifying pleasure for its own sake is a very uninteresting *cul-de-sac*. We worked that out a long time ago."

"Fair enough. But what do you do instead?"

Yann sat up and leaned against the side of the bed. "All the other things the embodied do. Give gifts. Show affection. Be attentive. Sometimes we raise children together."

"What kind of gifts?"

"Art. Music. Theorems."

"Original theorems?"

"If you're serious."

Tchicaya was impressed. Mathematics was a vast territory, far more challenging and intricate than physical space. Reaching a theorem no one had proved before was a remarkable feat. "That's positively . . . chivalric," he said. "Like a knight riding off to the edge of the world, to bring back a dragon's egg. And you've done that, yourself?"

"Yes."

"How often?"

"Nine times." Yann laughed at Tchicaya's expression of astonishment, and added, "It's not always that serious. If it was, it really would be as daunting as winning the hand of medieval royalty, and no one would bother."

"So you start with something easier?"

Yann nodded. "When I was ten years old, all I gave my sweetheart was a pair of projections that turned the group of rotations in four dimensions into principal bundles over the three-sphere. Ancient constructions, though I did rediscover them for myself."

"How were they received?"

"She liked them so much, she extended them to larger spaces and gave me back the result."

"Can you show me?"

Yann sketched diagrams and equations with his hands; through their Mediators, Tchicaya saw them painted in the air. To make sense of the group of four-dimensional rotations, you could project it down to the three-dimensional sphere of directions in four dimensions, by mapping each rotation to the direction to which it took the x-axis. All the rotations that treated the x-axis in the same way then differed from each other by rotations of the other three directions. This effectively sliced the original group into copies of the group of *three-dimensional* rotations—which was just a solid sphere with opposite points on its boundary glued together, since any pair of rotations around opposite axes became equal once you reached one hundred and eighty degrees. Like an artful rendering of depth in a painting, these striations made the topology of the larger group much clearer.

"The other projection inverts all the rotations first, so it turns the whole construction inside out." Yann demonstrated, smiling nostalgically. "I know it's sentimental, but the first time always stays with you."

"Yeah." The mathematics was simple, but it struck Tchicaya as having all the charm of an embodied child's handmade gift.

"So what about you?"

"I've generally had more success with flowers."

Yann rolled his eyes. "Your own first love. What was that like?"

Tchicaya contemplated lying, but he usually did it badly. And what would he say? He wasn't going to substitute someone else, writing Mariama out of his life.

He said, "I can't tell you."

"Why not?" Yann was twice as eager for the details, now. "How embarrassing can it be, four thousand years later?"

"You'd be surprised." Tchicaya struggled to think of a way to deflect the inquiry without piquing Yann's curiosity further. "There's a much better story I can tell you," he said. "About my father's first love. Can I trade that instead?"

Yann agreed, reluctantly.

"When my father was fourteen," Tchicaya began, "he fell in love with Lajos. It started in winter, when they used to sneak into each other's houses at night and sleep together."

Yann said, "Why did they have to sneak? Would their parents have stopped them?"

Tchicaya was momentarily at a loss for an answer; he'd never had to explain this before. "No. Their parents would have known. But it's more enjoyable to pretend that it's a secret."

Yann seemed slightly bemused by this claim, but willing to take his word for it. "Go on."

"By summer, they were giddy with it. They could touch and kiss, nothing more, but they knew it wouldn't be much longer. They'd go swimming together, walking together, waiting for it to happen. Aching this wonderful ache." Tchicaya smiled, hiding a sudden upwelling of sadness. He doubted he'd ever return to Turaev, to talk to the stranger his father had become.

"At the height of summer, they were walking on the outskirts of town. And my father witnessed the strangest, most terrifying event that had happened on Turaev for a thousand years. A spaceship descended from the sky. An ancient engine, spouting flames, burning up crops, melting rocks."

Yann was outraged. "And Lajos—" He struggled with his emotions. "Your father saw Lajos—"

"No, no!" Tchicaya was amused at the preposterousness of this suggestion, but he still warmed to Yann's response. He'd met bigots who would have assumed that an acorporeal would shrug off the notion that witnessing the local death of your first love would be of any consequence at all.

"Not even anachronauts land their spacecraft on top of people," he explained. "They do have instruments."

Yann relaxed. "So your father and Lajos got to meet the anachronauts. What were they like?"

"They'd left Earth fourteen thousand years before. Pre-Qusp. They used biological techniques to keep their flesh viable, but they spent a lot of time cryogenically suspended."

"*Cryogenically suspended.*" Yann was mesmerized. "I always

knew they were out there, but I've never met anyone before who's spoken to someone who's seen them in the flesh." He shuddered with vicarious otherworldliness. "What did they want?"

"When they left Earth, they knew they'd be overtaken by newer technologies; they knew they'd be traveling into the future. They knew there'd be established societies along their route. That was why they left. They wanted to witness what humanity would become."

"I see." Yann appeared to be on the verge of raising another objection, but then he let it pass.

"They had one particular interest, though," Tchicaya continued. "They told my father that they wanted to know what stage his people were in, in the eternal struggle between women and men. They wanted to hear about the wars, the truces. The victories, the compromises, the setbacks."

"Wait. How old is your father now?"

"About six millennia."

"So . . ." Yann rubbed his neck, perplexed. "Turaev was the very first planet they'd visited? After fourteen thousand years?"

"No, they'd made planet-fall six times before."

Yann spread his arms in surrender. "You've lost me, then."

"No one had had the heart to tell them," Tchicaya explained. "When they first made contact with a modern society, on Crane, it took a while before they were sufficiently at ease to reveal their purpose. But by the time they got around to asking questions, the locals had already gained a clear sense of the kind of preconceptions these travelers had. They'd been in cold storage for millennia, and now they were finally beginning the stage of their voyage that would justify the enormous sacrifices they'd made. Nobody could bring themselves to break the news that the sole surviving remnant of human sexual dimorphism was the retention, in some languages, of different inflections of various parts of speech associated with different proper names—and that expecting these grammatical fossils to be correlated with any aspect of a person's anatomy would be like assuming from similar rules for inanimate objects that a cloud possessed a penis and a table contained a womb."

"So they *lied to them?*" Yann was horrified. "On Crane? And on all the other planets?"

"It must have seemed like the kindest thing to do," Tchicaya protested. "And when it started, no one seriously expected them to reach another planet. When they did, though, word had gone ahead of them, so people were much better prepared."

"And this happened *six times?* Even if they were fed the same story on every planet, by the time they'd had a few chances to compare it with reality—"

Tchicaya shook his head. "They weren't fed the same story on every planet; that would have defeated the whole point. They'd traveled into the future in the hope of being entertained in a very specific way. On Crane, they'd revealed a lot about the kind of histories and practices they expected to encounter on their voyage, and so people played along with their expectations. The locals there told them that all the 'men' had been wiped out by a virus shortly after settlement, and made a big song and dance about the struggle to adapt: one faction trying to reinvent the lost sex; another, bravely pursuing monosexuality, finally triumphant. The anachronauts lapped it up, oohing and aahing over all the profound things this told them about gender. They made notes, recorded images, observed a few fake ceremonies and historical re-enactments . . . then moved on."

Yann buried his face in his hands. "This is unforgivable!"

Tchicaya said, "No one lied to them about anything else. They had some equally bizarre notions about the future of physics, but the people on Crane gave them an honest account of all the latest work."

Yann looked up, slightly mollified. "What happened next?"

"After Crane? It became a kind of competition, to see who could Mead them the best: make up the most outlandish story, and get the anachronauts to swallow it. A plague wasn't really barbaric enough. There had to be war between the sexes. There had to be oppression. There had to be slavery."

"*Slavery?*"

"Oh yes. And worse. On Krasnov, they said that for five thousand years, men had slaughtered their own firstborn child to gain access to a life-prolonging secretion in mother's milk. The practice had only ended a century before."

Yann swayed against the bed. "That's surreal on so many levels, I don't know where to begin." He regarded Tchicaya forlornly. "This is really what the anachronauts expected? No progress, no happiness, no success, no harmony? Just the worst excesses of their own sordid history, repeated over and over for millennia?"

Tchicaya said, "On Mäkelä, the people insisted that their planet had been peaceful since settlement. The anachronauts were terribly suspicious, and kept digging for the awful secret that no one dared reveal. Finally, the locals reviewed the transmission from Crane describing the first contact, and they realized what was needed. They explained that their society had been stabilized by the invention of the Sacred Pentad, in which all family units were based around two males, two females, and one neuter." Tchicaya frowned. "There were rules about the sexual relationships between the members, something about equal numbers of heterosexual and homosexual pairings, but I could never get a clear description of that. But the anachronauts were thrilled by the great 'cultural richness' they had finally uncovered. Apparently, their definition of 'cultural richness' was the widespread enforcement of any social or sexual mores even more bizarre and arbitrary than the ones they'd left behind."

Yann said, "So what happened on Turaev?"

"The ship had been tracked for centuries, of course, so the

mere fact of its arrival was no surprise to anyone. My father had known since early childhood that these strangers would be turning up, somewhere on the planet, at about this time. A variety of different hoaxes had been advocated by different groups, and though none of them had gained planet-wide support, the anachronauts rarely visited more than one place, so it would only require the people in one town to back each other up.

"My father wasn't prepared at all, though. He hadn't kept up with news of the precise timing of the ship's arrival, and even though he'd been aware that it would happen soon, the chance of planet-fall outside his own town had been too microscopic to worry about. He'd had far more important things on his mind."

Yann smiled expectantly, despite himself. "So when the flames died down, and the dust settled, and your father's Mediator dug up the visitors' ancient language from its files . . . he had to stand there and insist with a straight face that he knew nothing whatsoever about the subject of their inquiries?"

"Exactly. Neither he nor Lajos had the slightest idea what they were supposed to tell these strangers. If they'd read the reports on the anachronauts, they'd have realized that they could have claimed all manner of elaborate taboos on discussing the subject, but they weren't in a position to know that and invoke some imaginary code of silence. So all they were left with was claiming ignorance: claiming to be both prepubescent, and stupid." Tchicaya laughed. "After *six months* of longing for each other? Within days, or even hours, of consumation? I don't know how to translate that into terms you're familiar with—"

Yann was offended. "I'm not an idiot. I understand how much pride they would have had to swallow. You don't need to spoon-feed me similes."

Tchicaya bowed his head in apology, but he held out for precision. "Pride, yes, but it was more than that. Claiming anything but the truth would have felt like they were renouncing each other.

Even if they'd known their lines, I'm not sure that they could have gone through with the charade." He held a fist against his chest. "It hurts, to lie about something like that. Other people might have been swept up in the excitement of the conspiracy. But to Lajos and my father, that was just noise. They were the center of the universe. Nothing else mattered."

"So they told them the truth?"

Tchicaya said, "Yes."

"About themselves?"

He nodded. "And more."

"About the whole planet? That this was the custom all over Turaev?"

"More."

Yann emitted an anguished groan. "They told them everything?"

Tchicaya said, "My father didn't come right out and state that all their earlier informants had lied to them, but he explained that—apart from a few surviving contemporaries of the travelers themselves—there'd been nothing resembling sexual dimorphism in the descendants of humans, anywhere, for more than nineteen thousand years. Long before any extrasolar world was settled, it had gone the way of war, slavery, parasites, disease, and quantum indecisiveness. And apart from trivial local details, like the exact age of sexual maturity and the latency period between attraction and potency, he and his lover embodied a universal condition: they were both, simply, people. There were no other categories left to which they could belong."

Yann pondered this. "So did the intrepid gendographers believe him?"

Tchicaya held up a hand, gesturing for patience. "They were far too polite to call my father a liar to his face. So they went into town, and spoke to other people."

"Who, without exception, gave them the approved version?"

"Yes."

"So they left Turaev none the wiser. With an unlikely tale from two mischievous adolescents to add to their collection of sexual mythology."

Tchicaya said, "Perhaps. Except that since Turaev, they haven't made planet-fall anywhere. They've been tracked, the ship's still functioning, and they've had four or five opportunities to enter inhabited systems. But every time, they've flown on by."

Yann shivered. "You think it's a ghost ship?"

Tchicaya said, "No. I think they're in cold sleep, with their bodies frozen, and tiny currents flowing in their brains. Dreaming of all the horrors they'd wished upon us, in the name of some crude, masochistic notion of humanity that must have been dying right in front of them before they'd even left Earth."

As Tchicaya boarded the shuttle ahead of Yann, Mariama looked back and flashed him a brief smile. Her meaning was unmistakable, but he pretended not to notice. He didn't mind her knowing what he and Yann had attempted, or even how it had ended, but it drove him to distraction that she could deduce at least half the story just by watching them together.

He could have instructed his Exoself to embargo whatever small gestures were giving him away. But that was not how he wanted to be: hermetically sealed, blank as a rock. For a moment, Tchicaya contemplated reaching over and putting his arm across Yann's shoulders, just to devalue her powers of observation. On reflection that would have been petty, though, and likely to cause Yann all kinds of confusion.

Mariama sat beside Tarek. In the unlikely event that the two of them were lovers, Tchicaya would be the last to know. Behind him, the fifth passenger, Branco, strapped himself in place. Tchicaya turned to him and joked, "It doesn't seem right that you're outnumbered. You should at least have brought an observer along."

Branco said pleasantly, "Fuck that. The last thing I want to do is start mimicking all your paranoid games."

Branco had been part of the original coalition who'd designed and built both the *Rindler* and the Scribe. Yielders and Preservationists had arrived over the decades, exuding a kind of bureaucratic fog through which he was now forced to march, but as he'd explained to Tchicaya earlier, he'd become inured to the squatters and their demands. The Scribe was still available to its creators, occasionally, and with patience he could still get work done. The factions made a lot of noise, but in the long run, as far as Branco was concerned, they'd be about as significant as the vapid religious cults who'd once squabbled over contested shrines on Earth. "And you sad airheads can't even slaughter each other," he'd observed gleefully. "How frustrating that must be."

As they fell away from the *Rindler*, Tchicaya barely noticed the weightlessness, or the strange doll's-house/termite-colony view some of the modules offered as they shrank into the distance. The trip hadn't quite become as unremarkable to him as air travel in a planetary atmosphere, but on a planet even repeated flights along the same route were never as unvarying as this.

Tarek said, "Actually, we're outnumbered, three to two. If you're 'neutral,' you're a Yielder. There is no difference."

"Oh, here we go!" Branco chuckled and settled back into his couch. "It's a short trip, but please, entertain us."

"You're not fooling anyone," Tarek insisted heatedly.

"It's not important," Mariama said. Tchicaya watched her, wondering if she'd make eye contact with Tarek as she spoke. She didn't. "There are observers here for both sides. It doesn't matter how many there are." Her tone was calm, neither argumentative nor imploring.

Tarek dropped the subject. Tchicaya was impressed; she'd defused the situation without alienating Tarek, or incurring any debt to him. She hadn't lost her touch, she'd only grown more subtle. When Tchicaya had trailed after her as a tortured, infatuated child, it must have perplexed and frustrated her to find that she couldn't hone her skills on him. Anything above and beyond mere hormonal effects had been superfluous; she might as well have tried to learn martial arts by practicing on a rag doll.

Branco sighed with disappointment, then closed his eyes and appeared to doze off.

Most of the *Rindler*'s passengers had watched with a mixture of denial and dismay as Sophus's predictions had been borne out, and all their ingenious models had been dashed to pieces, once again, by the new spectrometer. Branco, however, had embraced the No Rules Theory wholeheartedly, and managed to extract predictions that went far beyond Sophus's gloomy verdict. Just because there were no preexisting correlations between the dynamics on the far side of the border, that didn't mean none could be created. Branco had designed an ingenious experiment that aimed to use the near side of the border as a kind of intermediary, to entangle different regions of the far side with each other. The dynamics revealed would still be a random choice from all the possibilities—or, strictly speaking, the near-side universe would split into decoherent branches, and in each, a different result would be observed—but at least the result would apply across more than a few square Planck lengths.

As they docked with the Scribe, Yann mused, "I think this is the first time I've come here with any possibility of being disappointed."

Tchicaya was taken aback. "You never had your hopes pinned on any of the old models? You never even had a favorite?"

"There were some esthetically pleasing ones," Yann conceded. "I certainly would have been happy if they'd survived testing. But I never had a good reason to expect it. Not until now."

"That's very touching," Branco said dryly, "but I see no reason why you should abandon your earlier stance."

Tchicaya challenged him, "You have no emotional stake in the outcome at all?"

Branco regarded him with amusement. "You've been here *how long*?"

Tarek went through the tunnel first, then Mariama. Tchicaya followed her. "Do you remember that playground?" he whispered. "With all the pipes?" She glanced back at him, puzzled, and shook her head. Tchicaya felt a stab of disappointment; he'd assumed that the sight would have triggered the same memory in her.

In the control room, Branco instructed the stylus. With his gravelly voice and deliberate singsong intonation, he succeeded in making every word drip with contempt, like a kind of sardonic poetry. "The phase relationships between the twelve TeV and fifteen TeV beams will be as follows." *They really are making me read this aloud.*

Tchicaya looked out the window, down at the immutable plane of light. He'd had vivid dreams about the border, imagining as he slept that the wall of his cabin was the thing itself. He'd hold his ear against it, listening for sounds from the far side, straining with his whole body, urging the signal across.

Sometimes, the instant before he woke, he'd see an iridescent film blossoming on the wall, and his heart would race with joy and fear. *Did this new infestation mean that he'd been found out? Or that his crime had never really happened?*

Branco looked up and announced with mock astonishment, "Am I finished already? Is that all I have to do?"

Tarek said, "For now. But I'm invoking my right to a functional audit."

"Hooray," said Branco. He pushed himself away from the control panel and floated by the window with his hands on his head.

Tarek took his place, and instructed the stylus to rise from the border. Tchicaya had heard about functional audits, but he'd never witnessed one before. A package of detectors, verified by the faction invoking the audit, was placed under the tip of the stylus, and the particles emitted were scrutinized directly, to be sure that they conformed to the agreed sequence.

Tchicaya was tempted to say something derisive, but he held his tongue. Whatever made Tarek believe that this was necessary, complaining about the procedure would do nothing to lessen his suspicions.

He used the handholds beneath the windows to drag himself closer to Mariama. "Where have you been hiding? I haven't seen you for weeks."

"I have a lot of meetings."

"I go to meetings, too."

"Not these ones," she said.

She didn't need to spell it out. She'd come to the *Rindler* hoping to work with Tarek on Planck worm design, and apparently the notion still wasn't dead.

The novo-vacuum was already the largest object in the galaxy, and it was growing so rapidly that its surface area would increase almost forty-fold while it was encircled at the speed of light. Even if the Preservationists discovered a potential method for dealing with it, there was no prospect whatsoever of surrounding the entire thing with conventional machinery to administer the cure. The only practical tool would be a self-replicating pattern embedded at the level of quantum graphs, able to "eat" novo-vacuum and excrete something more benign.

To supporters of the idea, these hypothetical Planck worms would do no more than reverse the disaster of Mimosa. To Tchicaya, the symmetry was false. The places lost to Mimosa—ordinary planets, unique as they were—had already been thoroughly understood. Learning just enough about the novo-vacuum to infect it with a kind of fungal rot struck him as a corruption of every impulse that made intelligence worthwhile. He had enough trouble forgiving that kind of cowardice in a child.

"So what do you think the prospects are?" He meant those for Branco's experiment succeeding, though if she cared to disclose her thoughts on anything further down the line, so much the better.

Mariama thought carefully before replying. "I'm almost persuaded that Sophus is right, but I'm not certain that Branco's ideas follow. When we have no access to any particular far-side dynamics, even plucking out a random correlated state seems like too much to ask."

Yann had been floating a polite distance away, but the room was too small for any real privacy, and now he gave up pretending that he couldn't hear them. "You shouldn't be so pessimistic," he said, approaching. "No Rules doesn't mean no rules; there's still some raw topology and quantum theory that has to hold. I've re-analyzed Branco's work using qubit network theory, and it makes sense to me. It's a lot like running an entanglement-creation experiment on a completely abstract quantum computer. That's very nearly what Sophus is claiming lies behind the border: an enormous quantum computer that could perform any operation that falls under the general description of quantum physics—and in fact is in a superposition of states in which it's doing all of them."

Mariama's eyes widened, but then she protested, "Sophus never puts it like that."

"No, of course not," Yann agreed. "He's much too careful to use overheated language like that. 'The universe is a Deutsch–Bennett–Turing machine' is not a statement that goes down well with most physicists, since it has no empirically falsifiable content." He smiled mischievously. "It does remind me of something, though. If you ever want a good laugh, you should try some of the pre-

Qusp anti-AI propaganda. I once read a glorious tract which asserted that as soon as there was intelligence without bodies, its 'unstoppable lust for processing power' would drive it to convert the whole Earth, and then the whole universe, into a perfectly efficient Planck-scale computer. *Self-restraint?* Nah, we'd never show that. *Morality?* What, without livers and gonads? *Needing some actual reason to want to do this?* Well ... who could ever have too much processing power?

"To which I can only reply: why haven't you indolent fleshers transformed the whole galaxy into chocolate?"

Mariama said, "Give us time."

"The equipment seems to have passed inspection." Tarek pocketed the detector package and began lowering the stylus.

Branco folded his arms and pondered this announcement. " 'Seems'? I'll take that as a general statement of Cartesian skepticism, shall I?"

Tarek replied curtly, "You're free to instruct it again."

Branco began repeating the sequence. Tchicaya was expecting him to rush through it this time, but instead he took pains to reproduce the same pacing and intonation as he'd employed originally.

Tchicaya caught Tarek's eye and said, "You know, you have as much to gain from this experiment as anyone."

Tarek frowned, as if the implication was not merely unjust but completely surreal. "You're right. That's why I'm taking it seriously." He hesitated, then added defensively, "Don't you think I'd prefer to believe that everyone was acting in good faith? I'd like to assume that. But I can't; there's too much at stake. If that makes me look petty to you, so be it. I'll answer to my descendants."

Branco completed his second recitation. Yann said, "Approved."

Tarek said, "Yes, go ahead."

Branco addressed the Scribe. "Execute that."

The Scribe remained silent, but a heartbeat later there was a sharp hissing sound from under the floor. Tchicaya had no idea what this could be, until he saw the realization dawning on Branco's face.

A fine crack appeared in one window, then another. Tchicaya turned to Mariama. "You're backed up?"

She nodded. "While I slept. You?"

"The same." He smiled uncertainly, trying to reassure her that he was prepared for whatever happened, without discouraging her from expressing her own feelings. They'd been through a lot together, but neither of them had ever witnessed the other's local death.

"Yann?"

"I'm covered, don't worry."

Branco and Tarek were in the same position: no one risked losing more than a day's memory. After his fourth local death, Tchicaya had ceased to feel genuine, gut-churning dread at his own fate—and he had some memories that led up to the moment itself—but in the company of others it was always more stressful. Wondering how much fear they felt, and how careful they'd been.

The hissing beneath them intensified, and the room began to creak. The windows had healed themselves, and the whole structure would be capable of a certain amount of self-repair, but if the border was lapping up against the Scribe, the wound it made would be reopened with every advance. The microjets were designed to compensate for the effects of bombardment with interstellar gas; shifts measured in microns were the crudest adjustments imaginable. The Scribe was not going to whisk them away to safety.

Tarek looked around nervously. "Shouldn't we head for the shuttle?"

Branco said, "Yes."

The wall behind Tchicaya emitted a tortured groan. As he

turned, it concertinaed visibly, the angle between two windows becoming impossibly acute. Tchicaya marveled at the sight. Air leaking from the Scribe couldn't be producing shear forces of that magnitude; the border had to be tugging on the structure beneath them. Nothing of the kind had ever been witnessed before. Beams constructed from a variety of substances, poked through the border, had always behaved as if the far-side portion had simply ceased to exist; there were no forces exerted on the remainder. Whatever Branco had triggered, he'd done more than displace the border by a few centimeters.

The wall flexed again, and the pair of windows that had been squashed together separated. Instead of reversing their original motion, though, they parted at the seam, like doors swinging open.

Tchicaya bellowed with fright, and reached out for something to stop himself. He succeeded only in clutching Yann's shoulder, and the two of them tumbled through the opening together.

For several seconds, Tchicaya remained rigid, preparing himself on some instinctive level for intense pain and a swift extinction. When neither arrived, his whole body began shaking with relief. He'd known that his suit would protect him, but the understanding hadn't penetrated far. He'd skydived from altitudes where oxygen was needed, and swum at depths where the next free breath was hours away, but black and starry space had remained the quintessence of beautiful danger: pristine, indifferent to his needs, predating every form of life. *Vacuum* was not a word that offered hope. He should have been snuffed out in an eye blink.

He looked around. The push of the escaping air had been firm but brief, so it was unlikely that they were moving very rapidly, but he was facing the wrong way to catch sight of the Scribe, the only meaningful signpost. The border itself offered no cues as to their velocity in any direction.

He'd been holding his breath deliberately, as if he'd plunged into water, but he realized now that the urge to inhale had vanished as soon as the suit's membrane had sealed off his mouth and nose. His body had shut down its lungs; the *Rindler*'s model could operate for days on anaerobic metabolic pathways. His skin felt slightly chilly, but he could see the exposed film of the suit on the back of his hand, silvered to retain heat. He extended his arm shakily so he could examine Yann, whose face had turned entirely metallic except for two holes for his pupils.

"You should have known it was futile, Tin Man, trying to walk among us. Robot nature always shows through." Tchicaya's teeth were chattering, but that made no difference; his Mediator grabbed his speech intentions and routed them away from his useless vocal cords, shunting them into a radio channel.

Yann said, "Believe me, the effect looks much stranger on you."

They were rotating slowly together, around an axis roughly perpendicular to the border. As they turned, the Scribe came into view over Yann's shoulder. The lower half of the structure was buckled and twisted, but the control room was still safely clear of the border. As far as he could judge, he and Yann were still four or five meters from the border themselves, and their trajectory was virtually parallel to it. This freakish alignment was sure to prove inexact, though, one way or the other.

He spotted a shiny Mariama standing at the ruptured wall, watching him.

"We're all right," he said. "Get in the shuttle."

She nodded and waved, as if he'd be unable to hear a reply. Then she said, "Okay. We'll come and pick you up." She vanished from sight.

Tchicaya instructed his Mediator to make his next words private. "Are we all right? I don't have the skills to determine our velocity that accurately."

"We're moving toward the border, but it would take hours before we'd hit it."

"Oh, good." Tchicaya shuddered. His right hand was still locked on to Yann's shoulder, the fingers digging in as if his life depended on it. He knew that wasn't true, but he couldn't relax his grip.

"Am I hurting you?" he asked.

"No."

Yann's metallic face brightened strangely, and Tchicaya glanced down. A patch of borderlight more intense than its surroundings drifted slowly by.

"What do you make of that?" Tchicaya asked. He was suddenly light-headed, from more than the shock of ejection. The Doppler-shift tints aside, he'd known the border as a featureless wall for centuries. The tiniest blemish was revolutionary; he felt like a child who'd just watched someone reach up and scratch a mark into the blue summer sky.

"I'd say Branco has succeeded in pinning something to the near side."

"We have physics? We have rules now?"

"Apparently."

Mariama said, "We're in the shuttle. Everyone's safe here."

"Good. No rush; the view is wonderful."

"I won't hold you to that. We'll be there in a few minutes."

The strange patch of brightness had moved out of sight, but after a few seconds another came into view. They were fuzzy-edged ellipses, traveling from the direction of the Scribe.

"They're like the shadows of reef fish," Tchicaya suggested. "Swimming above us in the sunlight."

Yann said, "Do you think you might be coming slightly un-hinged?"

As Tchicaya swung around him in their involuntary dance, he caught sight of the shuttle rising from the ruined Scribe. He smiled at the memory of Mariama's voice, promising to rescue him. On Turaev, if they'd given in to their feelings, it would have ended badly, burning out in a year or two. When this was over, though—

Yann said, "That's a bit ominous."

"What?"

"Can you turn your head back toward the Scribe? That might be quicker than me trying to put it into words."

Tchicaya twisted his neck. The border had formed a bell-shaped hillock, forty or fifty meters high, that had completely swallowed the Scribe. As his rotation forced him to stretch even more, he stopped fighting it and twisted his neck the other way, hastening the sight's return instead of trying to delay its departure.

The hillock was collapsing now, but as it did, a ring around it was rising up. Suddenly, Tchicaya noticed a whole series of lesser rings surrounding the first, like concentric ripples in water. They were undulating out from the center at great speed: the leading edge, the fastest component, in some kind of surface wave. The bulk of the wave was spreading more slowly. But it was still traveling faster than they were.

He searched for the shuttle, and found it, its exhaust a pale blue streamer against the stars. The thrust generated by the ion engine was very low; over time it could accumulate into a significant velocity, but the craft was about as maneuverable as a bathtub on ice. It might just reach them before the wave, and even accelerate away from the border again in time, but there'd be no margin left for any more surprises that might manifest themselves in the wake of Branco's intervention.

Yann read his mind, and declared flatly, "They have to stay clear."

Tchicaya nodded. "Mariama?"

"No!" she hissed. "I know what you're going to say!"

"It's all right. We're backed up, we're calm. Don't even think about it."

"It's a wave. It's a predictable phenomenon! I've computed a trajectory that meets all the constraints—"

"Predictable?"

"We can do it!"

"You've all voted on that, have you? Tarek? Branco?"

Branco replied laconically, "It's all the same to me."

Tarek said nothing, and Tchicaya felt a pang of sympathy for him. No one could reasonably expect him to put himself at risk, merely to spare his two adversaries the loss of their replaceable bodies and a few hours' memories. Yet if he did, many people would respect him for it. You had to be a utilitarian zealot, rotted to the core by dogma, not to admire someone who was willing to jeopardize their own comfort and continuity to preserve another's. Whether or not this required courage, at the very least it was an act of generosity.

Tchicaya said, "Stay clear! We can't afford to lose the shuttle!" This argument made no sense—the *Rindler's* stock of raw materials had not been depleted, and there were parts of the ship itself that could be cannibalized anyway, if necessary—but he wanted to offer them an unselfish-sounding alibi. "You have to gather all the data you can," he added, a little more cogently. "With the Scribe gone, every observation you can make is invaluable." The *Rindler* itself had powerful instruments trained on the border, but some crucial detail might conceivably depend on the shuttle's proximity.

Mariama did not reply immediately, but in the silence that followed Tchicaya knew that he'd swayed her.

"All right." Her voice was still strained, but there was a note Tchicaya recognized from their days on Turaev: a rare concession, not so much of defeat, as the realization that they'd been struggling over the wrong thing altogether. She understood the trade-off, and she knew that he and Yann were resolved. "Peace, Tchicaya."

"Peace," he replied.

Yann said, "You handled that well."

"Thanks." Over Yann's shoulder, Tchicaya could see the wave closing on them. It was dropping in height as it spread out from the point where the Scribe had been, but it wouldn't fall far enough to miss them. Tchicaya wondered if Yann would want to be distracted, or to confront what was happening directly.

"So well that I almost hate to do this. How strong do you think your legs are?"

"What?" It took a moment for Tchicaya to understand what he was suggesting. "Oh, no. Please—"

"Don't go squeamish on me; we don't have time. It would be hard to decide who to save if we were from the same modes, but I can start from backup with no delay. You'd be out of the picture for months."

That was true. The *Rindler* had run out of bodies, and there were currently about twenty new arrivals waiting. Tchicaya would have to join the queue. Normally, a delay like that would mean nothing compared to the centuries he'd lost to transit insentience, but Branco's experiment had just guaranteed that every day from now on would be unique.

"I've never killed anyone," he said. His stomach was knotted with revulsion at the thought.

Yann didn't quibble over the hyperbole. "And I've never died, in a body. Sex and death, all in one day. What more could an acorporeal ask for?"

The wave came into view again; they'd have a minute or less. Tchicaya struggled to clear his head. Yann was demanding no more of him than he'd demanded of Mariama. The sense of shame and selfishness he felt, at the thought of indulging his own visceral urge to survive at Yann's expense, was the right thing to feel, but that didn't mean he had to elevate it above every other consideration. Nor, though, did he have to annihilate the emotion in order to act against it. He would do what the situation required, because it would be a foolish waste for both of them to lose their bodies, but he wasn't going to pretend that he was happy, or indifferent about it.

He took hold of Yann's left hand, then released his iron grip on his shoulder so they could join right hands as well. He folded his knees up against his chest, then froze. The crest of the wave was thirty meters away. This was too complicated. They'd never have time.

Yann said calmly, "Give me your body. I've worked out the steps."

Tchicaya surrendered motor control, and they began to move together in a perfect, symmetrical ballet. It was as if his limbs had been gripped by a dozen firm, invisible hands, manipulating him without resistance. His back arched, his arms stretched painfully, but their fingers stayed tangled in a monkey grip as their legs forced their bodies apart, until their feet met, sole to sole.

Tchicaya said, "You made me an isotopy."

Yann laughed. "Nothing original, I'm afraid."

"It's the thought that counts."

Tchicaya had become disoriented, but as they swung around together his line of sight fell from the stars to the approaching wave. The muscles in his legs tensed, and the pressure against his feet grew until he felt as if his arms would be torn from his shoulders.

Yann said, "See you later."

Their fingers parted.

Tchicaya clutched at the emptiness between them, then stopped himself and wrapped his arms across his chest. He was ascending at a shallow angle, back toward the point where the Scribe had been. As the crest approached, he curled into a ball, and it raced past beneath him, a flash of silver licking at his heels as he tumbled.

An elaborate grid of colored lines scarred the inside of the retreating wave, like the map of some kind of convoluted maze. The pattern shifted as he watched. There was a tantalizing logic to the changes—the lines weren't dancing about at random—but deciphering it on the spot was beyond him. All he could do was record the sight.

Drained for a moment of every other concern, Tchicaya locked his gaze on the retreating enigma.

Everything had changed, now. Whatever Branco had revealed, or created, the wall between the worlds had finally been breached.

Chapter 9

"Everyone complains about the laws of physics, but no one does anything about them."

Tchicaya turned away from the control panel. He hadn't heard Rasmah entering the Blue Room.

"It's an old joke they used to tell, back on Maeder," she explained, crossing the wide, empty floor. "Which just goes to show how much work it takes to send a bad meme off to smallpox heaven."

"Don't count on having done that," Tchicaya warned her. "I believe the original version was 'Everyone complains about human nature.' When the second half became patently false, the meme just shifted context. You can tear the meaning right out of these one-liners, and they'll still find a way to keep propagating."

"Damn." She sat beside him. "So what *are* the laws, right now?"

"As far as I can tell, we have a macroscopic SO(2,2) symmetry, and E7 as the gauge group." He gestured at the display. "Nothing we haven't grabbed before, generically, though the details of the Lagrangian are unique." Tchicaya laughed. "Listen to me. I really am getting blasé about this."

"Seen one universe, seen them all." Rasmah leaned closer to examine the symmetry diagrams that the software had guessed from some partial results, and was now proceeding to test further with the Left Hand.

She glanced at the endurance clock. "Thirteen minutes? That's close to the record. You think this might—" Tchicaya glowered at her, and she laughed. "Don't tell me: I'm jinxing the result."

"Hardly. I'm just growing a little impatient with the idea that we keep grabbing dynamics, over and over, in the hope that one of them will turn out to be stable. It's never going to happen."

"You think not?" Rasmah pursed her lips. "Okay. It's no use just complaining, though. What do you want to do about it?"

Tchicaya made a gesture of helplessness.

She regarded him with disappointment. "Are you this lazy about everything?"

She was only teasing, but the accusation stung. Rasmah had been on the *Rindler* just six months longer than he had, but she'd already contributed substantially to several projects. Having helped to design the spectrometer that had been lost with the Scribe, she'd gone on to improve the design still further for the models used in both the Left and Right Hands. The Scribe's replacement had been planned as a single machine, but when attempts to renegotiate the protocols for its shared use collapsed for the seventh time, even the most ecumenical researchers had lost patience, and agreed to the duplication.

Tchicaya stretched his arms. "I've certainly had enough of staring at this for one day. Are you here to take over?"

"Yes." She smiled and added, "But I'm early, so I'm afraid you can't actually leave yet."

The destruction of the Scribe, and the end to cooperation between the factions, had delayed follow-ups to Branco's experiment, but once the two Hands were in place and gathering data, everybody on the *Rindler* had been riveted by the results. For months, the Blue Room—where the Left Hand's data was displayed, now that trips to the border were considered imprudent—had been packed with people twenty-four hours a day, and it was no secret that the Preservationists had reacted in the same way.

Branco's technique appeared to have confirmed Sophus's original assertion: the novo-vacuum did not obey any single analog or extension of the Sarumpaet rules. It was possible to correlate a macroscopic portion of the near side of the border with parts of the total far-side state that *did* obey specific rules, but each time the experiment was repeated, the rules were different. All of Sarumpaet's carefully reasoned arguments about which patterns of nodes in a quantum graph could persist as particles had been revealed as utterly parochial; the larger truth was, the ordinary vacuum that dominated the near side was correlated with sequences of graphs that behaved in that particular fashion, so it hid the fact that they were really just part of a superposition of countless other possibilities. The quantum subtleties that could, in principle, render the whole superposition visible were buried in the sheer number of details that would have had to be tracked in order to observe it.

The far side lacked the means to conceal its quantum nature in the same fashion, but if the view was less misleading, it remained confusing. Interpreting the new experiments was like trying to make sense of a jungle by watching an endless parade of exotic creatures cling briefly to the windows of a vehicle, stunned by the light, curious, or angry, but always flying off a moment later, never to return.

At first, every new set of laws had had their fifteen minutes of fame, but since none of them could be pinned to the near side for much longer than that, the novelty had begun to wear thin. Exhilaration at the cornucopia had given way to frustration. The experiments continued, but it had become a struggle to maintain even the symbolic presence of one sentient observer around the clock. Tchicaya supposed that this was fair enough: all the theorists were drowning in data already, and they had better things to do than sit and watch more come pouring in. For a week or two, he'd hoped that patient observation might actually lead him to a worthwhile discovery himself, but that was beginning to sound as crazy as looking for patterns in any other set of random quantum results.

"Oh, there it goes!" Rasmah wailed, as if she'd seriously expected otherwise. The patch of the border they'd pinned to the latest set of laws had just reverted to the old inscrutable glow. "What do you think would happen," she mused, "if we scribed some device that could function under the far-side dynamics, before we lost the correlation?"

Tchicaya said, "Even if it survived, what good would that do us? We've never been able to grab the same dynamics twice."

"What if we scribed a Scribe?"

"Ha! Like that Escher drawing?"

"Yeah." Rasmah pulled a face, suddenly aghast. "Though . . . that's a left hand drawing a right, and vice versa. We can't have that, can we?"

"Are you serious, though? Do you think we could insert a machine that could signal back to us in some way?"

Rasmah didn't reply immediately. "I don't know. What does the border look like, from the other side? Does it always look as if our physics is happening behind it? Or is something more symmetrical going on, where someone on the far side would catch glimpses just as varied and transient as the ones we're seeing?"

"I have no idea," Tchicaya admitted. "I don't even see how you could pose that question, in Sophus's model. You'd have to describe a specific observer on the far side, on whose terms you wanted to see things. But if the different far-side dynamics don't form decoherent branches—except over the tiny patches where we're forcing them to do so—what exactly are the laws the observer is supposed to obey?" The startled birds and butterflies fluttering against the window weren't even real; it was no use asking what they saw, staring back. The slices of different "universes" pinned against the border were more like the patterns formed by splattered insects. If they hadn't been dead, they would never have been seen side by side in quite the same way.

It was midnight, by the *Rindler*'s arbitrary clock. The lighting of public spaces changed with the cycle, and though many people happily slept through the daytime and worked all night, Tchicaya had ended up in synch with the light.

He stood. "That's it, I've had enough."

"You could stay and keep me company," Rasmah suggested.

"I wouldn't want to distract you." He smiled and backed away, raising a hand good night. They'd been circling each other at a distance for weeks, and his body had begun to change for her, but Tchicaya had decided that he would not allow anything to happen between them. While it would have been unlikely to end as swiftly, or as comically, as his experiment with Yann, he wanted to keep his life free of complications.

Tchicaya made his way around the ship, slightly removed from everything around him. The corridors were nearly deserted; maybe the Preservationists were having some kind of conference. The ghost town ambience reminded him of a hundred provincial cities he'd trekked through at night; on the empty walkways, the blaze of stars was like the view when you left the brightest streets behind, and the sky came suddenly to life.

He recalled a night he'd spent in a small town on Quine, thirty-six subjective years after he'd left Turaev: the mirror image of his birth in the moment of his departure. Three centuries had passed, in real time. He'd sat in an alley and wept for hours, like an abandoned child. The next day, he'd made half a dozen new friends among the locals, and some of the friendships had lasted three times longer than all the years he'd spent on his home world.

He still missed those people. He still missed Lesya, and his children and grandchildren on Gleason. And yet, he could never entirely separate that from the realization that part of the joy he'd felt in their presence had come from the sense that they were lifting him out of his state of exile. They had never been substitutes for the home and family he'd left behind; it had never been that crude. But every kind of happiness bore some imprint in the shape of the pain it had assuaged.

He heard footsteps behind him, outpacing his own. He stopped and turned to face the wall of the walkway, as if admiring the view, wiping his eyes with his forearm, less embarrassed by his tears than the fact that he'd be at a loss to explain them. If he'd still been on Turaev after four thousand years, he would have gone mad. And if he'd traveled and returned in the approved way, to find that nothing had changed in his absence, he would have gone mad even faster. He did not regret leaving.

Mariama said, "You look like you're about to jump off a bridge."

"I didn't realize you were following me."

She laughed. "I wasn't *following you*. What are we meant to do? Walk in opposite directions around the ship? All Preservationists must march clockwise? That would make for some long journeys."

"Forget it." He turned to look at her. It was unjust beyond belief, but right at this moment—having resolved for the thousandth time that he'd made the right decision—he wanted to rant in her face about the price she'd made him pay. After all her talk as a rebel child, after leading by example, after four thousand years as a traveler, she had now decided that her role in life was to fight to keep the planet-bound cultures—all the slaves she'd vowed to liberate, all the drones she'd promised to shake out of their stupor—safely marinating in their own inertia for another twenty thousand years.

He said, "Where are you heading?"

Mariama hesitated. "Do you know Kadir?"

"Only slightly. We didn't exactly hit it off." Tchicaya was about to add something more acerbic, when he realized that today was the day Kadir's home world, Zapata, would have fallen. That was only true in terms of a reference frame fixed to the local stars, not the *Rindler's* notion of simultaneity, and in any case no confirmation of the event would reach them for decades, but unless the border had magically altered its speed in distant regions, the planet's loss was a certainty.

"He's holding a kind of wake. That's where I'm going."

"So you and he are close?"

Mariama said, "Not especially. But he's invited everyone, not just his friends."

Tchicaya leaned back against the wall, unfazed by its transparency. He said, "Why did you come here?"

She shaded her eyes against the borderlight. "I thought you'd decided that we were never going to have this argument."

"If you think I've shut you up, now's your chance."

"You know why I'm here," she said. "Don't pretend it's a mystery." The glare was too much; she turned to stand beside him. "Do you want to come with me, to this thing of Kadir's?"

"You must be joking. Do you think I'm a provocateur, or just a masochist?"

"This isn't factional. He's invited everyone." She frowned. "Or are you afraid to spend ten minutes in the company of people who might disagree with you?"

"I spent ten *years* on Pachner."

"Keeping your mouth shut."

"No. I was honest with everyone I met."

"Everyone who asked. If the issue came up."

Tchicaya moved away from her angrily. "I wasn't sure of my plans, when I first arrived. And when I was sure, I didn't walk around with a banner that read 'I'm off to the *Rindler*, to make certain the same fate befalls as many other worlds as possible.' Does that make me dishonest? Does that make me a coward?"

Mariama shook her head. "All right, forget Pachner. But if you're so sure of your position now, why don't you come with me? No one's going to lynch you."

"It would be inflammatory. What makes you think Kadir wants the company of people who disagree with *him*?"

"There's an open invitation," she protested. "Check with the ship if you don't believe me."

She was right. Tchicaya's Mediator had filtered it out automatically; he'd told it to classify general announcements by known factional allegiances, to keep him from being distracted, and depressed, by news of events where Yielders were unlikely to be welcome.

"I'm tired," he said. "It's been a long day."

"You're pathetic." Mariama walked away without another word.

Tchicaya called after her, "All right! I'll come with you!" She didn't stop. He ran to catch up with her.

They walked in silence for a while, then Tchicaya said, "This whole iron curtain thing is insane. Within a decade, we'll find a way to pin some state to the border that will freeze it in place. If we worked on it together, it would take half as long."

Mariama regarded him coolly. "If we froze it, you think that would be enough?"

"Enough for what?"

"Enough to satisfy either side."

"Ideally, I still want to cross through," Tchicaya admitted. "We shouldn't have to flee from this, or annihilate it. We should be able to adapt. If the ocean comes a few meters inshore, you retreat. A few kilometers, you build a dike. A few thousand . . . you learn to live in boats. But if freezing the border turns out to be possible, and it rules out exploration, I'd just have to accept that."

Mariama was skeptical. "And you'd take no risks at all, from that moment on? You'd do absolutely nothing that had a chance of unfreezing it? You'd let it sit there for a hundred thousand years, undisturbed, and you wouldn't be tempted in the least?"

"Oh, I see. That's the logic that dictates the use of Planck worms? If you don't wipe the whole thing out of existence, some Yielder is certain to come along eventually, and unplug the dike."

Mariama didn't reply. They entered the module where the wake was being held, and walked up the stairs.

On the map Tchicaya consulted, Kadir's cabin had been merged with a dozen of his neighbors', producing a roughly circular room. Ahead of him, the entrance was wide open, and music wafted out into the corridor.

Mariama's clothes changed as they approached the doorway, forming a pattern of woven bands broken up by ellipses, in earthen colors. "You look good in that," Tchicaya observed. The comment elicited a reluctant flicker of warmth in her eyes, and she knew him too well to mistake it for insincere flattery, but she walked on into the room without a word. He steeled himself, and followed her.

There was quite a crowd inside, talking, eating, a few people dancing. Tchicaya could see no other Yielders, but he resisted the urge to ask his Mediator to hunt for friendly signatures.

Images of Zapata shone from the walls. The planet from space; aerial views of towns, mountains, and rivers. Tchicaya had spent forty years on Zapata, moving from continent to continent, never really settling down long enough to make close friends.

The life the settlers had unleashed on the sterile planet, though ultimately derived from natural terrestrial genomes, had been a little wilder and stranger than most. There were lithe winged cats in some of the jungles that could tear out your throat. Toward the end of his stay, it had been discovered that in one small, isolated town, deliberate exposure to harm by these creatures had become a "rite of passage" into adulthood—as if adolescence itself was insufficiently traumatic. The partially eaten bodies could generally be repaired, and at worst the Qusp could always be tracked down and recovered from the animal's stomach, so the ritual fell short of local death, but as far as Tchicaya was concerned, that only made it more barbaric. Better to suffer memory loss and discontinuity than the experience of having your jugular gnawed open—and better anything than the company of people who'd decided that this was the definition of maturity.

Children in the town who declined to participate had been ostracized, but once the practice came to light, the wider society of Zapata had intervened—with a concerted effort to improve transport and communication links. After a few years of heightened exposure to the possibility of simply walking away from the town and its self-appointed cultural guardians, no one was interested in being bullied into conformity anymore.

It was the kind of behavior that could only occur when people had been trapped for thousands of years, staring at the same sights, fetishizing everything around them, spiraling down toward the full-blown insanity of religion. You didn't need gates and barbed wire to make a prison. Familiarity could pin you to the ground, far more efficiently.

Mariama waved a small yellow fruit at him, half-bitten. "Try one of these. They're delicious."

"Good grief. Where do you think he grew them?"

"In the garden. Lots of people have set up plots for food. You have to tweak the genomes to get photosynthesis to work in the borderlight, but that's old hat, you just copy those ugly things the original builders put in."

"I must have walked past without even noticing."

"They're quite far back from the path. Are you going to try one?"

Tchicaya shook his head. "I've tasted them before. There can't be many; I'm not going to hog them."

Mariama turned to address Kadir, who'd appeared before them like a perfect host. She said, "Tchicaya was just telling me that he'd already tasted quetzal-fruit."

Kadir said, "You've visited Zapata?" He had probably intended to greet them politely then move on, but this claim could not be left unexamined.

"Yes." Tchicaya braced himself for a barrage of insults about travelers and other parasites.

"How long ago?"

"About nine hundred years."

"Where did you go?"

"All over." Kadir waited expectantly, so Tchicaya reeled off a list of towns.

When he'd finished, Kadir said, "I was born in Suarez, but I left when I was twenty. I never managed to get back. How long were you there?"

Tchicaya had been reorganizing his memories as they spoke, dragging the whole period upward in his association hierarchy. "Less than a year."

Kadir smiled. "That's longer than most visitors stay. What was the attraction?"

"I don't know. It was a quiet spot, I was tired of moving about. The landscape wasn't spectacular, but from the house where I stayed you could see the top of the mountains in the distance."

"That slate-gray color, against the sky in the morning?"

"Yeah. Completely different at sunset, though. Almost pink. I could never work that out." He'd raised the memories so high that it might have been yesterday. He could smell the dust and the pollen, he could feel the heat of the evening.

Kadir said, "I think I know where you were. Not the house, it wasn't built when I was there, but—do you remember the creek, north of the main road?"

"Yes. I was close to it. A few minutes' walk."

Kadir's face lit up. "That's amazing! It was still there? We used to go swimming in that creek. My whole family. All through summer, around dusk. Did you swim in it?"

"Yes." At the same time, the same season. Watching the stars come out, lying on his back in the cool water.

"Was the big tree still there? With the branch overhanging the deep end?"

Tchicaya frowned, summoning up eidetic imagery, constructing a panoramic view in his mind's eye and searching for anything meeting this description. "I don't think so."

"No, it wouldn't have been." Kadir turned to Mariama. "We used to walk out along this branch, about four meters up, and dive off backward." He spread his arms and swayed. "The first time I did it, it must have been an hour after sunset. I couldn't see anything, and when I hit the water I just kept sinking into the blackness. I was nine years old. I was terrified!"

Tchicaya said, "There was no deep water, when I was there. It must have silted up."

"Or the banks might have shifted," Kadir suggested. "I was there three hundred years before you. They might have built anything upstream."

Zyfete approached, and slipped an arm around Kadir's waist. She regarded Tchicaya warily, but it must have been obvious that he was not making trouble.

Looking away from her into the crowd, Tchicaya spotted Sophus, Tarek, Birago. He was conspicuous here; it couldn't be otherwise.

He said, "I have to go."

Kadir nodded, unoffended. He reached out and shook Tchicaya's hand. "I'm glad you saw Suarez," he said.

Mariama caught up with him outside.

"Go back in with your friends," he said.

She ignored him. "Was that so unbearable?"

"No. I never claimed it would be. I was afraid my presence might upset someone. It didn't. I'm glad."

"I suppose you think that's all pathological? The music, the pictures, the food?"

Tchicaya scowled. "So much for you reading my mind. It's ordinary nostalgia. I feel the same way about all kinds of places. There's nothing sick or obsessive about it. And because of that, it's hardly going to destroy him that he can't go back. His favorite swimming hole would have turned into a silted-up pond by now, anyway. He's been spared the disappointment."

"You really are made of stone." She sounded disappointed, as if she'd seriously expected a few minutes' reminiscing with Kadir to change his mind about everything.

"No one will have died, leaving Zapata. The rocks are gone. The trees are gone. If anyone really lived for those things, they'll find a way to re-create them."

"That will never be the same."

"Good." Tchicaya stopped and turned on her. "What exactly do you imagine he's suffering? He's thinking about the things he's experienced, and the things he's lost. We all do that. He hasn't been eviscerated. Nine thousand years is a long time, but no one sprang from the ground of Zapata fully formed."

"They've still been dispossessed," Mariama insisted.

"Of rocks. Nothing else."

"Of memories. Of meaning."

"You know that's not true! What do you think, we're back in the colonial era, on Earth? There *was* a time when it was possible for an honest, intelligent person to subscribe to a cosmology where their dead ancestors lived in the mountains, and if you angered the spirit of the waterhole the crops would fail for the next ten years. Where the land was alive, and unique, and sacred. And if some horde of barbarians came marching through, subscribing to an even more surreal religion and claiming everything in sight for some inbred fop in a powdered wig, what else would you do but fight for your land, and cling to your beliefs?

"No one is in that position anymore. No one can confuse *the landscape* with the inalienable things inside them."

Mariama replied pointedly, "Which would explain why you don't care at all what lies behind the border, and why you'd be just as happy to go and live in some abstract scape with the acorporeals."

Tchicaya was tongue-tied. He believed she understood the difference perfectly, but he knew he'd sound clumsy and self-contradictory if he backtracked to spell it out.

He said, "How many thousands of years should Zapata have remained unchanged? How many million?"

She shook her head. "That's not the question. It would have changed of its own accord."

"*When?* And how many children would it have smothered, before it changed?"

"You weren't smothered on Turaev. You got out in time."

"Not everyone did."

"Not everyone needed to."

They'd reached the stairs leading up to his cabin.

"You think I'm a hypocrite?" Mariama demanded. "Because I'm a traveler, and I'm championing people's right to stay put?"

"I don't think you're a hypocrite."

"I've *seen* change," she said. "Unforced, driven from within, not a response to some crisis that dictates the alternatives. That's painful in its own way, but it's better to go through that than have your whole way of life determined by some senseless accident that has nothing to do with anything.

"When I arrived on Har'El, there was a genuine renaissance

going on. People were reexamining their own traditions, not having them undermined by external events. Everything was fluid, everything was being questioned. It was the most exciting place I've ever lived in."

"Really? For how long?"

Mariama shrugged. "Nothing lasts forever. You can't have a whole world in perpetual upheaval."

"No, but when the upheaval ended the result was apparently not a world you were prepared to live in."

"My marriage broke up," she said. "And Emine wanted to travel. If she'd stayed on Har'El, I might still be there. But those are personal, idiosyncratic reasons. You can't start treating my decisions as some kind of measure of whether or not a whole society deserves to exist."

"That's true," Tchicaya conceded. He was beginning to feel both battered and invigorated; she'd always had to push him to the edge of defeat before he got his second wind. He'd forgotten how much he'd loved arguing with her, when they'd taken the opposite sides back on Turaev. The only part he hated was the very thing that made it so exhilarating: there was always far too much at stake.

He said, "But even if Har'El and all the other worlds deserve to be left in peace, that right isn't absolute." He gestured at the border. "How can you mourn the loss of Zapata, and then turn around and destroy something a thousand times more beautiful?"

"I'm not mourning Zapata," Mariama replied. "I've never been there. It means nothing to me."

"So because no one has been through the border, whatever lies behind it is worthless?"

Mariama thought for a moment. "That's putting it crudely. But however beautiful, and challenging, and fascinating it is, it's not worth losing what we already have."

"And if someone gets through and lives there for a day? Or a week? Or a century? When does the magic thing happen? When does their right to their home become equal to everyone else's?"

"Now you're just being jesuitical."

"I think that's the cruelest thing you've ever said to me." Tchicaya smiled, but she didn't soften.

"Freeze the border," he pleaded.

Mariama said, "*You* freeze the border, if that's what you want. If you do it soon, and if you do it properly, maybe that will convince us to leave it at that." She inclined her head, and he could see her assessing the idea, judging it to be the farthest she was prepared to go. "Freeze the border before we do anything more, and you might just save whatever lies behind it."

She turned and walked away.

Tchicaya watched her go, trying to untangle the negotiations he'd just stumbled through unwittingly. Without revealing any secrets, she'd all but declared that Tarek's Planck worms were visible on the horizon. The fanciful notion was finally taking real shape, and she'd responded by giving him one last chance to put his own case, and to listen to her own. One last chance to sway her, or to be swayed himself.

She had given as much ground as she could. Neither of them were envoys for their factions; their decisions counted for nothing with anyone else. Between the two of them, though, there'd be no more engagement, no more discussion.

Just this challenge. This ultimatum.

This race.

Chapter 10

"I've already designed the vehicle you're looking for," Yann insisted. "I just need some help to describe it in more palatable terms, so I can sell it to the others."

Rasmah said, "It's *not* a vehicle. It's software. And it's software for a nonexistent computer."

Yann shook his head. "That's just the mathematical formalism I've used. It's the best way to describe it—the most elegant, the most transparent. All we have to do now is disguise it." He added, deadpan, "You *can* obfuscate, can't you? Physicists have been taking simple mathematical ideas and obfuscating them for centuries. It must have been part of your training, surely?"

Rasmah took a swipe at him, and he flinched away from her. No doubt this was a habit he'd acquired during embodiment, when he'd managed to elicit a similar response from people on a regular basis.

With the queue for bodies growing ever longer as new arrivals flooded in, Yann had decided to remain acorporeal. Tarek had responded to this news at the weekly interfactional meeting with a long, paranoid dissertation on Yann's self-evident intention to use his new position to "corrupt" the *Rindler*'s processor network, infiltrating the Preservationists' communications and data storage systems, spying on them and undermining all their efforts. Fortunately, Sophus had spoken next, gently guiding Tarek back into contact with reality. Many things in the universe remained difficult and mysterious, but the causal structure of computer networks was not one of them. It would have required an act of cartoonish incompetence on the part of the *Rindler's* designers to create a network in which any of the abuses Tarek feared were physically possible.

Tchicaya said, "So you shift dynamics, once you're through the border? You navigate between them?" He had arranged for the three of them to meet in his cabin so that Yann could try out the idea on Rasmah and refine his pitch, before taking it to a meeting of all the Yielders. "The dynamic laws are like stepping-stones that only need to last for as long as you use them?"

Yann grimaced. "That sounds ugly enough, but it's not even close to the truth. The algorithm *never* obeys a sharply defined dynamic law; if it tried to do that, it would be doomed from the start." He thought for a while. "You know how a Gaussian wave packet can keep its shape in a harmonic oscillator potential?"

"Yes." Tchicaya felt a burst of confidence; that was just elementary quantum mechanics. In empty space, a particle's wave packet would always disperse, spreading out without limits. But if the particle experienced an attractive force analogous to the tug of a spring in classical physics, there was a certain shape—a certain Gaussian, like the bell curve of statistics—which was stable. Any tighter, sharper wave packet would necessarily have a range of values for momentum that made it spread out; that was just the uncertainty principle. The right Gaussian, though, in the right environment, was the perfect compromise between uncertainty in position and momentum, allowing the shape of the wave to remain unchanged as it moved.

"This isn't really the same," Yann admitted. "But it might sound persuasive if I put it that way."

Rasmah glanced at Tchicaya, exasperated. He made puppy-dog eyes back at her, pleading on Yann's behalf.

She laughed, and relented. "Why don't you just give me the description of the graph you want to scribe, and I'll grind through the calculations using my own picture of Sophus's model. If I can demonstrate that we'd get some information back through the border—something more than we put in—that might be enough to persuade people. I'll make sure I phrase my results in the ugliest possible way."

Yann said, "That's wonderful. Thank you!"

He passed something to Rasmah—Tchicaya's Mediator saw the fact of the exchange, but not the content—and then vanished.

Rasmah sighed. "You really think he's on to something? A quantum computer can simulate any quantum process; that's old news. It doesn't mean that there *is* a quantum computer underlying anything."

"No," Tchicaya agreed. "But qubit network theory doesn't claim that. It just says that when you get to a low enough level, you have nothing left to lose by treating the system *as if* it were software. It's like all the proofs in applied algorithmic theory that are based on imagining Turing machines. No one complains that the real universe is conspicuously devoid of paper tape."

"Old habits die hard," she confessed. "I'm still in mourning for the Sarumpaet rules, and they were disproved before I was born. They're what I was brought up on, they're what I've thought of all my life as the template for a physical theory. It's not easy adapting, even to Sophus's model."

"Yeah. I really am grateful to you for trying this," Tchicaya said. Since the factional rift had widened, it was more important than ever to keep all the Yielders open to each other's new ideas, and where he wasn't competent to contribute directly himself, he could at least act as a kind of broker, prodding the appropriate experts into action.

Rasmah seemed on the verge of pointing out that he might have expressed his gratitude to her more palpably, but then she smiled and accepted his words at face value.

"Okay. Here I go."

She turned her attention to something invisible to Tchicaya. For several minutes, she sat in complete silence.

Suddenly, she exclaimed, "Oh, I see! This is actually quite nice."

Tchicaya was excited, and slightly jealous. "Can you explain?"

Rasmah held up her hand for patience, retreating back into her private scape.

After a while, she spoke again. "Think of all the different dynamic laws that might make *topological* sense, in terms of the propagation of various kinds of particles that are defined as patterns embedded in a graph. I know that's horribly vague, but I don't think you'd want the version with added jargon."

Tchicaya said, "Okay. I'm thinking of them." He'd seen enough examples that they'd pinned to the border over the last few months to have some feel for what this meant.

"Now imagine each one is a quantum state vector in a big fat Hilbert space. All of them orthogonal to each other."

"Yes." Tchicaya had never had his mind restructured to enable clear images of more than three dimensions, but since Rasmah's Hilbert space was infinite-dimensional anyway, three was as good as any other number. "I'm doing that. Go on."

"Now imagine a new set of vectors that consist of equal amounts of *all* these dynamic-law vectors, and that are all orthogonal to each other. These vectors represent definite values of a variable that's complementary to the law vectors. Branco calls them law-momenta—which is a bit sloppy, because they're not true Lagrangian conjugates, but never mind."

"I'll try not to fret." Tchicaya thought of the directions on a map. If the dynamic-law vectors were north and east, then the new, unbiased, law-momenta vectors would be *north-west* and *north-east.* Both had equal portions of the old directions—if you counted west as being the negative of east, and only cared about the size of things, not their sign—and they were at right angles to each other. In three dimensions or more you needed to introduce complex numbers to pull off the same balancing act, but from there you could keep on going to any number of dimensions. The amounts of the original vectors you combined were just a series of complex numbers that moved around a circle in the complex plane; to get different vectors, all orthogonal to each other, you just moved around the circle at different rates.

"Now picture a state vector which has equal components when written as superpositions of the old set, or the new."

In two dimensions, that was easy: north-north-east lay at the same angle to north as it did to north-east, *and* the same angle to east as it did to north-west. In terms of the quantum mechanics Rasmah was describing, it had equal uncertainty in the two complementary variables: it did not obey a precise dynamic law, but nor did it have any precise law-momentum. It split the difference and compromised, in the most symmetrical way.

Rasmah continued. "These are the states Yann wants to scribe, because if you create one on the border, and then arrange to measure the same kind of state coming back, they yield the highest attainable probability of returning with information about the interior."

" 'The highest attainable probability'? That's a resounding declaration of confidence." Tchicaya had been hoping for something more reliable. He knew what quantum mechanics was like, but if his own Qusp could pluck certainty from the haze, granting him the ability to make unique decisions, surely Yann could work some similar trick with the vastly more powerful abstract machine behind the border?

Rasmah emerged from her visualization. "I know how that sounds, but it really is the best we can hope for. We're not *arranged* in the same way as the far side; we're stuck in a dynamic-law eigenstate, and that's always going to make things difficult."

"Yeah." Tchicaya was grateful for anything that took them beyond the current, artificial view of definite laws spread across the border, but it was sobering to realize how much stranger things became as the price of that advance. "I shouldn't be disappointed, but I keep underplaying the problems in my head: sweeping all the hard parts off to one side, where I don't have to look at them. If I faced the difficulties squarely, I'd probably just turn around and run."

Rasmah regarded him with a mixture of curiosity and affection. "You really do want to go through the border, don't you?"

"I think so. What about you?"

"Absolutely. That's what I came here to do." She hesitated, then added, "For a while, I thought I must have said something too extreme along those lines, and it put you off. But I don't think that's it. So what is it about me that you hate so much?"

Tchicaya shook his head vehemently. "Nothing."

"But we got halfway," she said, "and then you changed your mind." This wasn't a question. Their bodies had ceased the silent exchange of pheromones, and that in itself would have dampened her feelings toward him, but it must have been clear to her that he was the one who'd halted the process.

"You're very good company," Tchicaya said. "But you remind me too much of someone else, and I don't feel right about that. I don't want to confuse you with her; that wouldn't be fair on either of us." He frowned apologetically. "Am I making any sense?"

Rasmah nodded uncertainly. "The other thing I thought was, maybe you and Yann were still, somehow—"

"No!" Tchicaya was taken aback. "Where did you hear about that?"

She waved a hand dismissively. "Everyone knows."

"Actually, I think Yann might have forgotten."

"But there is no one else, in the present? Just this nameless competitor from the past?"

Not exactly a competitor. And not wholly in the past. But Tchicaya didn't want to explain any further. "That's right."

"Okay." Rasmah stood, and Tchicaya rose beside her. In part, he was glad that she'd cleared the air, though at the same time he felt a surge of resentment, now that he'd been forced to put his reasons into words. He and Mariama would never be together. Why was he letting her shape his decisions at all?

"You'll support Yann with this?" he asked.

Rasmah smiled. "Definitely. This is our best hope, and I'm sure I can sell it to the others. Suitably uglified."

The Blue Room was packed from wall to wall; it hadn't been so crowded since the Left Hand's first trial run. The room was near the bottom of its module, and it had already been expanded as far as possible in all horizontal directions; several unobliging neighbors above prevented it from growing upward. As relations had deteriorated, some Yielders and Preservationists had swapped cabins in order to be surrounded by fellow partisans, but the *Rindler* hadn't yet reached a state where every module was "owned" by one faction or another.

Yann paced the ceiling, ducking away from the tallest heads and shoulders—making his presence visible, but wisely desisting from trying to claim space that he could not defend with solid elbows. Other acorporeals came and went beside him, and no doubt he was conversing with some who weren't bothering to display icons. Almost everyone who'd been born acorporeal had now donated their bodies to new arrivals, effectively splitting the Yielders into two distinct communities, more so in some ways than the factions themselves. Tchicaya had mixed feelings about this; their generosity had given many more people a chance to participate in events on the ship, in the only manner that would not have been alien to them. But the acorporeals had been willing to change modes in the first place, so why couldn't the newcomers make do with software bodies? Maybe he had no right to think that way, having accepted the first such sacrifice himself, but the segregation by birth still depressed him, however well acclimatized to their condition the acorporeals were.

The Left Hand had scribed Yann's state almost an hour before, and they were still waiting hopefully for an echo. Rasmah had ended up translating Yann's purely algorithmic account into a kind of sophisticated scattering experiment: they were probing the far side by sending in an elaborately structured pulse that was capable of propagating relatively large distances. At least part of this pulse stood a good chance of bouncing off any structure that lay in its path, and coming back to them bearing an imprint of whatever it encountered.

This made it sound cozily familiar: a cross between radar, particle physics, and tomography. But the "distance" the pulse would travel and the "structures" it might or might not interact with were the raw topological details of an unknown superposition of quantum graphs, not properties of such elaborate near-side constructions as vacuum obeying Euclidean geometry, or the kind of matter that would reflect light or microwaves. Even the pulse itself had no real analogies in the ordinary world: it was not a particle, or a gravitational wave, or any kind of electromagnetic signal. It was a new form of dislocation in the pattern of threads from which all those mundane things were woven.

Rasmah cried out, "We've got something!"

People started jostling for a better view of the screen, though the image was being made available directly to everyone in the room. Tchicaya stubbornly stood his ground behind Rasmah for several seconds, then he gave up and let the crowd percolate around him, forcing him back.

He closed his eyes and saw, unobstructed, the first raw image of the returning pulse. It was a speckled, monochrome, pock-marked pattern, like a fuzzy shot of a cratered landscape, taken in such low light levels that you could count the individual photons. As he watched, the speckling of the image shimmered; it reminded Tchicaya of some kind of weird laser effect.

"Interference!" Yann crowed happily from the ceiling. "Wait, wait, let me—" An inset blossomed in the image, a huge, tangled, branching polymer, studded with loops and knots, built from nodes of every valence. Different parts of the pulse would have been modified in different ways by the same topology; Yann had used the interference between these altered components to reconstruct a typical portion of the kind of graph the signal must have passed through.

Rasmah said, "That's far from an unbiased superposition. It's not the sum of all random haystacks in there. There's no vacuum, but there's still order."

Tchicaya stared at the polymer. From childhood, he'd studied the Sarumpaet patterns, the quantum graphs that could maintain stability under the old rules. And for months, he'd seen the alternatives: all the different possible families of particles, deduced from the physics they'd trapped on the border.

This was like an amalgam that some magpie of a sculptor had created to sum up that experience, combining features from all of them—grabbing fragments of every kind of ordinary, vacuum-based physics and welding them together, without regard to such niceties as having to build a uniform, homogeneous geometry, or having to respect a simple set of rules that stayed constant over time.

Hayashi called out from behind Tchicaya, "Is that fractal? Can you give it a dimension?"

Rasmah invoked some further processing. "No. No dimension, integer or otherwise. The branching's not at all self-similar; there's no redundant information."

"Modify the probe pulse and send it again. Here are the details." Branco's voice rang out from midair, as if he were among the acorporeals; he'd declined to leave his cabin and join the crush. Some Yielders had been reluctant to grant access to the results to anyone who refused to declare their allegiance, but sanity had finally prevailed.

Rasmah said, "Thanks for the suggestion, but it will have to wait." The meeting that had approved Yann's experiment had set aside a week for the interpretation of the results, before any further action was to be taken.

Branco sighed. "Do it, don't do it. I couldn't care less."

Rasmah displayed Branco's proposal for everyone to see. It was a straightforward alteration to Yann's original state, accompanied by some calculations suggesting that components would bounce back to them in a staggered sequence that would make changes in the graphs over time easier to deduce. If this worked, it would give them a movie of the far side, in place of a single, still image.

Suljan yelled out, "We should try that, immediately!" Bhandari, in a far corner of the room, disagreed. People started voicing approval and shouting alternative suggestions from all directions. Tchicaya would have covered his ears, but his hands were trapped. This was bedlam, but it was intoxicating. It reminded him of the time he and a group of friends on Peldan had landed a remote-controlled vehicle on a passing asteroid: everyone wanted to grab the joystick.

Rasmah screamed, "Shut up!"

Something approximating silence descended.

"Read Branco's proposal," she pleaded. "Think about it. We'll have a vote in fifteen minutes. And if anyone feels like going out to stretch their legs in the meantime . . . don't rush back. You can vote from anywhere."

The noise rose up again, but there was no real note of discord. Rasmah slumped against the control panel.

Yann poked his head down in front of Tchicaya. "You're all completely mad. Someone's going to get crushed."

"Some of us have no choice about taking up space."

"There's plenty of room up here," Yann suggested helpfully.

"Yeah, right, just give me a hand up." The ship could probably have molded a tier of hanging chairs, but the ceiling was so low that this would have meant a constant risk of being kicked in the head.

"Some people are so inflexible. When Cass came to Mimosa, she insisted on a body. We obliged, but we made it small enough to fit."

Tchicaya had never heard this detail before.

"How small?" he asked.

Yann held out his hand, thumb and forefinger a couple of millimeters apart.

"You evil, sadistic bastards."

Tchicaya squeezed his way through the crowd back to the control panel. Rasmah looked frazzled but happy.

"What do you make of this?" he asked, gesturing at the polymer.

"It's too early for interpretations," she said.

"But it's structured, isn't it?" he suggested. "You said as much yourself."

Rasmah had grown more cautious. "It's not an equal superposition of all the things it could be. It's not a maximum-entropy quantum blancmange. That still leaves a lot of room for it to be disordered, in lesser ways."

Tchicaya didn't pursue the point, but the very fact that Yann's pulse had come back to them bearing information proved that there was some potential for setting up causal processes on the far side. Lawless as it was in the conventional sense, it could still support a kind of machinery. They could try to build more sophisticated exploratory vehicles. Perhaps, eventually, even bodies and Qusps.

More importantly, if they ever succeeded in doing that, the place they'd be entering was looking less and less like a featureless desert. When Tchicaya had arrived on the *Rindler*, it had still been conceivable that the world behind the border would be nothing but a different form of empty space, with no particular reason to contain even the equivalent of the tiny smudge of matter that enlivened the near side. They'd barely glimpsed the structure of the far side, but his first impression was that the hundred million cubic light-years of vacuum claimed by Mimosa had been rewoven into something orders of magnitude more complex.

"Do you think we should show this to the opposition?" Tchicaya asked. "It might give them pause, if they can finally see that they're not just dealing with a corrosive void."

Rasmah laughed. "You honestly believe they'd care?"

"Some would. And I don't see what we have to lose."

"Nor do I, but only because I'm sure they'll end up with exactly the same details, whether we inform them officially or not."

Tchicaya was startled. "You think someone's spying for them?"

"Of course."

"What makes you so sure? Do we have spies with them?"

"Not that I know of," Rasmah admitted. "But that's not a fair comparison. The most relaxed Preservationist is an order of magnitude more security-conscious than our most diligent supporter."

The vote was taken, returning ninety-two percent support for Branco's suggestion. Rasmah scribed the modified pulse, and they waited again.

Tchicaya sat on the console as people talked around them. "I never really thought we'd get this far," he admitted. "Even once I'd made up my mind to come here, it seemed like a mad, quixotic notion." He described the legend of the falling Sappers.

"I like that story," she said, "but it's not a good metaphor. Bombs hit the ground, and that's that. We're not facing a single, decisive deadline. Thousands of planets have fallen, but there is no moment when everything will be won or lost. So long as the border doesn't accelerate, we could hang on here for another thousand years, learning whatever we need to learn."

"Unless we lose everything to the Preservationists first."

Rasmah shrugged, as if that went without saying. Tchicaya hadn't told her about Mariama's ultimatum; the actual words had been so ambiguous that to most people they'd convey little more than the obvious fact that Planck worms were on the Preservationists' agenda. He hadn't given up hope of finding a way to freeze the border, but there was no clear path leading toward that outcome; randomly pinning dynamics was never going to do it. They had to look deeper, they had to learn more.

He said, "So you never doubted that this moment would come?"

"Never. Not for a second." She laughed. "You should see your face, Tchicaya. I grew up with the border, remember? My parents used to take me outside at night and show me this tiny little disk of light, where the brightest star in the sky used to be. Sixty years later, it was on top of us. I'd never felt as angry as the day we had to evacuate. Not just because I was losing all the places I'd known on Maeder. I hated running from this thing."

"You wanted to stay and fight?"

"I wanted to stay and understand it. I would have been on the *Rindler* from the start if I'd heard about it early enough. Instead, I went chasing rumors of another project. That fell through, and it took me centuries to make my way here. But I always knew we'd find a way through the border. The night before I left Maeder, I stood on the roof of my house and promised myself: next time, it won't just look as if I could reach up and push my hand into the far side. It will be possible. It will be true."

Tchicaya could easily picture her in this scene. "You're making me feel very old and indecisive," he complained.

She smiled. "I'm sorry, but that's because you are."

The console said, "Move your backside, please." Tchicaya slid off; data was coming through.

This time, he fought harder to stay beside Rasmah, peering over her shoulder at the console as the pulse appeared, and its interference pattern was analyzed.

Branco's refinement had been on target: the new set of images showed a graph changing smoothly. Again, this was just an average for the whole path that had been traversed, not any particular piece of the far side, but it was still as informative as, say, a sample of images of terrain from a million different Earth-sized planets of different ages. You didn't need to have the entire history of one specific world to get a qualitative sense of how things changed.

Rasmah set the image looping, and the Blue Room crowd fell silent. The intricate waves of knotted edges flowing through the graph were mesmerizing. Animations of standard particle physics could be austerely beautiful; watching something like pair-production, with the mirror-image patterns of electrons and positrons forming out of their parent photons and moving through the vacuum, you couldn't help but admire the elegant symmetry of the process. This was a thousand times more complex, without being random or chaotic. The still image had reminded Tchicaya of a clumsy sculptural collage, but that was only because he'd imagined all the separate parts still playing their old, vacuum-based roles. Seeing the integrated whole in action destroyed that impression completely. Rather, the old Sarumpaet-style patterns and interactions were beginning to look like repetitive attempts to imitate parts of *this*—like the work of some awful, sample-driven artist who took a tiny piece of someone else's intricately composed, wall-sized image and treated it as a decorative tile to be stamped out a thousand times in a rectangular grid.

Near-side physics did achieve the same kind of complex beauty, but not at this scale, twenty orders of magnitude smaller than a proton. You had to move up to the size of atoms, at least, and even the richness of chemistry appeared crude and stodgy in comparison. When atoms changed their bonds, it was generally a haphazard, rough-and-tumble process, driven at random by thermal collisions, or at best chaperoned by enzymes or nanomachines. These polymers of indivisible nodes and edges were reweaving themselves with a speed and precision that made the most sophisticated molecular factories look like children tossing snowballs.

Tchicaya heard someone clear their throat, nervous and tentative, reluctant to break the spell. He turned away from the console, curious and slightly annoyed, wondering what anyone thought they could add to this extraordinary sight with words. But the crowd moved respectfully away from the speaker, making space as if in encouragement.

It was Umrao, a recent arrival from Nambu who Tchicaya had only met once. He looked around shyly, even more nervous now that he had everyone's attention.

He said, "That's not particle propagation, but it's something I've seen before, in simulations. It's persistence, and replication, and interdependence. It's not a superposition of a billion different vacua—or if it is, that's only one way to describe it, and I don't believe it's the best.

"It's a biosphere. It's an ecology. Right down at the Planck scale, the far side is crawling with life."

Chapter 11

Tchicaya said, "We should tell them, now! Take them all the evidence. No, no—better, teach them Yann and Branco's method, and let them probe the far side for themselves. Then they'll know they're not being cheated with some kind of elaborate simulation."

Hayashi groaned. "And then what? They convince themselves that they're now facing the Virus That Ate Space-Time. While we've surrendered our sole advantage."

Pacing the ship, unable to sleep, Tchicaya had run into Suljan and Hayashi. When a casual exchange of views in the corridor had come perilously close to disclosing all the latest discoveries, he'd accompanied them to the Yielders' cafeteria, which was supposedly secured against listening devices. Other people passing through had become entangled in the debate.

Rasmah said, "I agree. This isn't going to sway anyone. Even if they're willing to interpret this as evidence for Planck-scale biota, and even if that destroys all their preconceptions about the 'Mimosan vacuum' . . . if you didn't care that much about far-side physics, why should you care about far-side microbiology?"

Yann's icon appeared, seated beside her. "Microbiology? These organisms are a few hundred Planck lengths wide: about ten-to-the-minus-thirty-three meters. This is *vendekobiology*."

Suljan picked up a mug and raised it threateningly. "What are you doing here? This is where the real people come, to metabolize in peace."

Yann said, "My mistake. I thought you might be sitting around singing the praise of everyone who helped win you a glimpse of the far side. But I can see you're more interested in getting in some valuable belching and farting time."

Hayashi reached over and slapped Suljan on the back of the head. "You're an oaf. Apologize."

"Ow. It was a joke!" He turned to Yann. "I apologize. I'm in awe of your accomplishments. I'm already working on an ode to your sacred memory."

Umrao looked embarrassed by all the bickering going on around him. He said, "I suppose we need more evidence if we're going to convince the skeptics, but for what it's worth, I've been doing some simulations." He summoned graphics, floating above the table. "The mix of replicators is probably not the same throughout the far side. There are other possible equilibria, other population mixtures that look more or less stable—and that's just changing the relative numbers of the species we've seen, not accounting for entirely different ones." The images showed both a graph-level view of these teeming communities of organisms, and a higher-level map of a possible set of neighboring regions.

"The transition zones tend to be quite sharp, and sometimes they just advance relentlessly in one direction at a constant velocity, like the border itself. But there are other situations where an intermediate mix of species forms in a narrow layer, and it stops either side from invading the other."

Tchicaya seized on this. "A kind of internal freezing of the border?"

Umrao nodded. "I suppose you could think of it like that. Except that our side of the border is completely sterile, so it's not really subject to the same effects."

"You don't think we could create a layer population like these, that worked with one side unpopulated?"

Umrao thought for a while. "I couldn't say. For a start, these are simulations, so I'm not even sure that any of this happens in reality. And we'd need to understand many things much more thoroughly before we set out to engineer a layer population with particular properties."

Suljan said, "Screw it up, and the border might just move faster."

Tchicaya gazed into the simulation. *Our side of the border is completely sterile.* All these millennia looking for life, scratching around on rare balls of dirt for even rarer examples of biochemistry, only to find that the entire substrate of the visible universe was a kind of impoverished badlands. Life had still arisen here, thirty orders of magnitude up the length scale, as heroic and miraculous as some hardy plant on a frozen mountain peak, but all the while, infinitely richer possibilities had been buzzing through the superposition that the dead vacuum concealed.

He said, "Keeping this quiet is insane. People have evacuated whole planets for fewer microbes than there are in one atom-sized speck of the far side."

"Not always enthusiastically," Rasmah replied dryly.

For a moment, Tchicaya was certain that she knew what he'd done. Mariama had revealed their secret, whispered it in a few well-chosen ears, to punish him for his hypocrisy.

That was absurd, though. It was common knowledge that compliance with the ideal of protective isolation had often been begrudging, and everyone suspected that there'd been cases where the evidence had been ignored, or destroyed.

"This could win us the Wishful Xenophiles," he persisted. "One glimpse of this, and they'd desert *en masse*." Not all Preservationists shared the view that cultural upheaval was the worst consequence of Mimosa; a sizable minority were more afraid that it might obliterate some undiscovered richness of near-side alien life. Four known planets dotted with microbes—whatever potential they offered for evolutionary wonders in a few hundred million years' time—might not be worth fighting for, and most people had abandoned hope that the galaxy contained other sentient beings, but unexplored regions could still be home to alien ecologies to rival Earth's. Now, that uncertain possibility had to be weighed against life-forms by the quadrillion, right in front of their noses.

"These aren't sophisticated creatures," Hayashi pointed out. "We can quibble about the definition of life in different substrates, but even if that's conceded, these things really aren't much more complex than the kind of RNA fragments you find in simulations of early terrestrial chemistry."

"That's true," replied Suljan, "but who says we've seen all the life there is to see?" He turned to Umrao. "Do you think these could just be the bottom of the food chain?"

Umrao spread his hands helplessly. "This is very flattering, but I think some of you are beginning to ascribe oracular powers to me. I can recognize life when I see it. I can extrapolate a little, with simulations. But I have no way of knowing if we're looking at the equivalent of Earth in the days of RNA, or if this is plankton on the verge of disappearing into a whale."

Yann said, "Now we're talking xennobiology!" Tchicaya shot him a disgusted look, though on reflection the hideous pun seemed inescapable. A complex organism based on similar processes to the primitive ones they'd seen probably would be about a xennometer in size.

Suljan wasn't satisfied with Umrao's modest disclaimer. "You can still help us take an educated guess. Start at the bottom, with what we've seen. I don't think we should try to imagine evolutionary processes; we don't know that these things are *primeval*, we just know that they seem to be ubiquitous. So we should ask, what else can fit in the same picture? The vendeks don't really prey on each other, do they?"

"No," Umrao agreed. "Where they coexist in a stable fashion, it's more like exosymbiosis. In totality, they create an environment in the graph where they can all persist, taking up a fixed share of the nodes. A given vendek in a given place in the graph will either persist or not, depending on the surrounding environment. At least in the sample we've seen, most do better when surrounded by certain other species—they don't flourish in a crowd of their own kind, but they can't make do with just any sort of neighbor. In microbiology, you get similar effects when one species can use the waste of another as food, but there's nothing like that going on here—there is no food, no waste, no energy."

"Mmm." Suljan pondered this. "No vacuum, no time-translation symmetry, no concept of energy. So even if there's another level of organisms, there's no particular reason why they should *eat* the vendeks."

"They might have subsumed them, though," Hayashi suggested. "Imagine the equivalent of multicellularity. A larger organism might have different vendeks playing specialized roles. Different 'tissues' of a xennobe might consist of—or be derived from—some of the species we've seen."

"I suppose so," Umrao said cautiously. "But remember, these things are much, much simpler than single-celled organisms. They don't have anything remotely akin to genomes. In most multicellular creatures, all the cells in all the tissues share their full genome, with different parts of it switched on and off. It's hard to see how vendeks could be regulated with the necessary precision."

Rasmah frowned. "Maybe multicellularity's not the right analogy. What's it actually *like*, on a larger length scale, to be immersed in these different vendek populations?"

Umrao shrugged. "For *what* to be immersed? I don't know what kind of organized patterns of information can persist, apart from the vendeks themselves. If we're going to model the behavior of some object, we need to know what it's made from."

Tchicaya took a stab at this. "Different vendek populations, with stable layers between them? A kind of honeycomb of different heterogeneous communities?"

Suljan said, "Hey, maybe they're the cells! Vendeks themselves are too small to play tissue types, but certain communities of them can be maintained within intact 'membranes,' so maybe our xennobes could regulate the population mixtures as a surrogate for cell differentiation." He turned back to Umrao. "What do you think? Could you look for a form of motility in these walled communities?"

"Motility?" Umrao thought for a moment. "I think I could build something like that." He began tinkering with the simulation, and within minutes he'd produced an amoebalike blob moving through a sea of free vendeks. "There's one population mix for the interior, and a layer around it that varies as you go from the leading surface to the trailing one. The leading surface acts like an invasion front, but it decays into the interior mix as it travels. The trailing surface does the reverse; it actually 'invades' its own interior, but it lets the external population take over in its wake. Perpetual motion only, though: this cell could never stand still. And it's a contrived setup. But I suppose there are all kinds of opportunities to modulate something like this."

Tchicaya looked away from the simulation to the mundane surroundings of the cafeteria. He was beginning to feel more optimistic than he had since he'd arrived, but this was all still speculation. To build a machine, a body, from anything like these "cells" was going to be a dauntingly complex endeavor.

He said, "We have to win time from the Preservationists. There has to be a truce, a moratorium, or this could all be wiped out before we learn anything."

Rasmah said, "You think they could make effective Planck worms, without knowing what they're dealing with?"

"You're the one who's convinced that they have spies."

"If they have spies, why should telling them anything buy us more time?"

"When did spies ever share their intelligence with the masses?" Tchicaya countered. "Suppose Tarek was looking over our shoulder right now, but everyone else remained in the dark?" He turned to Umrao. "I don't suppose you've investigated the possibility of Planck worms? A plague that kills the vendeks, and leaves a sterile vacuum in its wake?"

Umrao glanced around the table warily. "If any of what you just said was serious, I don't think I should answer that question."

Suljan groaned. "Forget about politics. We need more data!" He slumped down across the table, drumming his fists on the surface. "I was playing around with something last night, before I stepped out for a snack and ended up mired in this discussion. I think I might have found a way to extend Yann and Branco's technique, pushing the range about ten thousand times further." He looked up at Yann, smiling slyly. "The only way I could make any progress with your work, though, was to translate it all into my own formalism. Everything becomes clearer, once you express it in the proper language. It only took me a few hours to see how to scale it up, once I'd dealt with the mess you left us."

Rasmah asked sweetly, "So what was the great conceptual breakthrough, Suljan? How did you sweep our Augean stables clean?"

Suljan straightened up in his seat and beamed proudly at them all. "Qubit network theory. I rewrote everything as an algorithm for an abstract quantum computer. After that, improving it was simplicity itself."

* * *

On his way to the Blue Room, crossing the observation deck, Tchicaya spotted Birago standing by the starside wall. His first thought was to walk on by; minimizing friction by minimizing contact had become an unwritten rule of shipboard life. But the two of them had got on well enough before the separation, and Tchicaya was sick of only talking to Preservationists at the interfactional meetings, when the entire discussion was guaranteed to revolve around a mixture of procedural issues and mutual paranoia.

As Tchicaya approached, Birago saw him and smiled. He looked slightly preoccupied, but not annoyed at the interruption.

Tchicaya said, "What are you up to?"

"Just thinking about home." Birago nodded vaguely in the direction of the blue shift, but Tchicaya knew which star he meant. It had been chosen by the people on Viro before they were scattered, and Tchicaya had had it pointed out to him by the evacuees he'd encountered on half a dozen worlds. The spore packages had already been launched from Gupta, and the evacuees—who'd spread out to many different intermediate destinations, to avoid overtaxing the hospitality of the locals—would follow within a couple of centuries. "We're not losing this one," he said. "Not until the sun burns out."

Tchicaya had heard the slogan many times before. Whether it was a matter of being the oldest community of evacuees, or some other factor in the original culture, people from Viro always appeared more focused on their new home than on the loss of the old. Birago himself had no clear memories of Viro—he'd left as an infant, and moved from world to world a dozen times—but if his family had wrapped him in any vision of permanence, any sense of belonging, it was anchored to their future, not their past.

Tchicaya said, "There's good reason to be hopeful now." That wasn't giving anything away: the Preservationists would know, at the very least, that his side had had a series of breakthroughs.

Their understanding was snowballing; a concrete plan for some form of stable compromise could only be a matter of time now.

Birago laughed. "*Hope* is for when you have nothing else. When I was a child, no one around me would ever look up at the border and say, 'It's too big. We're too late. It's unstoppable.' We had no plans, we had no remedies; the only strength we had came from refusing to give up. Which was all very laudable . . . but you can't go on like that forever. There has to come a time when hope turns into something more tangible."

"Honey or ashes."

"Ah, know-it-all travelers." Birago smiled, but there was an edge to his voice. Picking up a few idiomatic phrases in passing didn't mean you understood anything.

"We'll both have certainty soon," Tchicaya insisted. "I can't believe it will be much longer now."

"*We?* What counts as certainty for you?"

"Safeguarding the far side."

Birago was amused. "And you think that could ever be part of certainty for us?"

Tchicaya felt a chill of disappointment, but he persisted. "I don't see why not. Once we understand this thoroughly, we'll know what is and isn't safe. No one runs around extinguishing stars out of fear that they might go supernova."

Birago gestured with his right hand, "There are tens of billions of stars to learn from"—then with his left, toward the border—"but there's only one Mimosa."

"That doesn't mean it will remain a mystery forever."

"No. But no one's patience lasts forever. And I know where the benefit of the doubt belongs."

Tchicaya arrived late in the Blue Room, missing the start of Suljan's experiment. Many more people had chosen to avoid the crush and watch from their cabins, so the place was far less crowded than before, to the point where there was space for furniture.

As Tchicaya joined Rasmah, Yann, and Umrao at a table not far from the console, Rasmah was saying, "I'm not optimistic about seeing anything new, such a short distance in. If the outermost mixture of vendeks is converting our vacuum at the fastest possible rate, there could be light-years of them behind the border."

" 'Light-years'?" Yann regarded her with amusement, as if she'd made some kind of category error: a liter of energy, a kilogram of space. The normal geometrical meaning of a quantum graph was intimately bound up with the presence of particles, and they were yet to unravel any simple notion of distance for the far side.

"You know what I mean," Rasmah retorted. "Ten-to-the-fiftieth nodes' worth."

Umrao said, "The hardest thing for me to wrap my mind around is the complete lack of Lorentz invariance. If you picture the graph's history as a foam—the edges all extending into surfaces, the nodes all extending into lines—you'd actually see *different* vendek populations if you re-sliced that foam in a different way."

Tchicaya grimaced. "Doesn't that imply that there's a preferred reference frame? Couldn't you assign yourself an absolute velocity, just by seeing what kind of vendeks you were made from?"

Umrao gestured with his hands in a fashion that Tchicaya's Mediator translated as negation. "Without any external cues to guide you, you'd always slice your own world foam the same way, and see yourself as being made from the same vendeks. *Other people* moving past you might see your constituents change, depending on their velocity relative to you, but you'd see them change in the same way. And both of you would be entitled to claim that you were the best judge of your own composition."

Tchicaya pondered this. "So everything ends up on the same footing as rest mass? It's as if speeding past an electron fast enough could make it look like any other particle at all—but in its own reference frame, it's still an electron?"

"That's right."

Suljan shouted triumphantly, "We have an echo!"

Tchicaya turned to face the screen. It showed a simple blip, the plot of a returning pulse. Suljan's method had coarser resolving power than Yann and Branco's, but that was what allowed it to penetrate further: his signal wouldn't reflect back from the middle of a vast sea of vendeks repeating the same population mix, so any return at all meant that it had encountered a larger-scale change.

Hayashi was beside Suljan at the console. "There must be a layer population, like Umrao predicted," she said. "Some ten-to-the-forty nodes from the border."

Rasmah leaned toward Tchicaya and whispered, "A hundred kilometers, in good old reactionary language."

Umrao was pleased. He said, "I wish we could tell exactly what the border mix changed into, though." He looked around the table. "Come on, there's a challenge for you. Range *and* resolution. How?"

Rasmah joked, "I'm sure using the Right Hand as well would do wonders."

Tchicaya said, "They'll be getting echoes, too, right now, won't they?" The two Hands themselves were about a hundred kilometers apart, so it was plausible that the scatter could reach them.

"Only if they know precisely what to look for." Rasmah raised her hands defensively. "Don't say it: I'm the one who believes in spies."

A sense of anticlimax had descended on the room; the result was important, but it didn't compare to their first glimpse of the Planck-scale structure of the far side. That there was macroscopic structure, too, was encouraging, but extracting further detail would be difficult. A hundred kilometers of solid rock would be no barrier to investigation, but a shift of vendeks was not like a change from crust to mantle, refracting and scattering seismic waves in a simple, predictable fashion. It was more like the boundary between two distinct ecosystems, and the fact that remnants of their expedition had straggled back intact after crossing a wide savanna didn't mean the adjoining jungle would be so easily probed.

Suljan said, "I think it's moving." Successive pulses were coming back with slightly different delays. The reflective layer was more or less keeping pace with the expanding border, but the signal showed it drifting back and forth. "Vibrating, maybe?"

Rasmah replied, "It's probably something changing in the border region, messing with the propagation speed." That explanation made more sense to Tchicaya; the signal was crossing a vast tract with potentially variable conditions, so it was more economical to attribute any delay to the vendeks it encountered along the way.

Suljan gave her a withering look. "More expert commentary from the peanut gallery. The returns are too clean, and too sharp; that much variation in propagation speed would broaden them detectably."

"Hmm." Rasmah didn't argue, but her eyes glazed over; she was checking something. When she emerged, she said, "Okay, you're right. And the changes are too fast and too regular; the source of the variation would have to be fairly localized, so it must be the reflector, not the medium."

Tchicaya turned to Umrao. "Any ideas?"

"I didn't see anything like this in the simulations," he said. "But then, I just remixed the vendeks from the border region. This layer might hold completely different ones."

The vibrations stopped.

Yann stared at the plot on the screen. "Just like that? No decay curve?"

The vibrations resumed.

Tchicaya looked around the room. Several people had left; apparently, the ringing of the far side's equivalent of a planetary ionosphere was of no interest to them. Anything that influenced signal propagation was of crucial importance, though, and if this layer could move, it might even break up and reveal something deeper.

The vibrations halted again, only to restart a few seconds later. "One hundred and thirty-one oscillations," Yann noted.

Rasmah said, "What's that going to tell us?"

Yann tapped his fingers against the table, one hand in time with the returning pulses, the other beating out the rhythm of the reflecting layer itself. Tchicaya resisted an urge to tell his Mediator to stop rendering Yann's icon; the constant drumming was annoying, but he'd never edited anyone from his sensory map before, and he wasn't about to start.

"One hundred and thirty-seven," Yann announced.

Tchicaya said, "You think there's some longer-period cyclic process, modulating the faster one?"

Yann smiled enigmatically. "I have no idea."

Suddenly, Rasmah groaned. "I know what you're thinking!"

"What?" Tchicaya turned to her, but she wasn't giving anything away.

She said, "I'll bet you anything that you're wrong."

Yann shook his head firmly. "I never gamble."

"Coward."

"We have no mutually beneficial assets."

"Only because you threw yours away," she retorted.

Umrao said, "I'm completely lost. What are you people talking about?"

"One hundred and thirty-seven," Yann counted. "One hundred and thirty-eight. One hundred and thirty-nine."

He fell silent. The vibrations had stopped.

Tchicaya said, "The slower cycle is varying, a little. Maybe lengthening. What does that tell us?"

Rasmah had turned pale. At the console, Suljan, who'd been paying no attention to the conversation at their table, suddenly leaned into a huddle with Hayashi. Tchicaya couldn't hear what they were whispering about, but then Suljan let out a long, loud string of obscenities. He turned to face them, looking shocked but jubilant.

"You know what we've got here?" he asked.

Umrao smiled. "I just worked it out. But we shouldn't jump to conclusions."

Tchicaya pleaded, "What conclusions?"

"Three consecutive primes," Suljan explained.

The vibrations had resumed, and Yann was calmly tapping them out again. Tchicaya calculated the next number in the sequence, and thought about trying to quantify the odds of the first three occurring by chance, but it would be simpler just to wait for the pattern to be broken or confirmed.

"One hundred and forty-seven. One hundred and forty-eight. One hundred and forty-nine."

On cue, the vibrations halted.

Yann said, "I wouldn't rule out nonsentient processes. We don't know enough about the kinds of order that can arise in this system."

Umrao agreed. "There's no reason evolution couldn't have stumbled on something useful about primes in the far-side environment. For all we know, this could be nothing more than an exotic equivalent of cicada calls."

"We can't rule out anything," Suljan conceded. "But that has to cut both both ways. It has to include the possibility that someone is trying to get our attention."

Chapter 12

"It looks as if the Colosseum is about to welcome us in," Rasmah said. "You first."

"I don't think so." Tchicaya held up his hand; it was shaking. They'd spent almost two hours sitting in the corridor outside the impromptu amphitheater where the Preservationists were meeting, and now the blank, soundproof wall in front of them was beginning to form a door.

"Turn down your adrenaline," she advised him.

"I don't want to do that," he said. "This is the right way to be. The right way to feel."

Rasmah snorted. "I've heard of traditional, but that's ridiculous."

Tchicaya bit back an irritated reply. If he was going to harness his body's natural agitation, he could still keep his behavior civilized. "I don't want to be calm," he said. "This is too important."

"So I get to be the rational one, and you get to be impassioned?" Rasmah smiled. "I suppose that's as good a strategy as any."

It had taken Tchicaya six days of arguing to push a motion through the Yielders' convoluted decision-making process, authorizing disclosure of the recent discoveries to the opposition, and he had hoped that it would be enough. The Preservationists would repeat the experiments, see the same results, reach the same conclusions. He'd set the chain of events in motion, and it would have an unstoppable life of its own.

Then the Preservationists had announced that two Yielders would be permitted to address them before they made their decision on a moratorium, and he'd found himself volunteering. Having worked so hard to create a situation where they were apprised of the facts and prepared to listen, it would have been hypocritical to back out and leave this last stage to someone else.

The door opened, and Tarek emerged, looking worse than Tchicaya felt. Whatever the body did in times of stress could be ameliorated at will, but Tarek had the eyes of someone whose conscience was robbing him of more than sleep.

"We're ready for you," he said. "Who's first?"

Rasmah said, "Tchicaya hasn't smeared himself in goat fat yet, so it'll have to be me."

Tchicaya followed her in, then hung back as she approached the podium. He looked up at the tiers of seats that almost filled the module; he could see stars through the transparent wall behind the top row. There were people here that he knew well, but there were hundreds of complete strangers, too; the ranks of the Preservationists had been swelled by new arrivals.

The audience was completely silent. There was an expression of stony resentment on some faces, an unambiguously hostile gaze, but most people just looked tired and frayed, as if the thing they hated most was not the presence of Yielders bearing unpalatable revelations, but the sheer burden of having to make an invidious choice. Tchicaya could relate to that; part of him longed for nothing more than a turn of events that would render all further effort irrelevant, one way or another, so he could curl up and sleep for a week.

Rasmah began. "You've seen the results of our recent experiments, and I'm going to assume that you've replicated them successfully. Perhaps someone will correct me if that's wrong, and the raw data is in dispute."

She paused. Sophus called out, "That's not in dispute." Tchicaya felt a small weight lifting; if there'd been a technical hitch, or some elaborate bluff in which the Preservationists claimed that they'd seen nothing, the whole discussion would have bogged down in recriminations immediately.

Rasmah said, "Good. You've also seen Umrao's simulations, and I hope you've performed some of your own. We could sit here for a week debating whether or not the structures we've called 'vendeks' deserve to be described as living creatures, but it's plain that a community of them—or a mixture, if you prefer a more neutral term—forms a completely different backdrop than the vacuum we're familiar with, or anything else most of us imagined we'd find behind the border when we made our way here.

"We've all pinned states with exotic dynamic laws to the border. We've seen tens of thousands of samples from the whole vast catalog of *vacuum-based* physics. But the far side's natural state, the closest it can come to emptiness and homogeneity, has access to all of those possibilities at once.

"I came here expecting to see physics written in a different alphabet, obeying a different grammar, but conforming to the same kind of simple rules as our own. It was Sophus who first realized how myopic that expectation was. Our vacuum isn't just devoid of matter; our universe isn't simply *sparse*, in a material sense. What lies behind the border is neither physics in a different language, nor an amorphous, random Babel of every possibility jumbled together. It's a synthesis: a world painted in hues so rich that everything we've previously imagined as a possible universe begins to seem like a canvas filled from edge to edge with a single primary color.

"We've seen hints, now, that there might be organisms far more sophisticated than the vendeks, just behind the border. There's probably nothing I can say that will influence your interpretation of the evidence. I'm not certain what it means, myself. It could be anything: sentient creatures longing for contact; a mating song between animals; an inanimate system constrained by far-side physics to lie in a state more ordered than our instincts deem likely. I don't know the answer, nor do any of you.

"Maybe there is no far-side life worth speaking of. Maybe there are just different pools of vendeks, all the way down. We can't tell yet. But imagine for a moment that the signal we're seeing comes from a creature even as complex as an insect. If life of that sophistication can arise in just six hundred years, then the far side must be so amenable to structure, and order, and complexity that it's almost inconceivable that we'd be unable either to adapt to it, or to render parts of it hospitable.

"Suppose we were handed a galaxy's worth of planets, all so near to Earthlike that we could either terraform them easily, or tweak a few genes of our own in order to flourish on them. What's more, suppose they came clustered together, so close that the time it took to travel between them was negligible: days or weeks, instead of decades or centuries. If we migrated to these worlds, it would mean an end to our fragmentation, an end to the rule that says: yes, you can see how other cultures live, but the price you pay will be alienation from your own.

"On top of this, imagine that interspersed among these Earthlike worlds was another galaxy's worth of planets, all dense with a riotous variety of alien life. On top of *that*, imagine that these worlds were immersed in a new kind of physics, so rich and strange that it would trigger a renaissance in science that would last ten thousand years, transform technology, reinvigorate art.

"Is that what the far side really is offering us? I don't know, and neither do you. Maybe there are some of you for whom it makes no difference: whatever lies behind the border, it can't be worth the price of even one more planet lost, one more people scattered. But I hope that many of you are willing to pause and say: Mimosa has brought tragedy and turmoil, and that has to be stopped, but not at any cost. If there is a world behind the border that could bring new mysteries, new knowledge, and ultimately *a new sense of belonging* to billions of people—a place that could mean as much to our descendants as our home worlds mean to us—then it can't be *unimaginable* that the balance could ever tip in its favor.

"People left families and nations behind them on Earth. They'd swum in rivers and walked on mountains that they would never see again. Were they all traitors, and fools? They didn't destroy the Earth in their wake, they didn't force the same sacrifice on anyone else, but they did put an end to the world as it had been, when humanity had been connected—when *the speed of light* was a phrase that meant instant contact, instant collisions of cultures and values, not a measure of your loss if you tried to achieve those things.

"I don't know what lies behind the border, but possibilities that seemed like castles in the air a year ago are now a thousand times less fanciful. Everything I've talked about might yet turn out to be a mirage, but if so, it's a mirage that we've all seen with our own two eyes now, hovering uncertainly in the heat haze. A few more steps toward it will tell us, once and for all, whether or not it's real.

"That's why I'm asking for this moratorium. Whether you recoil from the vision I've painted, or merely doubt its solidity, don't make a decision in ignorance. Give us one more year, work beside us, help us find the answers—and then make your choice. Thank you."

Rasmah took half a step back from the podium. Someone in the audience coughed. There was no polite applause, but no jeering either. Tchicaya didn't know how to read the indifferent silence, but Rasmah had been fishing for converts rather than searching for a compromise, and if anyone had been swayed by her message that would probably not be a response they'd wish to broadcast.

Tarek said, "We'll take questions when Tchicaya has spoken."

Rasmah nodded and walked away from the podium. As she passed Tchicaya, she smiled encouragingly and touched his arm. He was beginning to wish he'd gone first, and not just because she was a hard act to follow. Before a gathering of Yielders, a speech like the one she'd just delivered would have fired him up, filling him with confidence. Watching it received with no visible effect by the people who counted was a sobering experience.

Tchicaya reached the podium and looked up at the crowd, without fixing his eyes on any one face. Mariama would be here, somewhere, but he counted himself lucky that he hadn't spotted her, that her certain presence remained an abstraction.

"There is a chance," he said, "that there is sentient life behind the border. We have no proof of this. We lack the depth of understanding we'd need even to begin to quantify the odds. But we do know that complex processes that would have been inconceivable in a vacuum—or in the kind of hot plasma present in our own universe, six hundred years after its birth—are taking place right now on the far side. Whether or not you count the vendeks as living creatures, they reveal that the basic structure of this region is nothing at all like empty space.

"None of us arrived here armed with that knowledge. For centuries, we'd all pictured the 'novo-vacuum' as the fireball from some terrible explosion. I came here myself in the hope that we might gain something from the challenge of learning to survive inside that fireball, but I never dreamed that the far side could harbor life of its own.

"Life does not arise easily in a universe of vacuum. Apart from the Earth, there are just four quarantined planets strewn with single-celled organisms, out of almost a million that have been explored. For twenty thousand years, we've clung to a faint hope that the Earth would not be unique as the cradle of sentience, and I don't believe that we should abandon that hope. But we're now standing at the border, not between a desert with rare oases on one side, and a lake of molten lava on the other, but between that familiar desert and a very strange ocean.

"This ocean might be a desert, itself. It might be turbulent, it might be poisonous. All we know for certain is that it's not like the universe we know. But now we've seen something fluttering beneath the surface. To me, it looks like a beacon, a declaration of intelligence. I concede that this interpretation might be completely wrong. But if we'd ever spotted something a tenth as promising on a planet, wouldn't we be shouting with joy, and rushing to investigate?

"The homes and communities of billions of people are at stake here. One full year's delay would mean the certain loss of one more world." Tchicaya had agonized over the best way to phrase this; apart from starkly requesting an entire planet as a sacrifice, he had to tiptoe around the issue of exactly how close the Preservationists were to producing Planck worms. "But whole worlds have been evacuated before, to leave the rare life we've found with a chance to develop undisturbed. We can create far more sophisticated organisms *in vitro*, but we've still recognized in the simplest alien microbes both a chance to understand better the science of our origins, and a distant kinship with whatever these creatures might become. I'm willing to write off the vendeks as little more than Planck-scale chemistry, but even a slim possibility of sentient life on the far side, just beyond our grasp, has to count for at least as much as the possibility that the microbes we've left to their own devices will flourish into anything as rich as life on Earth.

"I'm not asking anyone in this room to abandon the values

that brought them here. But no one came here with the goal, or even the thought, of wiping out another civilization. If you believe there can be no sentient life on the far side, take the opportunity to prove yourself right. If you harbor even the slightest doubt, take the opportunity to gather more information.

"We're not asking you to wait for certainty. The far side is too large; however advanced our techniques became, there'd always be a chance that a part of it remained hidden. But after six centuries in which the border has been completely opaque, and a few weeks in which we've managed to see through it a very short distance, we're asking for one more year of exploration. We might never find out what's at stake here, but now that we have our first real chance to do more than guess, I don't believe we have the right to shut our eyes and refuse to look any closer.

"Thank you."

Tchicaya backed away from the podium. He hadn't felt too bad while he was speaking, but the discouraging silence that followed turned his stomach to water. Maybe the Yielders had merely decided to present the enemy with their best poker face, but the effect was still one of indifference verging on hostility. He instructed his Exoself to calm his body; whatever sense of urgency he'd managed to convey by allowing his stress hormones free reign, the effect had either succeeded or failed by now.

Tarek said, "Questions and comments."

Birago rose to his feet and addressed his former colleague. "The vendeks appear genuine to me, and I doubt that you could have engineered them into existence without us noticing. I'm much less confident about this so-called signaling layer. How do we know you didn't create it?"

Rasmah replied, "I'm not sure what you expect me to say. I suppose you could move the Right Hand away across the border and look for an edge to the layer, then see if the whole thing lies centered around the Left Hand. But if you seriously believe that we were skilled enough to create the layer at all, maybe you believe we could have disguised its point of origin." She spread her arms. "Look more closely, gather more evidence. That's exactly what we're asking for, and if you have doubts, that's the only cure for them."

Birago laughed curtly, unimpressed, but he resumed his seat.

Tchicaya had come prepared for accusations of fake data, but the idea that anything indisputably present behind the border could be taken as counterfeit had never crossed his mind. If the Preservationists did have spies, surely they'd know how ludicrous this was? But then, spies would probably only share that knowledge with people who would not be swayed by it.

Sophus stood. "I've studied this question, and I don't believe the layer could have been built from the Left Hand without us noticing, any more than the vendeks could. This thing is genuine, and it needs to be investigated. I came here to preserve civilizations, not to destroy them. The chance that we're seeing intelligence here is extremely slim, but this is a matter of the utmost seriousness.

"I support the idea of a moratorium. This need not be lost time for us; we don't have to stop thinking, we don't have to stop planning. A year in which we were forced to consider our next step very carefully—in combination with all the information about the deeper structure of the far side that might be gained as part of this investigation—could easily save more worlds than it costs. The border is expanding at half the speed of light; the success of any attempt to halt or reverse it will be *extremely* sensitive to the propagation speed of the agent we finally deploy. Rushing to adopt the very first solution we think we've found, when we could be refining it into something vastly more effective, would be a shallow victory. If we can clear our conscience of any lingering doubt that we might be committing an atrocity, while continuing to hone our weapons against this threat, we will be steering an honorable course between arrogance and timidity—between laying waste to whatever lies before us, and jumping at shadows."

Sophus took his seat. Tchicaya exchanged glances with Rasmah; they could not have hoped for a better ally. Tchicaya was glad, now, that he hadn't raised the same benefits for the Preservationist cause himself; they sounded far more credible coming from Sophus, and hearing them first from the opposition would only have put people off.

One of the recent arrivals spoke next. Tchicaya had never been introduced to her, but her signature named her Murasaki.

"There might be sentient life here, there might not," she said. "What difference should that make to our actions? Responsibility on our part can only arise through the hope of reciprocity—and many great thinkers have argued that sentient beings that bear no resemblance to us cannot be expected to conform to our own moral codes. Even on the level of pure emotion, these creatures will have arisen in a world we would find incomprehensible. What empathy could we have for them? What goals could we possibly share?"

Tchicaya felt a chill of horror. Murasaki spoke in a tone of mild puzzlement, as if she honestly couldn't understand how anyone could attach the slightest value to an alien life.

"Evolution works through competition," she continued. "If we don't win back our territory and render it secure, then as soon as these far-siders learn of our existence, they will surely find a way to push the growth of the border all the way up to lightspeed. While we still possess the advantage of surprise, we must use it. If there *is* life here, if there are creatures for whom the far side is a comfortable home, the only thing that changes is that we should redouble our efforts, in order to wipe them out before they do the same to us."

As she sat, a faint murmur rose up in the audience. If the Preservationists had resolved to give nothing away in response to the petitioners, their own members could still get a reaction. In all his time on the *Rindler*, in all his travels between worlds, Tchicaya had never heard anyone express a position as repugnant as this. Many cultures proselytized, and many treated their opponents' choices with open derision, but no champion of embodiment or acorporeality, no advocate for planetary tradition or the freedom of travel, had ever claimed that life in other modes was such a travesty that it could be annihilated without compunction.

These words could not be left unchallenged. The idea of genocide might have shrunk to little more than a surreal figure of speech, but in modern times there had never before been a situation in which the effort required to commit mass murder would not have been vastly disproportionate to even the most deranged notion of the benefits. If anything could still awaken horrors from the Age of Barbarism, six hundred years of dislocation, and the opportunity to eradicate something truly alien, might just be enough to end the nineteen-thousand-year era in which no sentient being had died at the hand of another.

As Tchicaya struggled to frame his response, Tarek said, "I'd like to answer that, if I may."

Tchicaya turned to him, surprised. "Yes, of course."

Tarek walked to the podium and rested his hands on the lectern. He looked up and addressed Murasaki directly.

"You're right: if there's sentient life behind the border, it probably won't share my goals. Unlike the people in this room, who all want exactly the same things in life as I do, and have precisely the same tastes in food, art, music, and sex. Unlike the people of Schur, and Cartan, and Zapata—who I came here in the hope of protecting, after losing my own home—who doubtless celebrate all the same festivals, delight in the same songs and stories, and gather every fortieth night to watch actors perform the same plays, in the same language, from the same undisputed canon, as the people I left behind.

"If there's sentient life behind the border, of course we couldn't *empathize* with it. These creatures are unlikely to possess cute mammalian neonate faces, or anything else we might mistake for human features. None of us could have the imagination to get over such insurmountable barriers, or the wit to apply such difficult abstractions as the General Intelligence theorem—though since every twelve-year-old on my home world was required to master that result, it must be universally known on this side of the border.

"You're right: we should give up responsibility for making any difficult moral judgments, and surrender to the dictates of natural selection. Evolution cares *so much* about our happiness that no one who's obeyed an inherited urge has ever suffered a moment's regret for it. History is full of joyful case studies of people who followed their natural instincts at every opportunity—fucking whoever they could, stealing whatever they could, destroying anything that stood in their way—and the verdict is unanimous: any behavior that ever helped someone disseminate their genes is a recipe for unalloyed contentment, both for the practitioners, and for everyone around them."

Tarek gripped the lectern tightly, but continued in the same calm voice. "You're so gloriously, indisputably right: if there is sentient life behind the border, we should wipe these creatures out of existence, on the mere chance that they might do the same to us. Then we can learn to predicate everything else we do on the same assumptions: there is no other purpose to life than an eternity of grim persistence, and the systematic extinguishment of everything—outside ourselves, or within us—that stands in the way of that goal."

He stood in place for several seconds. The room had fallen silent again. Tchicaya was both heartened and ashamed; he had never imagined Tarek taking a stand like this, though in retrospect he could see that it was an act of constancy, not betrayal.

Perhaps Tarek had left his own family and friends behind solely in order to fight for the security of their future home, but in the very act of coming here, he'd been transformed from a member of that culture into an advocate for something universal. Maybe he was a zealot, but if so, he was an idealist, not a hypocrite. If there were sentient creatures behind the border, however foreign to him, the same principles applied to them as to anyone else.

Tarek stepped back from the podium. Santos, another of the newcomers, stood and delivered an impassioned defense of Murasaki's position, in similarly chilling language. When he'd finished, half a dozen people rose to their feet simultaneously and tried to shout each other down.

Tarek managed to restore order. "Do we have more questions for Rasmah and Tchicaya, or is this the time to proceed with our own debate?"

There were no more questions. Tarek turned to them. "I'll have to ask you to leave now."

Tchicaya said, "Good luck."

Tarek gave him a reluctant smile, as if to concede that the two of them finally could mean the same thing by those words. He said, "I don't know how much longer this will take, but we'll keep going until we have a decision."

Out in the corridor, Rasmah turned to Tchicaya. "Where are those people from? Murasaki and Santos?"

"I don't know. It's not in their signatures." He checked with the ship. "They both came via Pfaff, but they haven't made their origins public."

"Wherever it is, remind me not to visit." She shuddered and wrapped her arms around herself. "Do we have to wait here for the verdict? It could be a while. And they will make it public."

"What did you have in mind? I don't think I could face the Blue Room."

"How about my cabin?"

Tchicaya laughed. "You have no idea how tempting that sounds, right now."

"That's how it was meant to sound." Rasmah took his hand; she hadn't been joking. "These bodies are very fast learners, especially when they have memories of a prior attraction."

Tchicaya said, "I thought we'd put an end to all that."

"This is what's known as persistence." She faced him squarely. "Whoever it is you're still hung up about, I promise you I'll make an impression that will erase all memories of the competition." She smiled at her own hyperbole. "Or I can try, if you're willing to make the same effort."

Tchicaya was tongue-tied. He liked everything about her, but some deeply ingrained part of him still felt as if it was a matter of principle to back away.

He said, "I'm seven times your age. I've had thirty-one children. I have sixth-generation descendants older than you."

"Yeah, yeah. You're a battered old creature, on the verge of slipping out of sentience into senility. But I think I can drag you back from the brink." She leaned closer; the scent of her body was beginning to regain significance for him. "If you have scars, I'll kiss them away."

"I want to keep my scars."

"That's all right. I can't actually erase them."

"You really are sweet, but you hardly know me."

Rasmah groaned. "Stop dividing everything by four thousand years. Your age is not the natural unit of time, by which all else must be measured." She leaned forward and kissed him on the mouth; Tchicaya did not pull away.

She said, "How was that?"

Tchicaya gave her his best Quinean wine-judge frown. "You're better than Yann. I think you've done this before."

"I should hope so. I suppose you waited a millennium to lose your virginity?"

"No, it just felt that way."

Rasmah stepped back, then reached out and took both his hands. "Come and wait with me for the vote. We can't do anything you don't want to do; it's biologically impossible."

"That's what they tell you as a child. But it's more complicated than that."

"Only if you make it complicated." She tugged on his arms. "I do have some pride. I'm not going to beg you. I'm not even going to threaten you, and say this is your last chance. But I don't believe we're wrong for each other, and I don't believe you're sure that we are."

"I'm not," he conceded.

"And didn't you just deliver a speech about the folly of making decisions without sufficient information?"

"Yes."

She smiled triumphantly. He wasn't going to argue his way out of this. Logic had nothing to do with it; he simply had to make up his mind what he wanted. One instinct told him that he should turn her down, because it was a decision he'd made so many times before that it seemed like a betrayal of himself to do otherwise. And another told him that if he didn't change, there was no point living even one more century.

Tchicaya said, "You're right. Let's put an end to our ignorance."

They went to Rasmah's cabin and lay on the bed together, still dressed, talking, occasionally kissing. Tchicaya knew his Mediator would make the vote known to him instantly, but he couldn't help but remain distracted. He'd done everything in his power to see that the Preservationists heard the whole case for the far side, but he couldn't rest until he knew whether or not they'd been persuaded.

Almost two hours after they'd spoken to the gathering, the news came through: the moratorium had been approved. No percentages had been released, but the Preservationists had agreed unanimously before beginning their debate that the majority decision would be binding.

Tchicaya watched Rasmah's face as the information registered. "We did it," she said.

He nodded. "And Tarek. And Sophus."

"Yeah. More them than us. But we can still celebrate." She kissed him.

"Can we?" Tchicaya wasn't being coy; he couldn't tell by mere introspection.

"I'm positive."

As they undressed each other, Tchicaya felt a rush of happiness, beyond sex, beyond his affection for her. Whatever hold he'd imagined Mariama had over him, it was finally dissolving. Their conspiracy over the power plant might have ended any chance that he could be truly at ease with her, but that hadn't poisoned everything he'd admired in her. He hadn't forfeited the right to be with someone who had the same strength, the same ideals as she'd once had.

Rasmah stroked the scar on his leg. "Do you want to tell me about this?"

"Not yet. It's too long a story."

She smiled. "Good. I didn't really want to hear it right now." She moved her hand higher. "Oh, look what we made! I knew it would be beautiful. And I think I have something that would fit here, almost perfectly. And here. And maybe even . . . *here*."

Tchicaya gritted his teeth, but he didn't stop her moving her fingers over him, inside him. There was no more vulnerable feeling than being touched in a place that had not existed before, a place you'd never seen or touched yourself. He lay still, and allowed her to make him aware of the shape, the sensitivity, the response of each surface.

He took her by the shoulders and kissed her, then did the same for her, mapping the other half of the geometry their bodies had invented. He was four thousand years old, but he was never tired of this, never jaded. Nature had never had much imagination, but people had always found new ways to connect.

Chapter 13

Tchicaya's Mediator woke him. It had just received a messenger from Branco, and judged it urgent enough to break him out of sleep.

He let the messenger run. He didn't want to close his eyes and risk drifting off again as he watched, so he hallucinated Branco standing in the darkened cabin beside the bed.

"This had better be important," Tchicaya said.

"I'm very sorry to disturb you," the messenger whispered. It was much more polite than Branco himself. "But this is something you'll want to hear. I'm only telling a handful of people. People I trust."

"I'm flattered."

The messenger gave him a look that suggested it was not immune to irony. "Someone has been trying to take control of the ship. I don't know who. The proximate, physical source of the attack was a spare communications link for external instruments, sitting in a storage area that hundreds of people have had access to.

"There was no chance of the attack succeeding. Whoever did this must be awfully naive about some of the technology they're dealing with." Tchicaya felt a frisson of recognition; hadn't Tarek imagined that Yann could "corrupt" the ship's network, just by running on one of its Qusps? "But it suggests a combination of foolishness and desperation that might not stop with this. So I'm telling a few reasonably level-headed members of both factions: you'd better find out who these idiots are, and keep them from going any further. Set your own houses in order, or you might all find yourselves walking the airlock."

The messenger bowed, and vanished. Tchicaya blinked into the darkness. "Walking the airlock" was a quaint way of putting it, but he didn't think Branco was bluffing. If factional squabbling reached the point where the *Rindler* itself was at risk, Tchicaya didn't doubt that the ship's builders would evict the squatters, one way or another.

He woke Rasmah, and shared the news.

"Why didn't Branco tell me?" she complained. "Why am I not trustworthy?"

"Don't take it personally. He probably just thought it would give the message more gravitas if it trickled through, instead of going straight to everyone."

She leaned over and kissed him. "I was joking, actually, but thanks for the reassurance." She groaned. "Oh, here we go."

"What?"

"Yann wants to talk to us." She hesitated. "And Suljan. And Umrao."

"We need to get together. We need to organize a meeting." Tchicaya picked up his pillow and put it over his face. "I can't believe I just said that."

Rasmah laughed and patted his arm. "We do have to discuss this. But you won't need to get out of bed."

Rasmah had her Mediator arrange the protocols, then she invited Tchicaya into a virtual Blue Room. His viewpoint drifted across the floor, toward a table where Rasmah, Yann, Suljan,

Hayashi, and Umrao were seated. He knew he was visible to the others as an icon, and he could alter his gaze and make gestures at will, but he had no real sense of being embodied in the scape; he still felt himself lying motionless on the bed.

Suljan said, "Any ideas, Tchicaya?"

"Who could be so foolish as to try this? I thought of Tarek, but that doesn't add up. Unless he's involved in some elaborate bluff."

Hayashi shook her head. "Not Tarek. I heard that the Preservationists split down the line on the vote, but he was definitely on the side of the moratorium."

"You're saying it was close?"

"Closer than I'd expected," she replied. "Almost forty percent against. Mostly new arrivals."

"Forty percent." Tchicaya had being fervently hoping that Murasaki and Santos were rare extremists. And it was still possible that they were; you didn't have to be sanguine about genocide to have voted against the moratorium, merely skeptical that destroying the far side would entail anything of the kind. Perhaps some of the newcomers had found the unfamiliar physics so bewildering that they'd decided they simply couldn't trust the evidence for the signaling layer, even with their own experts confirming it.

Yann said, "We shouldn't rule out some hothead in our own camp. Just because we've achieved the moratorium, that doesn't guarantee that we'll get everything else people want."

Suljan sighed. "That's very even-handed of you, but given the timing, it doesn't seem likely to me."

"It could have been a setup, though," Umrao suggested. "Someone who hoped their tampering would be detected, and get us all thrown off the *Rindler*—which would put back any prospect of the Preservationists unleashing their Planck worms by several centuries."

Rasmah said, "At the cost of every last trace of goodwill and

Greg Egan

cooperation between the factions. At the cost of everything we'd learn in the year of the moratorium."

"The neutrals would continue to do research," Umrao replied.

Tchicaya said, "Getting thrown off the ship is no good for either side. It must have been someone who really did think they could succeed."

"Succeed at what, exactly?" Hayashi asked. "They wanted control of the ship, in order to do what?"

Bhandari appeared suddenly, standing beside the table. "I hate to interrupt, but if any of you here are interested in reality . . ." He held up a framed image showing a view of one of the *Rindler*'s tethers. Six people were clinging to the cable near the top of one of the modules, slowly ascending toward the hub. Strapped to the backs of two of the climbers were bulky, box-shaped objects that looked as if they might have been built from the same modules as the instrumentation packages for the border experiments. Tchicaya didn't recognize the silver-suited figures, but he asked the ship to match their facial geometry with its manifest of occupants. The six were Murasaki, Santos, and four other newcomers, all of whom had arrived more or less together from Pfaff.

Rasmah vanished from the scape, and Tchicaya felt her shaking him by the shoulders. "Get up!"

He complied, momentarily disoriented.

"What?" he asked. "What do you think they're doing?"

"I don't know, but we have to be prepared for the worst." Rasmah grabbed her can of suit spray and hurriedly coated him. "Now spray me. Quickly!"

Tchicaya did as she'd asked. "The worst? What are you expecting?"

"They're headed for the engines, aren't they? Can you think of a benign explanation for that? I want you to go straight to the shuttle."

"*Why?* You're not turning protective on me, are you? I've

224

backed up last night. Even if we die here, I'm not going to forget you."

Rasmah smiled, and shook her head. "Sorry to be unromantic, but I'm thinking about more than us. If these people manage to remove the *Rindler*, someone has to be around to protect the far side. No one else I trust is any closer to the shuttle."

Tchicaya started pulling on his clothes. "Then come with me."

"No. Until we know what's happening, it's better we split up. They might have done something to the shuttle, it might be a lost cause. Better that only one of us goes there, while the other tries to stop them doing anything at the hub."

Tchicaya felt a surge of resentment, but this argument made sense, and she wasn't ordering him around for the sake of it. They had to move quickly, and it was pointless quibbling over who did what.

He asked the ship for a view of the shuttle. It was still docked in the usual place, and it appeared to be intact, though that hardly ruled out sabotage.

"You're going up after them?" he said.

"If the builders trust me enough to let me out there."

"How did those six get outside? Assuming Branco didn't toss them out."

Rasmah finished dressing. "They're on the tether that holds the module with the instrumentation workshop. They must have been pretending to be working on some sensor that needed to operate in vacuum." She glanced around the cabin with an air of finality, as if she was putting her memories of the place in order.

Tchicaya ached to hold her, but he didn't want to make it harder for them to part. As they stepped out into the corridor, he said, "If this all goes wrong, where will we meet?"

"My closest backup is on Pfaff. If it stops getting reassurance signals from here, that's the one that will wake."

"Mine too."

"That's where we'll meet, then." She smiled. "But let's see if we can achieve a swifter reunion."

They'd reached the stairs. Tchicaya said, "Be careful."

"Of all the things I came here to be, that was never on the list." She took his face in her hands, and touched her forehead to his. Tchicaya listened to her breathing. She was excited, and afraid, and she hadn't followed her own advice about adrenaline. She didn't want to be calm, for this.

Then she released him, turned, and bolted up the stairs without another word.

As Tchicaya took the stairs down toward the walkway, he asked the ship to show him the instrumentation workshop. There was some kind of half-assembled sensor sitting on the main platform, open to space, but he could see no obvious clues as to what Murasaki and the others intended. What did they think they were going to do at the hub? Hot-wire the engines and drive the *Rindler* away? That was never going to happen. It would be a simpler task than taking control of the whole ship, but not by much. Assuming they were being wildly optimistic, though, what good would it do their cause if they succeeded? Whisking everyone away from the border would only delay the work of both sides.

As Tchicaya panned around the workshop, he saw a dark, powdery stain on the floor, by the airlock.

"What's that?" he asked the ship.

"Blood."

The whole workshop was always in vacuum, and it would take much more than a minor act of carelessness to cut yourself through a suit.

"Can you show me when it was spilt?"

The ship showed him recorded vision from fifteen minutes before. As Santos stepped through the airlock, blood dripped from his fingers to the floor. His suit was only just beginning to silver against the cold; Tchicaya could still see his face. One nostril was full of red and black clots, only contained by the membrane of the suit, and the lid of one half-closed eye was encrusted with blood. He looked as if he'd been smacked in the face with an iron bar. Had he been in some kind of struggle with the others? It was bizarre.

On the walkway, Tchicaya saw Kadir coming toward him. They approached each other warily. Kadir spread his arms in a protestation of innocence. "I'm not with these lunatics! We disown them!"

"Do you know what this is all about?"

"I know that they opposed the moratorium, but I don't have a clue what they think this will get them. Birago's joined them now, but he's the only one I really knew. The others were never very communicative. They claimed they were travelers like you, but they were never at ease with anyone but each other. Whatever the faults of travelers, if you express an opinion they find unusual, they tend not to stop in midconversation and stare at you as if you'd sprouted wings."

"Where's Birago?" Tchicaya asked.

"Last I heard, he was standing guard at the entrance to the workshop, trying to stop anyone getting through and going after them."

"But he won't say what they want? There's no threat, no conditions they're trying to bargain for?"

Kadir said, "I think this has gone beyond bargaining."

"Is the Right Hand secure? Could they have used it, done something with it, without the rest of you knowing?"

Kadir shrugged. "The records say it's done nothing for days. But Birago helped build it. I don't know what he was capable of doing."

They parted. As Tchicaya reached the end of the walkway, Rasmah spoke in his head. "The builders let me out. I'm up on the cable." Even through an unvocalized radio channel, her Mediator made her voice as expressive as ever; she sounded both nervous and exhilarated, as if she almost welcomed the chase. "I'm a fair way behind our mutineers, but I think I'm gaining on them."

"You're outnumbered, and they're completely deranged." Tchicaya told her about Santos's appearance.

"Suljan and Hayashi are heading for another tether. They begged Branco to let them out before, but he fobbed them off, he said there was no need. I guess the builders changed their mind."

Tchicaya jogged through the bottom level of his own accommodation module. He was still three modules away from the shuttle. "So they thought they could deal with it, but then they realized they couldn't?" He struggled to make sense of this. The tethers clearly weren't made of anything smart enough to impede the rebels, or dispose of them directly; the insides of the modules were endlessly reconfigurable, but it probably never occurred to the builders that these cables would require any property but tensile strength. "What were they pinning their hopes on?" he mused. "Picking them off with debris-clearance laser? You'd think that would either be technically feasible, or not."

"Maybe they had some last-minute moral qualms."

"These people are either trying to hijack the ship, or to destroy it, and they're free to send backups wherever they like. Their memories are in their own hands. I doubt Branco would have had any scruples about vaporizing them, if it were possible."

Rasmah said, "He might have been outvoted."

Tchicaya asked the ship to show him an image of her. The lone figure was only about five or six meters up the kilometer-long cable, but she was ascending rapidly: gripping the slender braid of monofilaments with her knees, reaching up, dragging her body another arm's-length higher. At least at the hub she'd have a negligible velocity; if she ended up floating, he'd have plenty of time to reach her in the shuttle.

Tchicaya said, "Let me see through your eyes."

"Why?"

"Just for a moment. Please."

Rasmah hesitated, then sent him the vision. She looked down at the shiny globe of the module beneath her, then up across the spoked wheel of the ship, toward the faint glint of her quarry on the tether a quarter of a turn away. On her right, the dazzling plain of the border was as serene and immutable as ever.

"I'm not afraid of heights," she said dryly. "Stop fretting about me." She cut off the image.

"I'm not," Tchicaya lied.

"I just spotted Suljan emerging. Look, I'm not on my own here. Just get to the shuttle! If there's anything to tell you, I'll call back."

"All right."

As his sense of her presence faded, Tchicaya broke into a run. He'd been wasting time trying to piece everything together; he didn't need to know exactly what the rebels were planning. Rasmah's logic was sound. He hated not being beside her, but she'd trusted him with another task, and he had to dedicate himself to it, unswervingly.

He raced past people in the corridors and on the walkways, without stopping to shout questions or exchange hypotheses. If there was solid information being passed around, it would reach him eventually, wherever he was. Within minutes, he was dripping with sweat; the ship's bodies stayed reasonably fit by sheer biochemical fiat, but his own had been neither designed nor trained for speed. Refusing to be swayed by discomfort was easy, but there were limits that had nothing to do with pain.

Yann appeared suddenly, sprinting beside him. "Rasmah said

you're heading for the shuttle. How much free storage do you have in your Qusp?"

"Not enough for a passenger. I'm sorry."

Yann shook his head, amused. "I don't need a ride. I'm entirely used to not having my Qusp on legs, and I'm not worried about getting my memories elsewhere. But if you're stranded, you might need some assistance."

Tchicaya replied purely by radio, to save his breath. "That's a good idea. But like I said, I don't have storage for a second person."

"I didn't expect you would," Yann said. "I've prepared a toolkit; it's only a few exabytes, but it encompasses everything I know about the far side. Everything I've learned from Suljan, Umrao, and the others, and everything I've worked out for myself. Of course, all of this is useless if you don't have access to the border, so I'm organizing a vote on ceding control of the Left Hand to you."

Tchicaya didn't reply. Yann said, "You probably don't want all this riding on your shoulders, but believe me, we're doing our best to avoid that."

Tchicaya said, "What can they do up there?"

"Don't worry about that. Just get to the shuttle, and move away as fast as you can. We'll call you back once it's safe."

"Assuming the rebels don't steal the shuttle first." He checked the view; it was still in place.

Yann said, "They can't steal it; the builders have disabled it. Branco has agreed to release it once you're onboard. Now stop arguing, and take the toolkit."

Tchicaya instructed his Mediator to accept the package. Yann added cheerfully, "Let's hope you don't need it."

As Yann's icon vanished, Tchicaya swerved to avoid a startled pedestrian, who stared at him as if he'd gone mad. No one he'd encountered since leaving Rasmah had been in much of a hurry, and the closer he came to the shuttle, the more people seemed to be heading in the opposite direction: away from the *Rindler*'s sole lifeboat. Some planet-bound part of him found this surreal; there were few inhabited worlds where it would have been entirely pointless to abandon a burning ship in the middle of the ocean. Even in cultures where the loss of flesh was taken lightly, there were usually volunteers willing to make the effort to rescue endangered people who felt differently. Perhaps there were some crowded circumplanetary orbits where the shipwrecked could expect to be plucked bodily from the vacuum, but fleeing the *Rindler* as anything but a signal would have been raising optimism to new heights.

As he crossed the final walkway, Tchicaya asked the ship for a view of the entrance to the shuttle. There was no one visible, no one standing guard. He was on the verge of asking for a sequence of images covering the entire remainder of his journey when he spotted a group of people with his own eyes, ahead of him on the walkway. Four of them hung back, while a fifth approached, carrying a long metal bar.

Tchicaya slowed, then halted. The rebel kept walking toward him, briskly and purposefully. Tchicaya's Mediator could detect no signature, but the ship put a name to the face: Selman.

Tchicaya caught his breath, then called out amiably, "Talk to me. Tell me what you want." Selman continued toward him in silence. His face was even more damaged than Santos's; there was a ridge of scarlet running along the side of his nose, and a massive edema around the eye socket. His four companions were similarly marked. If this was a sign of internal disputation, the whole group should have torn itself to shreds weeks ago.

Suddenly, Tchicaya understood. Selman wasn't withholding his signature as a gesture of hostility, or in an attempt to conceal his identity. He had no signature, and no Mediator to send it. He had no Exoself. He had no Qusp. The rebels had improvised some kind of crude surgical tool, and plucked each other's digital brains out.

Tchicaya said, "Talk to me, and I'll find the right translator! We still have all the old languages." He wasn't expecting to be understood, but he could still provoke a response. Assuming Selman hadn't lost the power of speech entirely. Tchicaya didn't know how much neural tissue a *Homo sapiens* needed in order to be fully functional. Bodies like the *Rindler*'s had plenty of neurons in reserve, since the precise delegation of tasks between the digital components and the central nervous system varied widely from culture to culture. He suspected that even this reserve was less than the size of a complete ancestral brain, but a careful redesign might still have packed everything in.

With ten or twelve meters remaining between them, Selman stopped and spoke. Tchicaya couldn't even parse the speech into separate words; to his untrained ear it sounded like a continuous flow. This was the first time in his life that he'd begun a conversation with a stranger without the ground being prepared in advance, without two Mediators conspiring to bridge the gap. A moment after the utterance was complete, though, he recalled the sounds and understood them.

"Turn around and go back, or I'll beat you to a pulp."

Tchicaya replied in the same tongue, or what he hoped was near enough to be comprehensible. His Mediator had traced Selman's words back to a language from twenty-third century Earth, but it was compensating on the fly for the kind of variations that could arise over millennia in an isolated population of the original speakers.

"As opposed to what? Turn around and go back, and fry with the ship?"

Selman said, "If the builders are willing to take the ship away from the border, no one has to fry."

Tchicaya shrugged. "Flee or fry, it's all the same to us. The only thing at stake is access to the border, so every choice that would put an end to that is equivalent. You can fly us all the way to Earth, or you can crack our heads open one by one, but don't expect to get any more cooperation for one alternative than another."

Selman said, "Spare yourself the pain, then. Or the mess, if pain is beneath you." He stepped forward, swinging the bar. Tchicaya had no knowledge of martial arts; he delegated the problem to his Exoself, and watched the interaction as a detached observer until he was standing with one foot on the back of Selman's neck, and holding the bar himself.

"That wasn't even you, you bloodless worm!" Selman hissed.

"Oh, you noticed?" The other four were approaching; two of them were hefting large potted plants, a choice of weapon more alarming for its strangeness than its bulk. "None of this was necessary," Tchicaya said. "Whatever grievance you had, we would have given you a hearing."

"We gave our arguments peacefully," Selman replied. "Hours ago."

"What arguments? Evolutionary imperatives, and winning back territory? We're the ones who've lost two thousand systems. You haven't lost a single ship."

"So you expected us to sit back and do nothing? While you betrayed your own species, and wiped out the last vestiges of humanity?"

Tchicaya was still struggling to come to terms with the rebels' origins. To pass as ordinary travelers at all, they must have translated themselves into versions that ran on their Qusps, as well as their Trojan-horse brains. Lying in wait, impotently watching their other halves act, must have been a deeply unpleasant experience. The neural versions would not have been able to follow much, if any, of what was spoken around them—even when the words passed through their own lips—so the Qusp versions would have had to brief them later, whispering in private in their native tongue. Coming prepared to survive their own preemptive digital lobotomies had been prescient, though. Tchicaya was almost certain now that the builders possessed halt switches for all the ship's Qusps; that would have been the method they'd hoped to use against the rebels heading for the hub, before changing their mind and sending Rasmah and the others in pursuit.

The other four anachronauts stood before Tchicaya. One of them, Christa, said, "Let him go, and back away."

"Or what? You'll beat me to death with your rhododendron?" Tchicaya asked the ship, "What is that? Is it one of yours?"

"Originally, but it's been tweaked."

"Into something dangerous?"

"There's nothing obviously harmful being expressed in the leaves or stalk."

"And the roots?"

"I have no way of knowing about the roots."

Christa repeated, "Let him go, and back away. This is your last chance."

Tchicaya asked his Exoself if it could relieve both rebels of their pots without spilling the contents. It could make no promises.

He said, "I have nothing to gain by retreating."

Christa glanced down at Selman, her mask of grim resolve melting for an instant. She was stranded in a deranged, alien world, and she believed she was about to die.

Tchicaya said, "We can—"

She raised the pot to her shoulder, and started to shake the plant free. Tchicaya told his Exoself to keep as much as it could from falling; he sprang forward, grabbed the stalk, and forced the plant back into its container. As Christa toppled backward, his Exoself had him reach out with his other hand and secure the pot around the roots.

As he did this, in the corner of his eye he saw another anachronaut swinging the second plant by its stalk. The roots were already free of the pot, and the soil around them was falling away. Between the gnarled gray fingers of the roots were dozens of swollen white nodules. Tchicaya told his Exoself to prevent the nodules from coming into contact with anything solid. It knew how fast he was capable of moving, and how fast he needed to be. The task, it declared, was impossible.

The anachronaut slammed the roots of the plant down on the floor.

Tchicaya lost everything but his sense of motion. He was deaf and blind, falling, waiting for an impact. He'd been thrown into the air, so he had to come back down to the ground eventually. That made sense, didn't it?

The impact never came, but his vision was restored in an instant. His suit had turned fully opaque to protect his eyes; now it had decided that it was safe for him to see again. He was outside the *Rindler*, falling away from it. He could see the damaged walkway narrowing into two hourglass waists on either side of the ruptured section, pinching it off, stopping the flow of air. A skein of filaments was already beginning to crisscross the wound.

He looked around for the anachronauts. He spotted one in the distance, silhouetted against the borderlight, sharing the velocity he'd acquired from the *Rindler*'s spin but separated from him by the force of the blast. The limbs were fixed at unnatural angles; he was looking at a corpse. All the ships' bodies could switch modes and cope without oxygen, but between the explosion and the exposure to vacuum there'd been no prospect of anyone surviving unprotected. The rebels had had more time than anyone else to think about putting on suits before endangering themselves, but they'd apparently decided not to bother. That was either willful martyrdom, or the expectation that, whatever happened, no one was going to be left alive to come and rescue them.

Branco spoke. "Are you all right?"

"I think so." If his suit had been damaged at all by the blast, it had since repaired itself, and his Exoself reported nothing more than bruising to his body.

"I'll send the shuttle after you."

Tchicaya said, "Thanks." He waited, watching numbly as the necklace of the ship continued to recede. He was tumbling slowly around an axis that almost coincided with the direction of his motion; the *Rindler* never vanished from sight, but the horizon between the border and the stars wheeled in front of him.

Branco said, "Plan A might not be possible. They've glued the shuttle's release bolts in place."

Tchicaya pondered this, dreamily amused for a moment. The sheer strangeness of his situation had induced a sense of detachment; it was a struggle to think his way back into events on the ship.

"What's happening at the hub?"

"We reviewed what the climbers were doing earlier, in the instrumentation bay," Branco replied. "They were building a particle detector, with some powerful superconducting magnets. Which are now part of the devices they have with them."

"The fuel must be shielded, though? Against stray magnetic fields?" The antimatter portion was kept in a purely magnetic container; that had to be robust.

"Do you have any idea how many orders of magnitude difference there is between stray interstellar fields and the strongest artificial ones?"

Tchicaya took this question to be rhetorical. "How close are Rasmah and the others?" He didn't want to look for himself; he just wanted Branco to give him the good news.

"They're close. But the rebels are already at the hub, setting things up."

"And you believe they might be capable of spilling the fuel?"

"We can't rule that out. It will depend how good their device is. If they're smart, and if they have time, they could pump energy into two different flows that the containment fields couldn't restrain simultaneously."

Tchicaya said nothing. He closed his eyes. He'd screwed up, he'd let his guard down with the anachronauts, but Rasmah was unshakable. She'd stop them, if she got the chance.

Branco said, "We're now seeing flows developing in the fuel." His voice betrayed no hint of panic. After the loss of the Scribe, he'd told Tchicaya that he'd been through local death seven hundred and ninety-six times, but even if he was immune to existential qualms, the prospect of losing contact with the border had to be painful. "Listen to me carefully. There's no way we're going to get the shuttle free in the next few minutes, but we could use the debris-clearance laser to burn through the tether that's holding the module to which the shuttle is docked."

"What good would that do? The whole module is swarming with rebels."

"There are five known rebels—who we've managed to contain by reconfiguring some walls—but there are also three other people. All three are declared Preservationists, but they might still be your allies. If I throw the module clear of the *Rindler*, and everyone else is lost, they might get the shuttle free. And if the *Rindler* survives, at least they'll have a chance of getting back to us."

Tchicaya said, "Who are the three?"

"Alejandro, Wael, and Mariama," Branco replied. "I don't know any of them well. But you're the one who'd be left here with them, so you'd better decide whether that would be to your advantage or not."

The retreating ship was vanishing into the borderlight. Tchicaya didn't want the power to gamble with anyone's fate, but the rebels had left the builders with no choice but to juggle odious alternatives, and now Branco had dragged him into the same quagmire.

If the rebels were trying to destroy the *Rindler*, it was because they believed they had nothing more to do here, which meant that the Right Hand was already primed to scribe Planck worms without further intervention. Sparing everyone in the module wouldn't put the far side in any greater danger, so he should err on the side of saving those people, in the hope that they'd help him fight the Planck worms. If he was left here alone, drifting off into the distance, he might be able to control the Left Hand remotely for a while, but without the shuttle he'd eventually lose radio contact.

The rebels could still be mistaken, though. The first attempt to create the Planck worms could fail. If anyone aligned with the rebels remained, they could work to rectify those early mistakes; they'd have decades to achieve their goal, virtually guaranteeing that the far side would be obliterated. So maybe it would be safer to be left alone, to do whatever he could in the time he had.

It all came down to whether or not one or more of those three people had been swayed by the rebels, as Birago had been swayed. Birago, who'd always seemed passionate but reasonable, and nowhere near as fanatical as Tarek.

Alejandro, Wael, and Mariama.

Branco said, "We've worked out the strategy the rebels are using. It's not the best, but it is effective. If they're not stopped, they'll definitely spill the fuel."

Tchicaya said, "Cut it loose."

He stared at the horizon, watching for some glint from the laser in action, but that was futile. He couldn't see any part of the ship anymore, and the portion of the tether that was glowing white hot would only be centimeters long.

"Branco?"

"Nearly there. It will take a few more seconds. Rasmah's just reached the hub. She's fighting with two of the rebels." Branco chuckled. "Make that one."

Tchicaya's spirits soared. He asked the ship to show him the struggle.

There was no response. He asked again.

On the horizon, a dazzling bead of violet light appeared, out-shining the border. Then his suit shut off his vision.

Chapter 14

When the first, paralyzing wave of despair had left him, Tchicaya tried to contact Mariama. Without success, but he'd steeled himself for that further small blow. He didn't know which way the module had been flung, but with every minute that passed both of them were six kilometers further from the point where the *Rindler* had been, and it was possible that they were already too far apart for direct Mediator-to-Mediator contact. The module would have its own longer-range transceivers, but it was possible that they'd been damaged by the radiation from the *Rindler*'s fireball.

He had to be patient. If Mariama had survived, she would find a way to contact him.

Belatedly, it occurred to him to try the Left Hand. It responded. The vote Yann had spoken of had gone through in time: the Left Hand not only acknowledged his signal, it was willing to take instructions from him.

He had his Mediator construct a virtual replica of the familiar Blue Room console, and he placed himself before it. He merged Yann's toolkit with the interface, and summoned the first simple menu of possibilities. For several seconds, he was too afraid to do anything but stare at the screen. Then he scribed a probe that would enter the far side and return as quickly as possible.

Minutes later, the echo came back to him. The surface layer of the far side, at least, was unchanged, populated by exactly the same mix of vendeks as they'd seen with the first experiment.

He tried a deeper probe. The result was the same: nothing had changed.

Tchicaya left the scape. He watched the horizon hopefully, sifting through the possibilities. The rebels had chosen not to scribe the Planck worms before mounting their attack on the ship. Perhaps they'd feared that they'd encounter more determined resistance from their opponents, if the annihilation of the far side was already playing out right before their eyes. A premature assault on the border would also have weakened the position of the remaining Preservationists, if the mutiny had been crushed. In any case, the fact that they'd felt a need to destroy the *Rindler* implied that the rebels were not confident that the process would be unstoppable once it had begun.

If the rebels hadn't arranged for the loss of the ship to trigger the event immediately, there had to be some kind of timer counting down. If Mariama had got the shuttle free, she might have headed straight for the Right Hand, to pluck it out of the equation completely. If Birago had successfully corrupted it, the Right Hand would not take orders from her, and it was certainly more able to look after itself than the Scribe had been, dodging far larger shifts in the border. But Tchicaya doubted that it was equipped to defend itself from a determined assailant. The shuttle had more powerful engines; if it came down to brute force, she could probably bulldoze the Right Hand straight into the border.

If she reached it in time.

And if she was willing.

* * *

Three and a half hours after the loss of the *Rindler*, the border was transformed. Tchicaya didn't perceive anything approaching; he merely saw the expanse of white light replaced in an instant by an opalescent gray. He turned just in time to catch sight of the edge of the change as it vanished behind him.

The sphere of the border was so vast that the true geometrical horizon was a billion kilometers away, but to his unaided vision everything beyond about a million kilometers occupied a single line, too narrow to resolve. After replaying the event, his calculations could not rule out the possibility that the change had swept by at lightspeed. That would have made it literally impossible to see coming, and then the delayed evidence of the fleeing edge would have given the impression that it was traveling at half its true speed, crossing the million kilometers he could distinguish in about six seconds.

He checked with the Left Hand. Being closer to the border, its field of view was smaller than Tchicaya's, but its instruments left his senses for dead. It had tracked the change he'd witnessed, and judged it to be moving at the speed of light.

Not roughly, not nearly, but, to the limits of measurement, precisely the speed of light. Which meant that the Planck worms could not be pursued, let alone stopped.

The battle was over. The far side was lost.

Tchicaya caught himself angrily. The ability to move across the border at lightspeed didn't guarantee the power to penetrate the far side at the same rate. For all he knew, he'd just seen nothing more than a variation on Branco's surface-pinning effect.

He told the Left Hand to scribe another probe.

It couldn't. The border had retreated.

Retreated how far? The Left Hand couldn't tell him. How do you measure the distance to a featureless, immaterial plane of light? Once the border had slipped out of range of the particle beam of the stylus, the Left Hand had lost the ability to summon forth any kind of echo. It had scattered a small cloud of electronic fireflies, moving at about ten meters a second, to see when they were extinguished. So far, they all remained intact. It was no use tracking the brightness of the borderlight; each square meter of the border would seem dimmer as it retreated, but that effect was canceled out precisely by the fact that any particular instrument you aimed at it, with some fixed angle of view, would be taking in light from a larger portion of the border the further away it was. And there was no Doppler shift to reveal the velocity of retreat: the far side was being pared away, not pushed away, and the new, gray borderlight was being emitted from a succession of different surfaces, not a single moving source that could act as a clock.

The Left Hand had detected a microscopic lowering of the horizon against the backdrop of stars, which did prove that the Planck worms had corroded the far side into vacuum hundreds of thousands of kilometers away. But the line of sight from the Left Hand to the new horizon still only penetrated twenty or so meters below the surface where the border would normally have been; the growing crater could be as shallow as that limit, or it could be a million times deeper.

Tchicaya waited. The fireflies could still wink out at any moment. The Left Hand's engines weren't powerful, and it carried only a small reserve of fuel, but it could adapt to a shift in the border's velocity of a few meters per second.

After ten minutes, nothing had changed. The fireflies were still visible. The border was outracing them.

That did not mean that there was no hope left. But to move the Left Hand faster than the fireflies, to have any chance at all of catching the border, he would need the shuttle.

He was useless on his own, now. It all came down to three Preservationists, and whether or not the hint of life in the far side had been enough to change their minds.

* * *

Tchicaya woke his father with a tug of the hand.

"What is it?" His father squinted at him blearily, but then he smiled and put a finger to his lips. He climbed out of bed and scooped Tchicaya into his arms, then carried him back to his own room.

He put Tchicaya down on the bed and sat beside him.

"You can't sleep?"

Tchicaya shook his head.

"Why? What's wrong?"

Tchicaya didn't need to have the truth coaxed out of him. "I don't want to get older," he said. "I don't want to change."

His father laughed. "Nine isn't old. And nothing's going to change tomorrow." It was his birthday in a few hours' time.

"I know."

"Nothing's going to change for you, for years."

Tchicaya felt a flicker of impatience. "I don't mean my body. I'm not worried about that."

"What, then?"

"I'm going to live for a long time, aren't I? Thousands of years?"

"Yes." His father reached down and stroked Tchicaya's forehead. "You're not worried about death? You know what it would take to kill a person. You'll outlive the stars, if you want to."

Tchicaya said, "I know. But if I do . . . *how will I know that I'm still me?*"

He struggled to explain. He still felt he was the same person as he'd been when he was seven or eight, but he knew that the creature of his earliest memories, of three or four, had been transformed inside his skin. That was all right, because an infant was a kind of half-made person who needed to be absorbed into something larger. He could even accept that in ten years' time, some of his own feelings and attitudes would be different. "But it won't stop, will it? It won't ever stop."

"No," his father agreed.

"Then how will I know I'm changing in the right way? How will I know I haven't turned into someone else?" Tchicaya shuddered. He felt less dread now that he wasn't alone, but his father's mere presence couldn't banish this fear entirely, the way it had banished the terrors of his childhood. If a stranger could displace him, step by step over ten thousand years, the same thing would be happening to everyone. No one around him would be able to help, because they'd all be usurped in exactly the same way.

His father conjured up a globe of the planet and held it toward him, a luminous apparition painted over the gray shadows of the room. "Where are you, right now?"

Tchicaya turned the globe slightly with a gesture, then pointed to their town, Baake.

"Here's a puzzle for you," his father said. "Suppose I draw an arrow here, on the ground in front of you, and tell you it's the most important thing there is." He marked the globe as he spoke. "Wherever you go, wherever you travel, you'll need to find a way to take this arrow with you."

This was too easy. "I'd use a compass," Tchicaya said. "And if I didn't have a compass, I'd use the stars. Wherever I went, I could always find the same bearing."

"You think that's the best way to carry a direction with you? Reproducing its compass bearing?"

"Yes."

His father drew a small arrow on the globe, close to the north pole, pointing due north. Then he drew another on the opposite side of the pole, also pointing due north. The two arrows shared the same compass bearing, but anyone could see that they were pointing in opposite directions.

Tchicaya scowled. He wanted to claim that this was just a perverse exception to an otherwise reasonable rule, but he wasn't sure that was the case.

"Forget about north and south," his father said. "Forget about the stars. This arrow is your only compass; there is nothing else to steer by. You must take it with you. Now tell me how."

Tchicaya stared at the globe. He drew a path leading away from Baake. How could he duplicate the arrow as he moved? "I'd draw another arrow, each time I took a step. The same as the one before."

His father smiled. "Good. But how would you make each new one the same?"

"I'd make it the same length. And I'd make it parallel."

"How would you do that?" his father persisted. "How would you know that the new arrow was parallel to the old one?"

Tchicaya was unsure. The globe was curved, its geometry was complicated. Maybe it would be simpler to start with a flat surface, and then work his way up to the harder case. He summoned a translucent plane and drew an arrow in black. On command, his Mediator could duplicate the object faithfully, anywhere else on the plane, but it was up to him to understand the rules.

He drew a second arrow and contemplated its relationship with the first. "They're parallel. So if you join the two bases and the two tips, they make a parallelogram."

"Yes. But how do you *know* that they make a parallelogram?" His father reached over and skewed the second arrow. "You can tell that I've ruined it, just by looking, but what is it that you're looking for when you see that?"

"The distances aren't the same anymore." Tchicaya traced them with his finger. "From base to base and tip to tip, it's different now. So to make the second arrow a copy of the first, I have to make sure that it's the same length, and that its tip is as far away from the first one's tip as the bases are from each other."

"All right, that's true," his father agreed. "Now suppose I make things more difficult. Suppose I say you have no ruler, no tape measure. You can't measure a distance along one line and duplicate it on another one."

Tchicaya laughed. "That's too hard! It's impossible, then!"

"Wait. You can do this: you can compare distances along the same line. If you go straight from A to B to C, you *can* know if B is exactly half the journey."

Tchicaya gazed at the arrows. There was no half journey here, there was no bisected line in a parallelogram.

"Keep looking," his father urged him. "Look at the things you haven't even drawn yet."

That clue gave it away. "The diagonals?"

"Yes."

The diagonals of the parallelogram ran from the base of the first arrow to the tip of the second, and *vice versa*. And the diagonals divided each other in two.

They worked through the construction together, pinning down the details, making them precise. You could duplicate an arrow by drawing a line from its tip to the base you'd chosen for the second arrow, bisecting that line, then drawing a line from the base of the first arrow, passing through the midpoint and continuing on as far again. The far end of that second diagonal told you where the tip of the duplicate arrow would be.

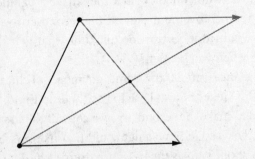

Tchicaya regarded their handiwork with pleasure.

His father said, "Now, how do you do the same thing on a sphere?" He passed the globe over to Tchicaya.

"You just do the same thing. You draw the same lines."

"Straight lines? Curved lines?"

"Straight." Tchicaya caught himself. Straight lines, on a globe? "Great circles. Arcs of great circles." Given any two points on a sphere, you could find a plane that passed through both of them, and also through the center of the sphere. The arc of the equator-sized circle formed where the plane cut through the surface of the sphere gave the shortest distance between the two points.

"Yes." His father gestured at the path Tchicaya had drawn, snaking away from their town. "Go ahead and try it. See how it looks."

Tchicaya copied the arrow once, a small distance along the path, using the parallelogram construction with arcs of great circles for the diagonals. Then he had his Mediator repeat the process automatically, all the way to the end of the path.

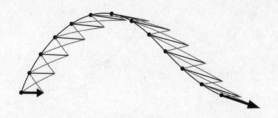

"That's it," Tchicaya marveled. "We've done it." A lattice of diagonals ran along the path, marking the way, carrying the arrow forward. No compass, no stars to steer by, but they'd found a way to copy the arrow faithfully from start to finish.

"It's beautiful, isn't it?" his father said. "This is called Schild's ladder. All throughout geometry, all throughout physics, the same idea shows up in a thousand different guises. How do you carry something from here to there, and keep it the same? You move it step by step, keeping it parallel in the only way that makes sense. You climb Schild's ladder."

Tchicaya didn't ask if the prescription could be extended beyond physics; as an answer to his fears, it was only a metaphor. But it was a metaphor filled with hope. Even as he changed, he could watch himself closely, and judge whether he was skewing the arrow of his self.

"There's one more thing you should see," his father said. He drew a second path on the globe, joining the same two points but following a different route. "Try it again."

"It will be the same," Tchicaya predicted confidently. "If you climb Schild's ladder twice, it will copy the arrow the best way, both times." It was like being asked to add up a dozen numbers twice, grouping them in different ways. The answer had to be the same in the end.

"So try it again," his father insisted.

Tchicaya complied.

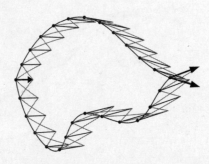

"I've made a mistake," he said. He erased the second ladder, and repeated the construction. Again, the second copy of the arrow at the end of the path failed to match the first.

"I don't understand," Tchicaya complained. "What am I doing wrong?"

"Nothing," his father assured him. "This is what you should expect. There's always a way to carry the arrow forward, but it depends on the path you take."

Tchicaya didn't reply. He'd thought he'd been shown the way to safety, to persistence. Now it was dissolving into contradictions before his eyes.

His father said, "You'll never stop changing, but that doesn't mean you have to drift in the wind. Every day, you can take the person you've been, and the new things you've witnessed, and make your own, honest choice as to who you should become.

"Whatever happens, you can always be true to yourself. But don't expect to end up with the same inner compass as anyone else. Not unless they started beside you, and climbed beside you every step of the way."

Tchicaya made the globe vanish. He said, "It's late. I'd better go to sleep now."

"All right." His father stood as if to leave, but then he reached down and squeezed Tchicaya's shoulder. "There's nothing to be afraid of. You'll never be a stranger, if you stay here with your family and friends. As long as we climb side by side, we'll all change together."

"Tchicaya? Can you hear me?"

It was Mariama.

"Loud and clear," he said. "Are you all right?"

"That depends what you mean by *me*. My Qusp is fine. Parts of my Mediator got fried; I only have a short-range IR link left. My body's not a pretty sight, but it's recovering."

The signal was coming to him via the Left Hand; she'd freed the shuttle and gone there in person. The long-range transceivers in both the module and the shuttle must have suffered irreparable radiation damage, which said something about the likely state of her body.

"What about the others?"

"Wael and Alejandro received similar exposure. They helped me get the shuttle unglued, but they weren't interested in sticking around, with no mod cons and such poor company. Birago's body seemed to be in better shape than mine, but the builders halted his Qusp, so he's as good as departed. When I left, the other rebels were all in a bad way; some of their bodies had reverted to undifferentiated goo, and even in the ones that were still intact and breathing, I'd be surprised if their minds have survived the repair process."

She was probably right; the bodies would make liberal use of apoptosis to kill off radiation-damaged cells, and there was no reason for them to treat neural tissue any differently.

Mariama said, "I went to the Right Hand first, but it had already scribed the Planck worms. It wasn't pursuing the border down, but I gave it a nudge in the opposite direction, too fast for it to reverse. If we find some use for it, I could go and drag it back, but I'm hoping the Left Hand will be enough."

"It will have to be." Nothing they did to the Right Hand would render it trustworthy.

"Branco told me about the toolkit Yann gave you, while he was cutting us loose, but I didn't have time to get a copy myself. The simplest thing might be if you send it to me now, before I go chasing the border."

"What?" Tchicaya stared at the red-shifted stars above the horizon, checking the view for any sign that he'd departed from reality and was hallucinating this entire encounter. "Why would that be simplest? You're coming to get me, aren't you?"

"That would be an awful waste of fuel. You don't need to be here, physically."

Tchicaya was silent for a moment. She was right about the fuel, but he couldn't accept what she was proposing.

"That's not true," he said. "If I stay out here, I'm going to lose radio contact, eventually. From sheer distance in the long run, but if the border has taken on a complicated shape, I might lose my line of sight much sooner."

"Then give me the key to the Left Hand. With that, and the toolkit, I can manage everything." She sighed. "Don't be precious about this. I don't like the idea of leaving you to drift away, but there are more important things at stake here. The time and the fuel I used fetching you could make all the difference to the far side."

Tchicaya felt a flicker of temptation. He could wash his hands of everything, and wake beside Rasmah on Pfaff. Mariama was being perfectly logical; time was against them, and apart from the secondhand skills that he could easily sign over to her, he was superfluous.

He wanted to trust her. Hadn't she earned that? They'd had no end of differences, but she had always been honest with him. It seemed petty and mean-spirited to keep on doubting her.

The trouble was, he didn't trust his own motives. Thinking the best of her would be the perfect excuse to absolve himself of all responsibility.

He said, "I'm not handing you anything. If you care so much about the far side, you'd better come and get me."

Mariama remained seated at the front of the shuttle as Tchicaya clambered out of the airlock. He nodded a greeting, and tried to smile. Her Exoself would be discouraging her from doing anything to interfere with her body's healing, by means both gentler and more precise than a blanket of agony; extrapolating from the raw pain of the minor burns he'd willingly experienced as a child was absurd. Still, the sight of her weeping, blistered skin made his guts tighten.

He said, "Hitchhiking in space isn't so bad. I've waited longer for a ride, on land."

Mariama replied through the IR link. "Try showing more flesh. That always works wonders."

On their way back to the Left Hand, Tchicaya received the first good news he'd heard since the moratorium vote. The horizon had stopped falling. The Left Hand was no longer seeing new stars creeping into view.

That in itself didn't fix the depth of the lost region everywhere, but the particular geometry was suggestive. The new horizon was exactly where it would have been if the Planck worms had failed to penetrate the signaling layer, where the vendek population changed abruptly, a hundred kilometers into the far side.

As they approached the Left Hand, the news became even better. The fireflies had finally begun to vanish, and the timing of their deaths confirmed the best possible scenario: the border had retreated to the signaling layer, and no further.

Tchicaya was elated, but Mariama said, "Don't assume this is the new *status quo*. Birago wasn't exactly confiding in me toward the end, but if what he's done here bears any resemblance to the work I was involved in with Tarek, the Planck worms won't have given up at the first obstacle."

"Meaning what?"

"They'll mutate. They'll experiment. They'll keep on varying themselves, until they find a way to break through."

"You knew how to do that? You had it all worked out?"

"No," she admitted. "But as soon as you showed us the vendeks themselves, they provided an awful lot of inspiration. Tarek and I didn't pursue that, but don't expect Birago to have passed up the opportunity."

They docked with the Left Hand, and carried it down to the point where the fireflies were disappearing.

Regaining alignment with the border took almost an hour, as a cycle of increasingly delicate adjustments brought the stylus into range. Once that was achieved, Tchicaya scribed a series of probes that would spread out laterally as well as moving straight in, improving their chances of gaining a comprehensive picture of the Planck worms. Unsurprisingly, now that the signaling layer was infected with Planck worms and exposed to vacuum, it was no longer vibrating, no longer tapping out primes. Tchicaya longed to discover the mechanism that had driven it, but he had to stay focused; trying to dissect the far-siders' ruined SETI equipment—if that was what it was—had to take second place to dealing with the plague the beacon had been unable to deter on its own.

As he launched the last probe, he turned to Mariama. "If you gave me all the details of the work you did with Tarek, there'd be no need for you to hang around."

She emitted a disgusted wheezing noise, the first real sound he'd heard her make. "Is that some kind of childish comeback, because I didn't want to waste fuel on making you cozy?"

"No. But I'm the one who came to the *Rindler* to protect the far side. There's no reason for you to keep crawling over broken glass for the sake of someone else's agenda."

Mariama searched his face. "You really don't trust me, do you?"

"To do what? To betray your own ideals? You always wanted to wipe this thing out."

"I never thought that would involve genocide."

"We're still not certain that it would."

She sighed, bodily. "So you're afraid that if we find a natural explanation for the signaling layer, my presence might suddenly become embarrassing?"

"Wouldn't it?"

"I voted for the moratorium," she said. "I voted to do nothing but look for signs of life, for a full year. Whatever happens, I'll honor that commitment."

Tchicaya experienced a twinge of shame, but he didn't back

off. He said, "Make up your mind. Are you here to protect the far side? Or are you here to relaunch the Planck worms in a year's time, if the far side proves to be sterile?"

Mariama shook her head. "Why do I have to choose? If there are sentient creatures in there, they deserve our protection. If there's nothing but an exotic ocean full of different kinds of Planck-scale algae, then the sooner it's rendered safely back into vacuum, the better. Is that distinction really so hard to grasp? What did I ever do to get lumped in with the rebels, in your head? When's the last time I displayed nineteenth-century morality?"

"Twenty-third."

"That just shows how little history you know. Most people who left Earth in that era did so precisely because they were out of step with contemporary mores. In this case, I'd say they were about four centuries behind the times."

Tchicaya looked away. Was she protesting too much? But she was just as entitled as he was to be contemptuous of the anachronauts' views. Being wise after the fact about the complexity of the far side, and the unwitting genocide the Preservationists might have committed, was like blaming the Mimosans for failing to anticipate the failure of the Sarumpaet rules.

The probes began returning. The Planck worms they revealed were dauntingly complex structures, at least as elaborate as the vendeks themselves. And Mariama had been right: they'd begun to mutate, to try out variations. The software counted thousands of strains.

Even if they were capable of adaptation, though, they were too simple to achieve it through anything but trial and error. Their designer had left them to fend for themselves, and in the end that would leave them as vulnerable as any other dumb pathogen.

Tchicaya addressed the toolkit, allowing Mariama to listen in. "Find a graph we can scribe that will wipe these things out— without moving deeper and damaging the native vendeks." As he spoke the words, this sounded like a breathtakingly optimistic request, but the Planck worms themselves had been seeded from a single point, so there was no reason why the antidote couldn't be introduced the same way.

There was a perceptible delay while the toolkit explored the problem. "I don't believe that's possible," it declared. "The Planck worms are exploiting the ordinary vacuum behind them: they set up correlations across the border that cause the vendeks to deco-here. I'm unable to find a method of attacking the Planck worms that wouldn't also destroy the whole vendek population in which they're immersed."

Mariama said, "What if the vendek population changes, deeper in?"

"Anything might be possible then, but until I know the details, there are no guarantees."

Tchicaya scribed probes to look deeper.

The second change swept the border as swiftly as the first. Through the windows of the shuttle, they saw the smooth gray plain transformed into a complex, striated pattern of dozens of bright hues. Tchicaya's heart raced; it was like watching a pool of acid eat its way down through featureless rock, exposing thousands of delicately layered sediments.

Mariama said, "The border must be motionless again, or we'd see the pattern changing. So the Planck worms have hit more obstacles. We might have killed them off, if we'd burnt away this whole layer first."

"Including whatever it contained," Tchicaya countered. "We have no idea what might have been there."

Mariama replied flatly, "Whatever was there, it's gone now anyway."

Tchicaya said nothing, but she was right. If he'd acted more swiftly, they might have cauterized the wound. If he was going to refuse to make decisions with imperfect knowledge, he might as well give up intervening and simply leave the far-siders to protect themselves.

The Left Hand had launched fresh fireflies immediately, but he wasn't going to wait for them. He told the shuttle to follow them down, keeping just enough distance to be sure it could decelerate in time.

The new border lay some sixty kilometers down, but its altitude was no longer constant; the shuttle came to a halt in the middle of a sinuous valley. The borderlight around them revealed the striations they'd seen from afar to be just one level of structure: the bands were crossed with networks of fine, dark lines, superimposed over shifting waves of increased luminosity. And this was just the naked-eye view of a ravaged landscape, exposed to the vacuum and thick with alien marauders. What the pristine depths contained on a xennometer scale, Tchicaya couldn't begin to imagine, but between these macroscopic structures and the vendeks themselves, the opportunities for complex life were greater than ever.

While they waited for the stylus to realign itself, Mariama said, "Can I ask the toolkit something?"

Tchicaya nodded warily.

"How complex an algorithm could you inject into the far side?" she said.

The toolkit replied, "On what time scale? If you give me long enough, there are no limits."

"How long would it take to inject yourself?"

"Scribing all the data directly with the Left Hand? About a hundred thousand years."

Mariama laughed in infrared. "What about other ways of doing it? What's the most efficient method that would be achievable with the hardware at our disposal?"

The toolkit fell silent, conducting an exhaustive search.

Tchicaya said, "What's this about?"

"We're blind up here," she replied. "All our time and effort is going into shuttling information back and forth across the border. Yann and the others have given you a lot of valuable knowledge, but the place where it needs to be applied is the far side."

The toolkit said, "I could scribe a series of graphs that would give rise to a far-side structure that would let me send data through the border as modulated light. That would take seventeen minutes. The total bandwidth would then be about one zettabyte per second. I could send myself through in a millisecond."

"In a form that could then travel deeper, away from the border?"

"Possibly. I could wrap the basic quantum processor in a shell of motile vendeks. It still might not be able to survive in every environment it encountered, but it could send out probes to explore its surroundings, and it could tweak the vendek populations in the protective shell as it moved."

"What about communications with the near side?" Mariama asked.

"I could try to maintain a shielded data cable back to the border, but the prospects for that look much poorer. The Planck worms are going to attack the border interface, and anything else that isn't moving faster than they are."

"Okay. But you could operate autonomously, once you were in there?"

"Sure."

Tchicaya said, "You want to just drop it through and tell it to improvise from there?"

"Why not? What's it up against? It's a lot smarter than the Planck worms. It would know exactly what it was doing."

"On one level." Tchicaya asked the toolkit, "How would you go about recognizing sentient life?"

"I have no idea," it admitted. "I have no information about that concept, beyond the rudimentary epistemological sketch that's stored in the conversational interface you're now addressing."

Tchicaya said, "I've spoken to cribs with more sense than that. We can't unleash it on the far side as a free agent."

Mariama closed her eyes. Clear fluid was spilling from fissures in her scalp and running down her face. She said, "My Exoself now tells me that this body's packing up. It thought it could repair itself, but there's too much damage. I'm afraid you're about to be stuck with a corpse."

Tchicaya reached over and took her hand, gently. "I'm sorry."

"It's all right," she said. "I've never gone acorporeal before, but I'm not a fanatic. A few days without flesh won't kill me." She smiled, splitting the skin on her face. "If you live long enough, you get to compromise on everything."

As Tchicaya watched, she let go of her body. Her breathing halted, and she slumped sideways. The flesh of her hand became rigid beneath his fingers; the individual cells had given up trying to maintain the integrity of the tissues they comprised, and had started to encyst, protecting themselves as best they could in case they were of any use for recycling.

Tchicaya felt tears spilling down his face. "Fuck." Mariama could no longer hear him; the IR link to her Mediator had worked via nerve and skin cells, and that was the only functioning route into her Qusp. She was deaf, dumb, and blind now, until he dug her out.

He made his way to the shuttle's tool bin, and selected something long and sharp. Then he strapped himself into the seat beside her, to keep himself from being pushed away by the force he applied.

Tchicaya knew that she was beyond harm, but he couldn't stop weeping as he cut into her flesh. He was not an acorporeal. He had never found a way to love her that entirely surrendered the notion that her body was the thing to cherish and protect.

He got the three devices out: three small, dark spheres chained together with optical cables. The Mediator and the Exoself both bore a fuzz of fine gray wires that had tapped into the body's nervous system.

Tchicaya consulted his own Mediator; it wasn't a great resource compared to the *Rindler*'s library, but it knew all about its own design. Given a disembodied version of the same hardware, with the radio transceiver fried, how could he reestablish contact?

His Mediator described the specialized hardware that could do this. The shuttle was carrying nothing even remotely similar.

Tchicaya contemplated the bloodied parts in his hand. He'd asked her once to leave him, so he could complete this task alone. Now he appeared to have had his request granted.

"There are no other ways to make contact?" he asked his Mediator.

"Not if the device remains disembodied."

He couldn't grow her a new body from scratch; there was no time. And the cells of the old one had already done their best; they would not be coaxed back into operation.

Tchicaya said, "What if it was inside someone else's flesh? Inside a body with another Mediator?"

"Where, exactly?"

"Where would it have to be?"

"Inside the skull. Or very close to the spinal cord."

That was the solution, then. Tchicaya steeled himself. He still wasn't certain where her loyalties finally lay, but he was even less certain that he could go on without her.

He stripped of his bloodied clothes, and peeled away his suit. Then he asked his Exoself to guide him. It knew the position of every nerve and blood vessel in his body, and it could move his hands with great precision.

* * *

The stylus came into alignment with the border. Tchicaya launched a swarm of probes, then instructed the toolkit to start work automatically as soon as the echoes began returning: designing a replicator that would burn away all the current strains of Planck worms, whatever the cost to the vendeks around them.

Mariama spoke. "What's happening?"

Tchicaya said, "You're behind my right kidney. My nervous system's just managed to link up with your Mediator."

This revelation only fazed her for a moment. "I didn't even think about communication. That body failed so suddenly, I didn't have time to make plans."

"Are you okay?"

"Absolutely."

"What are you simulating?"

"Nothing, yet. I've just been thinking in the dark."

"Do you want to share my senses?" It was what he would have asked for, himself, if their roles had been reversed: anything to anchor his mind to reality, even if it was secondhand.

Mariama hesitated. "I'd like access, thanks, but I'll make myself an icon with a viewpoint in a scape, and put your vision up on a screen. I don't want to start pretending that I'm inhabiting your body. Since I can't actually control it, that would just make me feel trapped."

"Right." Tchicaya felt a frisson of anxiety, but the notion that he'd invited in a guest who could mount a coup was pure fantasy. Every connection between his nerve cells and her Mediator was entirely under the control of his Exoself; right down to the molecular level, this body would only take instructions from the matching hardware.

"Keep talking while I do that," she said. "What's the situation with the border?"

Tchicaya brought her up to date.

Mariama was puzzled. "You're not scribing the interface?"

"What's the use?" he replied. "That would only tie up the stylus. We're better off trying to kill the Planck worms from the outside. That way, we can use their own trick against them: we can correlate them with the vacuum, make them decohere. It's a simpler problem. All we have to do is scribe something aggressive enough to take them on, but with a dead-end design that will fail completely at the next change of vendeks."

"You might be right," she conceded. "I hope it is that simple."

Tchicaya looked out across the rainbow-hued landscape. Everything that happened here—all the destruction wrought by the Planck worms, and by their putative remedy—would spread out at the speed of light across the entire border. The vendeks' diversity seemed to have acted as an effective barrier so far, but there could be gaps in that defense, threads or channels of identical populations running deep into the far side. He was gambling on a dizzying scale, like some dilettante ecologist in Earth's colonial era, trying to balance one introduced predator against another.

The toolkit spoke. "I'm afraid the Planck worms have been sneakier than I expected. The need to attack a new mix of vendeks hasn't filtered out any of the old mutations; they've all hitched a ride down with their successful cousins. So there are more than ten million different variants now. I can scribe seeds for individual replicators that would wipe out all of them, but that's going to take more than nine hours."

"Start doing that immediately," Tchicaya said, "but also start thinking about a single seed that could do the same job."

The toolkit pondered his second request. "I can't see a way to do that without scribing something every bit as virulent as the Planck worms. It would have to mutate, itself, in order to deal with all the variants, and there's no guarantee that it wouldn't either burn out prematurely, or not at all."

Mariama said, "We can't count on nine hours at the border.

And if it falls again before we've finished the job, the next time can only be harder."

"So what do you suggest?"

"I've told you what I think we have to do," she said.

"Drop something through that can work from the inside? And I've told you what's wrong with that. There are no magic bullets so smart that you can fire them into an uncharted world and expect them to repel an invader without destroying everything they're meant to be saving." He laughed bitterly. "It's hard enough believing that I can make those judgments myself."

"I know. Which is why you need to start making them from the other side of the border."

Tchicaya had suspected that this was where she was heading, when death interrupted her train of thought. He'd hoped to render the whole idea superfluous before she got around to putting it into words.

"You think I should send myself in?"

"The data rate would be fast enough. Seventeen minutes to build the interface, then about an hour to get you through."

"And then what? All our strategies for dealing with the Planck worms rely on correlating them with the vacuum. You can't do that from the inside."

"So you look for other strategies," Mariama insisted, "once you've gone deep enough to have a better idea of what's safe and what isn't. I'm not saying we should give up working from this side, but there are advantages to both. A two-pronged attack can only improve our chances."

Tchicaya had run out of arguments. He looked up at his reflection in the window, knowing she could see it. "I can't do this alone," he said. "I can't go in there without you."

He waited for some scathing rebuke. This was even more self-indulgent than demanding that she pluck him from the vacuum, when he should have been willing to drift stoically into oblivion.

The worst of it was, he still harbored doubts about her. How many chances to rid himself of her presence was he going to turn down?

Mariama said, "Joined at the hip, after four thousand years?"

"Joined at the kidney."

"I take it you won't let me go in by myself?"

"No. Think of this as extending the old protocols for the Scribe. There always had to be an observer from the other faction, to keep everyone honest."

Tchicaya tried to keep his voice lighthearted, but this felt like the final recognition of the way it was between them. He had always followed her, every step of the way. Out of Slowdown, away from Turaev. Even in the centuries they'd spent apart, his own travels, his own adventures, had only seemed possible once she'd blazed the trail. He was not ashamed of this, but he wished he'd faced it squarely much sooner. He wished he'd told Rasmah, when the rebels first showed their hand: *I am not the one to leave behind here. You head for the shuttle, I'll head for the hub. Anyone can toss saboteurs from the scaffolding. But not everyone could walk into the far side alone.*

Mariama said, "All right, I'll go with you. We can keep each other honest. But the process has to be set up so it doesn't jeopardize everything. If the border starts falling while only one of us is through, the vehicle will have to be programmed to interrupt the transfer, and dive without the second passenger."

"That makes sense," Tchicaya conceded.

"Which only leaves one thing to be decided."

"What's that?"

"Who goes first."

Chapter 15

Tchicaya looked out from the *Sarumpaet* into a lime-green sea. In the distance, glistening partitions, reminiscent of the algal membranes that formed the cages in some aquatic zoos, swayed back and forth gently, as if in time to mysterious currents. Behind each barrier the sea changed color abruptly, the green giving way to other bright hues, like a fastidiously segregated display of bioluminescent plankton.

The far side here was a honeycomb of different vendek populations, occupying cells about a micron wide. The boundaries between adjoining cells all vibrated like self-playing drums; none were counting out prime numbers, but some of the more complex rhythms made it seem almost plausible that the signaling layer had been nothing but a natural fluke. Even if that were true, though, Tchicaya doubted that it warranted relief at the diminished prospect that sentient life was at stake. The signaling layer might have brought him this far, but with millions of unexplored cubic light-years beneath him, judging the whole far side on that basis would be like writing off any possibility of extraterrestrial life because the constellations weren't actually animals in the sky.

The view he was looking at was a construct, albeit an honest one. The *Sarumpaet* was constantly "illuminating" its surroundings with probes, but they were more like spy insects than photons, and they had to return in person with the details of everything they'd encountered, rather than radioing back images from afar. His body, the vehicle itself—a transparent bubble like a scaled-down version of the *Rindler*'s observation module, with an added checkerboard of windows in the floor—and the gravity he felt, were all pure fiction.

He turned to Mariama's icon-in-waiting, complete up to the shoulders now. Her body was rendered as a transparent container, slowly filling with color and solidity from a trickle of light flowing down through a glassy pipe that ran all the way to the border. Tchicaya looked up along the pipe to the roiling layer of Planck worms, inky violets and blacks against the cheerful false pastels of the vendeks. Every few seconds, a dark thread would snake down toward him, like a tentacle of malignant tar invading a universe of fruit juice. So far, the vendeks had always responded by pinching off the thread and extinguishing the intruders. The *Sarumpaet* avoided sharing this fate by wrapping itself in a coat that mimicked the stable layers it saw around it, but though the Planck worms could only hope to achieve the same kind of immunity by stumbling on it blindly, once they did, they'd put it to a far less benign use.

Tchicaya was running his own private Slowdown, to keep the wait from being unbearable; the Planck-scale quantum gates of the *Sarumpaet* could have made the hour stretch out into an eternity. The toolkit was using its enhanced speed to broaden its search for new strategies, though as yet this had yielded nothing promising. The ten million individual Planck-worm-killers it had designed on the near side could have been scribed here in a fraction of a microsecond instead of the original nine hours, but most of them would have consumed the *Sarumpaet* itself in an instant. Tchicaya would not have minded mimicking the anachronauts and going out in his own blaze of glory, but only if he was unleashing a fire that was certain to be both effective and self-limiting.

Mariama was beginning to develop a chin. Tchicaya asked the icon if it was representing the proportion of data received through volume, or height.

"Volume."

The crisp image of her body began to soften, but it was the scape's lighting that was changing, not the icon itself. Tchicaya looked up to see a dark, fist-shaped protuberance pushing its way through the vendeks. An instinct from another era tensed every muscle in his simulated body, but he wouldn't need to make a split-second decision, let alone act on it physically; the *Sarumpaet* itself would determine when it had to flee. Dropping out of Slowdown to monitor events at a glacial pace would only be masochistic; he would speed up automatically as soon as the flight began.

The infestation of Planck worms spread out like a thundercloud. As the dark layer brushed the tube that represented the link across the border, the *Sarumpaet* launched itself down into the far side.

The single, brooding cloud exploded into a storm of obsidian, rushing toward the ship like a pyroclastic flow. Tchicaya had sprinted down the slopes of a volcano on Peldan, racing hot gas and ash, but the effortless speed of the *Sarumpaet* made this dash for safety even more nerve-wracking. The risk of being overtaken on foot was only to be expected, but the ship's pattern of data was propagating at close to the maximum rate the environment permitted. There was no such thing as lightspeed here, but he was nudging a barrier that was just as insurmountable.

As he glanced down, he saw that the visibility had diminished; the probes were traveling as far ahead as ever, but the *Sarumpaet* was racing forward to meet them. The toolkit would still have the crucial information it needed to adapt the ship's harnessed vendeks to changes in the environment, but the faster they fled, the less time it would have to cope with any surprises.

The first boundary was almost upon them, but they'd probed this one thoroughly in advance. As the ship crossed through the glistening membrane—an act portrayed as a simple mechanical feat, but which amounted to redesigning and rebuilding the entire hull—a motion within the scape caught Tchicaya's eye.

Mariama turned to him with a triumphant smile. "That's what I call an amphibious vehicle: glides smoothly from microverse to microverse, whatever their dynamic spectra."

He stared at her. "You weren't—"

"Complete? Ninety-three percent should be good enough. I packaged myself very carefully; don't take that decapitated progress icon literally." She looked up. "Oh, shit. That wasn't meant to happen."

Tchicaya followed her gaze. The Planck worms had already crossed the boundary. Some freeloading mutation, useless against the earlier obstacles, must have finally proven its worth. Their adversary was not dispersing, weakening as it spread; it was like an avalanche, constantly building in strength. If the Planck worms retained every tool they tried out, whether or not it was immediately successful, their range of options would be growing at an exponential rate.

"You have to hand it to Birago," Mariama observed begrudgingly. "The killer twist was his, not Tarek's or mine. We were too hung up on the notion of mimicking natural replicators—as if nature ever made plagues that were optimized for destroying anything."

"Humans did. He might have had some tips from the anachronauts."

They crossed into another cell of the honeycomb, as smoothly as before. Tchicaya wasn't entirely sure what would happen if the *Sarumpaet* failed to negotiate a population transition, but whether it was the Planck worms or some hostile strain of vendeks that rushed in and consumed them, they wouldn't have much time to dwell on their fate before they blinked out of existence. As local deaths went, he'd had worse.

He watched the Planck worms as they reached the partition; this time, they appeared to be trapped. However many mutations were part of the throng, they couldn't include an exhaustive catalog of all the possibilities. The toolkit was X-raying each gate and designing the perfect key as they approached; that strategy had to win out some of the time.

If not always by a wide margin. Tchicaya was just beginning to picture the *Sarumpaet* streaking ahead triumphantly, when the second barrier fell to the Planck worms.

He addressed the toolkit. "Is there anything we can throw in their way? Anything we can scribe that would act as an obstacle?"

"I could trigger the formation of a novel layer population. But that would take time, and it would only stretch across a single vendek cell." However long the artificial barrier held, the Planck worms would still percolate down along other routes.

They glided through a dozen more cells, maintaining a tenuous lead. Even when they appeared to be widening the gap, there was no guarantee that they wouldn't plunge into a cell to find that the Planck worms had reached the same point more quickly by a different route.

The honeycomb stretched on relentlessly; the *Sarumpaet* gained and lost ground. After eight hours of nominal ship time, they'd crossed a thousand cells. In near-side terms, they were a millimeter beneath the point where the border had last rested, and the chase had gone on for mere picoseconds. The Planck worms had spent more than two hours diversifying before they'd learned to penetrate these catacombs, but having found the basic trick they appeared to be unstoppable. So much for the strategy of burning away one vendek population and the predators trapped within it; that would have been like trying to cure a victim of bubonic plague by sterilizing a single pustule.

Tchicaya said, "If this goes on for a hundred kilometers, I'm going to lose my mind."

"We could go into Slowdown," Mariama suggested. "We wouldn't risk missing anything; the ship could bring us up to speed in an instant."

"I know. I'd rather not, though. It just feels wrong."

"Like sleeping on watch?"

"Yeah."

Three days later, Tchicaya gave in. The honeycomb could prove to be a centimeter thick, or a light-year; the probes could barely see half a micron ahead. They had no decisions to make; until something changed, all they were doing was waiting.

"Just don't go dropping out on your own," he warned Mariama.

"To do what?" She gestured at the spartan scape. "This makes Turaev in winter look exciting."

Tchicaya gave the command, and the honeycomb blurred around them, the palette of false colors assigned to the vendeks—already recycled a dozen times to take on new meanings—merging into a uniform amber glow. It was like riding a glass bullet through treacle. Above them, the Planck worms retreated, crept forward, slipped back again. The *Sarumpaet* inched ahead, but in fast motion the race looked even closer than before, their advantage even more tenuous.

As the Slowdown deepened, their progress grew smoother. After a full nanosecond of near-side time, they appeared to be leaving the Planck worms behind. After a microsecond, the worms slipped back out of range of the probes, and there was nothing to be seen but the *Sarumpaet* itself, and the honeyed esophagus down which it was gliding.

At sixty microseconds, the toolkit signaled an alarm and the ship dragged them back to full speed.

The *Sarumpaet* had stopped moving, in the middle of a cell of pale blue vendeks. "The probes can't go any deeper," the toolkit explained. "We've reached a new kind of boundary: whatever's behind it is qualitatively different from all the vendek mixes we've encountered so far."

Tchicaya glanced down into the darkness, as if his eyes could reveal something that the probes, responsible for the entire scene, had missed.

Mariama frowned. "Different how?"

"I have no idea. The probes don't even scatter back from the boundary. I've tried redesigning them, but nothing works. Anything I send down simply vanishes." For all its knowledge and speed, the toolkit had never been intended to act as much more than a repository of facts. It couldn't begin to cope with novelty in the manner of the people who'd contributed to it.

They sat and discussed the possibilities. Tchicaya had learned quite a bit from his faction's experts, and Mariama even more, but they needed a bigger group; on the *Rindler*, everyone's ideas had sparked off someone else's.

For weeks, they argued and experimented. They took turns sleeping for an hour each; even without any fixed, bodily need to recuperate, their minds were still structured to function best that way. The toolkit diligently analyzed vast lists of possibilities, sorting through the quantum states that might be swallowing all their probes without a trace, hunting for a new design that would avoid that fate and return with solid information.

Nothing worked. The darkness beneath them remained inscrutable.

They had no way of knowing how long it would be until the Planck worms came flooding down after them. On bad days, Tchicaya consoled himself with the thought that when they died, the Planck worms might be buried with them. On worse days, he faced the possibility that brute mutation would find a way through, where all their passion and borrowed ingenuity had failed.

On the thirty-seventh day, Tchicaya woke and looked around the scape. They'd tried all manner of distractions for the sake of inspiration, but no stroll through a forest, no mountain hike, no swim across a sunlit lake had led them to the answer. So they'd stopped ransacking their memories for places to camp, and returned to the unpalatable truth. They were stranded in an ugly, barren cave in the pockmarked rind of an alien universe, waiting to be corroded into noise by a billion species of ravenous sludge.

Mariama smiled encouragingly. "Any revelatory dreams?"

"I'm afraid not." He'd dreamed he was a half-trained Sapper from the legend, suddenly confronted by a new kind of bomb, falling beside it toward a landscape of shadows that might have been anything from a desert to a vast metropolis.

"My turn, then. Come on, get up."

"I will. Soon." She could just as easily conjure up a bed of her own, but taking turns with one imposed a kind of discipline.

Tchicaya closed his eyes again. Sleep had lost all power to assuage his weariness, but it was still an escape while it lasted. He'd understood from the start that their struggle was quixotic, but he'd never imagined such a dispiriting end. They'd spend their last days writing equations on paper planes, and tossing them into an abyss.

As he drifted back toward sleep, he pictured himself gathering up a mountain of crumpled paper and heaving it out of the *Sarumpaet* into the darkness below. If by chance some scrap went wafting through into another world, he'd never even know that he'd succeeded.

He opened his eyes. "We launch all our paper planes at once.

Then we throw a message back, and use it to clear away all the garbage."

Mariama sighed. "What are you ranting about?"

Tchicaya beamed at her. "We have a list of the kind of states the region below us might be in, and we have strategies for dealing with them all. But we still haven't found a probe that will cross through and return—giving us a definite answer, letting us know which strategy to use. Fine. We put the *Sarumpaet* into a super-position of states, in which it tries them all simultaneously."

Mariama was speechless. It took Tchicaya several seconds to interpret this response; he had rarely surprised her, and he had certainly never shocked her before.

She said, "Who cares about quantum divergence, if one world out of every quadrillion is the best of all possible worlds? That sounds like some desperate fatalist nonsense from the last days before the Qusp."

Tchicaya shook his head, laughing. "I know! *But it's not!* Answer me this: a quantum computer does a search for the solution to an equation, testing a few trillion candidates simultaneously. In how many worlds does it fail?"

Mariama scowled. "None, if there's a solution at all. But that's different. The divergence is all internal and contained; it doesn't split the environment into branches halfway through the calculation." A flicker of uncertainty crossed her face. "You don't think we could—"

Tchicaya said, "We're not in the near side anymore. Coherence is nowhere near as fragile here. Whatever this gulf is that we're facing, there's no fundamental reason why we shouldn't be able to stretch a single quantum computer all the way across it. And if we handle all the strategies with sufficient care, we ought to be able to manipulate the whole coherent system so that the failures cancel out."

She nodded slowly, then broke into an astonished grin. "We

reach out and swallow the problem; we internalize it completely. Then we can bludgeon our way through by trial and error, without the world ever seeing a single mistake."

They spent three days refining the idea, thrashing out the details with the toolkit and the ship. It was a complex maneuver, and it would require precise control over the ship's environment, both before and after it crossed through the boundary. The toolkit had had plenty of time to study the surrounding vendeks, and it understood the physics of this obscure *cul-de-sac* as thoroughly as that of the near-side vacuum itself. The second half of the problem could not be dealt with by direct observation, but that didn't mean they'd be taking a leap into the dark. Each strategy for making the crossing relied on a set of assumptions about the other side. Once they put the ship into a superposition of strategies, each component would know the kind of place it would end up in, if it ended up anywhere at all.

Tchicaya snapped awake, knowing the reason instantly. He'd been summoned to alertness by the tug of a trip wire that he'd installed, back on the near side, when he'd worked with the toolkit to construct a software container to sit between their minds and the raw quantum gates of the ship's processor.

Mariama was seated a short distance away, gazing out into the vendek cell. Tchicaya said, "Do you want to tell me what you're doing?"

She turned to him, frowning slightly. "Just rearranging a few things internally. I didn't realize I had so little privacy."

"I own this whole setup," he said. "You knew that when you came into it."

Mariama spread her arms. "Fine. Rummage through my memories; see if I care."

Tchicaya sat up on the edge of the bed. "What were you trying to expel into the environment?" At the border of the simulated Qusp in which her mind was cocooned, he'd replaced some of the more arcane facilities of the standard hardware—things she'd have no good reason to want to use, under the circumstances—with fakes that merely rang alarm bells. It had been a last-minute decision; the toolkit would have happily simulated the Qusp in its entirety, as the simplest means of guaranteeing that everything worked smoothly when it was piped through.

"Nothing," she said. "It was a mistake. I didn't even realize you'd put me in a cage, so I brushed against the bars by accident." She waved a hand at him irritably. "Go back to sleep."

He rose to his feet. "Are you going to tell me, or am I going to have to look for myself?" In an ordinary Qusp, the owner of the hardware could freeze the whole program and inspect its state at leisure. But the quantum gates here were implemented at too low a level; there was no room for that approach. All he could do was send in a swarm of utility algorithms to search for anything suspicious, while shuffling her working mind aside. That would do no lasting damage, but he had no idea how she would experience it. It could be extremely unpleasant.

Mariama regarded him calmly. "You do whatever you think you have to. I've already been flayed once."

Tchicaya hesitated. He did not want to hurt her, and if he was wrong, he'd never be able to look her in the eye again. There had to be another way to call her bluff.

"There's no need," he said. "I know exactly what you were trying to do." He wasn't certain of anything, but of all the possibilities he could imagine, one stood out sharply.

"Really? Do you want to enlighten me?"

"You brought in a stock of qubits entangled with the near side. You had to get rid of them now, or they would have shown up tomorrow when we prepared the ship." Anything that interacted with an entangled qubit would have its phase irretrievably scrambled. To a pure quantum system they'd be poison. They'd have to be carefully isolated, locked away somewhere inside her mind.

"You're right," she admitted. The expression on her face barely changed, as if this amounted to a minor clarification of her original story. "But I wasn't trying to use them. I was trying to get rid of them."

"Why don't you use them right now? Kill us both, right now?" However many she was carrying, she could not have imagined they'd be enough to do real harm to the far side. So the poison could only have had one target.

"I don't want to do that, Tchicaya. I want to go with you. Deeper in. As far as we can."

"*Why?*" Why had she dragged him down here at all? To give his version at the border an excuse to give up? Once he was also deep in the far side, battling the Planck worms like a valiant Lilliputian, it would be far easier to feel that he'd done all he could.

"To see what's there," she said. "To help protect it, if it's worth it."

"And help destroy it, if it isn't?"

"I never lied about that," she insisted. "I never told you that I'd fight for some exotic wasteland, over the lives of real people."

That was true. She'd told him exactly what she believed, and he'd still wanted her beside him.

Tchicaya sagged to his knees. He had the means to kill her, or to leave her behind for the Planck worms. The ship's processor would do whatever he asked. But nothing she had done was unforgivable. In her place, fighting for the same stakes, he would have lied, too, armed himself, too. How could he accuse her of betraying anything? For all he knew, if they'd taken different turns the last time they'd parted, they might have ended up in each other's shoes.

She walked up to him and cradled his head in her arms. "I'll get rid of them now," she said. "Will you let me do that?"

Tchicaya nodded. She took him by the hands and lifted him up. He constructed a safe route through the processor, and she ejected the tainted qubits, forming a tiny bubble of classical physics in the vendeks' quantum sea.

The toolkit completed its preparations for the *Sarumpaet*'s second launch. In principle, this was just another quantum computation, no different from the commonplace operation of turning a string of zeros into a superposition of every possible binary number of the same length. Treating the entire ship as an operand, though, meant expanding the infrastructure that performed the computation far beyond the original hull, wrapping the *Sarumpaet* in a second computer. This processor would rotate the part of the ship's state vector that described the propulsion system, giving it a small component in each of more than a quadrillion orthogonal directions. Then it would release the resulting superposition into the depths of the far side, and wait for the reply that would enable it to erase all its failures.

The scape made no attempt to portray the actual machinery in which they were embedded; an opaque shield moved into place around the hull, representing the fact that they'd ceased to exchange information with their surroundings.

The toolkit began a countdown from twenty.

"Give me liberty, and/or death," Mariama quipped.

Tchicaya said, "I'll be happier when we can drop the 'and'." He was more afraid of the possibility of a single success, diluted a quadrillion-fold, than he was of universal failure. "I don't know if I should wish you a peaceful local death. Does this count, or doesn't it?"

"Only if none of the strategies work."

"Then I won't say anything."

The toolkit said, "Zero."

Chapter 16

Tchicaya looked down through the panes in the floor into a borderless expanse of pale brightness, stretching out beneath the *Sarumpaet* like an inverted sky.

He turned to Mariama, relieved but confused. "That's it? It's over already?" The ship would not have sent out probes to explore their surroundings until the handshake across the boundary was completed.

The toolkit said, "No. The light represents information-bearing vendeks with which we've interacted, inadvertently. I'm afraid the shielding we emerged with was a bad choice; I've found something that works now, but they managed to crawl all over us first."

Tchicaya was horrified. "Catch them!"

"I'm trying. I'm weaving a net."

"*Trying?* You useless fucking machine!"

Mariama reached over and took him by the shoulders. "Calm down! We programmed a response to something like this, and it's all happening, as fast as it can. There's nothing more to be done."

When they signaled back through the boundary to consolidate their success, the *Sarumpaet* needed to be a complete quantum system, not part of something larger that included vendeks flee-ing through the far side. The entire maneuver depended on it. If they could not catch the vendeks, their presence would become an insignificant statistical fluke: for every branch in which they'd succeeded, there'd be a quadrillion in which they'd vanished from the picture entirely.

"We should have covered this," he said. "We should have cov-ered every eventuality."

"Covered it how?" Mariama retorted. "A superposition that in-cluded different shielding on emergence would still have emerged with the wrong shielding, some of the time. We were never going to banish every conceivable problem in advance."

She was right. They'd done as much as they could to prepare, and now they had no choice but to wait and see if the situation could be salvaged.

The light began to fade, slowly. The toolkit had netted a por-tion of the vendeks, trapping them in the structure it had woven and erasing their correlations with the ship. The light was only a metaphor; the task was not as hopeless as it would have been if they'd exposed a quantum processor to a random bombardment with photons. It was more like having a billion-piece jigsaw puz-zle stolen by a swarm of flying insects: difficult to reverse, but not impossible.

The sky beneath them turned gray, then pitch black.

The toolkit said, "That's all of them."

"How can you be sure?" Tchicaya asked.

"I can't be, absolutely, but all the subsystems that were most likely to have been affected are displaying interference patterns as sharp as they've ever produced in isolation. Unless the vendeks that happened to escape also happened to interact with us in a way that could mimic that result, we're in a pure quantum state."

Tchicaya could live with that much doubt.

The toolkit understood the physics on both sides of the

boundary, now. As it exchanged information with the machinery that had launched them, the state vector for the ship was rotated into an eigenstate for a single strategy: the one that had succeeded. Give that they'd launched themselves toward the boundary at all, the probability that they'd failed to come through was zero.

Mariama exhaled heavily. "I think that's the strangest thing I've ever been a part of." She held up her hands and inspected them. "You know, I half-expected to feel the amplitude come flooding into me. Moving from spine to fingertips, of course."

Tchicaya laughed, grateful that she'd found a way to break the tension. "We should have programmed in an oscillating factor, for that extra existential thrill." Not long after the Qusp had been developed, people had played around with all manner of quantum novelties, putting themselves into intentionally prolonged superpositions inside their skulls. But there was nothing even mildly strange to report about this: from the inside, each part of the state vector that described your mind experiencing something definite simply *had* that one, definite experience. Shuffling amplitude back and forth between two alternatives before finally letting one of them interact with the world could not be "sensed" as some kind of ontological ebb and flow.

As the shielding was removed from the hull, the bright expanse of vendeks reappeared beneath them. The inner workings of the ship still needed to be protected, just like the interior of any Qusp, but they could now live with the equivalent of sunlight on their faces. Sunlight, or a swarm of gnats. The *Sarumpaet* would keep sending out probes, but in this region some information would come to them for free.

"What now?" Mariama asked.

Tchicaya looked up at the bottom of the honeycomb; it appeared as black and fathomless here as it had from the other side. It would hold back the Planck worms for a while, but it would be hoping for too much to assume that they'd all dash lemminglike into oblivion. "We need to find out how deep this region goes, and exactly what it contains. Maybe we can build some kind of firebreak here, something that will stop the Planck worms once and for all."

They descended through the Bright as fast as they could, but their progress was erratic. The number of different vendeks here was thousands of times greater than in any cell of the honeycomb, and though there were no abrupt transitions, the environment was constantly changing. Currents of different physics flowed around them as the vendeks intermingled in new proportions and combinations. Umrao had largely anticipated the structures in the honeycomb, but these strange tides would probably have been too complex to show up in his simulations. Tchicaya could not decide if this place would be more hostile or more amenable to higher forms of life: the vastly greater diversity of the vendeks made it seem richer, but the honeycomb cells had offered a kind of stability that was entirely absent here.

The scape showed nothing beneath the ship but a distant haze, constantly retreating. The information-bearing vendeks—which Mariama dubbed sprites—seemed to pass intact through all the changing conditions, but they were refracted and scattered to varying degrees, so the visibility they provided was limited. The *Sarumpaet*'s artificial probes became lost in the currents even sooner; beyond about half a micron, only a tiny fraction managed to return.

It was impossible to guess how deep this region might be. Though the border was advancing through the near side relentlessly at half the speed of light, the precise meaning of this for the far side remained unclear. Viewed from either side, the border itself had to be expanding in a consistent fashion, but that left open the question of whether all, or most, structures in the far side sat motionless while the edge of their universe rocketed away from them, or whether the relationship was more like that of the cosmic expansion of the near side, where relative velocities grew slowly with distance. The honeycomb was certainly clinging to the border, but that was not a good enough reason to believe that everything else in the far side would be following close behind. Sweeping principles of homogeneity were wishful thinking here.

There was something deeply restful about moving through the Bright. With the scape's fake gravity insulating them from the ship's actual, bumpy passage, the *Sarumpaet* might have been a glass gondola hanging from an invisible hot air balloon, drifting through a planetary atmosphere after a volcanic eruption had shrouded the world in dust. Although there was nothing to see but the shimmering of the sprites, Tchicaya resisted the lure of Slowdown, and instead of retreating into virtual landscapes from their memories, they sat and talked about their travels. Mariama described the renaissance on Har'El, the excitement of the changes that had percolated up from nowhere. Tchicaya told her more about Pachner, and the similar vitality he'd seen at the approach of the border.

They were beyond arguing, beyond accusing, beyond holding up each other's earlier ideals as some standard against which they'd fallen. They had seen different things, lived different lives, and they had allowed it to change them. All they could do now was keep on climbing Schild's ladder.

Five tranquil days into the Bright, just as Tchicaya was beginning to fear that they risked being lulled into an irreversible torpor, they spotted a small, translucent structure drifting by at a leisurely pace. The sprites that the object modified and deflected reached them long before the ship's probes could journey out to form their own impression, and for nearly an hour it was not at all clear that this was anything more than an unusually stable and localized feature of the shifting currents. The sprite-image looked like an eddy of some kind, and if no circulating winds could be detected brushing across the *Sarumpaet* as it approached, the rules governing vendek flows didn't bear much resemblance to fluid dynamics.

Once they were close enough, the probes gave a more detailed picture. There were veins and pockets of vendeks inside the eddy that were like nothing they'd seen floating free here. Some of the mixes were similar to honeycomb populations; others were different again.

They tracked the thing for hours, and watched it negotiate the currents. As the free vendeks flowed over it and through it, the interior structures deformed wildly; these were not the kind of breezes that could stir a few leaves, they were shifts in the fundamental dynamic laws. Some species of interior vendeks died before their eyes; others seemed to be leached out, carried off into the wind. It was like witnessing an animal being sandblasted with bacteria and assorted foreign cells, fighting off some, incorporating others, surrendering whole lineages of its own. Twisting and reeling beneath the onslaught, but all the while continuing to function.

After eight hours of watching these feats of persistence, with neither of them willing to put it into words, Mariama finally declared, "This has to be alive. This is our first xennobe."

Tchicaya agreed. "What do you want to call it?"

"I named the sprites," she said. "It's your turn."

The internal structures that the probe revealed looked like knots of offal caught in a tornado, but not many creatures were beautiful to behold once you dug that deep. The sprites' gentler scrutiny gave an impression of something woven from the winds.

"An airflower."

Mariama was amused, but she didn't object. If the Bright was not actually much like air, nor did anything here lie within reach of one-word descriptions in near-side language.

They continued to follow the airflower, though it was drifting upward, back toward the honeycomb. The toolkit ventured no opinion on the question of whether or not this system was alive, but its observations had already yielded dozens of new methods for easing the *Sarumpaet*'s way through the currents of the Bright.

"Could it be sentient?" Mariama wondered. The airflower had shown no obvious reaction to their presence, but it wasn't actively probing its environment, and the ship was a fraction of its size. The tiny distortion in the sprite flow around the *Sarumpaet*'s hull would barely be distinguishable from the background shimmer.

Before crossing the border, they'd planned to initiate contact with the builders of the signaling layer by a simple act of mimicry: scribing a layer of vendeks of their own which beat out the same sequence of primes. Back in the honeycomb, that would have been straightforward; here, it would have been like trying to communicate by waving a white silk banner in a blizzard.

They consulted with the toolkit, and eventually settled on a reasonable compromise. They unfurled a sturdier kind of banner, flexible enough to cope with the vendek flows. Its precise geometry remained prey to the weather, but instead of encoding anything in its position, its degree of transparency to the sprites flickered between two states, flashing out the primes like a shutter held up to the light.

The airflower drifted on, apparently indifferent to the signal. They could only guess as to how it might pursue a conversation with its own kind, but if this creature had constructed the signaling layer in the alien environment of the far side's shallows—with the intention that it be noticed by beings from an even stranger realm—why would it remain oblivious to a version of the same message suddenly appearing in front of it?

It was possible that it was completely blind to the sprites. They seemed like the obvious basis for perception here, but the air-flowers might have evolved before them. If that was the case, it could take months of painstaking work to discover the creature's actual sensory modalities.

Tchicaya had asked the toolkit to run simulations of the known species of Planck worms interacting with the bottom of the honeycomb, and as he pondered his next move, the verdict arrived. By sheer force of numbers, the worms would almost certainly stumble upon the necessary mutations to find their way through. Once they managed that, they'd bring the near-side vacuum into play against the Bright, unraveling the intricate tapestry of vendeks into isolated deserts of homogeneous physics.

The toolkit had found no certain way to prevent this, but it was studying one possibility. It looked as if it might be feasible to transform the whole region into a kind of tar pit, deep enough to trap and drown every last species of Planck worm. The worms acted as conduits for correlations with the vacuum, but not every interaction with them induced decoherence. The honeycomb vendeks had made short work of some of the earlier would-be invaders, and a sufficiently diverse mixture of vendeks, tailor-made for the purpose, would have a chance of dealing with the entire current wave in the same fashion.

Along with every native inhabitant of the Bright.

"Would you sacrifice all of this," he asked Mariama, "to save whatever lies beneath it?"

She said, "Ask me that again when we know ten times more."

Tchicaya shook his head. "That's always going to be the right answer. Until it's too late for anything we do to make a difference." The toolkit's simulation was riddled with uncertainties, but to the extent that the risk could be quantified at all, within a few ship days it would cease to be insignificant.

"Don't be so pessimistic," she countered. "Don't assume that we're going to have to choose between utter recklessness and some paralyzing quest for perfect knowledge."

"Perfect knowledge? There could be a billion times as many sentient beings beneath us as the rest of the galaxy has ever contained, or we might already be looking at the pinnacle of far-side life—which might be a miracle of xennobiology but dumb as a cactus, or might be conscious in ways we're too stupid and parochial to fathom. How do you cope with that kind of ignorance?" Dwelling on it was enough to make his faithfully simulated body sick to the stomach. Part of him screamed that the only thing to do in the face of such barely comprehensible stakes was to bow out, to withdraw from any possibility of intervention—as if showing the appropriate humility was more important than the outcome.

But Mariama refused to be cowed by the gravity of the situation. "We keep exploring," she insisted. "We keep narrowing the gap between what we know and what we need to know."

"What I need to know is when we have no choice but to stop gathering information and make a stand."

Tchicaya gazed into the strange machinery of the airflower. This creature was a thousand times more sophisticated than anything that had been found away from Earth before, but if the signaling layer was an artifact at all, he did not believe that he was looking at its maker.

He said, "We need to go deeper."

With the refinements to its hull, the *Sarumpaet* traveled faster. For half a day they were alone in the Bright again, but then they began to spot more of the airflowers. The sightings became more frequent as they descended; at first they were seeing one or two an hour, but it soon reached the point where half a dozen were always in view.

Mariama suggested that they try to follow the path of the migration back to its source. "That could lead nowhere, but it's the only clue we've got as to where other life might be concentrated."

This made sense to Tchicaya. They moved the ship closer to the airflowers, and descended along the sparse trail.

Within an hour, the creatures were crowded around the *Sarumpaet* like coral spawn. When the toolkit probed the Bright itself, it appeared that the airflowers had latched on to a particularly stable current of vendeks; if this broke apart higher up, the specimens they'd encountered earlier might have pursued it as far as it went, and then scattered. The current was useless for transportation—you couldn't ride it like a thermal updraft, in a world without conservation of momentum—but whether the airflowers were using it as a navigation aid, as a feature to congregate around for breeding purposes, or merely as something to graze upon was impossible to say. The vendeks certainly diffused into the airflowers' bodies, but they still might have been anything from valuable symbionts, sought out by their hosts, to burdensome parasites that came with the territory.

"Can vendeks ever really be prey?" Tchicaya wondered. "They're the smallest stable objects, so there's no point seeking them out just to break them down into their constituent parts."

Mariama said, "There are no subunits that you can extract from them and treat as nutrients—nothing analogous to vitamins or amino acids—so when you eat for the sake of eating, you're infecting yourself. All food works like yogurt. But that doesn't mean that the only reason to seek out a particular kind of vendek would be to give it a new home. Nothing that crosses your path is going to move aside for you automatically here, so you have no choice but to convert whatever you encounter into a part of yourself. Sometimes the vendeks around you can be incorporated unchanged, but other times you need to have your own tame vendeks invade the graph ahead of you, chewing up whatever's there as they propagate through—in which case, you want them to be taking on adversaries that they can conquer easily, even if you're not planning to pillage the corpses for specific spare parts. Whether you call that predation or not is a moot point." She smiled. "Assuming that all this talk about larger organisms makes sense at all, and we're not just watching a few vendeks traveling in packs, lording it over the rest."

"I wish you hadn't said that." Tchicaya already found it eerie enough contemplating the identity of these xennobes. Humans had been nothing but a colony of specialized cells, but at least those cells had all been related to each other, and subdued to the point where they could pursue a common genetic goal. In the air-flowers, there seemed to be as many vendeks plucked into service from the surroundings as there were specialized ones that appeared only in the creatures' tissues.

"What's that?" Mariama had spotted something through the floor. She gestured impatiently to the scape, transforming the checkerboard beneath their feet into a completely transparent surface.

A dark shape was spiraling up around the column of airflowers, a sprite-shadow that the probes were yet to fill in. Seconds later, it began to take on details, the colors shifting wildly as the scape improvised palettes to encode the information, then judged them inadequate and started again from scratch.

The probe image showed a dense, branched network of tubes filled with specialized vendeks, cloaked in a more complex version of the eddies that wrapped the airflowers. The tube walls were layer populations, but they extended fine tendrils out into the trapped currents of the Bright. Controlling them? Feeding off them? The scape was unable to track all the dynamics; too much was happening for the probes to capture it all, and many of them were being captured themselves, lost among the vendeks they'd been sent to map.

The new xennobe was ten or twelve times larger than a typical airflower. As it soared past the *Sarumpaet*, Tchicaya instructed the ship to follow it. Going into reverse was disturbingly easy; the only thing resembling inertia that the ship possessed was the precise distribution of the hull vendeks that chewed their way through the Bright.

When they caught up with the xennobe, it was circling the airflowers closely, moving in on one target. As it struck, the probes showed the two cloaks of entrained Bright vendeks merging; it was impossible to tell if the airflower's covering had been stripped away or whether the creature pursuing it had deliberately exposed its own inner organs. As the process continued, though, neither party remained shielded from the other. Veins became entangled, endogenous vendeks flowed between the two. The airflower had made no attempt to flee, so it was either insensate, too slow, or a willing participant in the exchange.

Tchicaya said, "I don't know if I'm watching a wolf tearing open a lamb's throat, or a hummingbird drinking nectar."

"It might even be sex," Mariama suggested.

"Urk. I've heard of dimorphism, but that would be ridiculous. Besides, what are the gametes they're meant to be exchanging?"

"Who said anything about gametes? The mix of specialized vendeks inside the xennobes must control all their morphology. Animals share beneficial symbionts with each other, and pass them on to their young—but in this case, there's nothing else to pass on. Instead of having a genome, your heritable traits are defined by a unique blend of gut flora."

When the larger xennobe moved away from the airflower to which it had attached itself, and the remnant disintegrated into random currents in the Bright, Tchicaya said, "Wolf and lamb it is—or maybe rabbit and lettuce. And don't start reminding me about male spiders that die after mating; if there's no genome and no gametes, why call one creature a sexual partner of another, when at most it's really just a specialized dietary supplement?"

Mariama conceded the point, begrudgingly. "So do we follow the rabbit?" It had moved up along the column, outpacing the airflowers, apparently finicky about its next choice of meal.

Tchicaya glanced after it, then he looked down along the plume of airflowers vanishing into the haze. As much as anything, he wanted to know where the Bright ended. "Follow the food chain to the top of the pyramid? Or is that just naive?"

"There's no energy here," Mariama mused, "but there might be a hierarchy of concentrations of the most useful vendeks. Maybe airflowers strain some valuable species from the winds, or make them for themselves, and everyone else steals them from each other."

"Or goes straight to the airflowers. The Signalers could be herbivores, not rabbit hunters."

"That's true."

Tchicaya sent the ship in pursuit of the rabbit. When they finally caught it between meals, he unfurled the signaling device.

The rabbit froze in midflight. When the sequence was completed, it remained motionless.

Tchicaya waited hopefully for some kind of response. "Do you think we've frightened it?"

"It might just be wondering how to reply," Mariama suggested. "Some encounters must put you on the spot, even when you're half-expecting them. Like your father, cornered by anachronauts."

"I hope it's not trying to decide how to Mead us. But why would it need to lie, when it knows nothing about our expectations?"

"Maybe the airflowers are sentient, too," she joked, "and we caught it doing something that it senses we might not entirely approve of."

After fifteen minutes with no change, Mariama suggested repeating the sequence. Tchicaya started the banner flickering again.

The probes showed a series of topological changes spreading rapidly through the rabbit's plumbing. The process was too fast to follow in detail, but it culminated in the release of a rich brew of vendeks from deep within the rabbit's body. Most of the discharge flowed over the banner, but the portion that reached the *Sarumpaet*'s hull worked its way all around the ship, blocking out probes and sprites alike. The last thing the scape portrayed was the rabbit fleeing into the Bright.

Tchicaya addressed the toolkit. "What's happening? Is the hull intact?"

"It hasn't been breached, but it's not going to take us anywhere for a while. The foreign mixture has invaded a short distance, but it's not aggressively replicating or advancing."

"Can't you tweak the hull vendeks to break through?"

"I'm looking for ways to do that, but this mixture seems to have been optimized to make the problem as difficult as possible."

Mariama started laughing. "This is what you get for flashing your Rosetta stone at randomly chosen strangers. They glue you to the spot and run away."

"Do you really think that was more than a frightened animal?"

She shrugged. "Wouldn't it be wonderful if it was a shy cousin of the Signalers, out plucking fruit, who'll run home and tell the rest of the clan to come and take a look? But you're right; it was probably just a squid spraying ink in our faces."

They waited for the toolkit to find a way out. If the situation became desperate they could always try the superposition trick again, but the fact that they were hemmed in on all sides would complicate the maneuver: they'd have to leave part of the ship behind to clean up the failures of the part that escaped.

After almost two hours, the toolkit spoke. "We should be free soon."

Tchicaya was relieved. "You found vendeks for the hull that could invade through the glue?"

"No, but the weather is doing the job for us, from the outside. The glue is moderately stable, but it's not taking any kind of action to remain impervious to changing conditions in the Bright."

Mariama made a sound that was equal parts delight at this revelation, and disgust at her own slowness. "Of course! Anything static is doomed here. Stable mixtures of vendeks can endure for a while, but in the long run you need all the flexibility and organizational powers of a higher organism, just to keep up with the Bright. An entire xennobe might have managed to cling on to us indefinitely, but it would be a bit much to have to give birth to a dedicated assassin every time someone frightens you."

Tchicaya nodded appreciatively. "That must make technology difficult to get started. Vendeks are the material from which everything is made, so all engineering is bioengineering, but you probably couldn't expect any artifact less sophisticated than the most primitive xennobe to survive for long."

A crack of sprite-light appeared through the glue. Mariama sighed wistfully and leaned against him, wrapping an arm around his neck. It was the kind of unself-conscious physicality she'd often displayed when they were very young, before they'd even heard of sex.

She said, "Don't you wish we could have come here with nothing to do but understand this place?"

"Yes." Tchicaya felt no desire whatsoever to add a retort about her old allegiances. The factions belonged to another universe.

"For a thousand years."

"Yes." He put his arm across her shoulders.

Mariama turned to him. "Can I ask you something?"

"Sure."

"Do you think you would have traveled to the *Rindler* at all, if it wasn't for the power station?"

"I don't know. I can't answer that."

"But you still feel bad about it?"

Tchicaya laughed curtly. "It's not relentless crushing guilt, if that's what you mean. But I knew it was wrong, even when I did it, and I haven't changed my mind about that."

She said, "You know, I actually expected you to be grateful, because you got what you wanted. That's the last time I made that mistake with anyone."

"I bet it was. Ouch!" She'd punched him on the arm.

"But you just blamed me for everything, because I didn't fight hard enough against you."

"I didn't blame you," he protested.

Mariama gazed back at him neutrally.

Tchicaya said, "All right, I did. That was unfair."

"You made me feel like a murderer," she said. "I was just a child, the same as you."

"I'm sorry." Tchicaya searched her face. "I didn't know it still—"

She cut him off. "It doesn't. It doesn't still hurt me. It hadn't even crossed my mind for centuries. And it had nothing to do with me coming to the *Rindler*. I would have done that anyway."

"Right."

They stood for a while without speaking.

Tchicaya said, "Is that it? Are we at peace now?"

Mariama smiled. "Not histrionic enough for you?"

"The less catharsis I can get these days, the better." She'd smuggled in a weapon, she'd been prepared to kill him, and they'd still found a way to go on. But it had taken them until now to speak a few words and untangle the oldest, simplest knot.

"I think we're at peace," she said.

They continued down along the airflowers' crowded highway. Eventually the creatures began to thin out; presumably the

Sarumpaet was approaching the bottom of the vendek current that had attracted them in the first place—or at least the end of the weather conditions that rendered the current detectable from afar.

After the last airflower had disappeared into the haze above them, they tracked the current itself for another hour. When it finally came to an end, there was nothing. Just the Bright itself, empty and shimmering.

Mariama said, "I don't believe it! A river like that can't appear out of nowhere."

"We haven't seen any other currents as long," Tchicaya said cautiously. "But what does that prove? We don't know the limits of ordinary weather."

"I suppose some vendek mixes are just stable because they're stable," she conceded. "But xennobes have particular uses for stable combinations. I was expecting at least a pile of decaying xennobe corpses."

They circled around, examining the region with the probes. There was another persistent current, feeding into the first; it hadn't been obvious immediately, because the transition zone between them was far less orderly than the currents themselves. The vendek mix in the deeper current appeared to be decaying into the mix that had attracted the airflowers, catalyzed by a shift in the ambient weather; as they watched the probe image, they could see the transition zone drifting back and forth.

Tchicaya said, "Well, it's coming from deeper in. And I'm not going back up to try chasing rabbits."

They followed the river back toward its source. Within an hour, they'd hit a second transition zone—this time forking into two different upward flows.

A third transition.

A fourth.

Mariama said, "At least we're learning a lot of vendekobiology.

Can you imagine the kind of diagrams it would take to describe the Bright? I used to think the fusion reactions in a star were complicated."

"Students will curse our names. What more can anyone hope for?"

A fifth transition.

A sixth. Here, the current was flowing down to them, making a U-turn. If they were going to trace it to its origin, they would have to travel an unknown distance back toward the honeycomb.

Tchicaya was torn. They didn't know if this was an offshoot of a mighty river, the backbone to an entire xennobe ecology, or just a meaningless cobweb drifting through the Bright. They could end up chasing it back and forth, like a cat stalking a feather, until the Planck worms came raining down.

"If we don't spot another xennobe before the next transition, that will be the last," he declared.

Mariama concurred, reluctantly.

They stood together, staring into the haze. Tchicaya could think of no other strategy, once they abandoned this thread, than plunging straight down, hoping at least to hit bottom soon, yielding a purely physical measure of how much territory they'd be sacrificing if they built the tar pit for the Planck worms.

And if they never hit bottom, if the Bright went on forever? Then there'd be nothing they could do, nothing they could save.

Mariama said, "That's a sprite-shadow, isn't it? It's not just haze."

"Where?"

She pointed. Tchicaya could see a tiny gray distortion in the light. "If it's another airflower, that doesn't count."

The shadow grew, but the probes were still not reaching it. The object was much further away than they'd realized, and it was definitely not an airflower.

Tchicaya would have abandoned the vendek current to go after this new find, but the current itself was leading them straight to it. *This*, ultimately, was the source of the vendeks on which the airflowers had been feeding. And its sprite-shadow kept looming larger, while the probes remained oblivious to it.

Mariama said, "If this is a single organism, we've just gone from rabbits to whales. I thought the current must have come from necrotic decay, but this is so huge it wouldn't need to be mortally wounded; it could urinate a river."

The flickering outline of the shadow was roughly circular. "I don't think it's one creature," Tchicaya said. "I think we've found an oasis in the desert."

The shadow now dominated the view completely, a sight as overwhelming as the border from Pachner, but its exact form remained elusive. "We have to get those probes to go faster," Mariama complained.

A tiny patch of color and detail appeared suddenly at the center of the object, spreading slowly through the grayness. The framing effect was confusing; Tchicaya found it harder than ever to interpret the probe image. Things that might have been xennobes were moving around on a roughly spherical surface; the scape labeled them as being hundreds of times larger than the rabbits, but they looked like mites crawling over an elephant. The scale of the structure was extraordinary; if an airflower was the size of a daisy, this was a floating mountain, an asteroid.

The window of detail grew, revealing thousands of xennobes streaming about below them—the alignment of the *Sarumpaet*'s deck still made "down" point to the center of the far side, but it was impossible not to grant this minor planet precedence—and that was just the surface. Some xennobes were coming and going from the mouths of tunnels leading into hidden depths. As yet, the probes were spread too thinly to report on the new xennobes' anatomy in any detail, and like the others, their forms swayed wildly in the winds that wrapped around them, merging with their bodies. Yet some system at the core of each xennobe retained its integrity through all the changes sweeping over it, and the same organizational information was endlessly reencoded, endlessly preserved.

As the probe image spread out to encompass the entire colony, Tchicaya's heart leaped. He struggled to temper his excitement. His intuition didn't count for much here, and everything he was witnessing was constantly deforming, as if the whole vision was a reflection in liquid metal. He couldn't even pin down the source of his conviction, the one regularity in all the busyness beneath them that struck him as the signature of artifice over nature. But all technology would be built from nature, here. Nothing entirely lifeless could endure.

He turned to Mariama. "This is not an oasis. It's not a jungle. We've found the Signalers. This is their city."

Chapter 17

The *Sarumpaet* circumnavigated the xennobe colony, reconnoitering, apparently unnoticed. Tchicaya kept the density of the probes low, lest the rain of inquisitive devices cross the threshold of perception—or some more sensitive, artificial means of detection—and alarm the denizens. He had no urgent need to study these creatures' internal anatomy, and the details of the colony itself were overwhelming enough.

Veins and bladders and sheets composed of thousands of different vendek populations defined the structure, separated by an intricate warren of tunnels through which the free vendeks of the Bright continued to pass. The probes identified changes in the winds as they flowed through the colony; specialized vendeks were diffusing out of a multitude of reservoirs and modifying the raw weather, killing off some species, supplanting them directly, or interacting with them to create new variants. To Tchicaya, this looked exactly like air-conditioning for physics: the Colonists could probably cope with all but the most extreme natural changes in their environment, but it made sense that they'd find it less stressful to delegate some of their homeostatic efforts to their technology.

Hundreds of vendek currents snaked out of the colony, presumably waste products from both the thing itself and its inhabitants. A few were so stable that they completely resisted the passage of both probes and sprites, and they appeared in the scape as gnarled black roots twisting away into the distance.

Tchicaya saw nothing to dissuade him from his earlier conclusion, though everything was open to alternative interpretations. Termite mounds had air-conditioning, ants had mastered agriculture, and the Colonists might not have needed to expend even as much effort as social insects to bring their home into existence; it was possible that they were mere symbionts, mindlessly tending some giant natural organism. Mariama remained cautious, but she did not choose to play devil's advocate. They both had the same hopes now, and they both knew how easily they could be dashed.

They spent half a day debating the level of caution they needed to exercise. Whether these xennobes were the Signalers or not, they were likely to have far more potent defenses than the rabbit. It would be difficult to supervise any kind of complex interaction from too great a distance, though; if they hung back in their present orbit and sent down a drone, it would need to be largely autonomous.

The plan they finally settled upon was to send in a mobile form of their signaling banner, as large and obvious as they could make it, while following behind at a prudent distance. If the reception was violent, the tiny sprite-shadow of the *Sarumpaet* would be the less likely target.

If their mimicry of the signaling layer produced a promising reaction, they would move on to more complex exchanges, playing it by ear, hoping that the banner itself would prompt their hosts to respond in kind. Nothing the probes had revealed had offered any clues about the Colonists' preferred mode of interpersonal communication; sprites and other potential information-carriers flooded the colony, but plucking messages in an unknown language from all the influences modulating these carriers was beyond the standard Mediator software they'd brought through the border. Given time, Tchicaya would have happily observed the Colonists from a distance until everything about them, right down to the subtlest cultural nuance, was absolutely clear. He and Mariama could have descended from the sky expecting compliments on their perfect local accents and unprecedented good manners, like a pair of conscientious travelers.

It was not going to happen that way. The coming of the Planck worms would be unheralded, but the five percent error bars of the toolkit's best statistical guess had already been crossed. If the sky rained poison right now, as they rushed through their rudimentary preparations, they would not even have the bitter consolation of knowing that they'd been ambushed by unforeseeable events.

They'd reached the end game, ready or not. They'd have to walk a knife edge between recklessness and caution, but they could not afford to take a single step back.

The signaling banner spiraled down toward the colony, twisting and fluttering like an airborne tent in a hurricane, but pulsing steadily from translucent to opaque. The *Sarumpaet* followed, close enough to maintain a probe image of the banner that was only a fraction of a ship-second out of date. The probes could also ferry instructions from the ship to the banner, enabling the signal to be modified on a similar time scale as soon as the need arose.

From the deck of the *Sarumpaet*, Tchicaya formed a rapid series of impressions of the crowded world below, none of which he believed was worth trusting. The density and animation of the creatures made him think of the bustle of markets, of festivals, of riots. Of the crew of some ancient, oceangoing vessel battling a storm. In fact, all this violent swaying in the wind was probably about as exciting for the Colonists as a terrestrial animal's endlessly beating heart. For all he knew, this was what they looked like at their most indolent.

He searched for any hint of a flickering shadow from the banner on the surface below, but between the shimmering of the sprites and the erratic geometry of all the objects involved, that was too much to expect. Perhaps it was fortunate that the nearsiders would not arrive with anything like the drama of an artificial eclipse; even if these xennobes did belong to the same species as the Signalers, different cultures could still have varying degrees of sophistication, and an overblown spectacle might have terrified a group for whom the search for life beyond the border was a barely comprehensible endeavor, something that only an obscure, deranged minority would even contemplate.

On the other hand, since the banner had no significant effect on the ground, it was possible that no one would even notice it. It wasn't clear that any of the Bright's inhabitants focused the sprites to form an image; the rabbit had been close enough to the banner it attacked to sense its presence through a drop in overall irradiation, like a chill on the skin. It made evolutionary sense to expect all mobile xennobes to possess a detailed knowledge of their surroundings, but a sufficiently unnatural object might still be as invisible to them as a burst of neutrinos to a human.

The banner came to a halt at a predetermined altitude: some twenty times the Colonists' typical body size. Tchicaya gazed down at the crowd, wondering how he was going to distinguish panic from indifference. The Colonists weren't as shapeless as the airflowers; their network of vendek tubes bifurcated twice to give four distinct clusters of branches, and their geometry at any moment tended to reflect this. They looked like medical scans of the circulatory system of some headless quadruped, dog-paddling ineffectually in extremely rough seas. But if that intrusive probe image was unlikely to reflect the way they saw each other, by sprites alone they resembled tortured, mutilated ghosts, trying to break through into the world of the living.

Mariama said, "I think it's been noticed."

"Where?"

She pointed; a group of six Colonists had left the surface. As Tchicaya watched, they ascended rapidly, but as they grew nearer to the banner they slowed considerably. This cautious interest was not proof of anything, but it was an encouraging sign.

The Colonists surrounded the device, then began spraying it with a delicate mist of vendeks. "That's cooperative sensing!" Mariama exclaimed. "One of them illuminates the object, the other looks at the transmitted pattern."

"I think you're right." The group was arranged in pairs on either side of the banner, and the members of each pair took turns emitting the vendeks. The probes hadn't encountered this species of vendek before; perhaps nothing inside the colony warranted the same kind of scrutiny as this alien object.

The Colonists retreated and formed a loose huddle away from the banner. "What now?" Tchicaya wondered. "How do you react to a mutated version of your own stratospheric beacon suddenly appearing on your doorstep?"

Mariama said, "I just hope they realize they don't need to launch a new signaling layer in order to reply."

"Maybe we should try to make a more obvious proxy," he suggested. "Something that resembles one of their bodies."

"How would we decide which features to include, and which to leave out? We don't even know the difference between their communications signals and their waste products. We'd probably come up with the equivalent of a glove puppet of a monkey that smelled exactly like human excrement."

She had a point; even the six Colonists high above the din—and/or stench—of the colony were now bathed in a confusing fog of vendeks, and it was beyond the *Sarumpaet*'s resources to untangle their functions and meaning.

Tchicaya felt a sudden stab of pessimism. He believed he'd finally reached the people he'd come to find—but he had days, at most, not only to describe the Planck worms to them, but to reach a level of communication and trust that would enable them to work together to deal with the threat. However many subtleties, abstractions, and courtesies he omitted along the way, even conveying the core of the message was beginning to seem hopelessly ambitious.

He said, "Maybe we should change the signal right now, instead of waiting for them to reply? Just to make it clear that the banner's not passive?"

Before Mariama could respond, the Colonists began regrouping around the banner. In unison, they released a stream of vendeks, denser than before; in the probe image, it looked as if the six veined bodies were blowing soap films. The individual sheets met at the edges and merged, forming a bubble, enclosing the banner.

The Colonists retreated again, then sprayed a new mixture at the bubble. It began to drift after them, down toward the surface.

Mariama said, "They've grabbed it! They're towing it!"

The wall of the bubble was passing sprites, but it resisted the *Sarumpaet*'s probes—the only means they had to get instructions to the banner. They'd lost control of the device completely, now; they couldn't even reprogram its message, let alone command it to try to break out of its cage.

"We could make another one," Tchicaya suggested. "Right in front of their eyes."

"Why not see what they do with this one?"

"You think we should follow it?"

Mariama nodded. "They might release it from the container, once they've got it where they want it. They might even have their own signaling device down there."

Tchicaya was not convinced. "If they think it's just a message in a bottle, they're not going to talk back to it. And if we can't regain control of it, the last place we want to try scribing a new one is in the middle of some chamber down there."

"We'll only find out what they think it is if we go after it," Mariama replied. "Besides, we initiated contact *with this object*. We should stick to that, follow through with it, or we risk confusing them."

That did make sense. They had to be flexible, or they'd end up chasing their preconceptions down a *cul-de-sac*, but they also had to try to be consistent. Changing tack every time they feared that they might have been misinterpreted could bury any message beneath all the distracting shifts in strategy.

Tchicaya said, "All right, we'll follow it!" He instructed the *Sarumpaet* to pursue the purloined banner.

As they descended, it finally struck him just how extraordinary a sight they were witnessing. The banner was still flashing out its programmed sequence from within its container; the Colonists hadn't damaged it at all. *Towing* anything without destroying it, here, was a feat akin to putting a tornado on a leash. There were no simple analogs of the notions of pushing or pulling something, let alone any reason to expect it to respond by moving as a whole—like a nice near-side object made from atoms bonded together into a mildly elastic solid. You couldn't even rely on the local physics to *permit* something to behave, in uniform motion, as it had when it was stationary, however gently you conveyed it from one state to the other.

He turned to Mariama. "This is proof, isn't it? They have to be more than animals, to be able to move it like that."

Mariama hesitated, no doubt pondering the evolutionary advantages of a delicate touch when kidnapping other species of xennobe to fill with your parasitic young.

But she said, "I think you're right. I've been giving them the benefit of the doubt until now, but I think they've finally earned it."

The six Colonists touched down on the surface and proceeded along a narrow path that opened up in the throng ahead of them. The bubble appeared to be following a vendek trail laid by its creators, and the *Sarumpaet* stayed close enough behind it to avoid the crowd as it reclaimed the ground in the wake of the procession. Rather than rendering the flight deck in proportion to the ship's actual physical dimensions, the scape was constantly making choices of scale to keep the view of their surroundings intelligible, and the Colonists on either side of the ship appeared roughly as large as giraffes. Absurd as it was, Tchicaya found it difficult to suppress the feeling that they might look in through the hull and see him standing on the deck gazing back at them; he kept wanting to avert his eyes, so as not to risk frightening or provoking them.

Close up, the ship's probes revealed more of the Colonists' anatomy. Dwelling on the crude, wind-blown X of their overall shape was pointless; everything that mattered was in the vendek mixtures locked in the network of tubes. The toolkit struggled to annotate the images, hinting at the subtlety of the vendekobiology and the complexity of the network's topology. Tchicaya could only take in a fraction of what the toolkit was managing to glean, but the Colonists were manipulating their internal physics with as much precision as any animal controlling its biochemistry, juggling pH or glucose concentrations.

He caught Mariama's eye, and the two of them exchanged giddy, fearful smiles. Like Tchicaya, she was enraptured by the beauty and strangeness around them, but more painfully aware than ever of the vast gulf they'd have to bridge in order to protect it. The closer they came to the possibility of success, the more vertiginous the fall if they lost their grip. To be overrun by Planck worms in the honeycomb would have meant nothing but a bleak local death; here, they would be witnessing a whole world dying.

The procession entered a tunnel, angled steeply down into the colony's interior. As the density of sprites dropped, the scape experimented with the other ambient information-carrying vendeks. No single species could come close to matching the details of the probe images, but taken together they provided a fair description of the surroundings. From the Colonists' point of view, the Bright might well have been horribly misnamed; the conditions down here stood a far better chance of providing useful illumination, and the colony could have been perceived to lie in a somber landscape of permanent twilight.

Out of the full force of the wind, the geometry of both the Colonists and their architecture became more stable. The walls of the tunnel were formed from a basic layer population, but hundreds of other structures adorned them. Apart from the "air-conditioning" and "light sources," Tchicaya couldn't guess what purpose most of the structures served. They looked too complex to be decorations, but mere endurance required sophistication here; the air-conditioning wasn't perfect, and anything incapable of responding to the weather risked being scoured away by the Bright.

The tunnel branched; the procession veered left. The air-conditioning was becoming more aggressive about removing impurities; the ship and the toolkit had to work harder than ever to keep the hull intact and the probes viable in the presence of all the new cleaning vendeks. Tchicaya had contemplated a number of unpleasant fates since the anachronauts had blown him out of the 'Rindler, but being scrubbed from the environment like an unwelcome speck of dust was one of the most insulting.

After a second fork, and a section that zigzagged and

corkscrewed simultaneously, the tunnel opened out into a large cave. The physics here was more stable than anything they'd seen since the honeycomb; the weather had not been banished, but the turbulence had been subdued by an order of magnitude compared to the open Bright.

A stream of vendeks crossed the cave, rendered pitch black by the scape for most of its length, where the probes found it impenetrable. Near the center, the stream mingled with the surrounding free vendeks, expanding and becoming diluted before contracting back to its original width and continuing on its way. The probes could enter this region, which they portrayed as a sphere of gray fog; not all of them were coming back, though, and those that did reported that they'd almost lost control over their trajectories. Moving through the Bright had been difficult from the start, but some extreme, systematic distortion here was interfering with their attempts to navigate.

The toolkit collated all the evidence and reached its own conclusion. "There's curvature engineered into the graphs here. You can invade these vendeks where the current opens out, but in the process they reorient your time axis."

It took Tchicaya a moment to digest this. Patterns in a quantum graph persisted by replicating themselves in future versions of the graph, but "the future" could only be defined by the orientation of the pattern itself. If you sliced the space-time foam one way to find a graph with vendek A in it, but needed to take a slice at a different angle to find vendek B, the two vendeks would see time as lying in different directions, and mere persistence, on their own terms, would put them in relative motion.

So "reorient your time axis" was toolkit-speak for "change your velocity." The vendek current couldn't sweep anything along the way a river did, with pressure and momentum, but it could twist the local definition of being "stationary" progressively further away from its original orientation. In a sense it was like ordinary gravity, but on the near side the symmetries of the vacuum imposed a rigid austerity on the possibilities for space-time curvature. Here, the curvature had been tailored on the spot, woven directly into the graphs by the choice of vendeks.

"These people engineer space-time the way we do polymer design," he marveled. "Choose the right monomers, get their shape and reactivity right, and you can create whatever properties you desire."

Mariama smiled. "Except that they're more like microbes than monomers. Everything comes down to breeding and blending the right vendeks."

"So what is this? A waste-disposal system?" If they wanted to toss the banner away, they could have done that from the surface with their towing bubble, but this accelerated sewer might send it further, faster.

The Colonists had paused at the entrance to the cave, but now they began to move along a shallow spiral, inching their way down toward the velocity gradient. They weren't discarding the banner in the black river. They were going with it.

Tchicaya groaned. "I know what this is! We saw the rest of it, from the outside. It's a transport system. We're on the entry ramp to a highway."

Mariama agreed. "Maybe this whole place is just a tiny outpost, and the artifact is such a big deal that they're rushing it straight to the nearest expert."

The conga line of Colonists was winding its way toward the axis of the cave, actively fighting the effect of the black vendeks in order not to get dashed against the wall where the current exited. The *Sarumpaet* was still obediently following the towing bubble; if they wanted to break away from the convoy, they'd have to do it in the next few seconds.

There was no way of knowing how long the journey would take. They'd seen this highway disappearing into the haze, into the depths of the far side. This outpost was where the danger would strike first, where the people needed to be told what was coming so they could fight it, or evacuate.

But if the banner was being taken to the Signalers themselves, that could be the expedition's one opportunity to meet people with the knowledge and motivation needed to understand the warning at all.

Mariama said, "You don't want to back out?" Perhaps she was afraid that if this turned out to be the wrong choice, he'd hold her responsible for urging him down here in the first place.

Tchicaya said, "No. We have to trust these people to take us to someone who'll work hard to communicate with us. If that's not what they're planning, then we're screwed—but if we hang back and miss the chance to meet the experts, we're screwed anyway." Ahead of them, the banner was blinking feebly; undamaged still, but it had never been designed to modulate all the forms of illumination that filled the cave.

The bubble arced smoothly down into the gray fog of the entry ramp. As they followed it, the fog around them actually seemed to grow thinner; once the *Sarumpaet* began to surrender to the highway's demands, the probes had an easier task finding their way back to it—though the rest of the cave rapidly vanished from sight. Tchicaya felt a pang of frustration that he was insulated from any sense of the dynamics at play here. *What would it feel like, for a native, to be whisked into motion like this?* Would there be something akin to tidal effects, as different parts of your body were brought up to speed? It was a trivial thing to ponder, but he needed to cut through the barriers that separated him from the Colonists. He needed to imagine himself inside their skins, any way he could.

The convoy straightened out. They were in the center of the highway now, portrayed by the probes as a narrow tube of clarity surrounded by fog. The Colonists themselves had begun emitting some of the parasprites that had illuminated the tunnels and the cave; the bubble and its cargo blocked the view ahead, but Tchicaya could still catch glimpses of them, shy luminescent starfish waving their four legs lethargically. They were probably relaxing, free from the arduous demands of the Bright—or if those demands were trivial, perhaps this trip was so dull for them that they'd entered something close to suspended animation. The *Sarumpaet* was doing absolutely nothing to keep up with them; as far as it was concerned, everyone was motionless. The highway had them all free-falling effortlessly toward their destination.

Mariama asked the toolkit, "Can you tell how fast we're moving?"

"I have no direct access to the Bright around us, and interpreting the acceleration process we've just been through is difficult."

"Don't be such a killjoy; take a wild guess. In the broadest, most naive, near-side terms."

"We might be doing something comparable to relativistic speeds."

Mariama looked around the scape, her eyes shining. "Do you remember what Rasmah said?" She was addressing Tchicaya now. "When she spoke to the Preservationists before the moratorium vote?"

"Of course." Tchicaya had to make a conscious effort to summon up the memory, but he'd had a few other things on his mind.

"She was right," Mariama declared. "Her whole vision of this place was exactly right. Not in the details; she couldn't anticipate half the things we've seen here. But she understood precisely what the far side could mean for us."

Tchicaya experienced a twinge of irritation, bordering on jealousy. *What right did she have to share Rasmah's vision?* He was ashamed of himself immediately; she'd earned it, at least as much as he had.

"You've had a change of heart," he observed mildly.

"I told you I'd never fight for an exotic wasteland," she said, "but that's not what this is. And I'll fight for the Signalers because they deserve our help, but that's not the end of it. Not anymore."

She took Tchicaya's hands. "Some astronomically rare event created sentient life on the other side of the border, but that's all it was: bad luck, an accident of birth. We've found ways to live with all the hardships: the distance, the loneliness. That's a great achievement, an amazing feat, but that's no reason to sentence ourselves to repeat it for eternity.

"How can we go on living in that wasteland, when even space is alive here? *This is where we belong, Tchicaya.* I'll fight for this place because it's our home."

In the eerie calm of the highway, Tchicaya felt himself losing his grip on reality. A whole universe was at stake, and here he was playing stowaway on a road train? Unknown multitudes would die, because he lacked the nerve to tap the driver on the shoulder and make his presence known. He could get his message across to anyone, if he put his mind to it. He'd managed to converse with twenty-third-century zealots with flesh for brains; how much harder could a glowing starfish be?

When the highway began to disgorge them after barely two hours, he almost wept with relief. His gamble might yet fail to pay off, but at least it hadn't irrevocably sunk the whole endeavor.

As they spiraled out of the darkness, the *Sarumpaet* steeled itself for the worst contingencies the toolkit could imagine. The Bright had been a challenge, but there was no reason to believe that it was the most extreme environment the far side could contain.

Probes began returning. Parasprites flooded in. The convoy slipped out of the ramp into a vast, tranquil space. The toolkit analyzed the vendeks around them; the mixture was not honeycomb-stable, but it was like the Bright tamed, domesticated. The air-conditioning in the colony had gone a short way in the same direction, but it was like the difference between a mesh cage in the open ocean, keeping the largest predators at bay, and an aquarium of hand-picked species that could coexist and thrive with a minimum of drama.

The six Colonists were not alone here; the scape showed hundreds of similar four-branched xennobes moving around them in a multitude of neat, loosely defined rows, as if the place was criss-crossed with invisible escalators. Compared to the crush of the outpost, though, conditions were far from crowded. Layer walls undulated gently in the distance, dotted with parasprite lamps, but there was none of the density of structure they'd seen in the tunnels. High above Tchicaya—"above" according to the random orientation in which the *Sarumpaet* had emerged—other dark highways were visible.

"I believe we're in a railway station," he said. "The question is, where?"

Mariama declared confidently, "This is the big smoke. All space and comfort."

"Where we came from wasn't exactly a ghost town."

"No, just a small village with no entertainment, and no contraception."

Tchicaya scowled, but then he realized that she was being neither serious nor entirely flippant. Tossing a few anthropomorphic parodies at the least important of the ten thousand unanswered questions they faced might at least stop them wasting energy trying to fill in the same blanks with earnest hypotheses that were just as likely to be wrong.

As the Colonists crossed the atrium, alien cargo and its would-be puppeteers in tow, Mariama mimed cracking a whip. "Take me to your linguists," she said. "And don't spare the vendeks."

*   *   *

If they were in a city, they had no way of judging its size from within, no way of knowing if they were moving from building to building through something like open air, or merely navigating through the rooms of a single, vast, hermetically sealed structure.

They passed through narrow apertures and wide corridors; they wove through denser crowds; they encountered structures as baffling and varied as the machinery—or artwork, or gardens—of the outpost in the Bright. The probes gathered information, and the toolkit puzzled over it, but even when it made sense it was just another tiny piece of a vast mosaic. Grabbing hints of how the vendek populations were interacting inside some gadget—or pet—that they passed was all grist for the mill, but it was not going to make the whole city and its people snap into focus in an instant.

Still, Tchicaya clung stubbornly to the notion that it was better to observe whatever he could, and provisionally entertain some wildly imperfect guesses, than to close his eyes and surrender to the verdict that he might as well have been a flea aspiring to understand the culture of a great metropolis. The scale in that analogy was right, but nothing else was. Both he and his hosts possessed general intelligence, and however mutually foreign their needs and drives, there was nothing—including each other's lives, customs, and languages—that could remain incomprehensible to them, given time, patience, and motivation.

Time, they did not have, but he'd leave it to the Planck worms to declare when the supply was exhausted.

Mariama drank in the sights like a happily dazed tourist. She treated their purpose at least as seriously as he did, and she'd confronted every problem they'd faced with ferocious energy and clarity, but something in her temperament refused to admit that the corollary of that dedication could ever be despair at the thought of failure. They'd accepted a burden that was constantly on the verge of crushing them both, but he'd rarely seen her so much as tremble beneath the load.

The procession came to a halt in a huge chamber, containing a structure resembling a cluster of grapes the size of a whale. The surface of this object was like nothing the probes had seen before, and the interior proved even more surprising, killing them off completely. Other, slightly more familiar technology was arrayed around this bizarre leviathan.

The Colonists broke rank; three of them fussed around the towing bubble, while the others went to one wall of the chamber and returned with some kind of small device, or creature. Whatever they were fetching didn't need to be towed; it followed its summoners back under its own power.

When the Colonists burst the banner's bubble and lured their apparatus closer to it, Tchicaya moved the *Sarumpaet* away. He didn't want the ship caught up inadvertently in whatever they were about to do.

Sprayed by vendeks, the apparatus began to shine. It emitted sprites, not the related vendeks the Colonists seemed to favor.

Mariama said, "They're illuminating the banner with the right kind of lighting. The signal is encoded in its transparency to sprites; they understood that much."

"I think you're right." There was always a chance that they were misreading the action, but Tchicaya felt hopeful.

He surveyed the scene, trying to guess what would happen next. The banner was positioned between the sprite source and the giant bunch of grapes. Meaning what? *This* was their expert linguist? Another species of xennobe entirely, or some caste of the Colonists who sat motionless in this chamber like a bloated termite queen? He dismissed the notion immediately. They'd seen no other "castes." A few teeming xennobes in a crowded "hive," and he was starting to invent ridiculous insectile *non sequiturs*.

The Colonists moved back from the illuminated banner, and did nothing more. They floated at the edge of the chamber, branches twitching lazily in the gentle currents.

The toolkit said, "I've found a way to get probes into the un-mapped structure now. This is very strange."

Mariama said, "We'll be the judge of strange. Just tell us what they've found."

"Take a cluster of protons and neutrons, and compress it by a factor of a hundred million. That's what this is."

Tchicaya blinked, disbelieving. "We're looking at a nugget of squashed near-side matter?"

"Yes. It's wrapped in some complicated vendek-based layers that are helping to stabilize it, but basically it's a pile of ordinary nucleons with most of the empty space squeezed out of them."

Mariama turned to him. "It could be a kind of meteorite. With all the matter that's passed through the border, some microscopic speck might have encountered conditions that preserved it."

Tchicaya didn't welcome the conclusion this suggested. "So this room could be nothing but a museum display? I can't believe they'd go to the trouble of building the signaling layer, only to take the reply—proof of intelligent life behind the border—and stuff it in a cabinet for people to gawk at."

"Or study. People will come to study it."

"*When?*"

Mariama said, "If you want to draw crowds, maybe it's time we changed the loop."

Tchicaya sent instructions to the banner. It stopped counting out primes, and switched to a simple, ascending sequence of integers.

The Colonists responded with a flurry of activity: moving around the chamber, summoning new equipment. Tchicaya watched them, his hopes rising again. They had to realize that the banner was as good as alive, and ready to talk. Surely they'd reply now.

He was wrong. They aimed no shuttered sprite lamp back toward the banner, they flashed no answering sequence.

He switched to the Fibonacci series. This stirred the Colonists' branches a little, as if they welcomed the stimulation, but whatever the purpose of the equipment they'd gathered after the first change of message, it continued to be all they required.

They were happy to watch, but they had no intention of replying. They were politely, respectfully observing the alien emissary, but too cautious to engage with it and speed up the process of understanding its message.

"What do we have to do to get through to them?"

Mariama said, "We could push ahead with the mathematics leading to the GDL."

"Just like that? As a monologue?"

"What choice do we have?"

The toolkit had developed a Graph Description Language, a precise set of semantic conventions for talking about vendeks, Planck worms, and what would happen when they met. Given some moderately sophisticated mathematical concepts—which could be built up from elementary ideas based on integer exemplars—quantum graphs were far easier to talk about than anything as abstract and contingent as social structures.

If the Colonists weren't going to deign to reply, though, there'd be no way of knowing if the dictionary of concepts was coming at them too quickly, or even whether the basic syntax was being understood. They manipulated vendeks with skills that no QGT theoretician would dare aspire to, but that didn't mean they understood them in the same way. Humans had tamed and modified dozens of species of plants and animals before they'd had the slightest idea what DNA was.

Tchicaya started the program running. Without feedback along the lines of "Yes, we understood that, please skip ahead to something ten times harder," it would take four ship-days to complete. He could choose sections to omit, himself—but which ones? What concepts were obvious to a xennobe?

Mariama smiled tentatively. "They haven't left the room yet."

"It *is* an alien artifact. That in itself must merit some level of attention."

"They chose the primes," she said. "They picked the language, and it was exactly what we would have picked ourselves."

Tchicaya scanned the room. "We're missing something here." The Colonists had no faces, no eyes, and he had no way of telling what they were attending to, but they were far better positioned to observe the nucleon nugget than the banner.

He said, "They're showing *it* the banner. They're not even trying to make sense of the message themselves. They expect their meteorite to react."

Mariama was skeptical, but not dismissive. "Why would they think that way? Some kind of category error? They're intelligent enough to figure out that both these things came from the near side, but they have no concept of inanimacy? Because . . . everything here is living?" She grimaced. "Are you going to stop me before I start talking complete gibberish? Whether vendeks count as living or not, random collections of them would make very bad translators between xennobe languages."

Tchicaya said, "So are the Colonists suffering from animist delusions, or is this *not* a random collection of nucleons?" He addressed the toolkit. "Can you make any sense of its structure? What are the odds that nuclear matter in a star or a planet could be in a state that could come through the border like this?"

"Negligible."

"So someone wrapped it? Someone prepared it deliberately?"

The toolkit said, "That's more likely than it happening by chance."

Mariama said, "Don't look at me. Maybe someone was running their own secret experiments, but this was *not* a Preservationist project."

"Then whose was it? And what has it been doing down here?" Tchicaya asked the toolkit, "Can you model its dynamics? Is there information processing going on in there?"

The toolkit was silent for a moment. "No. But there could have been, once. It looks to me like it started out as a femtomachine."

Gooseflesh rose on Tchicaya's arms. Back on the *Rindler*, comparing their varied experiences of local death, Yann had definitively trumped him with tales of going nuclear.

He said, "It's the Mimosans. They're buried in there."

Mariama's eyes widened. "They can't be. The Quietener blew up in their faces, Tchicaya. How much warning would they have had?"

Tchicaya shook his head. "I don't know how they did it, but we've got to look for them." He asked the toolkit, "Can you map the whole thing? Can you simulate it?" The crushed femtomachine was vastly larger than the *Sarumpaet*, but having started from merely nuclear densities, it would have made far less efficient use of its graphs.

The toolkit said, "I'll try. It will take time to get the information out; the probes can only move it at a certain rate."

They waited. The mathematics lesson played on through the banner; the Colonists floated in place, patient as ever, expecting . . . what? *The femtomachine had talked to them, once.* It must have functioned long enough for its inhabitants to learn their language. Had it told them to make the signaling layer? Or had it commenced its own attempts to communicate with a sequence of primes, which they'd gone on to copy?

After almost an hour, the toolkit declared, "I have a complete model of the structure inside the *Sarumpaet*. Now I'm trying to repair some of the damage." It juggled connections, looking for gaps in information routes; it searched for redundancies that would allow it to reconstruct the missing pathways.

"There's a simulation of something resembling a primate body. With standard representation hooks into the model."

"Show us," Tchicaya said.

A person appeared on the deck in front of them, standing motionless, arms raised as if in defense against a blow, or an impact. The body did not resemble anything Tchicaya had inhabited himself, but it was a piece of software that made no sense unless the femtomachine had contained a sentient inhabitant.

"Can you trace back the sensory and motor hooks?"

"I'm trying. Okay. I've found it."

"You've found the mind?"

"Yes."

"What kind of state is it in?"

"Wait. I'm computing integrity signatures." Sentient software was always packed with check sums that would allow it to detect whether it had been corrupted. "Not scrambled, just frozen. Most of the physics that leaked in seems to have slowed down the strong force interactions, rather than damaging the quarks and gluons."

Tchicaya said, "Can you run it? Can you wake it?" He was shaking. He didn't know if he was digging a tenacious survivor out from beneath a rock slide, or breathing unwelcome life back into a mutilated castaway who'd escaped into a merciful local death. Too much was at stake, though, to let the Mimosan rest in peace until he learned the answer for himself.

The simulation twitched, looked around the scape, then dropped to its knees, sobbing wretchedly. "I'm going mad! I'm going mad!" The body being simulated had been designed to function in vacuum; it was even pretending to speak in infrared.

Tchicaya understood the words as they were spoken; his Mediator had turned the data into sounds in his head, and granted him the survivor's language immediately.

He knelt beside her and wrapped his arms around her shoulders. "You're not going mad, Cass. We're real. You're not home yet, but you're very close now. And you're among friends."

Chapter 18

Time was everything, and Tchicaya felt a streak of brutal pragmatism demanding that he press their only hope of a translator into service as rapidly as possible. It would be a false compassion that ended with all of them dead. But though Cass was undoubtedly sane, and increasingly lucid, she was still in shock. Before she could help them, she needed to make sense of her own situation.

Tchicaya told her about the signaling layer, and how the *Sarumpaet* had been led to this place. He said nothing about the Planck worms; he and Mariama were explorers from the near side, that was all that mattered for now. He invited Cass to complete the account, to bridge the gap between the events at Mimosa and this extraordinary meeting. Seated on a couch they'd conjured up for her, she told them some of the history of her voyage.

For the last of their experiments on the novo-vacuum, the Mimosans had sent clones into a femtomachine, in order to be closer to the event in real time. They had seen the nascent border expanding, and struggled to understand their mistake. In one branch of the femtomachine's uncontrolled superposition, they had reached Sophus's insight: the physics of the ordinary vacuum represented just one eigenstate for a quantum graph's dynamic laws.

Working from that starting point, they had devised a plan to spare the inhabited worlds from destruction. By modifying the border so as to make the emission of light sufficiently asymmetrical, the difference in radiation pressure could be used to accelerate the whole system. While the far side remained small, its mass as an object in the near side would be tiny (in fact, tiny and negative, since it had started at zero and lost energy as radiation). If it was left to others to tackle the problem decades later, the far side would have swallowed entire star systems—at the very least, Mimosa itself. If they acted now, they could send it flying out of inhabited space even faster than it was expanding.

When the border hit the femtomachine, they would have a chance to interact with it, but no fleeting, localized encounter would be sufficient to sculpt the borderlight into a propulsion system. They needed to buy themselves more time. Matching the border's velocity would have been ideal, but there was no prospect of achieving that. Their only hope was to find a way to keep working on the problem after the far side had swallowed them.

The Mimosans had choreographed a bravura quantum maneuver that would allow the femtomachine to inject a partial clone of itself through the border, and rotate all of its amplitude into the successful branch at the same time. But the passengers couldn't all pass through. The bulk of the femtomachine would have to become a device whose sole purpose was to implement the move, and only the acorporeals were structured in a way that gave them the power to rewrite their minds right out of existence, converting themselves into pieces of the quantum catapult. All seven had been needed, to make it work. Cass had been left to go in alone.

The first part of the plan had succeeded: the core of the original femtomachine had been re-created, in miniature, in the far side. But it had not been as mobile as its designers had hoped, and Cass had been trapped by changing conditions, hundreds of times. She had kept struggling to get the *Oppenheimer* into position, proceeding in fits and starts, but the vehicle's hull had become compromised, vendeks had flooded in.

If this had happened in the ferment of the Bright, Tchicaya doubted that any trace of the crippled machine would have remained a picosecond later, but the massed invasion by a single, tenacious species had effectively fossilized it whole. An unknown time later—near-side decades, or centuries—a group of intelligent xennobes had found the wreck. Subject to the same infestation themselves, they had revived the *Oppenheimer* with a vendek bred specifically to reverse the effects of the first.

Awake, but still trapped—nothing could remedy the fact that her vehicle was too primitive for the constantly evolving terrain—Cass had begun trying to communicate with her benefactors. Her own first message had taken the form of a layer population, vibrating, counting out the primes. From there, it had been a long, arduous process, but they'd eventually reached a point of limited mutual understanding.

Then the xennobes had vanished, prey to some shift in climate or culture; she had never discovered the reason. After decades had passed, another, related group had appeared, aware of the previous encounter, but speaking a different language themselves, and too impatient to learn to communicate properly. They had tried to carry her toward the border—knowing that this had been her original goal—without really understanding her nature. Moving anything through the far side was a delicate process, and their technology had not been up to the task. The *Oppenheimer* had become trapped again, damaged again. Invaded, frozen, and abandoned.

That was her last experience before waking on the deck of the *Sarumpaet*. She had no way of knowing whether the *Oppenheimer* had been towed here by the builders of the city, or whether the city had grown up around it.

Tchicaya was humbled; everything he'd been through was a stroll in the desert by comparison. He couldn't even offer her the comfort of hearing that her own failed mission had been completed from the outside.

But he had to press on. As gently as he could, he began explaining what had happened on the near side. Cass had long ago faced up to the likelihood that her actions had destroyed whole worlds, but she'd had no way of knowing how much time had passed, and he could see the wounds reopening as he described the numbers, the scale of the evacuation.

He compressed the machinations of the factions on the *Rindler* to the briefest sketch, but he made one thing clear: the vast majority of people had never intended to destroy sentient life in the far side. Most still wanted the incursion to be halted, but not at the cost of genocide.

For all the bad news that accompanied it, understanding the *Sarumpaet*'s presence seemed to solidify Cass's sense of reality. She could connect herself to the near side again. She could imagine something other than exile, and madness.

When Tchicaya finished speaking, she stood. "You want them to evacuate the Bright, so you can trap the Planck worms there?"

"Yes."

"And you'd like me to translate that message?"

"If you can."

"I'll need to be able to create vendeks," Cass explained. She had invented her own terminology for everything, but Tchicaya's Mediator was smoothing over the differences. "I don't understand the perceptual physiology, but there's a family of short-lived vendeks related to the parasprites that my first xennobe tribe employed for communication. Though what their descendants will make of any of this, I don't know."

Mariama worked with the toolkit to sort out interfaces with the software Cass had used back on the *Oppenheimer* to create the communications vendeks. While this was happening, Tchicaya rehearsed scenarios with her, possible responses from the Colonists. He wasn't entirely sure why she wanted this, but she appeared to be afraid of being caught out, unprepared.

"Everything's ready," Mariama declared. "As much as it will ever be."

They moved the *Sarumpaet* right up to the ruins of the *Oppenheimer*. The Colonists were still patiently looking on as the banner flashed out its mathematical lexicon.

Cass said, "I hope they really are expecting this. If I waved a papyrus at Tutankhamen and he started speaking to me, I'd probably run screaming from the room and never come back."

She sent the first vendeks out from the ship.

The scape painted a burst of color spreading out around them, fading rapidly as it moved. These vendeks did not last long in the room's environment; to Tchicaya's eyes, the signal looked faint by the time it reached the Colonists.

It was not too faint for them to notice. They sprang into action, gathering more equipment. If the Bright had made them feign constant excitement, this was the real thing; Tchicaya hadn't seen their bodies convulse so much since they'd descended from the surface of the outpost.

Reassembled in a huddle, armed with their additional machinery—recording devices, translators?—they finally found a reason to talk back.

Tchicaya wasn't privy to the exchange. Cass didn't talk aloud in her own native language, offering up sentences for direct translation, nor was there any running translation of the replies. She had never got far enough to integrate the xennobe language into the usual, Mediator-based scheme of things; she was working from her own mental dictionary of signals, memories of past conversations, brute-force software assistance, and guesswork. She made gestures with her body, frowned to herself, and emitted grunts and sighs, but most of the action was going on inside her simulated skull.

After almost twenty minutes, she paused to give the two spectators a brief commentary. "They expected me to speak in an ancient language, but they weren't quite sure which one it would be. We've sorted that all out now." She looked ragged, but she smiled.

Tchicaya was about to launch into a stream of lavish praise, but Mariama replied calmly, "That's good."

Cass nodded. "I think they trust me, more or less. At least they're willing to listen."

She resumed the conversation. Vendeks washed back and forth between the Colonists and the flea masquerading as a resurrected mummy.

More than four hours after the exchange had begun, Cass sat down on the deck and cradled her head in her arms. Three of the Colonists left the chamber.

Tchicaya waited. There'd be a reason for the hiatus: the Colonists were fetching another language expert, another translation device, a better dictionary.

Cass looked up suddenly, as if she'd completely forgotten that she was no longer alone.

"It's done," she said. "They understood me."

The Bright itself was of little value to their hosts, she explained, but it did contain several outposts from which they'd been attempting to learn more about whatever lay beyond. They hadn't constructed the signaling layer; they'd heard stories about the artifact, which had supposedly been built by an earlier civilization, but they had never had the means to verify its existence. They couldn't quite comprehend the nature of the threat she had described, but they did believe that she came from the outer reaches, and they had decided that they had nothing to lose by erring on the side of caution.

They would permit the creation of the tar pit. They would begin evacuating the Bright immediately.

The *Sarumpaet* rode the highway loop back into the Bright, escorted by Tännsjö and Hintikka—Cass's names for two of the Colonists who'd traveled down from the outpost with the banner. She'd explained to them that she'd moved from the wreck of her old vehicle into this new, smaller model, brought here by two colleagues who'd traveled all the way from her home; they found many aspects of this account baffling, but didn't expect to make sense of it until they'd learned much more. The legends about her had been full of obvious nonsense that they'd hoped to dispel, but they were patient, and they could wait for a more complete understanding.

"Do they know you're their creator?" Mariama asked.

Cass snorted. "That would be an overblown claim for me to make, when I didn't have the slightest idea what I was creating. But I haven't told them anything about Mimosa. All I've ever said is that I came into their world to try to keep it from colliding with my own."

The outposts in the Bright were all located unfavorably for their purpose, so they left the highway at a brand new ramp that Tännsjö and Hintikka fashioned from within, with tools they'd brought along for the purpose. Even more impressively, after forming the exit, the Colonists sent a signal into the structure that began to shift its operation into reverse. This expedition would not be able to get home by completing the loop in the original direction, and apparently it had never occurred to the highway-makers to have two opposing lanes running side by side.

The Bright was exactly as Tchicaya remembered it, but he had never expected to see Planck worms bearing down on him again the way they had in the honeycomb, unless it was at the moment before his death. The Bright was some three centimeters deep, but the Colonists had never mapped its limits in latitude or longitude. Tchicaya could only hope that if other xennobe civilizations unknown to the Colonists had sent their own explorers into the region, they'd see the tar pit coming, and flee.

The *Sarumpaet* launched the seed; it disappeared into the haze. For several minutes, there was nothing. Then an ominous sprite shadow appeared, a gray stain spreading across the sky.

This was as much as they could afford to witness. The Colonists would monitor the tar pit from below, but they would not see anything of the battle, if it was won here.

Tännsjö and Hintikka led the way back.

Once they were in transit, the highway sealed behind them, Tchicaya asked Cass, "What do they make of the fact that some near-siders almost wiped them out?"

"I told them that the top of the Bright was encroaching on our homes," she said, "which alarmed us, and made some of us act in haste. I think they could empathize with that; shifting weather's been known to have the same effect on people here, now and then. But I gather they're still a bit skeptical about the notion that the Planck worms could have killed everything in their path. They're also puzzled that the advance of the Bright could be such a big deal to us—given that we come from somewhere even more hostile."

Mariama said, "Do they understand that the border's still encroaching? That we're still losing territory?"

"Yes," Cass replied. "But they've offered to work with us, to do what they can to find a solution."

Tchicaya was bemused. "Don't you think that problem is a bit beyond them?" The toolkit had found no way to freeze the border. All the evidence suggested that the expansion was unstoppable.

Cass said, "Of course it is, right now. But they've come from nothing, to this"—she gestured at the highway around them—"in just six hundred years. Give them another near-side month or two, and they'll definitely be the ones leading the way."

They returned to the place Mariama had named Museum City. The tar pit would take time to stabilize, and until the Planck worms had either been trapped and killed, or failed to show up entirely, it would not be safe to try to drill through the mess and make contact with the border.

It had been less than a millisecond since the *Sarumpaet* had begun its flight. Tchicaya enjoyed imagining his own startled near-side version hearing the news that the Planck worms had been defeated, before he'd even had time to grow anxious about the fate of the mission. He'd made no firm plans for reversing his bifurcation, since he'd never really expected to return, but the less-traveled Tchicaya would probably be willing to be subsumed. If not, he only hoped that their continued separation would be justified, and they didn't merely dog each other's footsteps. If they both tried to meet up with Rasmah it would be awkward, though Tchicaya had little doubt which one of them she'd choose.

Cass gave Mariama xennobe language lessons. Tchicaya sat in on them, but he found them heavy going. Mariama made her own copy of the vendek-based communications software and began converting it into something a Mediator could work with, but filling in the gaps and formalizing the structures of the language was a huge task.

Tchicaya had expanded the *Sarumpaet*'s scape, building rooms beyond the observation deck, giving all three passengers privacy. He began sleeping more, eight or ten hours in every ship-day.

Mostly, he dreamed that he was back on the *Rindler*. It was strange to feel pangs of nostalgia, not for solid ground and blue skies, but for stars and borderlight.

The Colonists were intensely curious about the aliens, and eager to explain their own world to them. They dragged the *Sarumpaet* from group to group, place to place; if Cass had let them, they probably would have taken her on a tour of every city in their realm, talking to her nonstop all the way. In near-side terms, their history only stretched back about a year, and they had only explored a few thousand cubic kilometers of the far side, but by any local measure their civilization was orders of magnitude vaster than all of inhabited space. And they were far from alone: they'd had direct contact with twelve other sentient species, and they had secondhand knowledge of hundreds more.

Tchicaya listened to Cass's translations, and marveled at the things they were learning, but he could see how weary she was becoming, and he felt both a protective sympathy for her, and a lesser, parallel exhaustion of his own. He had dived into the far side unprepared, and whether or not he eventually made it his home, he needed to come up for air.

On their fifty-third night in the city, Mariama woke him, standing by his bed, shaking him by the arm. He squinted at her and willed the scape to grow brighter.

"It's about Cass."

He nodded. "She has to get out soon. The minute the tar pit's safe to traverse, we need to start drilling."

Mariama sat on the bed beside him. "She's started talking to me about staying on. Seeing out her original project, in some form or other: freezing the border, pushing away the far side. Whatever can be done to stop the evacuations."

Tchicaya was horrified. "That could take centuries!" He only meant far-side time, though on reflection he wondered if that wasn't optimistic.

Mariama said, "I don't know what she's thinking. That they'll crucify her outside, if she dares to emerge without a solution? Or maybe it's more personal. Either way, I don't think she can hold out that long. It's too open-ended, and she's taking it all too personally. She's already been through enough. Will you try to talk some sense into her?"

"Sure."

"Thanks." Mariama smiled. "It'll come better from you. I'd sound too much like someone who's simply angling for her job."

Tchicaya wondered for a moment if he'd misunderstood her, but she'd managed to be oblique without the slightest hint of ambiguity.

"Why do you want her job?" he said.

"I'm ready for this," Mariama declared. "It's exactly what I came to the *Rindler* to do."

"You came to the *Rindler* to work with Tarek on Planck worms!"

"I came to the *Rindler* to give people a choice," she said. "There are limits to the way that can be achieved, complications that I never anticipated, but working with the Colonists to find the solution would be an entirely honorable compromise."

Tchicaya shook his head in mock admiration. "So you get to live exactly like a Yielder, while retaining your Preservationist credentials? Very slick." He made it sound like a joke, but he was angry. He could forgive her the almost tongue-in-cheek self-serving spin. What he hated was the fact that she'd set her sights so far beyond his own, again.

He wasn't ready to stay. He couldn't live among the Colonists with her, when the arrival of every other near-sider was an eternity away. He'd planned to meet Rasmah on the other side of the border. He needed to see the stars at least one more time.

"You'll go mad," he said.

Mariama laughed. "That's what my mother used to say, about travelers. Wandering from planet to planet, until they could no longer remember their own names."

"Sounds romantic, doesn't it? No wonder you couldn't resist." Tchicaya's anger was fading, but the ache beneath it remained. He reached out and put his arms around her. There would never be an irrevocable parting, so long as they were both alive, but the gulf she was planning to create between them was the widest and the strangest he'd ever faced.

"What will I tell the version of you next to my kidney? She'll think I made you walk the plank."

"She'll understand. I'll give you a messenger for her."

He pulled away, and held her at arm's length. "What is it with you, that you always have to go further than anyone else?"

"What is it with you, that you always have to tag along?" Mariama ran her hand over his scalp, then she stood and walked to the doorway.

She stopped and turned back to face him. "Before I go, do you want to make love?"

Tchicaya was speechless. She had never once spoken of the possibility, since he'd willed an end to their first chance on Turaev.

"Now that I'm more your type," she said, spreading her arms wide, as if showing off some enhancement to her appearance.

"More my type?" he replied stupidly. He couldn't detect any change in her.

Mariama smiled. "*Acorporeal.*"

Tchicaya threw his pillow at her. She retreated, laughing.

He lay back on the bed, relieved. Nothing could have lived up to four thousand years of waiting. Except perhaps an original theorem.

* * *

Cass stood on the observation deck, listening patiently to Tchicaya's appeal. Mariama had made herself scarce, and even the Colonists had finally noticed that their living legend began to emit incomprehensible streams of vendeks if they didn't give her an occasional day off.

She'd done enough, he said. No sane person blamed her for her lack of omniscience. The Mimosans' plan to accelerate the far side had been ingenious, and she'd struggled valiantly to try to make it work, but the rules had changed, the prize she'd been reaching for had retreated into the distance. Other people could carry on in her place; the end result would be the same. And if she needed personal redemption, couldn't that come from passing on her knowledge of the far side to someone rested, someone fully prepared for a second long haul?

Cass appeared calm, even slightly distracted. Tchicaya wondered if she'd taken in his words, if he should repeat himself from the beginning.

"I want to go swimming," she said suddenly.

"Swimming?"

Cass nodded earnestly.

"All right."

Tchicaya began to gesture at the scape, but she grabbed his arm. "In real water," she insisted fiercely. "Real molecules of water."

Tchicaya unclenched her grip on him, and held her by the shoulders. "Okay. As soon as we get out, you can do that."

"I swim in real water; that's who I am." Her face contorted, and she emitted a long, anguished moan. *"I didn't want to be changed this much!"*

"I'll help you," he promised. "I'll get you out of here."

On her last day in Museum City, Cass steered the *Sarumpaet* unescorted through the corridors and tunnels, searching for something. "I asked Hintikka, and she made some inspired guesses, but we never got around to investigating all the possibilities. The Colonists don't really understand graphs, but they have a system for describing vendeks that maps quite well on to our picture, if you know how to make allowances for the parts that don't match up."

They veered from wall to wall, scrutinizing various living gadgets: lamps, air conditioners, fragrance dispensers, parasprite telephones, humor replenishers—Mariama's name for the sacs full of endogenous vendeks that the Colonists imbibed to keep themselves in peak condition.

They probed the gadgets, and the toolkit did its best to infer the fine structure of the vendeks they contained. Tchicaya had no idea what Cass was hunting for. She had bidden farewell to the Colonists earlier, formally handing her diplomatic role on to Mariama. He didn't know how well that notion translated, but Mariama had begun conversing with the xennobes for herself weeks before, and she seemed satisfied that her newcomer status would not be a handicap. Her own new ship had been prepared; she'd named it in honor of Tarek, in spite of the fact that he was still very much alive. But as she'd pointed out, there were only so many dead people.

"Not quite," Cass muttered. She pulled the ship away from something whose most polite anthropomorphic equivalent was probably a spittoon.

Mariama glanced at Tchicaya inquiringly.

He said, "Don't ask me. We'll know when we find it."

The tar pit had stabilized, and the toolkit's models suggested that the Planck worms would have drowned in its depths. Other, grimmer scenarios could not be ruled out entirely, but as the *Sarumpaet* made its way back to the border it would seal the tar pit behind it; even if the ship was lost, they would not be opening up an easy channel for the Planck worms.

The worms would certainly have destroyed the interface across the border, but he and Cass would build their own, as close as possible to the old one; it shouldn't be hard to catch the attention of the equipment on the Left Hand.

From there, they would transmit themselves to Pfaff. It was on the route to Earth, and Tchicaya would accompany her at least that much of the way.

Cass said, "Here it is."

Tchicaya looked up at the toolkit's display, a schematic of a graph, drawn node by node and edge by edge, superimposed over the larger scape portraying their busy surroundings.

It took him a moment to spot what she meant. Between two vendeks that resembled ornate ironwork, there was a plain, narrow, highly symmetrical layer.

It was the Diamond Graph. The state from which the whole near-side universe was believed to have arisen. Stable here, in this tiny sliver, cushioned between the right two vendeks.

The seed for a universe, lying in the gutter.

Cass gestured at the scape and summoned the image closer, placing it before them on the observation deck.

"That's what I went looking for," she said. "A glimpse of *that*. Only I never expected I'd come this close. And I never thought there'd be so much else attached." She smiled uncertainly, then pushed the graph away.

"I think I'm ready to go home."

References

Quantum Graph Theory is fictitious, but the spin networks on which Sarumpaet's work is based are part of a real theory, known as loop quantum gravity, discovered by Lee Smolin and Carlo Rovelli. There is a considerable literature on this subject; two comprehensive review papers are:

> "An Introduction to Spin Foam Models of Quantum Gravity and BF Theory" by John C. Baez, in *Geometry and Quantum Physics*, edited by Helmut Gausterer and Harald Grosse, Springer, Berlin, 2000.
> <www.arXiv.org/abs/gr-qc/9905087>

and

> "The Future of Spin Networks" by Lee Smolin, in *The Geometric Universe*, edited by S. A. Huggett *et al.*, Oxford University Press, Oxford, 1998.
> <www.arXiv.org/abs/gr-qc/9702030>

I'm indebted to John Baez, who very kindly explained several points to me directly, as well as posting numerous articles on the news group *sci.physics.research* making these ideas more accessible to nonspecialists. Of course, any errors I've committed in describing the real theory, and any absurdities in the way I've imagined its future, are my fault entirely.

Decoherence is a real phenomenon, and it is widely accepted as playing a major role in the absence of detectable quantum effects in macroscopic objects. Its role in relation to the superselection rules that forbid superpositions of certain kinds of quantum states is more controversial. These ideas are discussed in:

Decoherence and the Appearance of a Classical World in Quantum Theory by D. Giulini, E. Joos, C. Kiefer, J. Kupsch, I.-O. Stamatescu, and H. D. Zeh, Springer, Berlin, 1996.

I learned about the construction known as Schild's ladder from:

Gravitation by C. W. Misner, K. S. Thorne and J. A. Wheeler, W. H. Freeman, New York, 1970.

who cite an unpublished lecture by Alfred Schild on January 19, 1970, at Princeton University.

Supplementary material for this novel can be found at <www.netspace.net.au/~gregegan/>.